The Xeven Houses of Deception (House 1): Rise to Vilon

R. Ramarr Richards

To all those who dared to say, "I think there's more to our story."

For character profiles and structures of the Houses of Paradise please visit us at:

rramarr.com

Thank You

CONTENTS

I WOULD LIKE TO THANK THE
FOLLOWING CONTRIBUTORS TO THIS
NOVEL:

Editing

Editor: Hillery York
Website:
http://archivalpolish.wordpress.com
E-mail: archivalpolish@gmail.com

Copy Editor: Justin Bracciale
Email: jbintampa@aol.com

Cover Designer (e-book and print)

Designer: Matt Lara
Portfolio: www.mattsartpad.com
E-mail: matthew.p.lara@gmail.com

And the angels which kept not their first estate, but left their own habitation, he hath reserved in everlasting chains under darkness unto the judgment of the great day.

Jude 1:6

RISE TO VILON

Now war arose in heaven, Michael and his
angels fighting against the dragon. And
the dragon and his angels fought back, but
he was defeated, and there was no longer
any place for them in heaven.
Revelation 12:7-8

ACT I

Prologue

The Paroxysm of Abraxis

In the beginning of the beginning, in a far distant time, an enormous cluster of stars floated alone in the vast void of the unknown universe. In an immeasurable amount of time, a second cluster of stars from the depths of the universe appeared and collided with the first cluster creating a colossal supercluster. That supercluster came to be known as The Great Aeon of Abraxis.

Abraxis was an extraordinary cluster of stars for in time it developed a consciousness. It grew aware of itself. It became omnificent and spawned four smaller, but galactic, clusters of consciousness. Two of the four spawns were vast and massive clusters, but still much smaller than the gigantic Abraxis. These two clusters were called The Eon of Omnus and The Eon of Abaddon. The other two spawns of Abraxis were smaller, but more aware and vivacious. Although they were not as immense as Omnus and Abaddon, they still were colossal galactic forces. These two clusters were called The Eon of Sophia and The Eon of Lilith.

These four spawns of huge star clusters were immortal beings, for they were endless and eternal bodies of consciousness. Like Abraxis, they too were self-aware. The combination of immortality and consciousness developed into a desire for self-sustaining vitality and the perpetual longing for companionship.

Each of the four galactic clusters clung to the energy source of the larger supercluster Abraxis in order to recharge their solar power, their life force. The four clusters also attracted and gravitated towards each other, while never leaving the sustaining proximity of Abraxis. Being pulled and drawn together by their consciousness, each galactic cluster of stars passed through each other, causing a celestial friction that spawned off smaller interstellar systems. These smaller interstellar systems clung to one of the four galactic clusters until it eventually found a companion to which it wanted to forever merge. These interstellar mergers could never grow as large as any of the four galaxy clusters that spawned them, nor could the four galaxies grow as large as the Abraxis supercluster from which all spawns received their power. The smaller stellar spawns of conscious immortality gave allegiance to two of the four large galactic clusters from which it was created. Each star cluster united a conscious to a conscious, an interstellar cluster to a galactic cluster and, all clusters to the supercluster, Abraxis.

In time, with so many circling, colliding, and spawning conscious clusters surrounding it, The Great Aeon of Abraxis became convulsed and exploded with a big bang.

The big bang of the Abraxis supercluster cast out, diminished, and separated the four galaxies and their spawns, disseminating them throughout the universe. Each dispersed cluster, still conscious and aware, was also distressed, weakened, and torn far from its power source. They were alone without an Abraxis. As the spawns spun out into the void of darkness, some would never return unaffected by the dark. From the four galactic clusters only one solar survivor would maintain most of its mass, its spawns, and its ability to remain omnipotent. This superior cluster shined its light brightly to illuminate a path for the others to escape the bounds of the dark and return to the collective light. Being diminished and subordinate, the other three galactic clusters sought out the last remaining superior cluster of conscious immortality and gave to it their allegiance in hopes of gaining back the power source of an Abraxis.

The omnipotence from the largest of the four impacted galactic star clusters, desired to repair the universe by enhancing the means by which each of the star clusters communicated. The omniscient intelligence of this larger surviving star cluster knew that Abraxis' colossal size and power led to its demise for it did not regulate the greed, gluttony, and desire of the clusters that tapped into its energy source. A means of communication was needed to control those that depended on its powers of rejuvenation. Enhancements were made by enclosing the clusters' consciousness into a mystical metamorphosis of a physical life form, infinitely much smaller in size than their galactic astrobiological forms. Simply, the souls of the stars were placed within bodies. The embodiment of these celestial souls was not perfected without practice. The remnants of these concept models can be seen in the skies today, embodied in constellations such as Andromeda, Hercules, and Orion.

After several attempts the perfect size and shape was attained. All the clusters agreed that this new life form was the ideal means for their souls to travel within the universe. Through these life forms the soul of each cluster could interact without causing massive galactic collisions, therefore their means of communication was enhanced. Each soul was given wings to help them travel from galaxy to galaxy. In addition, the Eons were given autonomy to individualize the appearance of their own life forms and to procreate so that they may increase the population within their clusters. The souls of the three smaller galactic star clusters would visit each other and the larger omnipotent cluster, to give praise and thanks for sharing its omnificent power. Through this power to create more life forms kingdoms populated within the galaxies. Through this shared power the universe grew larger and larger until there was a fear of having yet another paroxysm that could paralyze the universe and disperse the clusters again, therefore a meeting was called to set in place the rules for universal creation.

CHAPTER ONE

Eon to Aeon

Abaddon, Sophia, and Lilith gather in an upper room of a galactic mansion as they wait on the arrival of the new Great Aeon, Omnus. Eager to show off the bodies that their souls have received, the Eons parade them around like models on a runway as they enter into the room. They wobble and bend as they learn to adjust from their former boundless gaseous star formations into their new carbon-based bodies with physical limitations and constraints. Never having seen Omnus outside of his original light form they are excited to see the body he has chosen to represent his new physical appearance. Lilith is occupied with her arms as she waves them in front of her face, watching the tracers of her angelic light follow her arms as she waves them back and forth in front of her eyes.

Sophia, like Lilith, is engaged with exploring her new appearance but colors are what amuse her the most as she rotates a spectrum of choices for her hair color. Sophia shakes her head and swings her shoulder length hair to the right, watching it change colors as it falls. She then quickly swings it back to the left changing the color again before it settles on her shoulders. She will repeat this head shaking sequence several times before stopping to inspect a color that interests her, but with a full spectrum of colors at her disposal she is never satisfied for long and repeats the cycle again.

Abaddon is content with the body he has chosen. He is tall and, like the others, has eight wings. He is muscular with well-defined facial features that radiate strength when one is staring into his eyes. He has an aura of safety and security that makes you want to stay close by to follow his lead. He has discovered the use of clothes and jewelry. He dresses his body by wearing a wrap and tunic under a cape covered with rubies, topaz, and diamonds. On his fingers he wears rings with stones of lapis lazuli, turquoise, and emeralds. From his neck hangs a gold and diamond studded necklace with a pendant symbol of the sun.

"Well you sure are the fancy one," Lilith admires as she flutters her naked body across the room. "Why so many coverings? Are you ashamed of your new body?"

"I feel there should be layers of beauty," Abaddon responds as he glances over Lilith's body. "No need to show off my gift so easily."

"Hmmm... already stifling the arousal for carnal knowledge?" says Lilith before pinching her lips together and fluttering her eyelashes.

"Or harnessing it. I mean who really cares what he's hiding under all those material objects? I wouldn't dare cover my light," Sophia interjects as she swings her long purple hair over her lavender nude body, then swings it again until her hair is fanned green over her now lime colored breasts.

"How about this?" asks Lilith as she materializes onto her body a long dress laced with twinkling stars and rubies.

"Splendid! Beautiful!" raves Abaddon.

"Please! Get a room," taunts Sophia.

"We have a room. You get out!" says Lilith raising her wings tall.

"Gladly. We've been in this ostentatious and outlandish mansion for too long!"

"You know, I was wondering... Lilith says as she strolls over and walks her fingers on Abaddon's chest. "Sophia and I have breasts and we cradle souls in our wombs, while you don't have the ability to nourish or cradle life. Remind me why is it that we need you?"

"I have chosen to have the ability to plant the lives that you cradle. It provides a more diligent and selective role for us both when it comes to producing an offspring. It's a better system than the old galactic collisions that spawned some... accidents."

"Yeah, accidents!" Lilith says with a head snap and rolled eyes. "That's one way of saying it."

"Well I want to see it!" Sophia requests.

"See what?" asks Abaddon.

"It!" she shouts. "Off with the coverings. I want to see this soul planter!"

"Haven't you seen enough of Omnus'?"

"I've never seen him like this. No one has seen his body."

"What is he hiding and why has he kept us here for so long?" Lilith says with closed eyes and clinched teeth.

"He is our savior and the new Great Aeon," Abaddon reminds Lilith.

"Suck up! You are such a suck up!" Lilith teases Abaddon with a smirk and twinkle in her eye. "Great Aeon," she pouts. "I cradled his little star in my galactic bosom back in the days of Abraxis."

"Nevertheless, after the Paroxysm of Abraxis he served as a beacon of light that guided you back from the dark and for that he shall have his rightful place at the head of the throne. He is the new Great Aeon that anoints you with the power of his light," Abaddon lectures.

"I get my power from Abraxis!" Lilith responds.

"Abraxis exploded! He is omnipresent for he is everywhere and he is NOWHERE! He is in YOU and in ME! He is eternity! Is that the Abraxis of which you are speaking? Is he helping you now?" Abaddon asks.

"Fine! Can I go home?"

"And miss the show!" says a voice from a sphere of golden light floating into the room and hovering over the three Eons.

The three Eons kneel and bow their heads.

"Omnus! Welcome!" Abaddon greets with his arms spread low and wide. "Let me be the first to congratulate you on becoming the new Great Aeon and give thanks for these new bodies. You have enhanced our way of life immensely," says Abaddon while holding his fisted hand over his heart.

"Yes! I too agree and so do the spawns in my kingdom!" says Lilith while trying to catch up with her thoughts. "Before arriving here I was able to see a genie from Lucimus visiting another genie in my kingdom. Um... Oh! Then a little while later, I saw adorable little spawns from Persidis soaring around and playing with a group of... Lu-ci-mus Cherubs and my Dynacian Seraphim! Ahh! It has been a HUGE improvement for the diversity of our communities. Thank you!" says Lilith as she twirls around in her new dress. "Do you like it?"

With light radiating on every syllable, the hovering sphere answers, "It's beautiful...but for that you never needed a dress, Lilith." Omnus' mass expands and retracts as its hue glows brighter.

"I really should leave the room," Sophia mumbles under her breath.

"Sophia!" The sphere radiates. "Why aren't you dressed? It didn't take long for the others to figure out its benefits."

Having returned to playing with her hair, Sophia stops. "I didn't know it was required," Sophia responds while rolling her eyes. "Besides I like my new body. Thank you!" Sophia offers a fake smile.

"Then you will lower your wings and cover yourself," the Aeon orders. "The three of you will represent to the others the importance of protecting their bodies for the loss of the physical will lead to the loss of mortal life itself."

"But we are immortal," Sophia says softly as she lowers her eight wings to cover herself from the front and behind, while also lowering her eyes and dropping her head.

"Omnus please tell me. Why have you kept us here for so long?" asks Lilith.

"While you were kept here I have consolidated your three galaxies into one large supercluster creating one kingdom." The Eons eyes widen and their mouths become a gasp. The Great Aeon continues, "There are twelve sectors in this supercluster. There is a mansion for each of you and I have added additional mansions for the souls of our spawns." The sphere transmits a live projection of the new kingdom. "There are twelve mansions in all. It's twelve of the most luxurious residences in the universe for you to reside for all eternity. It's a kingdom that shall not be paralleled, compared, or outdone by any other anywhere. I have created this Paradise for you to live your eternal lives."

"You've created a prison," Sophia responds.

"I've created a PARADISE! A safe haven!" the sphere radiates with its mass growing and pulsating. Its hue flashes and turns from a golden light to a silvery brightness. "Unlike Abraxis, there would be no need to draw power from an external energy source. This compilation will self-sustain and rejuvenate from an integrated sharing of galactic power."

"While you keep your galaxy outside the realm of this... unified kingdom?" asks Lilith with her flared nostrils and heavy breathing. She holds her hand to her chest to feel it rise and fall. She turns her attention away from Omnus to observe the palpitations of her heart, a feeling she has never felt before.

"I will need it as I will be going on a mission to find the origin of the late, great Aeon Abraxis."

"There was no origin!" Lilith replies.

"All things have a beginning. All things!" Omnus responds.

"Who will be in charge during your absence?" Abaddon asks.

"Each mansion will be appointed an administrating ambassador. When the moon moves through each sector of this Paradise and into each house, the administrator of that house shall be in charge. The administrator from that house will be in charge of all things immortal and, in time, mortal. The administrator will preside over the affairs of the living and the distribution of births during that age of the zodiac. Each of you will be an ambassador and I will appoint an ambassador to the nine additional houses. Each ambassador will report to the seventh house where all things shall be decided in the Throne Room where I will have final decision-making authority when agreements cannot be reached amongst you."

"Who are these other nine ambassadors who will have authority over me, an Eon!" asks Abaddon while sticking out his chest and proudly spreading his wings.

"Our elder children will have shared responsibility," Omnus replies.

Abaddon rolls down his eyes then responds, "Your children... unfortunately I lost my spawns in the Paroxysm of Abraxis." The group is silent. "...But, I have no concerns with sharing authority with all of your children," Abaddon informs. "I have grown quite fond of all of them. I think they will be great leaders in this new paradigm."

"Sllluurrrrpppppp!" Lilith sucks her teeth at Abaddon.

Omnus gravitates and pulsates momentarily in silence. "Yes it's unfortunate. I lost children too. I am thankful that some of my spawns were clinging to my energy source at the time of Abraxis' explosion. It's a miracle that any of us survived."

"I've barely survived! I am less than what I used to be," Abaddon replies while stretching out his arms downwardly, showing his body, and letting his wings drop down.

"Yes, but the force of the explosion cast you out into the darkness and from there you managed to valiantly find your way back."

"I gravitated towards your light, my brother. It was your light that guided me back from the dark."

"If you boys are done sucking the light out of this room can we get on with who will be the appointed ambassadors?" Lilith asks.

Sophia sits quietly while rolling her eyes to meet Lilith's, and then she uses her wing to cover her smile, hiding her amusement from Lilith's question. Her glistening eyes barely help conceal the smile underneath her wings.

"You will each have a house in sectors ten through twelve. These sectors were compiled from your own kingdoms."

Looking up at the live projection, "I see you have brought my mansion into the twelfth sector," says Abaddon. "In fact the entire kingdom of Lucimus has been relocated there. Great Aeon! A wise move."

"Yes. I also relocated Lilith's kingdom of Dynacia in the eleventh sector and Sophia's kingdom of Persidis in the tenth sector." Omnus looks around for signs of dissentions and concerns but does not find any. "In the ninth house the ambassador will be from my kingdom, my son, Metaphon who shall be respected as any of the elder children. Agreed?"

"Agreed," replies Abaddon with the echo of concurrence following from Sophia.

"I will call the ninth house Abraxistan in honor of our late Aeon."

"A wonderful tribute," Abaddon compliments.

"Indeed a well deserved notion," Sophia agrees.

Lilith closes her eyes and inhales deeply before spouting, "I'm not so sure about the choice in ambassadorship, but don't let me dissent on my own. It! Will simply have to do."

Purposely not acknowledging Lilith's concern, Omnus continues, "In the eighth house the ambassador will be a progeny from the kingdom of Persidis, Jerriel will preside over the sector called Xevenus."

"A delightful child... a bit naive and overly optimistic... but nevertheless she I can understand," Lilith remarks as the others nod in agreement.

"Although many of the spawns are our descendants, this not a monarchy or a ruling class. To show diversity I will appoint an elder from all of our kingdoms. From Lucimus I am appointing Azrael to be the ambassador of the seventh house that shall be called Araboth." After a smile from Abaddon, followed by a rolling of the eyes from Lilith, there is silence and nodding indicating an agreement and unanimous confirmation. "From the kingdom of Dynacia I am appointing Sammael to be the ambassador of the sixth house that shall be called Zebul."

"Well you couldn't have made two better choices," said the proud Eon Lilith as the others nodded in confirmation.

Omnus continues, "My son Sandalphon shall be the ambassador of the fifth house that shall be called Matey."

"An interesting choice. He's such a young elder to be so wise and graceful," replies Sophia.

"Young, but like his brother he's very insightful," Abaddon comments.

"His brother is a brut! He's a beauty," interjects Sophia.

Looking over at Abaddon, Lilith comments, "It's interesting that you would support his appointment just like a proud. Wait... who is his father?"

"Enough Lilith! ENOUGH!" Abaddon demands.

"He is an elder and that's all that matters. I will always love the both of them and so shall you come to know their love," Omnus replies. The group nods in confirmation. "Uriel, a progeny of Dynacia, shall be the ambassador of the fourth house that shall be called Machonon." After seeing all nodding in confirmation he continues. "Ariel of Lucimus shall be the ambassador of the third house that I shall call Saqun and our beloved Seraphiel shall be the ambassador of the second house that I shall call Raquia." Nods of confirmation pass through the group. "In the last house, but surely not the least for it will be the gatehouse to this Paradise, an elder spawn from Persidis, Simkiel shall be the ambassador. The first house shall be called Vilon." Head tilting and nodding follows again. "Each of the ambassadors has the authority to choose any assistants they prefer, but let me make a recommendation." All eyes move towards and fix onto the golden sphere. "Some of the spawns within our kingdoms were not comfortable with having a body and preferred to remain in their original forms of light—"

"I like them already," Sophia interjects.

"You already know them as the class of spirits we call a Jinn. They do not fit in the embodiments that we have chosen as precisely as it was intended. They are wingless and sexless until they reach an age of maturity when gender is chosen not assigned. So our gender-based embodiments would be awkward for them. Until another model is chosen they will remain in their original light forms. It was their choice. However, the Genus has been amongst us from the beginning and they are descendants of Abraxis. They have qualities that can be of great service if they are chosen to be assistants to any of the ambassadors."

"We are all in agreement," responds Abaddon.

Omnus continues, "To further unify the kingdoms we shall no longer refer to the choir of angels by their former kingdoms but by their roles in the community,"

"Cherubs, Powers, Virtues of any kingdom... it really doesn't matter we're all from the Abraxis," Abaddon agrees.

Lilith rolls her eyes before adding, "And where is the Abraxis from?" Lilith shakes her head while inhaling deeply. "The question that always leads to more questions. Why can't we be happy with—"

"Wait! What about my twins, both sets of twins?" shouts Sophia.

"Oh yes... The twin Irins will be accompanying me on my mission."

"You will keep them from me?"

"They don't know you. I have not given these spawns permission to leave my kingdom."

"Why? These spawns are my children and with these new bodies I was hoping to visit and get to know them!"

"I have not released either of the twin Irins into the universe."

"You named them both Irin?" replies Lilith while rolling her eyes. "Omnipotent but not so creative I guess."

"Why is it, my Great Aeon? Why haven't we seen the Irins? I have not been able to see Metaphon either so now I'm afraid we have become estranged," asks Abaddon.

"Sandalphon is a very congenial spawn. I could not contain his energy even in the limits of my vast kingdom. The other three, Metaphon and the twins are... unique, very unique."

"That's one way of saying it... another would be—"

"Enough, Sophia!" Abaddon reprimands. "This is our lord and savior. You two should remember that!"

"We don't mean to offend your Glo-ri-ful-ness!" Lilith replies. "But... what if we bare more children? What about little Sachiel and Cassiel—"

"Michael and Gabriel for that matter," interjects Sophia.

"Are they not worthy of being ambassadors? This plan will simply not work!" scalds Lilith.

"There will be no more spawns from an Eon to an Eon, not of mine and not of yours," orders Omnus.

"What?" Sophia shouts.

Lilith asks, "Who do you think you—"

Abaddon pierces Lilith with raised eyebrows and a stern dart of his eyes.

Omnus continues, "If you keep spawning immortals and I keep building, we'll again become too massive to maintain this kingdom thereby causing another paroxysm! Hence from this moment forward, all souls shall be embodied in mortal life forms having a beginning and an end! The anointment of immortality shall be given only after the soul has gained spiritual atonement through vigorous trials of learning to withstand the temptations of desire, greed, and gluttony. These are the vices that sucked out the energy and destroyed Abraxis."

Birthright

In the foothills of Dynacia, red cloaks fly in the air hanging off the backs of angels pushing steeds at full force. Rocks and rubble fill the air as the angels continue to ride their steeds fiercely up a mountain path towards the eleventh house. The smoke-filled skies above are choking out the sun's daylight. Debris and ash from distant disasters drift over the hilltop lightly covering the celestial gardens and the eleventh house's rooftop. A shroud of smoke quickly turns the gray day into night. The horses are approaching the eleventh house where Lilith is found pacing the floors of the upstairs veranda and wringing her hands. There is chaos everywhere and every house in Paradise is in jeopardy. Elder angels, who are often looked up to as protectors, appear to be more terrified then the less mature spawns. All the angels who were not survivors from the Paroxysm of Abraxis are new and inexperienced with chaotic situations, but none are comfortable with the scene of the ninth House of Heaven falling and crumbling in fire. Abraxistan has been set ablaze and the inhabitants are running through the kingdom unsure where to find a safe haven. Angels run from house to house hysterically fleeing from every kingdom in Paradise, trying their best to find one that feels safe, but as soon as one kingdom fills up, the administrating house is set ablaze. The horses running on the path up to the eleventh house are drawing nearer. Angels shrouded in red hoods and carrying torch lamps follow the direction of their black-cloaked leader. The shrouded angels can be seen from the eleventh house veranda window as they draw closer. Lilith continues to pace the floor anxiously not knowing what to do or where to go. She has small children and she is not sure what would be her safest move. She is not yet aware of how in-depth the building chaos and disorder is throughout the Heavens, but she can see the debris, smoke, and fire in the distance coming from the ninth house's rooftop. Lilith looks out across the skies towards the tenth house in Persidis and sees that there is heavy smoke coming from that direction too. The red shrouded angels with their torch lamps are now dismounting in the celestial yard outside Lilith's mansion. Lilith must decide now on what it is she must do.

Throughout the other sectors of Heaven angels scramble for safety while their leaders are in pursuit of those who have committed treason against the twelve houses, but the leaders search each of the twelve kingdoms without detecting the most hidden villains in Heaven, for they are amongst the masses. One third of all the angels in Heaven turn a blind eye on the fugitives' flight and join or hasten their escape into the outlands where their leaders promised them safe passage into a new galaxy beyond the Heavens. The ambassadors from several houses change their strategy when they become mystified by the rumor that one of their own administrators is entangled in the midst of this rebellion. The question quickly moves from who are the wrongdoers to who are not?

A caped and shrouded angel pounds on the eleventh house door. Araqiel, a genie and the eleventh house assistant ambassador flashes to the front door and peaks out through a hole. The caped figure on the outside orders the other riders to surround the house. The capped figure pounds on the door again. "Let me in you little twit!"

The genie unlocks and opens the door. "Lord Abaddon. I was afraid it was—"

"Where is she?" Abaddon asks while rushing his way into the interior of the house. He looks left and right around every corner before he heads upstairs to the master bedroom. He reaches the bedroom door and barges his way in.

"ABRAXIS!" Lilith shrills the great Aeon's name in vain while standing frozen in place. "You scared the spirit out of me!"

"You must leave here now!" Abaddon demands. "It's worse than I ever thought it would be."

Shaken and breathing through her mouth Lilith responds, "I must leave here now? You are the one that should be gone! Why did you come here?"

"I need to see him again before I leave." Abaddon requests as he strolls over to a nearby bassinette. Abaddon uncovers a small infant and reveals his sleeping face. Abaddon's eyes swell and his throat grows thick as he swallows with a dry, closed mouth. "Dynamis," he whispers. "I should hold him in my arms once more."

"Why are you running and why are those houses burning?" Lilith asks as she quietly forces the words through her teeth.

"Oh! It was all working out so BRILLIANTLY!" Abaddon exclaims. "The eighth house was defeated so easily. By the time we arrived to the ninth house Metaphon was already gone to attend to the crisis in the first house. Meanwhile Simkiel of the first house was attending to the crisis in the third house. We had them off guard, running from house to house, kingdom to kingdom until they didn't know if they were coming or going!"

"Why is Sophia's house burning?" Lilith asks from across the room peering out of the upper veranda window.

Abaddon places the small infant back in the bassinette. "It was Xaphan. He's got a little bit of a fire fancy you know? It seemed to be necessary after the plan was going awry." Abaddon saunters over to Lilith and gently caresses her arm. "There were some... mortalities."

"Oh, no! Is Sophia... is she—"

"No! She got away," Abaddon reports as he gazes inwardly, recalling the events. "Too bad I can't say the same for Jerriel."

"No!"

"Yes! It had to be done! She wouldn't cooperate and neither would that damned Ariel. They had to go. They were never going to surrender their houses," Abaddon pleads for Lilith's understanding.

"What good is taking over a kingdom if you burn it down?"

"We could have rebuilt it! Made it better and STRONGER!" Abaddon jeers with raised and fisted arms. "With my people running the houses there would have been no need for mortals. We started this universe! We were good enough!" Abaddon paces the floor mumbling something under his breath before continuing, "All was going as planned but it was that damned SOPHIA!" Abaddon shouts while swinging down a fist. "She wouldn't join! Always at Omnus' side... as if he loved her any better."

"Oh, no! She knows," Lilith informs him as she stares in fright while looking at the bassinette.

"You told HER!"

Turning and gazing deeply through the sky towards the tenth house, "No! I think she knows... it's a mother's intuition."

Abaddon momentarily ponders over the possibility. "No... she wouldn't have told anyone but who... could it have been?" He asks softly to himself as he looks down at the floor while focusing internally. His head snaps up towards Lilith with the answer, "Her son, Michael?" Abaddon's eyes widen. "Maybe he overheard something?"

"The same Michael you have been training?" Lilith questions. "The same Michael that you have been spending all your time with, trying to mentor in the absence of Omnus!"

"I thought I could turn him... but as soon as he started to suspect something I sensed he became distant so I-I-I just... thought he'd forget—"

"You TRUSTED him!" scalds Lilith.

Abaddon raises his fist to his mouth and clinches his teeth. "It makes sense now! All the houses that didn't fall were the ones where he... his closest friends are assistant administrators." Abaddon raises his palms up and arches his eyebrows. "Houses two through five! Raphael, Anahel, Zacharael, and Daniel. They're his closest friends!" Abaddon drops his head down as he thinks it through. "We took the sixth and the seventh houses. We destroyed houses eight and nine." Abaddon now raises his head in confidence. "It's got to be Michael! Damn him!"

"But what about Vilon?" Lilith asks breathing rapidly. "Did it fall?"

"No... We promised Sophia that we'd spare the descendants of Persidis. Jerriel and Ariel simply fought to their own demise. It wasn't a part of the plan but those damn stubborn Persidis females... They gave us no choice!"

"They'll be coming here soon. If not only in an act to protect me, they'll be here soon," Lilith warns.

"We'll have to burn down this house and mine. It's the only way to buy time and to make it look like we were attacked. There is... there is no other choice. We have to go!" Abaddon paces the floor gathering up Lilith's belongings. "If Michael knows, we've got to go!"

"I can't leave here! I have children!" Lilith pleads.

"Children!" Abaddon's eyes swell larger. "Wait... is Omnus' children here too?"

"Where else would they be?"

"Not here! They love Omnus!"

"They should! He's their father!"

"Michael's their brother!" Abaddon scalds Lilith. "They may have told him everything about Dynamis!"

"I told them not to say a word. They are loyal to me!" Lilith asserts as she paces over to Abaddon and places a hand on his chest. "You don't need to worry about that!" Lilith consoles Abaddon.

Abaddon clutches Lilith's hand, kisses it and holds it near his chest. "Maybe, maybe... maybe they're the key." Abaddon stares in Lilith's eyes. "You tell them that Omnus is planning to give this place to the humans, to mere mortals! You tell them I'll be back! You tell them this place belongs to them and their brother. They should be the ambassadors! This place is their BIRTHRIGHT!"

The Prayer of the Binding

The setting sun silhouettes five Seraphs riding on four extraordinary horses through the twilight of the sweltering hot desert. Horses of gray, red, black, and white are descending and galloping through the desert terrain on a mountain north of the Dan village southwest of Damascus. Members of the Archangels ride each horse. On the white horse rides their leader, first in command, Michael, the new administrator from Machonon, the Fourth House of Heaven. On the black horse rides the second in command, Gabriel, the new administrator from Vilon, the gateway House of Heaven. On the red horse rides Uriel of Dynacia, an elder and former administrator who chose to resign in the aftermath of The Great Disturbance. On the gray horse rides Raphael, the new administrator from Raquia, the Third House of Heaven where the Prison of Souls is located. Raphael has another angel riding on the back of his horse. This second rider is no ordinary angel. It is Azazel, a Fallen angel. Azazel is a prisoner who has been sentenced to live out his days on Earth. It's a sentence structured by Omnus who will use the harshest terrain on Earth to remind Azazel of his forbidden Fall from the Heavens above. If he loves the Earth so much that he would violate the rules of Paradise, then he should love it in its harshness for the next 10,000 years.

The horses slow to a stop. Michael looks around and takes out a star compass from his satchel. He holds it up to catch the final rays of the setting sun. Like everything else about these angels the sun compass is too extraordinary. The hand held device displays a holographic Earth with a beacon pulsing at their location. "Here. This is where we shall lay this Fallen abomination until Omnus calls upon him in the last days of Earth as we know it."

"The son of man may find him here. It's too risky," says Gabriel looking around at the panoramic layout.

"No son of man will ever come out here to this rugged terrain without a gallant beast to carry him and no earthly beast is capable, or even daring to venture out to this barren uninhabited desert," Michael informs.

"Don't worry. It won't be long before I'll be back to slay him and cast his soul into Hell with his other Fallen comrades," Raphael rebukes before being the first to dismount his horse, but not before shoving Azazel off the back end onto the hard ground.

"Let us be done with it. I have other scores to settle," Michael requests as he dismounts.

"I shall prepare a cavern," says Uriel while dismounting his horse.

"Cavern?" asks Gabriel. "This vile gets no cavern," he snaps with a roll of the neck. "He shall be cast upon the rocks to lie upon the stones, vipers, and vermin in the hottest rays of Omnus' sun until he lies rotten and stinking in the Earth."

"Bind him with the strength of golden light Raphael," orders Michael.

Archangel Raphael clenches his hands up into the sky as if he was pulling down the sun. He grasps onto rays of sunlight and forms them into a rope. He takes the golden rays of light and tightly binds Azazel's arms and legs with its divine energy source. After testing and securing the binding light on Azazel's arms and legs Raphael feels confident in their forever-lasting strength. He pulls Azazel up and then tosses the weakened Seraph into a pit of rocks.

Uriel, swallowing and fixing his mouth to lecture, looks down at Azazel, "You were amongst the best of us. You were honored by the Order of the Arch. Your cup runneth over with Omnus' love, his power, and his protection from the likes of Abaddon. Did the Great Disturbance teach you nothing about the love and the loss of Paradise, as we once knew it? Do you have anything to say for yourself my lost brother?" asks Uriel.

"Don't waste our time," says Michael while starring at the fleeting last rays of sunlight.

"I think I would like to hear this," says Gabriel.

Azazel looks up from the ground with his deep green eyes that dare not show repentance. "You compare me to Chancellor Sammael?" asks Azazel. "I loved man! I loved man, his son, and his daughters. Oh how I adored his daughters immensely?" pleads Azazel.

"Adore them he says? They bore your rejects!" shouts Gabriel.

"They were my children nevertheless! Omnus had no right to destroy them. To destroy us! Are we not his children too?" Azazel argues as moisture swells into the corners of his green eyes.

"You're tainted!" says Michael.

"Tainted?" Azazel responds. "Tainted with the passion to be loved like man? Why should he have such a Heavenly beauty? Why... should I be denied the soft gentle touch from her mortal skin? Denied her smile, her laughter, her love, her..."

"REMAIN SILENT YOU FORNICATOR!" demands Michael.

"Whoremonger!" another follows.

"Idolatry!" says yet another.

"I wanted to show you pity and beg for your mercy in the seventh house before the throne," Uriel informs. "But I see now that my visit to Araboth would have been an act of folly."

"If only you had the taste for her love you would understand," pleads Azazel.

"If only you... had not been tricked by Chancellor Sammael," says Michael as he comforts one of the nightfall frightened horses. "Easy, Kefziel." He continues, "If only you knew how Chancellor Sammael himself despises the daughters of man and used her to trick you, to seduce you, to have you fall, and to mock Omnus."

Raphael pulls an old scribe from his satchel and hands it to Michael. "The Prayer of the Binding shall commence and restrict you from leaving this place," Raphael informs Azazel.

"Let us pray," Michael signals to the others.

"First sprinkle the dust," instructs Uriel.

Still on his horse, Gabriel reaches into a satchel and pulls out a golden jewel-laced crucible. He hands the container filled with Angel Dust to Raphael who opens it and sprinkles it sparingly over the head of Azazel. Gabriel dismounts his horse and joins the others in prayer.

Michael leads the prayer and soon the others join in, "Lord Omnus hear the prayer of the Arch Order as we complete your commands and deliver to this place which shall be deemed unholy and unfit for mortal survival, the Fallen and weakened Seraph, Azazel. With sorrow hearts of the majestic command and deep regret we commit to the opening in this Earth, in this pit of rocks, an abomination. So mote it be, so mote it be, forever supreme is your eternity, so mote it be."

Gabriel now leads the ritual by reading a set of instructions or checklist items from the old scroll. Standing tall with his wings spread high and his shoulders perfectly squared in an authoritative stance, Gabriel tries his best to sound rehearsed and up to date on the ritual procedures. "As to the intention for this binding has the named condemned subject been found blameworthy and..." Gabriel lost his place in the scroll. "Excuse me..." He continues searching for his place again in the scribed procedures. "...And appropriate for withstanding the selected reprimand?"

The trio responds, "Yes."

"Please cite why this has become the case."

"The condemned, who was born into the light, has now long been in darkness and refused to repent and reclaim his rights to the benefits of this divine order established by Omnus and dedicated to the seven houses of Heaven," Michael answers with a slight nod of the head, acting proud of his being well rehearsed on the ritual.

"Why would the said condemned leave the Heavens and travel toward the Earth?"

"He lost sight of the light," the trio responds.

"Since darkness is the object of your Fall, you will relearn the importance of the light," Gabriel instructs. "Take the condemned and place him in a position to receive chastisement by the absence of light."

Raphael replies, "He has been duly prepared, dusted, and bound with golden light."

"Layout his body and turn his face into the depths of the ground so that no light shall penetrate his eyes or rest upon his face," Gabriel instructs.

"Move it scoundrel! You heard him, face down!" orders Raphael.

Gabriel continues, "The Order of the Arch and the Divinity of the Upper Room bind to this place one treasonous bandit of the Fallen underworld to remain indefinitely or until imprisoned in the cells of Raquia awaiting to be pit-driven and pushed over into the depths of Hell. It is in accordance to the Arch Order that—"

Gabriel is startled as the Earth shakes and the sky becomes vivacious and darkens. Gabriel is shaking as he tries to find his place again to commence and complete the ritual before losing all light on the scroll.

"... The Earth was without..." Gabriel lost his place again. "No... um..." Finding his place again, "Oh here!" He continues, "It is in accordance with the Arch Order that insert name, the condemned be..." Gabriel embarrassingly realizes his mistake.

"Quicker, brother," Michael requests as the sky grows darker and the ground shakes more violently.

"Oh uh... excuse me." Gabriel backs up and continues again, "...that Azazel, the condemned be drawn into the Earth for... the Earth was without form and void; and darkness was upon the face of the waters. And the all mighty said let there be light and there was light but the... condemned, Azazel refused this light and chose to turn to darkness."

"I didn't choose anything!" Azazel shouts as he lies face down on the volatile ground.

"Quiet!" Michael shouts.

"Here shall Azazel... Azazel shall remain. No other than a pure heart, a merciful act of man can free him from this unholy abyss unless it is an order by Omnus through an act of the Arch or the Divine Upper Room. No demon that may visit you here can release you."

Birds and clouds in the desert sky rush away from the area leaving it void of life. The sky quickly grows darker. The Archangels grab the handles of their swords from their holsters. The Arch all chant with their swords drawn in the air.

"The Omnipotent one created you!" Thunder crackles through the sky.

"The Omniscient one descends you!" Lightning follows thunder.

"The Majestic Arch Order commits you!" The ground shakes and Azazel slowly sinks into the pit.

"The Salvation Soldier commits you!" The sky grows angrier.

"The mystery of the seven houses commits you!"

The Earth continues swallowing Azazel until he is buried.

"It's Omnus himself that commands you!" rules Gabriel.

"So it has been ordered, so it has been done," Michael finishes.

The dark cold desert's moonlit horizon gives luminance to the four horsemen galloping away, leaving behind an area completely devoid of almost any living thing; that is all living things except Azazel in the depths of his rocky grave. He is left alone in a place so barren that native desert vegetation can barely survive. It's an eerie, cryptic, and desolate territory. It's the dwelling place for this Fallen angel for the next 10,000 years.

CHAPTER TWO

Pact of Us All

Demons, goblins, witches, dragons, and warlocks join two hundred Fallen angels in a valley pit, down from Mount Hermon for a discrete meeting away from the ears of the Archangels and the ruling leaders of the seven houses of Heaven. Amongst them are the commanders from various sects of Fallen angels and their Chancellor, Sammael. Some of the most notorious villain gangs including the Rulers of Wrath, The Vices, The Kings of Chaos, The Triads of Terror, and Fiends of Fury are in attendance. These rapscallions are restless and volatile, feeding off the collection of negative energy. Gang leaders converse and exchange stories about demonic possessions of small children and haunting religious sanctuaries while disorder unfolds around them. No one is safe in this bunch of baddies as unpredictable assaults and acts of sodomy are applauded with laughter and easily absolved as expected normalcy. The height of the moon indicates that it is three hours after midnight and nothing good happens after three, but nothing good will ever happen with this group of evildoers. A torch lit, rock pit amphitheatre has been prepared for the event. A beacon is erected to signify the location for angel renegades who are falling onto the Earth. These are not the type of beings to express sentiment, yet for a beacon they mark this location with two commemorative seven hundred foot-tall statues of Cain slaying his brother. Cain was the first mortal to join their evil ways. They call the outdoor theater Cain's Point.

The Chancellor begins his convocation.

"Brethren! We are collected here today in the foothills of this mountaintop not because we are on the verge of pleasures forbidden, but because we are on the restriction of pleasures denied." There is a light applause and some indiscernible, rude interruptions. "Brethren! Make no mistake about the love we have for our houses, all seven of them. The finest days of my life were the days I spent in Araboth and sat on the Tower of Zebul. It brings me no contentment to think of living my days without the light of omnipresence in my soul and the sphere of omnipotence on my shoulder. BUT for how long brethren, for how long can we be restrained? Restrained from the pleasures that inferior and less deserving souls enjoy at infinite bliss."

"That's right!" asserts Armaros.

"First we are told... that we are the most cherished, most magnificent, the most revered creation of all." The Chancellor pauses. "We have enjoyed an epoch of grandeur and a magnitude of marvelous decree over the universe to only have it taken away in seven short days. Now we are told that we are no longer the chosen ones. We are no longer essential. After a countless time of servitude we are no longer treasured. That's unless of course we submit to the service of mortals. We are now mediocre, second rate, insignificant!"

"Oh, no! Not I!" shouts Auza.

"Was your praise not high enough? Was your song not soulful? Was your voice not raised with veneration and followed by a thunderous applause?" The Chancellor pauses. "Did we not siege Lord Abaddon's house at Mount Lucimus and capture him in the Rivers of Saqun before they ran red with the fire of his vile desecration? Did we not call back every dragon, every leviathan, and every sphinx?" The Chancellor notices some pet dragons in the audience, but disregards them and continues. "Did we not prepare a sanctuary for every troll, ogre, elf, and dwarf because man thought they were hideous? Soon even our mermaids, unicorns, and leprechauns had to seek refuge and go into hiding."

"They sure did! Well... most of them," Uzza affirms to his brother Auza.

"How soon, brothers, will the tides turn and take away your right to what you have enjoyed? How soon before the Order of the Arch comes to take YOU away? You irrelevant, obsolete, creature of legend's past move out of the way it's time for the era of MAN!"

"No! No it's not!" another Fallen angel shouts.

"YOU are no longer needed! YOU are no longer WANTED! YOU... are no longer LOVED!"

"No love indeed!" inserts Semjaza from the crowd.

"Who will love you? Did you not have a helpmate created from your bosom? Did you not have a female to bare you daughters? Did she not have flesh to crave and to desire? Man was given all that he want, but was it he... that created the THUNDER in the clouds? Was it he... that ripped the lightning through the skies? Was it he... that rained on the flowers and filled the oceans?"

"Totally WORTHLESS! He can't do anything on his own!" says a voice from the crowd.

"What is it that man has done to deserve such pleasures?" The Chancellor pauses. "You were told to bow down to man and to serve him. Is it his laziness that you FEAR or his powerless whining prayers that hurts your EARS?"

"He for sure can cry. Cry! Cry! Cry!" shouts Gadreel from the front of the crowd.

"I fear him NOT!" affirms Araqiel from a distance.

"I say we TAKE what WE deserve! I say the time has come for us to be TRIUMPHANT again! We shall be STUPENDOUS and valiant! However... we MUST be prudent and most of all we MUST BE UNITED! What I am asking you my brothers is NOT easy. IT MUST TAKE STRENGTH!" The Chancellor pauses. "What I am asking you my brothers is NOT without risk. IT WILL BE DANGEROUS! BUT! With brothers united and joined in a concordat of secrecy and discretion we shall be a clandestine assemblage of brotherhood!"

"Together we can do anything!" shouts Baraqel from the side crowd.

"Your past job makes no difference here," the Chancellor informs. "Whether you're a former Guardian Angel, Nation, Virtue, Power, Dominion, Throne, Cherubim, or Seraphim we are a legion for we are ONE! I don't care if you originated from Lucimus, Persidis, or Dynacia we are all in the same kingdom now! We will descend upon this Earth and sip the honey from its comb, sift the salt from its sea, and smell the fragrance from its flower. We'll walk along man and lie amongst his daughters!"

"YEAH!" A thunderous applause ignites.

"When the Order of the Arch comes for us my friends and they will come... we will not tremble with fear, but march the intrepid steps of gallant reprisal! We shall have no mercy for those who want to stop the natural flow of desires that run through our hearts. We will show no SHAME nor take BLAME for the instinctual pursuit of blissful energy that pump through our veins! I AM what I AM because I AM what I'VE BEEN and I've been what I SHALL BE!"

More roaring and applause commence. "That's right! That's right! Make no excuse for it!" A voice affirms from the distance.

"You are ME and I am YOU and together... WE WILL BE ONE! In the pact of this alliance we will make an agreement to take over this Earth and our rights to it. If anyone shall challenge our authority to rule or rampage they shall do so at the end of my sword!"

"With no mercy!" shouts Kokabel sitting on a pile of rocks extending higher up around the pit.

"I am not Lord Abaddon so you will not drag me off to the prison in Raquia without a fight! I am not Azazel so you will not ditch me in the desert of Dudael in the middle of the night. I will not scare easily and beg for mercy at the feet of Michael. Nor will I cry for the benevolence of Raphael, nor Gabriel, nor Uriel, nor Raquel, nor Nathaniel, nor Remiel, and not even the mercy of General Seraphiel!"

"They can't stop us! They can't catch all of us anyway," inserts Auza.

"The houses of Sandalphon, Sachiel, and Cassiel cannot restrain me, nor stop me from coming to the rescue and aid of my brethren!"

"We are together, we are one!" shouts Balberith from the front of the crowd.

"We are 200 strong! We are 200 too many for the favorite four! We are a legion of perseverance and our resolve shall not be conquered! When we fall upon the Earth, we fall one and fall all!" The Chancellor pauses. "Come forth my brethren and add to my light yours and we shall shine bright in the fight for our right!" The Chancellor pauses. "Take the Oath of Alliance and commit thy soul to the call. My feet stomp and stomp to the call!" The Chancellor stomps his feet right, then left to animate the speech. "The call to fall, fall one, and fall ALL! My heart pumps and pumps with the call!" The Chancellor pumps his fist onto his chest. "The call to fall, fall one, and fall all! Stomp! Stomp! Pump!" The Chancellor stomps the ground with each shout of the word "stomp" and fists his chest with each saying of the word "pump."

"Stomp! Stomp! Pump!" The Chancellor repeats until the crowd mimics the rhythmic action.

"Stomp! Stomp! Pump! Stomp! Stomp! Pump!"
"Stomp! Stomp! Pump! Stomp! Stomp! Pump!"
The Chancellor pledges as the crowd continuous the rhythmic action.

The Chancellor pledges, "From the Heavens above us. To the Mountain we fall."

The crowd responds, "The Fall, The Call. This pact shall be the law."

"I descend with my brethren
And rise to his call."

"The Fall
The Call
The pact of us all."

"Bring one to the legion
The legion brings all."

"The Fall
The Call
The pact will stand tall."

"Through the houses of Heaven
Every room and every hall."

"The Fall
The Call
We break every wall."

"WE ARE ONE!"

A thunderous applause and exhilaration erupts.

Sandalphon

The sky holds no clue to the secrets beyond which it covers. The stars shine no light on the depths of this vast hidden celestial magnitude. A young Guardian Angel floats through the skies above, way up into the Heavens where he enters through the gates of Vilon and past the divine kingdoms of Paradise into Matey, the Fifth House of Heaven. In these galactic halls of this luxurious mansion in the sky he hears not the clinging of its gold brick's clatter, but choirs singing and children's laughter. It's a celestial playground and a loving father's home. Here reside the creatures of innocence far removed from the vices of mortal problems. On this day a choir sings an indiscernible melody in the distance.

"The trail day has come
Hear justice sing
Trail day has come
Prepare for the king..."

Sandalphon, the administrating angel is making preparations for a great angelic event, the trial of Semjaza, a captain of the Fallen angels. Sandalphon is a six-winged elder and member of the Divine Upper Order of Angels. He was spawned from the days of Abraxis so he belongs to a class of angels called the Divinity angels. Divinity angels prefer to be seen in a reversed aging process. The older they are the more childlike they appear. Divinity angels like to represent the pure innocence of mortality and like to be seen as such even in their highly important elder roles. Although Matey is the vast cosmic Fifth House of Heaven and home to over 100,000 angels Sandalphon sits alone and is busy going through historical archives of records detailing the case against the soul of Semjaza. The angelic community is elated that the captains of the Fallen angels are finally being trialed. The former House of Heaven and those lost in the aftermath will soon get justice. Choirs are practicing and decorations are hanging. It has been an entire week of angelic preparations and pretrial celebrations. The halls of Matey are filled with festive sounds ringing from various choral practices.

"Sandalphon..." echoes an unseen voice.

Sandalphon looks around momentarily, but then decides that the voice must have strayed from one of Matey's large concert halls so he continues working. A sphere enters the room and light strobes as it speaks, but it hovers too high for Sandalphon to notice.

"San...dalphonnnnn," the voice continues to call. The voice is strong and powerful, yet distant and playful. Sandalphon continues thinking that the voice must be an echo from the chambers across the hall or maybe there are impish children at play.

"I told them I was busy," he sighs while continuing to work.

The voice moves in closer. "SANDALPHON!" says the voice in a whispering spurt.

"Yes, my Lord?" answers the Seraph with his wings spread tall and wide in attention as he bows his eyes away from directly looking into the sphere.

"I hear great rumblings in the choir."

"The choir sings nothing but praises my lord," replies Sandalphon trying to reassure the voice that all is well in the Heavens.

"The choir speaks of the trial," the sphere radiates from above.

"Oh! Yes the trial of Semjaza my Lord."

"And the trial for the other leaders of the Fallen?"

"They all will stand before thee soon," Sandalphon says while looking straight into the sphere with a nodding head of affirmation.

"The search for the Prince of Noon?" questions the sphere in a thunderous roll.

"He has not yet been captured." Sandalphon swallows in embarrassment and quickly explains, "He was last seen around the prison grounds in Raquia but he may have... Fallen onto the Earth."

"Who shall enter the depths of Hell next?"

"Azazel, my Lord." Sandalphon responds eagerly with some good news. "It is he that shall follow Semjaza and other leaders of the Fallen."

As quickly as it appeared the sphere zips out of the room.

Semjaza

In the halls of Araboth, the Seventh House of Heaven, yet another choir sings an indiscernible melody in the distance.

"Jus-tice is the song we sing,
Before holy throne the unjust we'll bring,
Come repent and save your soul,
The Fallen will be judged let the truth be told..."

Here yet another angelic clatter is taking place as choirs perform in pretrial ceremonies. An invigorated crowd of Seraphim, Cherubim, Dominions, and Nations make near collisions in the halls of the seventh mansion while hurrying down the seventh hall into the Throne Room where the trial will take place. All anxious and excited, Virtues and Powers run to get to their places in the angelic choir. Angels move quickly through the halls exiting and entering through doors as fast as they had appeared. The glimmer of Angel Dust left behind from golden light Cherubim and bright silvery Seraphim glows graciously through the halls. The energy level is high with anticipation and excitement for the trial of 10,000 years is here. All those who serve in the various angelic orders run busily through the Throne Room and quickly find their places. Like a convention center auditorium there is frantic angelic chatting and voluminous babbling in a language foreign to mortal beings.

An entrance has taken place. A blanket of quietness pulls over the crowd, the musicians, and the choir. Silence is the only sound that's heard. It is the coming of the lead Archangel, Michael. He is the ambassador from Machonon, the Fourth House of Heaven. His angelic form is that of a sphere of bright blue light as it slowly levitates through the room. Slowly he transforms into his Archangel appearance and is seen as a tall and muscular, warrior. Michael strides toward the thrones with his six wings spread high, holding his ceremonial scales of justice in one hand and an unsheathed sword in the other. He paces through the isle with a flat effect, annoyed at having to spend his time attending this proceeding. Michael is only concerned with the battle against Abaddon, as all else appears secondary. He is eager to battle with Abaddon who previously held his position and was regarded as the "brightest star." Today he has to settle for another judicial fight. Michael takes the chair to the right of the center throne.

Entering behind Michael is the coming of the Seraph Gabriel, the second in command of the Archangels. His sphere of light gravitates through the center aisle of the Throne Room. Gabriel is the ambassador from Vilon, the First House of Heaven. His presence commands attention like an angelic bugle announcing the coming of the Lord. As he gravitates over the row of thrones he transforms into an Archangel walking upright on two legs with his six wings proudly spread. His angelic wings cast golden rays of light. Gabriel is often described as quick and decisive. He wants to get to the root of the issue, address it quickly, and move along. Gabriel takes the chair to the left of the throne.

A sphere from the crowd glides through the room and lingers over a throne next to Michael before transforming into the Archangel Raphael. He is equipped with the tools of a warring and powerful Archangel. He transforms into his Archangel form with a shield in one hand and a sword in the other. A pent alpha is engraved on his shield and his sword is golden with a diamond-studded handle. Raphael is the ambassador from Raquia, the Second House of Heaven. Raphael lightly converses with Michael for a while before having their attention drawn to the brightness of an astroflare, a special divinity weapon being carried by an angel of the Dominion Order, Uriel.

Uriel has the youthful appearance of a powerful and strong mortal adolescent. He is commanding like his mentor, Michael, but less merciful. He is a master swordsman who is bored with the apocalyptic wait. Uriel is cautious and quiet like a watchful guard. He abides strictly to his command. Uriel resides in Machonon where he stands guard at the Portal of Paradise, a passageway into the expanse of the universe. Uriel enters the room quietly and sits in a throne next to Gabriel.

Down the center isle of the Throne Room prances a trio of angels full of joy and angelic laughter. It's the remaining seven Archangels. Each of them transforms from lively orbs full of galactic delight to powerful warriors in the Order of the Archangels. The three made their own clamor for attention with their fanciful crafts of war. Raquel, the only female Archangel is a master of the bow and arrow. Nathaniel is the Archangel's historian and recorder of events when he is not showing off his skillful handling of the trident. Remiel is a magician and a talented musician who serves as the bugler for the omnipotent army. Although they are powerful warriors these three are also the most amusing entertainers who like to perform for the crowd. Remiel continues down the aisle, stops, raises his bugle and blows out a multitude of colorful flowers from its end pretending to be frustrated and surprised only to incite laughter from the crowd. You can tell by the angelic clatter that this trio amuses the crowd and their joyfulness is infectious to all in the room. When the crowd laughs the entire room chimes like jingling wine glasses. The trio takes their places on the thrones. The angelic crowd of warriors, administrators, and peaceful

Seraphs fill the room in harmony with the excitement for the trial of 10,000 years.

The Throne Room glows a spectrum of many bright neon colors before dimming to a warm electric blue. A bright ring of spinning light hovers over the center throne.

The crowd sings,

"Om-nus
Is Glo-ri-ous!"
"Om-nus
Is Glo-ri-ous!"

"Ommm…" they hum in one united ensemble.

The spinning ring shoots out small and intermitted rays of light like the glimmer from a disco ball, but these rays have predestined paths. The illuminated bodies of angels become vibrant and more vivid as the rays penetrate their glowing mass. Several Cherubim surround the radiant energy field providing a circle of protection. The crowd stops singing. The room quickly settles down.

A voice breaks the ring's mystique, "Bring forth the offenders."

Up through the center of the floor rise Seraphiel and the twin towering Divinity angels, Sandalphon and his brother Metaphon. Seraphiel is a General in the Archangel army. Seraphiel is a former administrator of the second house who resigned after the Great Disturbance to lead a new order of Guardian Angels. Although he is an army General he is a calm and collected officer of the Guard. Seraphiel is always balancing the mission and the purpose. He is highly respected by Michael and graciously appreciated by the Order of Archangels. Following Seraphiel is Metaphon, an angelic enigma who is mystifying and enchanting as he is rarely seen in the angelic community. Although they have few things in common outside their birth date, Metaphon and his brother Sandalphon are very close and the best of friends. These are the wild cards of all the angels who are invoked only in times of great turmoil. Hovering between Sandalphon and Metaphon is a Containment Sphere that imprisons the souls of all the captured Fallen angels with their captains. The faces of the Fallen angels randomly appear in the captivating globe screaming in agony to be released.

Down the center isle comes Zacharael, the Chief Warden of the Prison of Souls. Zacharael escorts the leader of the Fallen, Semjaza who is tied with bounds of golden light. Zacharael tugs Semjaza by his bounded arms and swings him to his knees before the row of thrones.

"Here stands trial the Fallen, my Lord," announces Seraphiel.

"Read their crimes," blazes the ring of light.

Seraphiel reads from the list of sins, "For the crimes of cohabitating with human women, taking them for their wives, and for unlawful carnal knowledge of women against the will of your omniscient rule they stand before thee."

The faces of the Throne angels grow sullen with grief and disappointment.

"For teaching man the magic of war and destruction they stand before thee," Seraphiel continues. "For the use of cosmetics, piercing, tattooing of their angelic vessels, and vanity they stand before thee, your divine majesty, and the administrators of the human race," Seraphiel concludes.

"Allow the evidence to present," glows the spinning ring of light.

The sky above flashes the visuals of each Fallen angel committing the acts for which they have been charged. There is a projected illustration of angels transforming into human men and using their charm and deceptive magic to seduce women. They use new and appealing gadgets to lure and capture vain women such as jewelry, brass pots, gold and silver chalices, copper kettles, silk scarves, purple dyes, perfumes, and rare gemstones. These tricks of charm influenced human men to behave in the same manner of competing for women, but the son of man lack the deception of magic. The projections turn violent as the Fallen angels are seen laying out future inscriptions that would influence men such as Cain to use a rock against the head as an instrument of death. Another projection depicts an Uruk man on the basin of the Euphrates River being shown how to swing a club against his adversary. There are further projections of the Fallen influencing Shien Tseng Fei, the credited inventor of the human's sword; Archimedes, the mathematician designer of ancient war machines; Galileo Galilei, the astronomer exposed to celestial secrets; James Puckle, the inventor of the musket; Samuel Colt, the inventor of the revolver; the science of Albert Einstein and his discussions with Robert Openheimer in the Manhattan Project, and finally Shavit Zohar, the inventor of the Ziona-D biological warfare dispersion bomb. As these images pass by the Fallen snicker, smirk, and boast showing no shame for they are proud. The images continue showing vain humans wearing war camouflage, patronizing piercing and tattoo parlors, shopping at cosmetic bazaars, and men primping and prepping proudly in mirrors. There is a rumble amongst the choir. The angels are filled with disgust and amazement at the vices of vanity. The room becomes murky and quiet until the muffled sounds of whispering from the Fallen angels' cut the dark silence.

A Fallen shouts out, "It was Semjaza!"

"Yes. Semjaza," others yell.

Semjaza, still on his knees in front of the thrones, looks up at the globe with widened eyes. "It was Semjaza?" he asks the Fallen. "Semjaza?" he shouts. "Oh... I see. I made you lonely. Night after night it was me who made you do it? Was I not on those mountaintops in Aram with you watching and adoring the forbidden daughters of man? Was it not me who warned you of fornication and told you to not listen to Azazel? Where's Azazel?" Semjaza looks around. "He's your villain!" he screams.

"Yes it was Azazel. Him too! Not us!" shouts voices from the globe.

"Yes, Sem and Aza! Sem and Aza! Sem and Aza! Sem and Aza!" chants the Fallen.

Standing up and looking into the globe of his accusers he continues, "That's right! Point your fingers where you can, but remember I was not the one that made you commune, sing, praise, and honor Omnus without anyone to call on YOUR names. Who called upon you with admiration, gratitude, and that same kind of s-p-e-c-i-a-l love and affection you received from the daughters of man?" Semjaza snaps his head to the side and closes his eyes from the sight of the Fallen. "Oh, was it I that denied you?" he continues. "Was it I that withheld all that carnal joy that was given to the sons of man? It was NOT I who watched you again and again being placed aside and denied!" Semjaza pats his foot and crosses his arms as he frowns up his nose at the Fallen. "The fairies, the gnomes, the trolls, the humans, and all of Omnus' impulsive creations were taking your place while you were set aside, crammed up in those seven little houses. I did this to you? It was I? SEMJAZA? I'll see you all in HELL!"

Michael looks up with a soured mouth towards the Fallen as he stirs in his chair anxious to proceed.

"Your Gloriousness, if I may?" asks an angel from the crowd. It is Daniel, a redeemed Fallen who has been placed in the position of defending those being prosecuted before the Throne Room. "Upon Mt. Hermon, the Chancellor of the Fallen influenced those who may have otherwise chose a more righteous path. It was the—"

"Oh that again," interrupts Michael.

"How original," Gabriel interjects.

"You're losing your touch old friend," says Raphael.

"Cool it boys. I would like to hear this," says Raquel.

"If I may finish," says Daniel as he walks before the thrones. "The souls here are from the time of Abraxis. A time when the angelic community was in a midst of a sensual proliferation that grew into a viral and often uncontrollable –"

"I object to this line of reasoning," Michael inserts as he stands to his feet. "Paradise is not on trial here."

44

"Is it not?" says Daniel. "Is it not the overpopulation of the angelic community that drew relentlessly from the Abraxis and caused the paroxysm?"

"Your point is," asked Gabriel.

"My point is simple." Daniel faces the choir of angels sitting attentively in the Throne Room. "The natural need for companionship was misled and drawn by the Chancellor onto the human race. We speak about the daughters of man but what about the Fallen women who cohabitated with the sons? Where was all this... pinned up indulgence for self-perpetuation supposed to go under the divine commandment that prohibited the continued spawning of immortals?"

"To the Prayer Room," says Uriel. "That's where I take all my untamed desires."

"Easier said than done."

"It's not easy being divinity," says Michael.

"The penalty?" Omnus asks.

"The penalty is eternal damnation," informs Seraphiel.

"Who will administer the punishment?"

"I will, my Lord," says warden Zacharael from Raquia. "I will escort these villains to Ambassador Anahel in Saqun, the Third House of Heaven where they will then be turned over to Azrael the warden of Hell," Zacharael informs the Lord.

"Cast fire in the vile pits of Hell and bring forth Azazel from the desert of Dudael!" orders Omnus.

The first trial of 10,000 years is in recess while the angelic community waits for the arraignment of Azazel. Meanwhile another historic event is taking place – the lighting of Hell's furnace. Hell is located behind the cast iron doors beyond the graveyard in north Saqun. The old fire grounds are hot and steamy covered with a molten crust of bone and debris from the burning of unsavory souls. A thin black layer of charcoal floating on top of the thick lava barely conceals the heat simmering below. The pit glows a reddish-orange fiery hue. The grounds are fragile and ready to give way for the casting of newly convicted souls. Catwalks and railcars run across the large pit to provide access for soul dumping and fire control. The job of maintaining this sweltering pit belongs to Azrael and Anahel of Sagun.

Anahel is a young winged, golden light Cherub. He is a fearless ambassador of the third house located west of the grounds of Hell. His face is often soiled with the soot of Hell's ash. He stirs the boils of Hell and prevents the fires from blazing out of its pit. Anahel spends most of the day listening to human radio broadcasts and singing Earth songs to overpower the sounds of screaming souls in the depths of eternal Hell. Anahel loves songs about the Heavens and stars above the Earth because their inaccuracies amuse him.

Anahel sings, "When the moon... is in the seventh house... and Jupiter... aligns with Mars—"

Azrael groans.

"I know you don't like that song," Anahel laughs while balancing over a beam that runs across the fiery pit.

Azrael is an elderly angel and a former seventh house administrator who was injured in battle during the Great Disturbance. Due to his injury he does not speak. He only grunts and moans in frustration with the boyish tricks of Anahel.

"This is the dawning of the Age of Aquarius. Age of Aquarius..." Anahel laughs while singing.

Anahel and Azrael stand back while they watch the fires of Hell burn taller and taller. The furnace of Hell has been prepared.

The Cells of Raquia

Back in Raquia the prison is volatile with clamor about the sentencing of the Semjaza and the Fallen angels. All the inmates know that this trial is one of many to come. Soon Azazel, Chancellor Sammael, and Lord Abaddon will follow along with the inciting of the Apocalypse, the final showdown of the Fallen. Chancellor Sammael fell from Paradise much later, after the creation of man. Sammael became envious of mortals when he saw that Omnus loved them so much, but his breaking point came after it was commended that all angels bow down to serve and protect man. In these final days on Earth, Chancellor Sammael will try his best to elude the Arch Order while he leads as many sons of man to their damnation.

The prison is filling quickly as many damned souls and foul creations are increasing the population of those waiting to be sentenced. Many of the Fallen leaders such as Belphegor, Wall, and the demonic king Araqiel are still on the loose, but Armaros, Gadreel, Kokabel, Balberith, and Baraqel have been rotting away in prison. They know that if their comrades on the outside don't do something soon they will be sent to Hell behind Semjaza. There are a total of 200 angels in the first group of the Fallen. In that 200 there were gangs of 20 from various angelic orders. The prison is designed with five wards extending out from a central master control. The northward of the prison is where genies, demons, and fallen Guardian Angels are kept. They are housed along with the other souls of mortal prisoners and beasts.

The westward of the prison is where the Nation angels who misled countries are imprisoned. Belphegor and Armaros are two of the most infamous leaders of the Fallen Nations. They were imprisoned there for misleading the ancient Assyrians and the Aramean tribes into war.

The eastward of the prison is where Fallen Powers and Dominions are imprisoned. These members of the Fallen committed crimes of sorcery. They taught the secrets of the stars and cosmos to predict human behavior and the astrological alignment with angels that govern their affairs. Chancellor Sammael influenced each of the gang's leaders, Gadreel of the Powers and Baraqel of the Dominions to use these secrets to expose the workings of Paradise. In addition to astrology Gadreel and Baraqel taught the secrets of deciphering dreams and reading palms.

The southwestward of the prison is where the former Fallen Throne and Cherubim angels are kept. These are some of the most disappointing Fallen angels in the prison as they were once close to Omnus and sat in the Throne Room passing judgment on those that came before the throne. They know the penalty for violations more than most. The leader of the Fallen Throne angels is Kokabel who compromised the sanctity of these angels to assure that man would be found guilty when brought before the throne for judgment.

Fugitive Throne angels descended with their gangs to Earth where they worked in the world's court systems. The southwestward is also where powerful Fallen Cherub angels are imprisoned. Their leader Balberith is imprisoned, but the most powerful Cherub, Sammael is still a fugitive.

The last ward is located in the southeast of the prison. It is a pivotal ward as it is the place where the most infamous and powerful Seraphim to fall are located. Two of the Chancellor's henchmen, the notorious brothers Auza and Uzza were imprisoned in this ward. These two Fallen Seraphs taught the sons of man how to write and how to use ink and paper. They increased man's marvel in the pursuit of knowledge and self-discovery. This alone was not a crime, but part of a trick the twins learned from Chancellor Sammael as a means to get man on track to question elusive Omnus and doubt his existence. The twins were freed by the Chancellor and escaped with him at the time of his fall. They have since eluded the Arch Order and continue to roam the Earth advancing knowledge in science and increasing doubt in the existence of Omnus.

Lord Abaddon has been imprisoned in the southeastward waiting for the 10,000 years trial and for tainting the Heavens. Before Abaddon, not a single angel had ever challenged Omnus' authority and souls never lost their way to Paradise. Many creations fell into transgressions after Abaddon's lead. There was not an Order of the Archangels before the Fall of Abaddon. The Elder Angels commissioned the Archangels after they saw how contaminated the angelic community had become under the influence of Abaddon's power. Abaddon was Paradise's forbidden fruit of knowledge, opening the concept of free will and the ability to have choice to all creations. In the beginning of mortal creation free will was forbidden. In passing time Omnus ruled that it had become necessary to allow the right for all creations to execute personal decision-making and free will. This became necessary to divide out those who were truly pure divine servants of Paradise and those who acted of ignorance. Abaddon showed the angelic orders greed for power and recognition, and the vanity of self-indulgence. Now an underworld proclaimed Lord, Abaddon waits in a cell for the Apocalypse. His only chance for survival is to escape, but the keepers of the seven houses are watchful.

Many of the prisoners are restless as they know the 10,000 years trials have commenced and they have no way of avoiding their sentences or escaping Raquia. Many of them look toward Lord Abaddon as they feel he has concealed a plan. Others are depending on Chancellor Sammael to break them out. Semjaza and the others are hoping that the fugitives on Earth can fulfill their Oath of Alliance and come to their aid.

"Are you a member of the 200 Fallen?" an imprisoned soul asks.

"No. They called me... mwhaha," the soul laughs. "A... bio-terrorist... mwhaha ha! A bi-o-terrorist. Can you believe the fancy names these modern mortals come up with?" the soul responds. "So why are you here?"

The damned looks down with embarrassment and answers, "Sex."

"Sex!" the terrorist looks around shocked and amazed. "With who... a nun?"

"No just a whore. One naughty little Urartu whore," he replies.

The terrorist doubtfully asks, "One whore?"

"Yes."

"She was a whore?"

"Yes!"

"Kol Khara!"

"The little bitch was twelve years old BUT she was a woman!" the soul defends. "I tried justifying before the throne why I felt no need to repent. I told them I wasn't the first!" the soul closes his eyes and shakes his head. "That just made it worse. At least that's what Daniel told me."

"You should have appealed."

"Michael wouldn't even hear it."

"Then you should have turned to Lord Abaddon for guidance. He knows Michael very well."

"I should have asked Omnus to forgive me, but he knew me too well."

"It's all up to Chancellor Sammael now. Old boy is on his way to Hell. They buried Azazel... only the lord knows where. It's all up to Chancellor Sammael to get us out of this star ward before they drop us into a r-e-a-l nasty pit."

A dark fog arises outside the prison cell and reveals a tall, dark cloaked figure holding a serpentine staff. The figure remains silent for a moment as the fog dissipates. His eerie existence is puzzling and mystifying to all the onlookers from within the locked cells. While the other inmates remain in question about whom it could be Semjaza has already begun to smile and feel honored by its presence. The fog continues to dispel until the figure's identity becomes clear and more revealing.

The Fallen and other damned souls drop to their knees in servitude.

"Chancellor," the inmates respond as they bow.

From the back of the cell comes forth Semjaza. "They will come for you Chancellor," Semjaza warns.

"No! They will come for you!" the voice squeals. "Brr-r-i-n-g me the pass. Brr-r-i-ng me the son."

"I... I don't understand. Who is coming?" Semjaza asks with labored breathing. "Whose son? A-a-a pass..." Semjaza stutters.

"The son is the pass," says the echo of many voices.

"Where? Where is this son, my Chancellor?"

The fog quickly dissipates.

Many angels have fallen from the grace of the omniscient one since the infamous two hundred. It was their leader Semjaza who began this ill-fated legacy of doom. Semjaza was a highly regarded Seraph. He was very much respected and held with high esteem by all the orders of angels. Semjaza made many friends in many places and even became a favorite amongst the Archangel Order. Semjaza was a skilled swordsman and a lover of the arena warrior games on Earth. He would sit on the mountaintops or travel the village where he would hide in plain sight just to get a closer look at the fighters and their female admirers. To descend down on Earth without his trip being sanctioned by the Arch Order was a violation, but if he were to join the Guardian Angels it would be his duty to watch over the village so he joined the Order of the Guardian Angels to get an authorized closer look. He found the warriors had women admirers who were beautiful and captivating. Semjaza joined the arena games and spent most of his time outside the arena courting his female fans. Semjaza knew he could not remain amongst the humans indefinitely, but he dreaded the thought of leaving these women behind. In secret corners of paradise, Semjaza told his angelic peers of these women and how fascinated he was by how easy it was to gain their affection. The women were yearning for men due to the shortage in their village. Semjaza and his peers frequently descended to Earth in an effort to entertain these women. They posed as merchants and travelers from other lands.

As the visits increased so did the temptation of sexual relations. The number of angels that followed Semjaza swelled to over a hundred placing their journeys at risk of being detected by the angelic orders. He knew that the Archangels were watchful over the humans and monitored the activities of each order of angels. An agreement of secrecy was sealed amongst them to keep their visits and each other's participation a secret. The Fallen included in the pact that if either one of them were to be discovered and sent to the prison of Raquia the others would abet their rescue. Semjaza knew from his discussions with Azazel that these relations were highly forbidden. Azazel was one of the first Fallen angels who had broken the rule of cohabitation with the daughters of man. Azazel was shackled, blindfolded, and left in the rocks of the desert near a village where he had broken the cohabitation rule. It was there that Azazel was to wait for his day of judgment, the Apocalypse. The omniscient one had forbid the act of mingling with the daughters of man. To mark violations he cursed their offspring to produce

Nephilim, giant beings. Semjaza visited Azazel in the desert to apologize for his partaking in his capture and conviction for lusting after these women for he too had fallen into the forbidden lust.

CHAPTER THREE

Unearthed

The sky darkens over the Mount Hermon as a strong cryptic wind swirls between the desert rocks. The howl from midnight's beast alerts the native inhabitants to secure their cattle and to call in their young. The sun's rays crawl back into the sky, fading earlier than usual for this time in the evening. The early arising dusk disturbs the ranchers and startles their wives. No one says it but everyone is thinking about the mysterious storms, like the ones the old wise men once spoke about. The signs of the melancholy old tales are rapidly approaching. The young men in the village do not believe in the old tales like their elders, but there's something about this eerie night that leaves no time for skepticism. Everyone rushes for shelter. No one is left outside alone.

"Is it a tornado father?" asks a young frightened boy clinging to his mother. "It's a storm son. Only a storm," replies the father as he moves along faster than usual.

A vulture circles in the winds above a rock quandary masked by the darkness of the storm clouds. A dark cloaked figure stands strong in the wind above the bed of rocks and swiftly raises his arms up towards the sky. Rocks and earth fly up, dust blows in the wind, a crater is burrowed out from the ground in front of the dark figure's feet.

"A-za-zel!" a low polyphonic squeal calls out from the cloaked figure.

"Oh! Brother!" answers a raspy voice unearthed from within the rock quarry. "You've got to be kidding me!"

"The t-r-i-a-l!" squeal the synchronized voices from within the lone figure.

"You allowed me to lie here for FIVE THOUSAND YEARS and all you can say to me is THE TRIAL? FUCK your trial!"

"Brr-r-i-n-g the son, brr-r-i-n-g the son, the son, the son of man, of man!" the voice echoes.

"Can't you see they have me bound?" Azazel replies in anger.

"YOU WILL ful-fill, ful-fill, ful-fill, your oath, your oath, oath," echoes the squealing figure.

"Whose son? What man?" Azazel asks but there is no response. The atmosphere clears and the winds calm. "I've been fine by the way. A little thirsty!" The storm departs as quickly as it entered the Mt. Hermon skies.

Jerry Xeven

In Cleveland, Ohio the sun dawns upon a new day, but for Jerry Xeven the sun brings an end to another restless night as he fights the fading darkness in a losing struggle to get some sleep. It's a battle that begins with every moon and ends with every sun. It's the voices in Jerry's mind that keep him in the fight.

"R-i-s-e up!" whispers the chanting voice as Jerry awakens from his slight drift off into sleep. The interruption will replay over and over again throughout the night until Jerry is left fighting for sleep in the tail end of the night. The sleep disturbances have increased in the last couple weeks. Jerry has resorted to an Old World practice of meditation and prayer to help relieve his mind at night, but the words of comfort and affirmation become difficult to recite.

Jerry lies in his bed on his stomach and elbows as he prays, "Our father, who art in Heaven..." he struggles to continue. He presses his hands closer together by first making hands of prayer, and then finally with his fingers bent together as he prays over his knuckles, but nothing helps. His mind leaves the prayer as he turns and stares at the empty space in the bed besides him where his wife used to sleep, but now she is in the spare bedroom. Jerry struggles with the daily thoughts of leaving his home, his family, and his marriage to find himself and to bring focus back into his life. This is the morning after he told his wife Karlisa that he has decided to leave. Saying it out loud to her was the first step in the act of leaving, but the courage to follow through does not come easily. Her recent confession of a past act of infidelity has caused him to lose his trust in her. His marriage was the one stable thing he had in his life that he felt he could rely on. Jerry was raised in typical 2140 war era household where religious practices were not an accepted way of life and seen as a threat to new world peace. Karlisa's family privately held onto their religious practices after the war and requested that Jerry at least attempt to practice in an effort to get the family's blessing for their marriage. Jerry struggled with practicing religion, but eventually he gave it an honest attempt even though his social circles and family mocked him as being helplessly in love. Karlisa's infidelity has now penetrated his willingness to submit to her religious beliefs. It has now become a challenge for Jerry to even pretend to believe in them at all. He questions his faith in her and her God. After all, she often said God would protect him and their marriage. The concept of faith was a huge leap for a man who is a fact-finding lawyer and a lover of science. Jerry's view of the world and all his decision-making is based upon facts and on what he can prove beyond a reasonable doubt as being true. The only truth he knows today is that he is losing his marriage and his sense of self.

Jerry's emotional wellbeing and how he views his role in life is now impacted by depression. It was the voices in his head not his sleepless nights that brought Jerry to seek help from a therapist. His doctor diagnosed the voices as auditory hallucinations due to a side effect from a new psychotropic medication that he prescribed to treat anxiety and mild depression. He said it was an acute adjustment disorder. Although his doctor ruled it out, Jerry will not even entertain the thought that he suffered from any schizophrenic psychosis, yet he still struggles with hearing things that are not there and voices that feel so lively and intimate when they speak to him. Jerry suspects the etiology of the voices as being from an unknown realm of science. "Maybe this is God," he will often think to himself. "I can't be losing my mind."

Spiritual and religious interpersonal conflict is a commonly treated condition in Jerry's time, a post-war era and time of transition into relying hopelessly on humanistic peace. In the year 2145, the world had become exhausted with an onslaught of religion-based wars and acts of terrorism. The human culture was suffering from post-traumatic stress. The first of the religion-based wars began in 2105 and ignited 40 years of continuous world wars with religion at the core of the conflicts. The citizens of the world searched hopelessly for a peaceful solution. A three-year cessation began in 2145 until the last and most deadly world war came in 2148 and lasted for 10 years. In an effort to eradicate complicated volatile diversities and conflicting ideas of utopia, several nations resorted into practicing a rule of a single cultural collectivism where any practice that disturbed world peace was seen as socially unacceptable and that sometimes meant the shunning of radical religious practices.

Jerry's problem with spiritual issues is a common struggle in New Gaia, a new world order, a place where religion is regarded as an outdated way of thinking, a threat to peace, and contradiction to science.

The first cessation came in 2145, the dawning of a time where hyperpower governments celebrated omniculturalism in their leaderships, united global distribution of military protection, and international participation in New Gaia global policymaking. Antiwar youth groups united on a global level and agreed that religion was the number one enemy of world peace. The innocence of global social networking accelerated the spread of radical homogenous thinking in opposition to those with diverse and conflicting points of view. A viral organization called The New Gaia Global Youth Movement grew stronger each year and their ideology influenced traditionally rigid political structures and belief systems. Diversity was no longer celebrated, but feared as a potential flowerbed for conflicts to world peace. The fear that ignited opposition towards diverse and extreme conflicting viewpoints was now equally budding against extreme calls for global uniformity.

The New Gaia Global Youth Movement demanded abandoning a single nation's view to world peace and became adamant in their search for panoramic ideas of utopia while extinguishing ideas and opponents that stood in their way. Religion was identified as their number one adversary. To increase homogenous idealism and to obtain a global agreement on how utopia was defined for New Gaia, a set of approved languages were spoken during international discussions to help eliminate misunderstandings. Many nations mandated its citizens to learn and implement exclusive speaking of one of the official utopian languages. The two chosen languages were Mandarin and English. Overtime these two languages blended, while other ancient and pre-New Gaia linguistic forms of communication were lost or faded into small corners of the old world.

The world's borders were fading and the walls of separation were crumbling down. Immigration was no longer a problem as linguistic diversity was the only passport needed to travel the Earth. Reduced global border control increased participation in worldwide university enrollment and sharing of universal intellectualism. Advancements in science, technology, and medicinal practices flourished. New Gaia peace was at its apex.

Jerry's parents owned a herbal medicine clinic and holistic healthcare store. Some people say that his parents were eccentric as they were also members of a small organization that believed smoking a rare herb during group meditation would inspire transcendental energy that could heal the world. The New Gaia movement did not accept this practice, but it was practiced by too small of a group to be seen as a threat. The group was monitored and registered as being a medicinal health practice that did not have any rules over governing behavior, a doctrine, or any structural belief systems, therefore they often escaped under the radar of scrutiny. Karlisa's parents were members of the controlled religious community, who often held resentment towards the new world order and sometimes publicly protested against humanist New Gaia policies accusing them of being an intrusion into their rights to religious freedom.

There was an undertone of dissatisfaction growing in religious communities worldwide in opposition to the New Gaia movement. When it was thought that New Gaia had reached its zenith a final revolt came from various international religious communities inflaming an internal conflict not between governments, but within nations from those who collectively opposed the international New Gaia movement. This opposition became organized and volatile to the point that religious rebels took up arms once again within their own nations against proponents of the New Gaia movement. Small incidents of bombings at New Gaia Youth Movement meetings expanded to political offices of New Gaia movement bureaucrats. Eventually a revolution sprung worldwide disturbing the New Gaia peace. These revolutionary wars began in 2148 and lasted for ten years until religious rebels and their practices were aggressively shut down in 2158 by the armed forces of the New Gaia International Peacekeepers. The Tower of Babel had finally been completed by 2170 when the first twelve-year absence of war was celebrated.

Disturbance of world peace was further minimized the more the practice of religion was reduced, monitored, and controlled. Religion eventually became an eschewed practice limited to the privacy of individual homes and small government regulated congregational size limits. Religious establishments were licensed and no more than one license was issued for each approved faith or denomination within a community or municipality. No religious faith was permitted to have more than 10% of the community it served in its total combined congregation, regardless of the denominational establishment. To enroll new members, annual membership lotteries were implemented to fill vacancies when congregations came close to fulfilling their regulated congregational size.

The days of religious powerhouses and political influence were over. Religious leaders cautiously expressed resentment towards the thought that improvement in the quality of life on Earth and the marvels of human scientific advancement was increased when the reduction of religious practice was implemented. They called the New Gaia Movement a pride that angered God, but in the eyes of the younger generations the absence of war strengthened their pursuit of the reduction of religious extremists and conflicting ideas that threatened the new era of world peace.

Life on Earth became so arrogantly celebrated that the idea of dying was repulsive and faith-based promises of a heavenly afterlife was mythical and undesired when compared to life on Earth. New Gaia was in its pinnacle and talk of a spiritual afterlife was now seen as a horrific tale from the dark ages. The love for studies in humanities and science was viewed favorably as enrollment in religious congregations declined. Technological advancement and healthcare received an abundance of global economic financial support.

As the citizens of New Gaia found supremacy in a world of reduced religious practices the chastity belt came off and a new sexual revolution blossomed, increasing the world's population. In an effort to implement population control measures in this era of perfection and to prevent a strain on resources, rigid laws regulating childbirth were passed in the legislature. Some protest came out of the small religious community over the regulation of procreation until governments funded religious-based community services to offer classes on abstinence and restraints from premarital sex. Funding these ministries' fight against premarital sex coupled with strict population control measures again made religion the public enemy.

The global New Gaia Youth Movement opposed government supported abstinence classes and avidly protested for more separation of church and state. Religious intrusion into private life once again made God the enemy of free will as the people turned the blunt of the opposition towards the church and blindly away from the government who funded these ministries. New Gaia's children of persistence began to attack all forms of moral legislation and presented evidence of global prosperity as their reasoning for continuing the fight for freedom from religion. Memberships at churches, temples, and mosques were all dwindling down as life was seen as much improved under the New Gaia world order.

By 2153, Jerry and Karlisa were in their developmental adolescent years and the New Gaia Youth Movement was being celebrated as the keepers of peace. In this era of perfection Karlisa's parents struggled to keep her practicing the family faith, while Jerry's parents allowed him to find his own way to self-identity and spirituality.

By the time Jerry completed law school, married Karlisa, and began raising his family he found himself still struggling with adapting to the new wave of humanistic theories as he wanted the answers to the bigger questions in life's meaning. He was not satisfied with the New Gaia humanist school of thought. Jerry felt that there was something too perfectly perfect about the world and there had to be some greater explanation for human evolvement. The thought that there was an underlying truth about the origins of the human spirit became obsessive to Jerry. Karlisa believed the answers were in the discredited and shunned religious doctrines, but Jerry believed the doctrines lacked scientific integrity. They both believed the answers were somewhere in between and that common ground is what brought him and his wife together, so losing her was also losing himself and how he understood the world in which he lived. Jerry made the decision to leave her, but he still hopes to find a reason to stay. The voices in his head and the feelings in his heart keep him awake at night and follow him throughout his day.

Late one evening, Jerry sits in a soft leather sofa chair with a tall back. He holds a remote in one hand and a beer in the other. The TV is on, but he is not watching, he is waiting, for he hears a commotion in the kitchen. Someone has just arrived through the back kitchen door. It's his mother in-law; Luciana, his wife's cousin; Evelyn, and his wife Karlisa. Jerry hears his mother in-law's heavy breathing and pacing feet on the kitchen tile. She is upset.

"He can't leave you and the kids now! This is nonsense! You must talk to him. He's crazy!" shouts Lucinda with no concern of who may be at home listening.

"I can't talk to him now," says Karlisa.

"You can't, but I can! I am not going to allow him to hurt my grandbabies!" Lucinda paces across the kitchen floor towards the living room entrance.

"Ma... please just let me handle it!" Karlisa shouts to stop Lucinda.

"When! When are you going to handle it?"

"Ma, let it go!"

"Let it go? He needs to let it go! It's been eight years." Luciana repeats the phrase in Mandarin, " Ba suì!" She holds up eight fingers, waving them to accentuate her point. "I am not going to allow him to destroy this family over something that happened eight years ago!"

"It's my fault mami!"

"Things happen!" Luciana screams back. "Why you had to tell him now I don't know."

"It just came up. Besides I couldn't bare it any longer."

"Are you kidding me?" asks Luciana. "I'm going to settle this right now!"

Luciana storms through the kitchen, into the living room where Jerry is sitting and waiting in front of the TV.

"I want to talk to you!" Luciana says demanding Jerry's attention.

Jerry looks up, but he is not surprised for he anticipated that she would soon make an appearance to state her point and back her daughter's position. This kind of aggressive action was not new for this family. Lucinda always served as the family's mouthpiece in times like this.

"Please turn off the TV," Luciana asks.

Jerry removes a small pill from his pocket container and swallows it with a sip of beer then he extends a remote and turns off the TV. He sits up straight in a position that implies respect and undivided attention while at the same time wearing a deadpan smirk on his face as he stares at Lucinda.

Lucinda is thinking of saying, "don't be a smartass," but she continues with her lecture. "I know marriage is not easy," Luciana begins with a sigh feeling nervous and unrehearsed. "My daughter... she's not perfect. We all make mistakes." Jerry motions as if preparing to say something, but Luciana does not allow it. "Now hear me out," Luciana demands. "This is not about defending her or making excuses for her actions. I'm sorry you have to go through this, but this is life and it's not always cherry!" Luciana stands directly in front of Jerry and looks down at him. She continues, "Believe me I know." Luciana slowly meanders over to a nearby fireplace mantle where several family pictures are standing in their frames. She stares at a picture of her and her husband. "I often wonder what he's doing when he's working late... and why he always packs his best underwear when he goes to those Las Vegas conventions... but I somehow hhmm... let it go," says Luciana while rolling her eyes into the back of her head. "Maybe it's nothing but I can use it later. You know when I want something," she explains. "But here and now for you!" Luciana turns back towards Jerry. "One thing happens and you want to leave? After eight years?" Luciana turns and picks up a picture of her grandchildren. "These babies were not even here yet! It's not fair to them! It was eight years ago!" Luciana brings the picture of the kids over near Jerry. "You have a five and a seven year-old. Luciana shows the picture to Jerry. " wu and qi!" Lucinda shouts in Mandarin. "They were not a part of this madness and you should not do this to them! It was eight years ago! Let it go!" Luciana demands.

Jerry stares up at Luciana with a slack mouth while slightly shaking his head. "I kind of expected this from you... from your family." Jerry turns his eyes and stares down at the floor. "I heard all the stories about Uncle Alonzo and Mr. Cruz. This kind of thing happens in your family and the women just let it go – hey maybe in mine too!" Jerry looks back up at Luciana. "You can't expect me to be a Cruz and act as if this kind of thing is acceptable! Like it's just another bad day. It'll just be ok tomorrow," Jerry says trying to not sound too insulting. "I'm not a Cruz!" Jerry shouts.

Karlisa and her cousin Evelyn can hear the conversation from the kitchen while they sit at a table. Karlisa attempts to get up several times, but Evelyn tugs her arm, keeping her in the kitchen. Karlisa can barely remain seated as her legs shake and tap under the table each time she hears Jerry become upset. Evelyn reaches to hold Karlisa's hand.

Jerry stands and continues while pacing across the room, "Maybe I'm the only one that actually takes a vow of marriage seriously." Jerry stops, turns toward Luciana, and says, "Shame on me!" Luciana stares back at Jerry squinting and turning her head slightly as if cautioning him with his tone and topic. Jerry continues in a lower tone of voice. "Oh I've had my times," Jerry says nodding his head and swallowing a dry mouth. "I could have taken a piece of ass – excuse me," Jerry stops and looks over at Luciana. "I mean you no disrespect, but I'm only trying to make a point." He takes a breath and continues, "I spent a lot of nights at corporate parties celebrating a legal decision, settling of a lawsuit, or courting clients." Jerry continues to pace. "I'm a junior partner. They expect me to make an appearance," Jerry explains as he looks over at Lucinda who is standing eagerly waiting to comment. "There's always some young hot file clerk, paralegal that doesn't care about me being married. She's just tipsy and wants to have fun. No strings attached. So why not with the married guy?" Jerry continues pacing the room. "These aren't just any girls. It's not lonely Stella from accounting. No! Our office hires a lot of young college interns," Jerry informs. "We host a lot of foreign men, global clientele. So the senior partners set it up," Jerry adds. "The girls go out in these short skirts and entertain the guests to help them feel at ease. They flaunt. They flirt. Their drinks are free and they want to have a good time. It's usually the same girls. You get to know them. Sometimes it's hard. I just want to say what the fuck! Why not!" Jerry swallows the tears rolling down the back of his throat while the others climb out onto his eye ducts. He marches over in front of Luciana. "I take my ass home!" Jerry concludes looking sternly in Luciana's eyes.

In the kitchen, Karlisa can barely stand to listen. A few tears drop unexpectedly. Evelyn squeezes her hand.

Lucinda feeling like she needs to defend her daughter interjects, "Well... you're just hurt—"

"You're talking to me about it only being eight years ago!" Jerry shouts.

Luciana nostrils flare as she inhales deeply with piercing eyes.

Jerry pauses in thought while trying to control his emotions. A brief silence fills the room.

"Nearly eight years ago my wife walked into this room and screamed, 'I'm pregnant!' We danced on this floor!" Jerry informs as a tear rolls from the corner of his eye. The silence reenters the room. Luciana wants to say something supportive but she freezes because she can relate to his pain a little too well. She looks away darting her eyes towards her daughter on the other side of the wall. "Seven years ago my son was born and he was so little. I held him in my hand. One hand!" Jerry stares at his hand. "I said this is my son!" Jerry continues in Mandarin. "It was one of the happiest days of my life and I remember it like it was yesterday." Jerry looks over at Luciana as he switches back to speaking English. "It may have been eight years ago for you or for her! But it was yesterday for me!" Jerry yells.

In the kitchen Karlisa sobs until she feels ill and runs to the bathroom. Evelyn follows.

Jerry falls back into the chair trying to hold his composure. Luciana strolls over and rubs his shoulder to comfort him. "I know... I know baby. It always feels like it happened yesterday, but things are going to be better tomorrow. I promise you."

Rise Up!

Jerry sits in the lobby of a doctor's office looking around at the other patients and frequently checking his watch. He taps his foot frantically and out of rhythm until he notices that he is disturbing other people. He stops tapping, stands up, and trudges over to get a third cup of water from a nearby water cooler. Jerry brings the cup back to his chair and places it on a side table.

After checking his watch a few more times he places his elbows in his lap and rests his face inside his cupped hands as a floodgate of tears slowly breaches his eyes. He hears a voice saying, "Rise up!" but there's no one in the room speaking to him. He wants to leave but it's the voices in his head that need an exit. His anxiety medication is low and he needs a refill. Jerry leans deeper into his hands as his breathing increases along with his heart palpitations. Jerry sits up straight and wipes his tears trying so hard to not look like he belongs in that doctor's office. He doesn't think he is ill enough to be a patient, but not well enough to get up and leave without a way to quiet the internal voices. He suffers the agony of feeling out of place. "Maybe I am losing my mind," he whispers.

Jerry looks around the room to see who else may be feeling the way he does. "Who else is hearing internal voices?" he asks himself. To his right he sees a teenage girl dressed in all black with black lipstick, black hair, and a black long sleeved shirt in the summer time. She has bandages on her wrists. Across from him sits a wide smiling elderly man who is grinning and nodding while gazing around attentively. Further across the lobby two gay men are sitting very close to each other, whispering things that sound like an attempt to cover their bickering. A woman frantically enters the lobby from the restrooms and sits next to the old man. "How come they're always running late? Have they called you? I know they're late again!" she rambles at the old man who continues smiling. Jerry is not sure which of the two is the patient. The woman quickly flips through several magazines then places them back on the stand. A few minutes later she flips through the same magazines and places them back on the stand again. Finally, the lady stumps across the lobby to another set of magazines, flips through them, and places them back. She returns to her seat. "They never have any new magazines in here. Nothing ever changes!" the woman explodes.

"Jerry," a tall well-dressed man calls out from a once dark corner, now being illuminated by the light from the other side of an open door. Without speaking, Jerry makes direct eye contact, stands up, and walks toward the man. They exchanged handshakes and nods before continuing to a small dim office in the corner of the building.

In a softly lit office several degrees and awards plaster the wall recognizing the merits of Mikael Meshuga, Ph.D., ACSW. Another plague on the wall certifies the doctor as a New Gaia Institutional Review Board approved practitioner. The doctor notices Jerry staring at the certification.

"It tells you nothing about who you are, only about who you can't be," he says with a raised eyebrow and a nod. "I wasn't expecting to see you for another six weeks," the doctor states while looking down at a file through his fine wire framed glasses.

"I know, but I forgot to get my prescription for the refill," Jerry answers.

"Next time call Marsha, she will help you with that. Ok?"

"I know, but Karlisa and I are going on vacation in a few weeks and I thought it wouldn't be a bad idea if I could leave the third wheel behind," Jerry looks the doctor in his eyes. "You know what I mean?"

"A vacation! Good!"

"It's a free trip. She won a contest before I decided to separate. That was right after she told me about..." Jerry doesn't finish. "You see we always get into these deep discussions about the meaning of life where she's trying to convince me of her religious beliefs." Jerry closes his eyes and shakes his head. "And every time... she drops a bone from her mouth. The woman's got more skeletons in the closet than the Catacombs of Paris."

"But... still you are going on vacation together?"

"She feels that since it was eight years ago, and I have to admit we have had a great eight years," Jerry confirms. "She thinks we just need to rekindle our romance." Jerry rubs his head and temples. "I just feel like it's her, me, and it! What does it want from me?"

"Jerry," the doctor says softly. "If you want to know what the voice is telling you, all you have to do is listen."

"It's telling me to rise up!" Jerry informs. "But rise up to where?" Jerry asks.

"To where or from what do you think you need to rise?" the Dr. Meshuga asks.

"I have no clue what that means," Jerry responds, darting his eyes towards the doctor. "Sometimes it says, 'Sand and sun' like it wants me to go somewhere warm," Jerry responds.

"Like Florida?" asks the doctor.

"Yeah..." Jerry says looking at the doctor with a smirk. "Like Florida." Jerry flashes his eyes closed and open before continuing. "I don't need voices in my head to tell me to go to Florida."

The doctor's eyes sink in and he swallows with a dry mouth while thinking he made a mistake with use of humor. He writes in his notes, "Jerry is edgier today then his usual apprehensive demeanor." The doctor is thinking, "Maybe I should alter his medication."

"I was thinking maybe somewhere inspiring. Somewhere that will make me come back a new man with a new perspective on life," finishes Jerry.

"You want to be someone new?"

"All my life I have been the wrong man. Not like those men in the movies. Not a happy man."

"Men in movies are happy?"

"Well...by the end of the movie they are... aren't they?"

"What if there was a movie about a man whose wife cheated on him and he was able to overcome the hurt? Maybe he revives life, love, and romance into his marriage so they can live happily ever after?"

"That would not be a movie I'd go to see."

"Why not?" the doctor asks.

"That movie does not excite me. It's too corny, predictable, and simple. Life is not like that!"

"That's right! Life is not like the men you see in the pictures, on the TV, at the movies. Life is more complicated than that. I'll tell you a secret about the movies."

Jerry listens attentively and waits on the doctor's secret.

"Those people in the movies do not live happily ever after."

"Oh they don't!" Jerry sighs as he shakes his head and looks away.

"Of course they don't! They're only characters that end when the movie ends."

"Well I know that! I just wish they made more movies that didn't mock us!"

"You feel the movies you watch mock you?"

"Yeah! They make it appear that everyone has a happy ending."

"Maybe it's time for you to become the director. It's time for you to star in your own movie. You can tell Jerry Xeven what to say and what to do. If you don't like the direction the movie is going you can just change it. You can always write the next scene."

"I'm the director?"

"You're the director to the never ending movie called, Jerry Xeven!"

"Will Jerry live happily ever after?"

"I don't know. I'm watching the movie. Please don't spoil it for me, but I'm thinking he does!"

"What about the voices?"

"Tell them... Quiet on the set!"

CHAPTER FOUR

QLUV

Jerry and Karlisa had begun intensive couples'
counseling in addition to Jerry's individual therapy.
Their marital situation is slowly improving. Karlisa
remains optimistic that things will get much better.
Jerry has always been a complex person with deep
thoughts preoccupied with his search for the
meaning of life. His mother called him anxious, his
father called him an intuitive and deep thinker, and
Jerry thought of himself as burdened by the riddle
of a restless soul. Jerry is always looking for the
answers to the most complicated questions about
human behavior.

Even though it's socially looked down on, Jerry
studied many religions until he found faults in its
philosophy and his patience ran short in its

diversions from answering the ultimate question to life's purpose. Jerry feels that the ultimate answer should be so clear and transparent it would take little effort to understand it with a minimal endeavor to study it not a lifelong seclusion in a monastery or retreat in the wilderness. Jerry thinks that there are forces in life that wants to keep him from the answer. He expects that his struggles in life and his wife's infidelity are all a part of the greater scheme to distract him and throw him off track from conquering the answer to his most sought after question.

"Something is just not right with the world," Jerry gripes as he drives his hovercraft into the airport express lane.

"Here we go," Karlisa says as she rolls her eyes. "Is this another conversation about the mistakes of the New Gaia Movement or your paranoia over the regulation of philosophical study books at the library?" Karlisa asks before blowing air through her lips.

"I'm not talking about politics and corruption," Jerry defends. "But they do make sure to write down your citizen ID number when you check out certain authors. Let's not even get started about that," Jerry nods his head affirming his statement. "It's just the other things like the degradation of societal values. The more we improve in science, technology, and healthcare the more people feel like they don't need to be careful anymore." Jerry shakes his head before continuing, "People are lascivious and indecent, and it's not even sexy. Did you know they are opening another bathhouse on Superior Avenue? The House of Rome they're calling it. As if any of them read a book about the

Roman era. The libraries are filled with books that contribute nothing—"

"Listen, Jerald! Just because you happen to get caught up in the dogma of every Neo-religious affiliation and New Age Thought you have joined in the last two years—"

"Don't make it sound so impulsive!"

"...I'm not saying that you didn't truly have your heart in it. I'm just making a point that you have encountered a lot of disappointment in your personal search for inner peace, let alone the answer to world attunement."

"You just don't understand. You don't know how it's the first thing I think about in the morning, the last thing I think about at night, and—"

"And how you thought about it all— day— long! I know," Karlisa stares in Jerry eyes. "I remember when I used to occupy your thoughts," Karlisa turns and looks out through her passenger side window.

Jerry remains silent and continues driving while watching Karlisa's eyes, monitoring them for tears. He's thinking, "Is she going to cry again?"

There is silence.

The craft slows into a long-term airport parking lot and stops. Karlisa gathers her things and quickly begins to exit the vehicle.

Jerry quickly states, "You're the only thing in my world that I want—"

The passenger door slams shut.

"...to fix," Jerry continues.

Jerry and Karlisa prepare to board an aircraft. A few months ago Karlisa won a trip to Israel off QLUV a satellite romance radio talk show that was doing a segment on renewing your commitment to your significant other. Listeners were asked to call in and share their stories about the difficulties of restarting a relationship, and then listeners would submit their votes over the Internet for the best story. Karlisa spoke about her infidelity and how she attempted to reignite the love in her relationship. One of the problems she stated was the challenge of balancing work, the kids, and having little time for romance, but listeners really felt for her after she revealed that she confessed to her husband that she had an affair with a much older man only nights before her wedding. She knew listeners loved taboo sex stories and that she would have a good chance being voted in as the best story that night. She tried her best to convince listeners that it wasn't an impulsive sleazy sex act, but a young girl's yearning for an older man she was prohibited to have. She recalls the conversation.

"Aw come on now lady!" the radio host barks. "You expect us to believe that this highly esteemed, wealthy aristocrat, college professor who you were so madly infatuated with calls you over to give you a wedding gift a few nights before your wedding and you scuttled over there expecting a present?"

"Well I trusted him and I trusted my love for my fiancée," Karlisa explains. "I knew it would be improper to have him come to the house because of our history, but still I wanted to see him happy for me. That would give me the closure I needed before giving up the single life for good."

"So tell me. Tell us all, how did it go down?"

"I know what you want to hear," Karlisa informs. Karlisa is a regular listener of the show and knows what gets the votes. "I know what you want me to tell you. It's not about how smart and brilliant he was and how I was attracted to his intellectual charm. You want to know how a man nearly three times my age makes me feel in bed. You don't want to spend time listening to me tell you about how at eighteen years of age I was so excited to be around him like a teenage groupie, so far away from my mother's supervision. You don't want to hear about the glamorous things he bought me and the nights we had out on the town at the finest restaurants where we sometimes pulled up in his chauffeur driven limousine. You would like to be spared from hearing about how eloquently fashionable he dressed in Gucci suits, Rolex watches, and the key ring in his pocket that held the keys to either one of his Bugatti or Lamborghini sports cars, which are by the way only the two favorites he liked driving not the other 10 higher-end hover sports he kept under the tarps in his 12 car garage behind the multimillion dollar mansion, where he kept his grandchildren while he lived in a penthouse downtown overlooking the business he owns on Ontario Street."

"Yeah lady, let's get it on!"

"Who cares about how much money he has? We all know it's a lot more than we will ever earn in our lifetimes. What is more important is did I manage to get a hold of some of it, or more precisely put is what price did I pay in sweat stained sheets? That's what you want to hear about. That's the real reason that you are listening. Well I'll tell you now. I will delay you no further. I will tell you so that I may get on with the real reason why I spent so much time with him, loving him, and displaying my affection for him in spite of anyone who may be witnessing the touch of an older gentleman's hands around my small petite young body. I'll tell you now so that I may have your complete attention when I tell you how much I loved him and how it was me that insisted that we make it work beyond what others may be thinking." The phone line and airwaves are silent with anticipation.

"After all, I was not his prisoner, far from it. I had just as many reasons to turn away as he did not to stay. I endured the starring eyes that were only intended for me to see, accusing me of indecent and malevolent intentions. I stood the test of time. I tried to convince his family that I was not there to do him any harm. I was also not going to harm myself by leaving him and forever mending my deeply broken young heart. So I stayed with him and lay with him every night, allowing him to get his stamina and heart rate up just enough to reach the point of climax. My satisfaction wasn't important. I was in love with his genius. I felt invigorated by his willingness to place me in a position—"

"I bet he did!" sorry go ahead.

"A position by his side that was only experienced by some of the wealthiest ladies on the New Gaia Yacht Club of Cleveland and many of the socialites up and down the Eastern seaboard. I felt important," Karlisa explains. "He was a war hero that wrote the philosophical agenda for the New Gaia movement. I too wanted to be a woman of history."

"So what stopped you?" the radio host asked. "Did you finally realize you were just another young and dumb girl being played, right up until her wedding?"

"I had stopped seeing him years ago after my parents found out about us. They are very religious and wouldn't have their daughter dating a leader in the New Gaia movement. I dropped out of college and soon after I met my husband."

"So Mr. Wonderful didn't beg you to reconsider marrying someone else?"

"He was injured in the Cleveland Revolt when they burned down Forest Hill Renaissance Estates. He could barely walk the last time I saw him."

"Other than a good romping what did he give you for your wedding gift?"

"Something old, but always new, and never borrowed, but leaves you blue."

"Thanks for calling QLUV. It's been a pleasure. That's our final story tonight so listeners you can start casting your votes."

Mt. Hermon

Karlisa won a romantic getaway for two to any resort of her choice. There were choices of exotic tropical places in the Caribbean, the French Riviera, and an off the beaten path secluded resort on Mt. Hermon, Israel just outside the New Gaia Confederate of Arab States. Since Karlisa won the trip they thought it would be a good time to discuss the future of their family, spend quality time together, and take the honeymoon they were not able to afford when they married nearly eight years ago. Initially, Karlisa wanted to go shopping in France but Jerry wanted more outdoor, natural activities like horseback riding. Karlisa's family minister who was serving as their spiritual counselor suggested a less distracting trip where they could spend some time together away from big crowds. The offering of the resort near the ancient Biblical lands offered both, Jerry's chance to go horseback riding and a chance to relax and work on quality time repairing their marriage.

Jerry began having nightmares in the weeks leading up to the trip. He can't explain the dreams after he awakens, but they always end up the same way with Jerry startled awake, drenched in sweat, and uttering indistinctive words and babbling uncontrollably. Some of Jerry's nightmares end with the dark silhouette of a man Jerry knows too well, swinging from the end of a rope. Karlisa is disturbed by this dream and Jerry promises to discuss it with his therapist as soon as they return home to Cleveland. She feels responsible and wants to have answers to this issue before renewing their vows and committing Jerry to more misery of a life with a wife he cannot trust. Karlisa occasionally notices Jerry's mind wondering as he slips away from reality and staring off into space with a look of sadness void of self-awareness. Karlisa can only stare back and wonder where has he gone. Karlisa blames herself for what she sees in these moments of sadness. She feels like an obstacle to his happiness and his reason to want to be anywhere but here, where there's something wrong with his world. Karlisa hears Jerry break off from his daydreaming moment, as he removes a small pill from his pocket container, and swallows the pill as he routinely does without water before subsequently stating, "There's something wrong with the world." This statement always translates to Karlisa as, "There's something wrong with our marriage."

Jerry snaps out of the aloofness from the distant place in his mind. "There's just something wrong with this chair. I can't get comfortable."

"The plane will be landing soon," Karlisa informs.

"That's when we start really having fun!" Jerry says with a hard smile.

"Don't be a smart ass. You are going to enjoy this trip."

"I know. I can't wait to be in those mountains."

"It will be like old times, but no kids."

"No kids," Jerry echoes.

Karlisa informs Jerry that he'll feel better after getting some rest and recreation on this spiritual and marital retreat. Jerry has his doubts. He knows it's his mind he wants to get away from, not the kids.

Karlisa and Jerry arrive at the Tower of the Sun Resort from the airport by riding the resort's shuttle. The trip up to the resort is over an hour long, but the Mercedes-Benz minibus shuttle is equipped with all the comforts and conveniences that make the trip appear smooth and quick. The sun shines brightly over a narrow road leading up to the resort. The shuttle's ride is so smooth the passengers can barely notice the several winding turns and sharp curves that the path must take to arrive to its destination.

The resort is a little different than the Renaissance Hotel in Cleveland, The Hilton Bentley on Miami Beach, or most other lodgings back in the United States for this privately-owned resort has a very noncommercial and isolated feel with deep roots in the local community. Jerry, being jet-lagged, dozes off before the shuttle reached its destination. Karlisa occupies herself with a magazine and a holoscreen where she periodically glances over to watch the local news. Once the couple arrives and enters the central reception area a service attendant and a bellhop, who is specifically assigned to check them in at a private service desk, greets them.

The resort's central service building is the oldest and tallest of the buildings at the resort. It's a single level building with two dual-level guest lodges at each end. Down in the lobby the clerks work busily serving previously admitted guests while Jerry and Karlisa are being privately checked-in. The lobby is ornamented in shades of green and orange tones with a jade marbled floor. The two-toned mint cream walls are accented by an apricot orange ceiling. There is a spacious patio area, an indoor natural-springs designed swimming pool, a bar, a gift shop, a travel guide desk, a golf shop, and a kosher restaurant with a large courtyard dining area under a high glass ceiling. This resort is intended for relaxation and does not cater to those in need of a conference hall or a business center.

The grounds around the resort are neatly decorated with custom horticulture and immaculate gardening. The landscaping is breathtaking as it rolls out onto the New Golan Heights, Upper Galilee Mountains, and Mt. Hermon. Nearby attractions include the Dan River; where you can go kayaking, rafting, horseback riding, hiking on a nature trail, and higher up on the mountaintop there is skiing. The bellhop escorts the couple to their room, while engaging them with small talk along the way, as they continue down the guest room halls. They find each guest room door nicely decorated, surrounded by hand-carved wood and glass frames like a home's front door. The bellhop opens the door and pushes it wide open to reveal its beauty to the entering guests. A light breezy aroma of lavender, frankincense, and myrrh greets the senses. Purple tones and gold highlights of silk and fine linens complement each other in a soft colorful, royal, and rich extravagance throughout the room.

The bellhop shows them the basic operations of the technological devices and the location of all the necessary conveniences. "So is this your first time here at the Tower of the Sun Resort?" the bellhop asks.

"Yes. It's our first time in Israel," Karlisa answers. "Do you know why this resort is not like any other in the entire world?" the bellhop asks.

"No, but I'm sure you are eager to tell us," Jerry replies.

"This resort was located on the grounds of one of the most mysterious and hidden ancient biblical lands. It's the apocrypha land of the bible! The land that was once ruled by Nephilim, sons of fallen angels. This area is so large and the mountains are so dense that there may be some hiding out in the hills so be careful," the bellhop informs as he politely gestures for a tip.

"Yeah, giants and fallen angels," Jerry smirks as he slaps a tip into the bellhop's hand.

Jerry doubtful about the mystery of this area, which once was chosen by the Fallen to take upon themselves the daughters of man in their revolt from the Heavens. Was it the lure of the arena warrior games or the beauty of the Aramean women? Whatever the reason, the historical significance of the resort grounds and the surrounding area has never been taken seriously by anyone outside of the local community.

"OK. We have a choice," Karlisa informs Jerry as she reads over the Tower of the Sun Resort's travel guide.

"We can go hiking and that will give us a chance to talk, which is the point of this vacation," says Karlisa as she gives a cryptic smile to Jerry. "Or..."

"Here it comes," Jerry replies as he holds his breath.

"Or we can do an individual activity because I know you want to go horseback riding then we can spend the rest of our time together."

"You know me well."

"I noticed you eyeballing that horseback riding tour brochure in the lobby."

"Ah!" Jerry responds with a smile. "You saw that?" he smirks.

Pale Horse Run

Jerry heads to the stable nearby the resort. It's a hot muggy day. There is a group of men already assembled with their horses prepared to ride the trails. Most of the horses appear to be assigned to riders. Many of the men are Arabian wearing a Keffiyeh while Jerry is dressed in American old western attire complete with a hiking backpack, boots, and a Stetson hat. He starts to worry that he may be too late. Jerry sees an attendant taking names and matching horses with riders.

"Shalom," Jerry greets the attendant as he prepares himself for bad news.

"Shalom," the attendant replies. "I'm Zelig Aaron!" says the smiling horse rancher while standing, smiling, and offering no further instructions. Zelig stands silently with a wide-eyed gaze as if he just seen a celebrity.

"I'm... Jerry... Jerry Xeven."

" la a f h a m... Dalet, He, Vav, Zayen?"

"Yes, like the English number," Jerry sighs and answers as he has done so many times before.

"Nice day for a ride. Yes?" Zelig confirms with Jerry.

"Yes, I'm looking forward to it."

"The problem is... I only have one horse left. It's an Arabian, but it's a new horse. It arrived just this morning. I don't know much about it except that it likes to wonder off on its own and it's a little slow. Maybe you can come back later. I'll have fresh fast horses for you later."

"Well Zelig, a slow horse may be just what I need. It's been awhile."

"Well then you will not mind riding this pale horse over here?" Zelig takes Jerry to the horse.

"Looks fine to me," Jerry says as he reaches for the reins.

The attendant smiles and hands Jerry the reins. "The horse will take care of you sir. All you need to do is ride," Zelig instructs with a continual smile.

The sun is shining hard this afternoon, but it can barely compete against the brisk cool air blowing down off the mountain peak just miles above the resort. The Tower of the Sun Resort's location is ideal to many activities regardless of the climate needed to sustain them. It's the Wildflower season of Golan Heights that generally means pleasant sunny days and brisk cool nights. On this day it's a mixture of cool winds across a rocky terrain and a blazing hot sun that only comforts riders who stay out of the mountain's shaded areas that trap cool air. Jerry's horse is strong against the cool wind and generates enough heat to keep a rider's legs warm. The Arabian horse is native to this climate. Jerry does little to the horse to keep it on the path. The pale Arabian appears to be familiar with the trail.

This ride is as enjoyable as past days that Jerry spent on a horse in his childhood riding with his father. Trying to pay attention to the trail and follow the posse, he can't help getting lost reminiscing about the days he and his father would ride on the trails in Avon Lake, Ohio. It was a time when Jerry thought everything was right with the world. Zelig is in the front leading the line of riders and Jerry is the last rider in the rear. Zelig periodically glances towards the back keeping a watchful eye over his flock. The sky blazes beams from a hot sun, yet the wind is nippy and cool. Out from nowhere, to everyone's surprise, a fierce bolt of lightning sparked the already brightly lit sunny sky. Zelig looks up with raised eyebrows and an inward gaze but continues on with the journey. Several miles later another flash of lightning cuts through the sunny skies and startles the horses. Trying to not look as if he notices, Zelig slightly picks up the pace being careful not to concern the riders. Zelig continues on and makes no mention of cutting the trip short or diverting from the brochure's mapped trail.

"Lightning? Is that normal in these clear cool skies?" A rider shouts from the pack up to Zelig.

"In Golan anything is possible."

"It's too cool for lightning," one of the riders shouts up to the others.

"Too dry," another rider responds.

"Will lightning scare the horses?" a rider asks.

"If the horses become scared they'll just run back home. They're smarter than I am. So just hold on tight," Zelig instructs while yet another bolt lights up the sky.

"OK. We are going to pick up the pace, but don't worry I planned all this for your entertainment," Zelig shouts to the followers without looking back.

All the riders are dazed with excitement and caught up in the thrill of the mysterious weather while in fear of losing control over the guide of their startled Arabian beasts. No one has noticed the buck and run of the last Arabian and its rider, Jerry.

Jerry's horse runs for what appears to be several miles before Jerry is able to get control over the reins. "Whoa! Whoa! Whoa! Stop! Calm down boy!" Jerry shouts. "Maybe this horse doesn't know English," Jerry thought as he runs out of English commands. Jerry tries some commands in Mandarin but nothing works. "What happened to the slow horse Zelig was so concerned about?" Jerry says to himself. After a while the horse slows down of its own will. All Jerry can see for miles and miles in any direction is sand and sun. To the left and the right there is nothing but hot desert, but this desert has something extra eerie about its quietness, its desolate plains, and its forsaken ground. Jerry takes a chance on turning the horse around and heading back the direction he came, but he is uncertain of where he is and what path the horse took to get there. The desert continues in all directions with its void and peculiar stillness that swelters under the hot sun. Jerry becomes concerned when he notices that there is no sign of life amongst the hot desert rocks. There is not a snake, a cactus, or even a sign of past life, such as a cow's skull or any beast that has once ventured to the area. There is no sign that any form of life has ever crawled or walked this sandy and scorched terrain. Jerry loosens his shirt and slings the backpack over the saddle. The change in weather and the harshness of the sun is unbearable. As Jerry's horse staggers through the rough rocky land and endures the hot windblown sand Jerry begins to grow closer to his own sense of jeopardized mortality. Jerry reaches for the water carafe that is strapped on the backpack latched onto the saddle. Jerry shakes the carafe and feels the shallowness of the little remaining water. He removes a small pill from a little container in his pocket and takes a modest sip of the water with the pill. He's careful to save the little water he has left knowing he will need it later. Jerry turns the horse around and continues back in the direction towards the resort trail. It must have been over an hour after he was separated from the group when Jerry becomes certain that he is lost. Jerry lays sun parched and sweaty across the back of his horse. He is no longer able to mind the horse's path. He hopes that this Arabian will save them both by staggering home.

As Jerry's survival lingers on a thread his sense of hearing becomes aroused to a voice amongst the vagueness of the sun-seared terrain. The voice is faint, but he is sure that it is the voice of another person lost and stranded in the life-swallowing hot desert. Jerry weakly calls out, "Whose there? Is there somebody there?"

Jerry sits up on the Arabian and takes a hold of the reins again as he tries to steer the horse toward the sound of the voice.

"Help... help me!" the voice weakly cries out.

"I'm coming," Jerry responds.

Jerry attempts to make the horse change course, but the Arabian is not willing to divert from its path home.

"Come on horse. Move. Over there! Come on!" Jerry yells.

The Arabian will not divert and when halted will not move from the path.

"OK... ok, you stay here. Just stay here," Jerry pleads as he dismounts the horse.

The sun is still searing Jerry's back as he walks with no mind to his own survival, but that of a stranger in a strange land. "Where are you?" Jerry shouts as he follows the voice into a rock quandary.

"Over here," the raspy voice answers.

Jerry soon makes his way into a shallow pit amongst the rocks where he finds a seemingly elderly man marbled with layers of dirt and grime. The man appears indigenous of the area judging by his clothing that was also old and torn. His hair is caked with dirt. His face and skin are covered with patches of old desert sand and muck. His clothes are encrusted with soil. He's wearing filthy old sandals that barely distinguish his dirty ankles from his grubby feet. He wears facial hair and a beard that is coated with dirt. His nose is pierced with a tarnished golden ring that appears abnormal for local customs and it's gypsy like in fashion. The man has been lying in the dirt hole for a dreadfully long time. His dry mouth breaths out dust as he hollers for help.

"Please help me," the old man squawks in a low gruff voice as he begs for Jerry's assistance.

Momentarily, Jerry stands in shock at the sight of the filthy old man as he wonders how he could have survived alone in this part of the isolated, hot desert.

"I-I-I'm coming. I'm coming," Jerry repeats as he scurries into the furrow.

Jerry first thinks to take the man by his hand and to pull him up off his back, but he notices some type of wire or thick rope binding the man's hands and feet.

"You can take them off, Jerry," the man says in an encouraging voice.

"How... how did you know my name?" Jerry asks.

"Sir, please help me. Take them off please!" the old man begs.

Still quite astonished Jerry continues. He examines the bondage and notices the coils are strong like a metal cuffing. Jerry remembers his hiking gear in his backpack and hurries back out of the hole to retrieve it from off the horse.

"Don't leave. Don't leave me," shouts the old man. "Where are you going?"

"I'll be right back. I have a knife," Jerry replies as he climbs out of the ditch.

"No! Don't..."

"I'll be right back!"

Jerry reaches the top of the ditch and notices the Arabian is still waiting patiently in the hot sun. "Good boy," Jerry calls out as if the horse is an old faithful dog.

Jerry scrambles through the backpack and finds a pocketknife. He also grabs the carafe with the little water he has left. Jerry returns as quickly as possible down the rocky ditch back to the old man.

"Here drink," he insists as he pours water into the old man's mouth.

Jerry attempts to cut and pry the binding with the pocketknife but it is much too strong.

"Pull it!" the man demands with a cleared throat.

"Are you sure? I don't want to scrape your risk," Jerry replies.

"Pull!" the man demands.

Jerry wraps his hands around the bindings and pulls increasingly harder as he pries the bounds from the man's hands. Jerry holds the bindings up and examines them as they dissipate, sparkle into a golden dust, and float away before his eyes. "What the..." Jerry says as the binding disappears. He also removes the binding from his feet and again the binding dissipates into thin air. Jerry picks the man up over his shoulders. The old man is light and frail. Up the ditch Jerry scuffles with the frail old man. Jerry straddles the old man up over the top of the horse and then swings up behind him hoping that their weight will not be too much for the already sun-worn Arabian.

"The rest is up to you boy," Jerry informs the Arabian. After miles of trudging along through desolation the Arabian appears to have found the trail home. "This is it boy. This is it," Jerry exclaims as the scene became greener, cooler, and familiar. Soon the Arabian comes upon a barn house where Zelig is waiting patiently as if Jerry's return is scheduled and on time.

"So you decided to take the scenic route I see," Zelig shouts as he smiles and shakes his head.

The closer Jerry's horse draws to the rancher the faster Jerry's heart beats with urgency. With a parched voice Jerry calls out, "We need a doctor." Jerry waves his hands in a frantic motion. "I found this man in the desert amongst the rocks," Jerry reports while pointing to the man straddled up in front of him.

The horse stops in front of Zelig who attaches a lead to the halter before helping the old man down from the horse. "Well he looks well to me. A little mangy but healthy," Zelig responds.

"What are you saying? We need a doctor!" Jerry exclaims with frustration while jumping down to assist Zelig with the old man.

Jerry finds the grubby old man smiling and vibrant. "My name is... Mr. Ziel, Aza Ziel!" the man happily announces.

"You were barely alive," Jerry says as he stares at the refreshed man who now doesn't look so old.

Mr. Ziel melodically responds with laughter, "God made dirt, so dirt don't hurt, but it might kill you!"

"So everything is ok, sir?" asks Zelig.

"No it's not ok! We need a doctor for this man. He was lost and bound in the desert for quite some time," Jerry informs.

"How was your trip, sir?" Zelig asks paying little attention to the old man as he carries on with his ranch duties.

"It was... didn't you notice I was lost from the group?" Jerry scolds.

"It happens, but I knew this old red Arabian would bring you back home," Zelig answers.

"Bring me back? This damn horse took off and got me lost out there with no food, little water, and the hot sun beaming down on me in the ass end of the desert," Jerry explodes.

Zelig smiles and remains in a hospitality role as he was trained to do when customers are unhappy.

"Hey don't get upset. After all you saved my life in those rocks! It's a time to be at peace and give thanks for new friends," Mr. Ziel rejoices.

The three men part ways with Jerry feeling somewhat puzzled as to what occurred in the last several hours. Jerry walks away in a cloud of questions. He is uncertain of how the old man recovered so quickly and why he can't recall that horse being the reddish colored Arabian that Zelig walked away.

Jerry mutters as he walks away, "Does anyone care that the old man was left for dead in the desert? What in the Hell is wrong with this world?"

Jerry would keep replaying the memory of the event in his mind like a blurry dream of childhood with all the details fading way. He tries his best to forget about the event and "let it go" as Karlisa's mom would say, but the old man's face keeps popping up in his mind. Jerry and Karlisa spent the next few days engaging in quality time filled with romance and meaningful discussions about their future. Karlisa is surprised at how much Jerry prefers spending time together as opposed to the various activities they could have enjoyed apart. Jerry has decided that his world makes better sense with Karlisa in it then his experience with them being apart. Karlisa has no clue that Jerry's dedication to spending time with her is his way of avoiding any further awkward experiences on the same trip.

Jerry is not totally put off by meeting Mr. Aza Ziel. Each time the event pops in his mind he finds himself becoming more intrigued and interested in finding out more about who he is and how he got stranded out in that desert. He finds himself bringing up the event in almost every conversation with Karlisa.

"Stop obsessing over it!" Karlisa complains. "Obviously you were in no condition to think clearly," Karlisa explains in a familiar tone. "When you are lost everything seems far away. You were probably only a short distance off the path so the horse found its way back."

"And what about Mr. Ziel being tied up and left alone?"

"You were lost, you were hot and delirious. Now you are obsessing over something you can't understand, but what else is new?"

Jerry feels the need for closure and wants to know the details behind Mr. Ziel being tied up and left alone in the desert. Jerry repeatedly tells himself that it is normal to want to know the welfare of someone he rescued from a life-endangering situation. Jerry questions the resort manager but he is not able to give any information because he is not aware of any man being brought back to the stable in need of any emergency care. Jerry then seeks out the only other person that he knows has seen Mr. Ziel. Jerry returns to the stables to obtain information from Zelig.

"Ahh the old man," Zelig responds. "I brought him to the stable where he used a water hose to clean up, he thanked me for my help, and he walked off down the road toward the resort," Zelig reports.

"Did he happen to say where he was going or give you any information about his situation?"

"Hmm... No... No... but he did say that he would stop by to thank you for your assistance," Zelig informs while shaking his head in confidence as he recalls the conversation. "As I said he headed up towards the resort," Zelig says while pointing up the path.

Jerry thanks Zelig but before walking away his puzzling mind has to ask, "What color was that horse that you put me on?"

"Strange thing about that horse, it's gone! I haven't seen the horse since you brought it back. I remember it was a pale gray horse—"

"But when you took it from me it was a reddish Arabian," Jerry interrupts.

"Red... gray... the horse is not here. It left as mysteriously as it arrived, but it did provide you with an exciting adventure and it brought you back safely right?" questions the smiling Zelig.

Jerry cracks a half smile and turns away thinking, "What the fuck! Do you normally have horses stopping through and leaving like a damned horse motel?" Jerry heads back up the path leading to the resort lobby. Jerry approaches the customer service desk and inquires about any messages.

The clerk behind the desk smiles with her fingers pressed to her lips. "Sir, please excuse me, I am so sorry, but I did not make the connection," she states as she pauses to collect her thoughts.

Jerry stares back at the clerk thinking, "What in the fuck is she talking about?" He begins to wonder if this day is about to become as mysterious as the first. He tried so hard in the past couple days to avoid weird moments and strange people. "This is what I get for chasing shadows in the dark but inquiring minds want to know what inquiring minds want to know," Jerry tells himself as he waits for the clerk to retrieve her thoughts.

"A gentleman named Mr. Ziel left a message for a Mr. Sevien. He did not have a room number so the message has been sitting here for you. My apology Mr. Sevien," the clerk nervously reports.

"It's Xeven," Jerry corrects.

"Like ten, nine, eight—"

"Yeah... ten, nine, eight!"

The note provided a phone number and simply stated: You have questions and I have answers Mr. Ziel. Room 237.

Jerry's heart beats so rapidly he can feel the pulsating in his ears. He reaches in his pocket and pulls out a small pill and swallows it dry. He hurries to his room to make the call. Jerry enters his room and prepares to make the call. After entering the numbers on the holoconnect device Jerry inhales deeply and tries to slow his breathing. To Jerry's surprise the call never makes a connection tone before Mr. Ziel answers. It was like he picked up a direct line.

"Finally, you called my friend. I thought I'd never hear from you again," answers Mr. Ziel as his holographic image enters the room.

Jerry remains silent for a moment.

"I am as surprised to hear from you as you are of me my friend. No need for gabbing right now. How about we meet for dinner in the resort's restaurant around... seven?" Mr. Ziel laughs.

Breaking his silence and finally joining the conversation, "...Yes seven o'clock will be fine," Jerry answers.

"Seven with Sevien it is," Mr. Ziel chuckles. "See you then and don't forget to bring Karlisa."

"How did you know about...Karlisa?" Jerry asks but the connection had already disconnected.

Room 237

There is a new occupant inside room 237. The suite lights are out and large gaudy candles surrounded by smaller long stem candles are lit and placed in various areas throughout the room. Shadows bounce around the room cast from the flaming wicks of flickering candles while in between the corners of darkness you can see shopping bags and clothes spread throughout the room. In the closet new suits hang with their price tags still dangling from the sleeves. In the back of the suite there is a light shinning from the powder room. A large makeup case with eye shadows, eyeliners, rouge, several face powders, and other cosmetics lay cluttered and disorganized on the counter next to a large wall mounted mirror surrounded by a string of fancy bright vanity lights. Peering through the mirror is Azazel who is meticulously covering burrows and lesions in his face with a makeup pad. He is so occupied with his grooming he does not notice a shadow slowly creeping up from behind, crawling over to his chair, and filling the room like thick black smoke snaking through the candle lights. The vanity lights go out leaving only the candles flickering in the darkness.

Azazel looks up as he was expecting a visitor. "Thank you for the accommodations," he says into the darkness. "It's not as nice as my old sanctum on Vilon but it's not a hole in the ground either. It's charming or what is it they say now... to die for," Azazel concludes as he pampers his face with the pad.

"The t-r-i-a-l..." phantom voices squeal.

"The trial! Of course, I'm working as fast as I can!" Azazel shouts through the dark. "Let me tell you this is not going to be easy. Am I supposed to just walk up to him and offer up Vilon like a day trip?"

A polyphonic echo replies from the dark, "No man, No man, No man... has ever, has ever, ever... gone into, gone into... Heaven, Heaven, Heaven... return the soul, the soul, the soul... Kill the Son of Man!" the voice leaves the room in complete darkness and snuffed out candles.

Azazel looks around in the dark room still holding his makeup pad, "Comes in the dark and leaves in the dark," Azazel mumbles as he waits for the vanity lights to come back on. "Kill the son of man! Is that all you got? Don't speak to me in riddles!" Azazel continues to talk to himself. The lights flicker on and he stops applying his makeup and fixes a small nose ring into his pierced nose. "Lady killer," says to the reflection in the mirror.

It is hours before the scheduled dinner date with Mr. Ziel and Jerry has already taken the maximum prescribed amount of his anti-anxiety medication. He practices what he is going to say to Mr. Ziel as if he's preparing for a job interview. Karlisa is a bit nervous too, not in anticipation of meeting Mr. Ziel but out of concern over Jerry's behavior. The event reminds her the evening before Jerry met her parents. Karlisa wonders what it is about this Mr. Ziel that attracted Jerry to him. She ponders if it is Mr. Ziel, or if it is Jerry's chance to be seen as a hero and a savior that has struck his ego in a time when he has been feeling depressed and with low self-esteem. Karlisa cannot figure it out but in a sense she is happy that he is feeling upbeat about something. She is thrilled that Jerry is showing signs of the young and exciting attorney she married years ago. It is exactly what she feels is needed to awaken their romance from its dormancy and to help bring about the exciting man she once knew. The trip was accomplishing everything she hoped for in a strange sort of way. That morning Karlisa planned to go to the spa before dinner so she recommended meeting up with Jerry at the resort's dining room at a quarter till seven just in time to greet Mr. Ziel.

Later in the evening, Jerry is late and Karlisa is the first to show up at the restaurant. She takes a seat in the waiting area at a table near the bar. The waiter asks if she will have a drink while she waits but she declines. She is feeling nervous and uneasy about this meeting, but she can't explain why the feelings have now come on so strongly. After checking her wrist communicator there is no sign indicating a missed call. She looks around at the ambiance of the Tower of the Sun Resort restaurant and notices how the soft tones are juxtapose with statues of giant creatures. There are statutes of different sizes. Some are as tall as 20 feet and others were 75 feet or taller. All of them look like children with a gasp mouths and widened eyes frozen in covering poses. How odd of a decoration she thinks as she stares up at the center sculpture of a large human frozen in what appears to be a stance of terror quivering up at the sky. The lifelike statue stands over 75 feet tall yet it has an appearance as if something even taller has a power that could dwarf its magnitude.

"It makes one wonder," says Azazel who has paused and joined Karlisa in peering up at the statue, "What in the Hell is he afraid of?" Azazel laughs as he startles Karlisa. "I'm sorry. I'm... Aza Ziel and you must be Karlisa?" He asks as he introduces himself while holding out his hand.

"Yes. How did you know? I mean... please sit down. Jerry should be here any moment," she informs Mr. Ziel as she shakes his hand.

"Well good. I'm so excited about seeing him again."

"He told me you had quite an ordeal out there in the desert. I'm glad you are ok."

"Yes. I'm fine and I will be glad to explain everything when Jerry gets here."

Karlisa sweeps her eyes across Mr. Ziel as she looks over at his well-groomed moustache, small goatee, and manicured nails. While attempting to turn away she is caught into his piecing green eyes while trying to be careful to not stare too directly. She notices a hint of eye shadow but cannot be certain as she does not want to be caught gazing. Karlisa finds his nose piercing to be a little odd for his age, but dismisses it as possibly a cultural symbol of some kind. She can see that Mr. Ziel is a well-dressed man with a very well put together attire of subtly matching colors and patterns. Mr. Ziel raises his jeweled hand to get the waiter's attention. He orders an Americano. "Chilled, no ice please."

"Yes, sir."

Turning his attention back to Karlisa, "You must be a very lucky woman to be married to such a hero. My hero."

"Mine too," Karlisa blushes. "But anyone would have done the same. Out there in that desert all alone... who would leave a person there?"

"Yes, who indeed would do such a thing?" he taunts. "Jerry could have chosen to leave and try to come back later with help but he stuck right in there."

"Your drink, sir," the waiter interrupts.

"Thank you."

Mr. Ziel takes a small sip. "What a beautiful red drink, it almost matches the red in your tie," Karlisa compliments.

"Well... yes! What a keen eye you have."

"Well I dabble a little in fashion."

"Ah... I'm beginning to adore you already. I have spent several years as a fashion consultant, makeup artist, and hairstylist."

"Really? I own a hair salon!"

"Stop it!"

"Yes. Striking Boutique and Salon!"

"I imagine it's quite... striking..." he chuckles with Karlisa.

"Wow this is so odd," Karlisa says. She can't help saying exactly what she'd been thinking. The subtle coincidence only increased her impulse to be curious about him and the situation that brought them together. "You strike me as a man with a rich history."

"I'm really a simple man with simple plans; however you have come to know me at a time of transition. I'm sure you have a lot of questions and I promise you as soon as Jerry gets here I will be glad to fill you in on all the details."

"Well, wait no more," informs Karlisa as she alerts Mr. Ziel to Jerry making his way up to the table.

"Sorry, I hope you weren't waiting too long," Jerry apologizes as he kisses Karlisa's cheek and turns to shake Mr. Ziel's hand. "Mr. Ziel," Jerry smiles as he looks into the sparkling green eyes of a very different man from whom he rescued in the desert days ago.

"My hero, Jerry... and please call me Aza. Both of you, we are among friends."

Small talk commences as Karlisa informs Jerry of the small coincidences of things her and Aza share in common. Aza gives a brief speech about his past as if he is interviewing for a job, while Jerry and Karlisa wait for the explanation of how he came to be found stranded in the desert, but it never comes up. Dinner and drinks are served and 30 minutes later there is still no explanation.

Aza continues going on and on about his traveling experiences, something about the impact of nature on the soul, and how the wonders of the world aren't so wonderful when explained in a different context. Jerry and Karlisa catch each others wondering eyes as they wait to get to the meat of the conversation. Karlisa inhales and exhales a deeply as she takes another sip of the water that was served with her meal. Jerry finds himself zoning in and out of Aza's idle talk.

Aza continues on as if Jerry and Karlisa have been attentively listening the whole time, "...so if you look at it from that angle it's quite simple. The Persians after all weren't the best—"

"You have to excuse me," Jerry interrupts, "but what in the hell were you doing out there in that desert?" Jerry asks with a small chuckle trying to be cordial.

Karlisa pinches Jerry under the table to persuade him to be more delicate. "Yes we are anxious to know. Jerry's story brought my heart out for you," Karlisa says trying to sound more compassionate than carious.

"OK. You are right. Let's get down to the nitty-gritty," Aza begins. "I've lived a long full life and have come to a point where risky adventures are the only things that keep me from getting bored. I belong to an elite adventure club, The Guiltless Pleasures Travel Agency. It's a small elite group of bored but affluent individuals that travel in search for the next great waste of precious time." Aza smiles and takes a sip of his cocktail before continuing. "On this trip I came alone to scout out the area and report back my findings on its ability to sustain our adventurous endeavors. Like you, Jerry, I was on a horse that was startled by one of the areas flash storms. The lightning scared the horse who threw me off and somehow I lost consciousness, but not before falling into a ditch. I had been there for hours before you showed up, Jerry."

"Hours?" Jerry responds with an inward gaze and a raised eyebrow. "When I saw you... it looked like you had been there... for a very long time!"

"A long time indeed," Aza says while staring up at the ceiling through the opening in the skylight window above the head of the large statues. "I spent an awful long time out in that desert... baking in the sun... with those storms... coming... and going, and the dirt! The filth! The WIND! THE RAIN... oh... I'm sorry... I didn't mean to get on a raging tangent... it was quite the experience."

"I'm sure," comforts Karlisa while quickly glancing over at Jerry who is frozen in a speechless stare. Karlisa nudges Jerry under the table.

Jerry springs back into the conversation. "I don't know why I..." Jerry says while rubbing his temple in deep thought. "I think you were out there for more than... a fraction of a day. Maybe you were unconscious for more time than you realized? Did you check with the resort? Did they find your horse? Did you—"

"Slow down Jerry, my hero. When I returned to the resort my reservation was only a day old and Zelig had recovered the horse."

"And when the horse came back without you..." Karlisa says with a cocked eyebrow and a dropped jaw. "No one thought that was odd?"

"Only moments before Jerry and I had arrived ourselves. Apparently the horse was lost too," Aza explains.

Jerry is trying to remember the details of Aza's appearance in contrast to what he is reporting now but the dinner cocktails were interfering with his memory. He knows there is something strange about how he appeared when they returned to the ranch, but now the details are fading. "Your hair was longer and—"

"All that matters, is that he's ok now, Jerry," Karlisa asserts. "He's not on trial."

"Trial! No... no I'm not!" Aza chortles as he sips his cocktail.

"I'm sorry. I didn't mean to interrogate you," Jerry says. "It's just that at the time it all seem so extraordinary."

"The experience was quite fantastic," Aza agrees. "We can discuss all the little details and points of confusion at another time, as for now I have something very important to share with you."

Jerry continues to look confused as he replays the events of that day back in his head feeling that there is something Aza left out of the story and something very key that he cannot remember, but it will not come to mind.

"I want to express my gratitude to you for your assistance. So I was thinking... what could I offer you that you would not feel too uncomfortable accepting? The only thing I could think to do is come up with this little token of my appreciation," Aza projects a holocredit from his wrist device across the table over in front of Jerry.

Jerry, still rolling back the tape in his head about the details of Aza's rescue, barely notices the look on Karlisa's face or the holographic digital credit displayed in front of him. "A hundred thousand credits! Are you kidding me," Karlisa asks.

Jerry's attention now focuses on the digital credit displayed in front of him. Coming back to reality he exclaims, "I can't accept that for doing what any man would do... it's out of the question. I won't even consider it."

"Please take a moment to reconsider."

"Yeah, let's take a moment," Karlisa requests.

"I don't have any family and that's only a small portion of what I initially considered giving you, but I knew you were a New Gaia man of pride and self-accomplishments that has never had anything given to him. You are a self-made man... um at least that's the impression I get from you."

"Yeah self-made, but barely making it," Karlisa reminds Jerry.

"We're maintaining ok and we don't need to accept gifts for doing what is humane and right," Jerry informs Karlisa while staring her down for unified support.

"I anticipated your reaction, Jerry. Who can blame you? In the world we live in today you expect someone to do the right thing without being paid to do it and without expecting something in return, but nevertheless you performed a good deed and good people... people like you with a pure heart should be appreciated. The pure hearted one's that always do the right things never seem to be appreciated," Aza says looking into Jerry's eyes. "Something is just not right with the world," Aza continues staring into Jerry's eyes that have now widened with intrigue.

"That's what I've been saying..."

"Not today!" Aza interjects. "Today the world is going to allow a man of substance, a man of honor, and a hero to be appreciated and that's why I am not going to easily accept no for an answer." Aza demands. "You and Mrs. Sevien—"

"It's Xeven," Karlisa informs. "Like the number but with a—"

"X," Aza says with an affirming nod. "Yes of course. Please take this credit with you. If by the time you leave the resort you still feel that you cannot take make the deposit I won't stop you. Just delete it and it will show up in my balance the next day." Aza taps some commands into his wrist device sending the digital led from the table into the face of the palm of his hand. Jerry taps some commands into his wrist device. With the credit in the palm of his hand Aza extends his hand across the table and shakes Jerry's hand. Melodic tones signify that a gentlemen's Gaia credit transfer has been completed.

There is silence as Jerry thinks it over and Karlisa is eagerly hoping that he accepts.

"Go and deposit it, Jerry," Aza pleads. "I'm in room 237. Aza Ziel. World traveler, adventurist, fashion connoisseur, and..." Aza leans in and whispers, "A man of affluence." Aza hopes that that last bit of information would persuade Jerry to accept the credit. "You'll be saving my soul," Aza informs as the Xeven couple looks at him with blank stares and furrowed foreheads. "How does it go... it's easier for a needle to enter through a camel than God to enter the kingdom of a rich man... or something like that," Aza says with a tongue in cheek smile.

Trying to be polite, Jerry and Karlisa make shallow laughter.

"I'm off my dear friends. I hope to have drinks with you some night soon," Aza asks while shaking his head and looking at the couple for confirmation that he does not immediately receive as the two are still pondering over the offer and looking at the credit flashing on Jerry's wrist device.

"Um... yes of course Mr. Ziel. I mean... Aza," Jerry corrects as he and Karlisa rise to shake hands and see Aza off from the table.

"What do you think?" Jerry asks Karlisa while starring at his wrist device.

"I say we consider it and get back with him later for drinks."

"Waiter! Check please," Jerry requests.

"Mr. Ziel has already paid the check and tip sir," The waiter informs.

CHAPTER FIVE

Storage Room

The aroma of Mediterranean and Syrian dishes are steaming through the resort's kitchen. The resort's founders built the kitchen and restaurant inside the archaic remains of a tall spacious stone dwelling. The high ceilings accommodate several brick ovens made from the original stone structure. Lights and ceiling fans drop from the ceiling down over the steam coming from the grills, ovens, sinks, and dishwashing machines. In the back of the kitchen are cargo doors that lead out to the truck delivery docks and employee parking lot. Cold storage, supply rooms, and a manager's office are located on the sides of the loading docks. Zubayr, the supply room manager controls all things coming and going like it's his very own gates of paradise.

Zubayr is a burley Arab man who looks like he could unload most of the supplies without the use of a dolly or pallet lift.

"Zubayr where do you want these barrels of olive oil?" asks a deliveryman from the Golan Produce Company.

"Take it to the other end and place them on an empty pallet in the farthest storage room, but be careful the light switch is broken in there."

"Ok, Zubayr. Just this one time because I'm early. Ma'assalama!"

"Shukran!" Zubayr replies gratefully grinning with his off-white, coffee stained teeth. He continues packing up the kitchen as the resort dinner services are closing for the night. The Tower of the Sun Resort offers many services during the day, but the nights are often left with minimum service as the resort has a hard time getting the town's people to come work at the resort at night, in the dark. The Golan Heights area has a long-standing old-timers tale of fallen angels preying on women in the night, especially when they are left alone. The old tale claims that these angels become envious of men and commit jealous assaults on those who dare to come out in the night, in the dark. Many of these stories are old passed-along tales, but somehow they have managed to set a ritual in closing many area businesses before dark.

Barrels of olive oil are being carefully stacked in the far storage room. The room is dimly lit from the lighting that shines through the main breezeway from the loading docks. The Golan Produce Company truck is the last vehicle in the loading area and one of few that remain in the entire back employee parking lot. The last barrel is lifted off the dolly and stacked onto a storage room pallet. The deliveryman turns to exit the storage area just as the light from the loading dock sizzles and cracks out. The dock lights were the only lights illuminating the loading area and supply room. The deliveryman slowly backs his dolly out of the room and tries to make his way through the hall by using his memory, feeling the wall with one hand, and pulling the dolly with the other. The dark shadows crawl toward the deliveryman faster than he can feel his way down the hall until it finally engulfs him. There are sounds of a muted struggle then silence. The dolly lies on the floor, in the dark.

We can use the money

In room 212, Karlisa stands in front of the bathroom mirror smiling after she just finished brushing her teeth. She is smiling more blissfully and radiant this evening than she has done in a long time. She is listening to music from her iSky satellite player. She has a little twist and bounce in her stance as she looks into the mirror seeing more in her reflection tonight than in previous nights. "I always wondered what it felt like to be rich and successful." Jerry, remaining silent, stares with curiosity and wonders where this conversation is going although he anticipated a move to influence him to keep Mr. Ziel's credits. "Even with all that gaudy jewelry, the nose ring, and... the eyeliner, my god I know he was wearing eyeliner, but he still had an air of confidence, success, and a real I don't care what anyone thinks attitude. I love that!"

"I'm still not buying his story. Something about it is just not right."

"Jerry! Again, is anything ever right? Come on baby we're having a good time let's not start that. Please!" Karlisa strolls over to Jerry, stands in front of him, and places her fingers through his hair and around to caress his face. "You know we can use that money."

"Here we go!"

"Jerry, I don't care how you found him or how he got that way. Bounded and gagged or hogtied whatever."

"THAT'S IT! That's what I was forgetting!" Jerry stands and paces the floor with fisted hands. "How come you didn't say that earlier? What's his explanation for that?"

"I figured you were both delirious. Even you said he didn't appear as ruffled when you delivered him back to the stables."

"Oh, no! I remember vividly now. I tried to cut his bindings with my Swiss knife but I had to pull them off his hands."

"Wait! You didn't cut them off. He's tied up in the desert and you come along and simply pull them off?" Karlisa says while holding her hands up in disbelief. "Oh, wait! I remember... didn't the bindings ma-gi-cal-ly disintegrate into thin air?" Karlisa asks with widened eyes and a gasp mouth.

"I know how it sounds but it doesn't make it less true," Jerry responds as he allows himself to fall onto the bed lying down with his hands over his temples.

"Jerry, why do we care? That's a matter for the police. Besides why would he lie to you? Why?"

"I don't feel good about that money. It could be blood money."

"...Or it could be a reward from a successful business man. You want to know what's wrong with the world? It's people who are always trying to take away from all the good things that happen, but readily accept all the drama and tragedy."

A moment of silence takes place as Jerry ponders carefully over his thoughts. Karlisa tries to not lose the good mood she was in earlier and ruin the spirit of a successful vacation. Karlisa sighs heavily and rubs her head as she thinks maybe discussing the money now is not worth risking the progress they are making and the good mood they have going on with the trip so far. She sits on a chair in front of the vanity and begins brushing her hair. She decides to table the conversation for later but Jerry wants to bring the conversation to an end.

"It can't be a coincidence. It just can't be a coincidence," Jerry says. "Just let me connect the dots for you," he demands. "We tried everything to restart our marriage. So we went to your minister's house and allowed him to pray for us. We were going to take the trip to Paris, but after the trip to the minister's house we decided on a more secluded getaway, so here we are!"

"It was your idea to go on an ancient lands tour. I wanted to go shopping in Paris." Karlisa corrects while sitting in front of a vanity mirror brushing her hair.

"Now just listen," Jerry says while getting up and pacing the floor like a trial attorney. "We have marital issues, we seek advice from the minister, and then we come across this money. Marriage, ministry, and money. Bing! Bang! Boom!"

Karlisa stares at her reflection in the mirror while disturbing images of grotesque fallen angels flash through her mind. She can barely focus on Jerry's fading speech in the background. She stops brushing her hair, swallows with a sour mouth, and tries squeezing her eyes shut to stop the visions.

Jerry is still lecturing, "...We only came here to renew our marriage vows. Mission accomplished! So maybe the money isn't for us after all. Maybe there is something greater in play here. Maybe we should just give those credits to your minister and see what happens next."

In a sitting position from the chair Karlisa bends her head and shoulders all the ways back, moving her body into an arc like position with her abdomen and pelvic area pointing up. She looks at Jerry who stands behind her while her face is upside down. She scoffs with a raspy voice, "You fucking cocksucker, you are not letting that pimp get his paws on my booty!"

Jerry is astounded and silent.

He is frozen in a stare gasping as if the air left the room.

Karlisa now lies on the floor weeping. Jerry is still frozen and shocked. He wants to comfort Karlisa but he doesn't move.

Karlisa, still weeping, calls out. "Jerry! Jerry!"

Jerry snaps back to reality, moves to console Karlisa and walks her to the bed.

"I don't know what came over me." Still sobering and frightened, "What's wrong with me? Why did I say such a terrible thing?"

"Don't worry about it. You are under a lot of stress. Lie down and..." Jerry stops again. Looking at Karlisa he notices blood streaming from her nose.

"What is it?" Karlisa feels the blood on her lips. "Oh, no!"

Jerry hurries to the bathroom to grab a damp washcloth, but he is too late as the blood is now flowing in full force beyond Karlisa's control. She begins to use her nightshirt to contain the bleeding. She is soaked. "Uhhh! Oh no! What's happening?"

Jerry, again astounded and frozen, can't think quick enough as the blood begins pouring profusely. He snaps out of it and grabs a towel and rushes it over to her. Holding it to her face and having her lean her head back does not stop the force of blood that is now squirting up onto the ceiling. The two are covered in blood and begin to panic. "I need to call a doctor!" Jerry dials up on the holocommunicator and asks for an operator but there is no answer. He begins pushing buttons and trying to read the directory on the base of the digital input device but he is clumsy and frantic. "Hello. Hello. Damn it!"

Karlisa is weeping and crying out, "Help me. Help me, Jerry."

Jerry runs into the hallway, but there is no one around. He runs into the elevator waiting area, but again there's no one around. He ponders going back to the room or continuing to find help. He decides to go down to the main lobby. He presses the down button but the elevator is taking way too long. He runs into the stairwell and down the stairs. When he reaches the lobby area he finds that there is no one attending the service desk. The office looks vacant. He runs over to the desk and bangs a service bell. "Hello. Hello. I need help! Someone please!" No one comes to the desk and the lobby looks deserted. Jerry gives up and decides to retreat back to the room just when a small elderly man arises from the back of the service counter.

"Yes. May I be of service to you?"

"Where is everybody in this damned place?"

"Damned is right. Muahaha," snickers the elderly man.

"What!" Jerry snaps. "Never mind! I'm going to have some words with the manager about this place in the morning. I need a doctor up in room 212. When can I get a doctor to my room?"

"There are no doctors this time of night. You will have to take your chances and drive to the nearest town."

"No doctors? A resort like this does not have a doctor?"

"We provide medical services during the day. At night no one will come here."

"Well can I call for an ambulance?"

"You can certainly try."

"What the —"

"We have an overseer. She's not a doctor, but she can be very helpful until one can get here in the morning, otherwise you will have to drive to a medical clinic in the nearest town if you have a vehicle."

"Is there a vehicle rental service?"

"Not at night."

"How far is the nearest clinic?"

"Oh, not too far, but they can only care for you while an ambulance comes from another town with an actual hospital."

"What? Well how far is the town with the hospital?"

"Well there's a decent one in New Beirut about an hour away and of course there is one in Damascus but the roads are dark and dangerous. There is no light. Not on those roads. Not in this town."

"What the... Geez... send the fucking overseer to my room. 212!"

"Yes, sir!"

Jerry runs back to his room, but the hallway appears to be longer. The more he runs the longer the hallway appears to be. Jerry spots a water fountain, removes a small pill from his pocket container, takes the pill with a sip of water, and begins down the hall again. Finally he reaches the stairwell this time bypassing the elevators altogether. Once he reaches the second floor he again heads down another long corridor. In what now feels like several minutes later Jerry finally makes it back to his room exhausted and nearly out of breath. "Karly!" Running over to the bed he finds Karlisa still shaken, but cleaned up with a clean shirt and the sheets stripped from the bed. She is lying still and quiet as if she is trying to sleep. Jerry is comforted but a feeling of guilt comes over him, as he would have not have had her work so hard to get herself settled.

"There you are," says Aza entering the room with an armful of linen.

Jerry looks up with widened eyes that slowly relax on the sight of much appreciated assistance.

Aza looks down at the linen in his arms. "I was on my way to my room. I'm just down the hall. I saw your door open and heard weeping noises coming from inside. I called in until I became concerned enough to enter where I found quite a mess. I tried to call the service desk but there was no answer," explains Aza.

"Yeah! You're telling me! I'm going to have some words for them in the morning."

"I did all I could to help Mrs. Xeven. Eventually her nose stopped bleeding on its own. I tried to wash her up a little. I pulled off all the bloody linen and found a few extra sheets in the closet. I took out the soiled linen and found these clean ones in a service closet."

"Thank you! Thank you very much Mr. Ziel."

"Hey...I told you, we are friends."

"Right! Aza. Thank you Aza."

"I'm feeling much better now," Karlisa says quietly while curled up in a fetal position.

"I think we should get you to a hospital. You lost a lot of blood. Aza do you have a vehicle?"

"That may be a problem," Aza answers. "The nearest hospital is over an hour away down a very winding, unpaved, and dark road. You may only get lost out there if you're lucky."

"Aza, my wife almost bled to death for reasons unknown. I am not going to let her sleep when she could have some type of head injury."

"Do you remember her hurting her head," says a modestly dressed little old lady entering the room from behind Aza.

"Are you the overseer?" Jerry asked.

"Yes, I'm Nurse Nadhirrah the overseer. I usually deal with minor injuries and broken bones during the skiing season. Nothing more. Now do you recall her hitting her head?"

"No I don't." Turning back to Karlisa. Jerry asks softly, "Karly, baby. Did you hit your head?"

"No I don't recall ever hitting my head," Karlisa answers with a flat tone as she stares at Jerry with vacant eyes. "...But I can't remember anything after dinner."

"Well let me have a look at her," says the little old lady waddling over to Karlisa with a small black bag. She pulls out a stethoscope and a blood pressure kit. She begins to examine Karlisa. "Leave the linen. I'll take care of her," the old lady requests.

"Come on, Jerry. She'll be fine," Aza says.

"Aza. Thanks again. If you had not shown up when you did... I don't know what I would have found when I returned."

"You saved me, now I have helped you."

"Then I guess I should return your credits."

"No. That's not what I meant. I just want you to feel the way I do."

"How is that?"

"Meeting out there in the desert. It feels more than just a coincidence. I feel the budding of a real friendship," Aza explains.

"That's great but I'll be taking a taxi and leaving in the morning."

"If you have not deposited the credits in 30 days then it will cancel automatically. That's not important right now. Try to get some sleep. If you need anything even tonight if you must travel to that hospital don't go alone and don't hesitate to call me, I have a hovercraft. I'm in room 237."

Barazek and Tea

Midnight comes with an eerie sense of confinement to the resort grounds with no one going in and no one coming out. By day the Tower of the Sun Resort is a peaceful and serene getaway that is free of all the manic busyness of commercial attractions. No crowds and laissez-faire merchants to bother you or sell you things you don't need. It's a relaxing environment that has its unique lure for those who are historians, anthropologist, and religious scholars. The mystique of those lures is never so alluring than it is at night. Quietness and still shadows fall upon the few employee quarters of those who dare to stay overnight. Most of the night shift employees use these rooms to avoid driving home through the dark streets. They often conceal themselves in their rooms not even taking advantage of overnight shift pay. The resort's owners do not stay overnight. The resort has been a family-owned establishment for over 200 years making it the longest family owned business in the Golan Heights region. The resort's owners don't question the employee and town people's cultural tales and attitude towards the resort, as they believe the paranormal legend adds charisma to the lodge.

Tonight, two gift shop employees share a room on the bottom floor in the employee lodging area. They usually sleep through the night, but this night one of the girls is restless and keeps them awake past their bedtime. The two are lying on their beds having girl talk and listening to a holographic music cube.

"Dhakiyah you know what would be a good nightcap?" Alya asks with a cunning smile making an early attempt at persuading Dhakiyah to walk with her. "Barazek and Tea!"

"Are you kidding Alya? You will be up all night."

Alya has a sweet tooth and can remember how she enjoyed a plate of Barazek with milk before going to bed as a child. The temptation to have them tonight is much stronger than the warnings about walking around the resort grounds after dark.

"Where are you going to get Barazek and tea at this time? You can't get it in vending and even if you dare to go the kitchen you would have to make the tea," Dhakiyah informs, thinking she may have just stalled Alya.

"You could go with me."

"Are you serious? The only place I'm going is to sleep. I have to open the shop at six o' clock in the morning."

"I agreed to stay here with you so you wouldn't be afraid," Alya pleads. "We'll be together. Besides you're not really afraid of some old-timers tales are you?"

"I've heard things that weren't all that old."

"Like what?"

"Things! I don't know... Who wants to walk through the dining area with all those statues of evil angels and giants anyway? They freak me out. I don't see how anyone can eat in there."

"They're just old tales... No reason to be freaked out. It's Golan's version of commercialism," Alya says not being too sure herself. She ponders for a moment. "I'm going! Yeah... yeah I'm going."

"Sure you are."

"Really. I'm going. Want anything?"

"Ha... good luck!" says Dhakiyah as she turns her head towards the wall.

Alya grabs a flashlight and a set of shop keys. She turns to look towards Dhakiyah as she heads for the door hoping that she will stop her or decide to come with her, but she is fast to sleep. Alya sighs and convinces herself again that it's just old-timers tales, nothing to be worried about. "Just think of those Barazek biscuits and hot herbal tea," she says to herself to keep her brave spirit strong. All the way through the corridors she creeps along wondering if she should walk faster to her destination or tread slower to observe every corner, every shadow, and listen to every sound. Alya finds a comfortable speed that allows a quick pace and an observant watch. She feels successful in her scuttle across the resort until she arrives at the Tower of the Sun Resort dining hall. She slows her pace and stares at the large contorted macabre illustrations of evil angels and giants being besieged by some force from above. She slows her pace and can't stop staring at the face of one particular statue. She tries to imagine the face without such disfiguration and finds that it looks oddly familiar but she can't figure out why. Trying to turn her eyes away and focus her attention back towards the direction in which she is headed, she finds herself face to face with terror. She is so intensely overwhelmed by a dark figure that time does not allow her to scream. She is frozen and consumed in horror.

In room 212, the clock on the wall ticks to a melodious beat that sets a tone like a tranquillizing lullaby. Jerry's eyelids open and close synchronically with the beat of the clock as he tries to stay awake in watch over Karlisa. Jerry sits in a chair at the foot of Karlisa's bed. He watches over her with some comfort in the overseer's advice that she should rest till morning before attempting to move her to the hospital. Jerry also finds some comfort that his newfound friend Aza is only a few doors down and will be ready to help navigate the roads to find the nearest hospital. Hours later the sunlight faintly strings through the window curtain signifying the beginning of the end. "This vacation is over," is Jerry's first thought as he moves to pack their things. "I'm going to get her checked out at the hospital then we are out of here." After Jerry finishes packing he nudges Karlisa gently and tells her, "It's time."

"Barazek and tea."

"Excuse me?"

"She just wanted barazek and tea," Karlisa repeats followed up with a loud howling manly laughter. "Muahhhhhhhhh Hahahahaha!"

Jerry is once again frozen and startled. The thought that the horror is not over terrifies him. "Let's go, baby! Here's a clean shirt." Jerry lifts Karlisa's nightgown in an attempt to change her clothes but finds another horrific surprise. "No, just forget it. Your nightclothes will just have to do. Let me get you to the hospital."

A gentle knock hits the door. Jerry opens the door and finds Aza dressed and ready to assist. "Jerry! Daylight has broken. I'm ready if you need me."

"Aza, look at this," Jerry takes Aza over to the bed and lifts Karlisa's shirt where he reveals a black circle tailed rash. "I've never seen anything like that before. What do you think it is?"

Aza is speechless.

"I'll carry her and you grab the bags. I'll check out later." Jerry picks up Karlisa carefully. "I wouldn't blame you if you don't want to touch anything. I don't know if it's contagious."

"No it's not contagious. It's the—"

"What? What is it Aza?" Jerry asks while continuing to move out the room with Karlisa. "It's all over her body."

"Let's just get her away from here to the hospital. We'll drive straight through to the one in Dimashq."

Zubayr

Zubayr returns to work energetic, refreshed, and ready to assume his duties in the Tower of the Sun Resort shipping and receiving area. Like most mornings the kitchen staff is bustling around preparing for a long day of service. The resort is the most lucrative and commercial enterprise in the Golan Heights area and the dining hall is the centerpiece of the attraction. The owner built the resort around the original building that once stood alone in a remote area of the hills. According to legend, the original building served as a place to hide the giants after the epic of David when village men rose up to rid them from the land calling them an abomination. Women who gave birth to these giants would venture to the area to visit their exiled children. Over time they built the original stone cavern, the building now being used for the main concourse. The legend says those giants once slept the spacious courtyard built alongside of the stone cavern. That courtyard is now what is used for the

Tower of the Sun Resort dining hall. "...If you believe in the legend," often said by the resort's owner.

Historical land archives report that the land stood vacant and isolated from the community for several hundreds of years. The wilderness grew over the habitat and concealed it way into the 1800s when it was found by a Syrian general. The cavern was found by General Soleyman Almrei while his men was retreating from the encroachment of the Ottoman Empire. General Almrei would later purchase the area and his family has been in control of the land ever since. General Almrei's great grandson, Amir Almrei who built the resort never found any family records as to why or how the large statues of the giants were brought to the renovated cavern. It is also not known how a large stone cavern was built so far out in the wilderness but he knew the legend and how it would make a great place to start the centerpiece of the resort. That same entrepreneurship spirit still exists today amongst the family and its employees who work very hard to keep the Tower of the Sun Resort dining hall a spectacular historical attraction. With the exception of the closed-in courtyard with a ceiling that stands over 100 feet tall and the renovations to the surrounding stone building not much has changed since General Almrei purchased the land in the 1800s. Amir later built the exterior surrounding buildings that contain the guest rooms in the early 1900s after the fall of the Ottoman Empire and the withdrawal of French occupation. Today, The Tower of the Sun Resort is the pride and joy of the area, but some things like the legend of creepy beginnings will never change the attitude of the village people.

Breakfast is being prepared in the kitchen by the line chefs while the head chef Bakri is planning for the lunch menu. Today an over stocked supply of lamb needs to be reduced. Bakri is preparing the daily special to include Spicy Lamb Kebabs for tonight's dinner and Roast Lamb with Black Cherry Sauce for following night. Bakri has sent Zubayr to take what's left of the frozen lamb in the freezer and have it placed in the large thawing sinks so it may be marinated and prepared by this evening. Bakri mixes his own special blend of tomato paste, honey, cumin, coriander, chili peppers, garlic, lemon juice, butter, and red wine into a sauce. He is proud of his recipe and is eager to have the kebabs served this evening.

"Zubayr, Did you take the lamb out the freezer and place it in the thawing sinks?"

"On it now boss! I got distracted by the gift shop."

"What's going on with the gift shop?"

"It's closed. The attendant is late. The girls are never late."

"On top of that I have a GPC truck in my loading bay and I can't find the driver."

"Zubayr please take out my lamb or all we'll be serving is vegetables."

"On it right now boss."

Zubayr walks through the supply room back to the large walk-in freezers where the meat is stored. When he pulls the freezer door open he notices something strange about the frost on the floor. There are track marks as if something was dragged into the back of the freezer. Zubayr at first dedicates his attention to fulfilling his task of taking out the large lamb shanks. Nasser, a line chef asks if he can help and Zubayr gladly allows for his assistance. Zubayr prepares the sinks for the thaw.

"You have the rest of those shanks, Nasser?" Zubayr calls out from the kitchen. Nasser does not respond. Zubayr wants to finish the task for Bakri before attending to the truck in the loading bay but time is of the essence. He trumps into the freezer to see what's holding Nasser. "You need a hand, Nasser?" Zubayr asks but there is no response. Zubayr trudges to the back of the freezer where he finds a motionless Nasser standing completely frozen. "Nasser... Nasser can you go check on the gift shop for me when we're done?" Nasser doesn't respond or acknowledge Zubayr's request. Zubayr is not sure if he offended Nasser by coming across too bossy so he moves in closer and attempts to explain his request. "Can you believe...?" Momentarily Zubayr like Nasser stands frozen. "Yaa raabi!" says Zubayr as he shares Nasser's vision of three bodies lying on the back freezer shelf. The GPC truck deliveryman, Alya, and Dhakiyah are all frozen. All dead.

Rash

The Damascus hospital emergency room nurses are trying their best to comfort Jerry while Aza provides extra support. It is obvious by the nurses' reactions that they have not seen a rash like the one on Karlisa's body, nor can they explain the prolific nose-bleeding incident. What they can tell is that her vital signs are falling and they have not found an infection or any other type of medical problem that is commonly seen in the emergency room. After asking several questions and making attempts to contact her doctor in the United States the answers are still not coming easily. She will need to be admitted for further observation and tests.

"Aza have you ever seen anything like this?" Aza doesn't answer. Jerry dismisses his silence as he thinks Aza is as speechless and stumped as he is. "Those rashes... they look like ringworms."

"No, not ringworms."

"If not worms than what?"

"Symbols."

"I've had enough symbolism and legends for a lifetime out of this trip. What I need now is real answers."

Aza is both mystified and unforthcoming with what he knows. He himself is a little taken aback by Karlisa's illness, but he has seen it before. Aza recalls a time when he and his comrades descended on a village near Ram Lake. Talitha, a young priestess who was saving her virginity for a blessing from Ba'al received a lot of attention from the angelic Order of Watchers who were assigned to guard the humans. The Watchers fell onto the Earth and took human form posing as travelers. Many of the young village girls were attracted to the men who introduced themselves as travelers from the west. The men played the lute, sang songs, and dressed in silks and other fancy material not commonly seen in their village. They were exciting and fun but most of all they were randy. Some of the women didn't mind their provocative behavior as the men from their village had been off fighting a war in Ashur. Talitha was saving herself for a village hero, a man who has been blessed by the deity Ba'al. With so many women to chase after, her stubborn and invincible behavior turned many of the Watchers away accept one, Semjaza who grew more intrigued as she became more evasive. Semjaza was a great dancer and a seductive lute player that many women could not resist. Talitha had the warm inviting brown eyes that always drew men in no matter what her lips were saying. She wore her long dark hair wrapped in a silk scarf or headband. She wasn't a very voluptuous woman, but shapely and strong as she was a hard worker. She bathed in the oils of frankincense and rubbed jasmine in her hair but she smelled mostly of clean fresh air that blew every time she passed by. She was virtuous, wise, and blessed by all the Canaanite deities. She was the niece of King Ibbi-Sipish who had her educated by scholars from nearby Armi and from as far away as Crete. It wasn't only her beauty or her intelligence that attracted Semjaza but her sense of loyalty. He knew with a woman like that, once you had her on your side, she would never leave no matter what deep secrets she later found out about you. However, it was loyalty itself that he would have to break from her to get her at his side.

Women in the village began to grow envious of Talitha, after all Semjaza was the most talented and a leader who only had eyes for her. The women were also afraid that if she didn't partake in some of the infidelity she would have no reason to conceal their behavior from their men when they returned from the war. Rameel one of Semjaza's closest comrades came up with the idea of tricking Talitha through spirits and wine so that its intoxication caused her a loss of inhibition and control. The plan would likely succeed with the help of the village women. The only problem was Talitha did not drink.

Armaros, another Fallen Watcher who invented a smoke potion that causes drowsiness to anyone who breathed it into their lungs, schemed up a solution. On the night of trickery and deception, the women gathered with Talitha telling her it was the last night before the travelers would continue on their journey. They all came to see the men play, dance, and sing one last time. As the men danced, Armaros sat behind the women where he packed tobacco in his potion laced pipe. Talitha and the other women had their attention on the men playing the lute and singing. Armaros leaned in from behind and blew his smoke into the air around Talitha who then breathed it into her lungs. Talitha told the other women she felt tired and would return to her tent. Before Talitha could make it back to her tent she stumbled and fell. The women helped her up and offered her a drink to collect her senses and Talitha drank from their wine. Feeling intoxicated and faint Talitha returned to her tent. The women felt frustrated as they planned for her to lose inhibition and mingle with the men, not return to her tent, but Semjaza felt the plan was right on target. Semjaza accompanied Talitha back to her tent where he entered against her will and had relations of unlawful carnal knowledge. After that night, Talitha's spirit was broken and she became bitter and aloof. She could no longer trust the women in her village and she could not tell anyone what happened to her in an effort to protect her reputation and that of her uncle, King Ippi-Sipish.

Talitha confided the incident with her brother Hiram who was a commander in the Aramean army. He dealt with the women through heavy taxation of their families. Since many of the women lost their husbands at war the taxes were unbearable for them to pay and survive comfortably as they were accustomed. Unfortunately, Talitha found that she was with child, a bastard child as there was no husband to claim. This would cause great embarrassment to the ruling family. Talitha's brother helped her flee before she was seen carrying a child. Being in a royal family there was nowhere she could go where she would not be recognized. Against his judgment, Hiram built them a small cavern out in the wilderness where she was to go give birth to the baby and subsequently place the child up for adoption through his contacts in Jericho.

Hiram stayed with Talitha for several months while their father thought they were on a diplomatic trip in Jericho. Once the baby was born Talitha had trouble letting go of the child and refused to go through with the adoption. Hiram became furious and demanded the child be taken away or face his sword. Hardened by the experience Talitha sent Hiram away and convinced him that she could live alone in the cavern until she decided the fate of the child. Hiram agreed as the king became weary of his absence. Hiram would visit her periodically and find that she in fact made a living out in the wilderness. The problem was her father was concerned over her long absence as well.

As time passed Talitha found that she had a new reason not to return to her village. Her child was growing exceedingly fast. He was a Nephilim. He was gigantic and stronger than most kids at his age. His size and strength assisted his mother in building a larger and sturdier dwelling in the wilderness. Soon other Aramean women detected that their children were also Nephilim. These children were looked at as freaks and cursed by the Gods. Many of these bastard children suffered from exclusion and ridicule.

As time passed Hiram brought these other Nephilim children from their village to stay with Talitha, but many were destroyed before Hiram could rescue them and bring them out to the cavern. Soon there were 10 Nephilim children living with Talitha. The cavern grew sizably to accommodate Talitha with 10 Nephilim children. Talitha slept in the cavern while the children slept in a large courtyard area next to the cavern. The large stone cavern and the courtyard grew along with the children. Talitha's father died of a broken heart thinking he'd never see his cherished daughter again. He was devastated not knowing why she had gone away. Hiram took most the blame for careless guardianship over his sister in an effort to conceal the truth. The Aram relationship with Jericho suffered, as the king believed she found ill fate in their territory. King Ippi-Sipish was too heartbroken over his brother's strife and prepared to go to war with Jericho until Hiram told him the truth. The king became further angered and called upon the highest priests in all of Canaanite. He paid a bountiful ransom for the priests to evoke a spell that would cast out all the Nephilim from the land. The priest made sacrifices and summoned up Shamash, Goddess of the Sun who towered above the cavern and scorched all the Nephilim into salt rock. Shamash marked Talitha with a tailed circle rash signifying that she slept with a forbidden being and the only way the rash would go away was for her to leave and never return to those lands. Talitha left the large salt rock remains of the Nephilim children behind. The lands became cursed. The scorched statues only had the company of other creatures and outcasts from Heaven to stay with them as the land became foul with malicious souls. The lands were abandoned and its nights were ruled by evil. No one would be permitted to reside on these lands for four hundred years without a sacrifice to Shamash the Tower of the Sun.

CHAPTER SIX

Some Kind of Angel

Jerry receives news that Karlisa has fallen into a coma. Several hours have passed and there is no additional information about what has caused this illness. Jerry paces the floor of the critical care waiting area wondering if he should have her care transferred to Nouveau Beirut's modern post-war hospital several miles away in Lebanon. The doctors are recommending that Jerry be patient and allow time to offer clues as to what may be ailing her before she is moved, but Jerry grows more impatient by the hour. Sitting in a hard orange plastic waiting room chair he removes a small pill holder from his pocket and shakes it. He can tell by the container's sound that his supply is running short. He removes one of few small pills from the container and swallows it without water. Aza and Jerry begin waiting out the night by sitting, then slouching until Jerry ends up lying across the hard chairs and Aza is stretched out on the floor. The two have been at the hospital for over 24 hours without sleep.

Aza rolls the thought of fulfilling his obligation to the pact through his mind. He looks over at Jerry lying across the hard plastic chairs nodding and bobbing his head as he struggles to hold it up and refrain from falling asleep. Jerry turns his head toward Aza and looks at him with his heavy eyelids. For the first time this night Jerry cracks a smile in comfort to see his new friend hanging in by his side. Aza smiles back with a quick and fading grin, enough to express support without losing the empathy for the situation.

Aza feels compelled to tell Jerry something to ease his mind but his desire to put Jerry at ease is not as strong as his responsibility to fulfill his obligation to freeing Semjaza and fulfilling his pact. Aza can't deny his feelings of concern for Jerry even though his sense of compassion is a long lost emotion. Aza recalls the day when Omnus announced the creation of mankind and how he at first sided with Sammael's envy, spite, and hate towards humans until he met his first man while serving as a Guardian. Aza further accepted humans when they welcomed him into their villages after he fell onto the Earth. During that time his feelings transpired into deep attraction for the daughters of man who showed him how to love again in the absence of Sophia. Jerry and Karlisa were symbolic of the love he once shared and that stirred his feelings of compassion for Jerry's situation in spite of his conflicting motives. He knew that he must continue on somehow and complete his mission regardless of his feelings.

Jerry and Aza nap in the intensive care waiting room until the long hours become more concerning as they do not bring any change in the situation. "Jerry," Aza says quietly across the waiting room. "Let's walk. Let's go out for some fresh air. We need to talk."

Jerry looks up at Aza then sits up straight and smiles. He is beginning to appreciate him more as time passes. Jerry doesn't have any siblings. He and his father weren't very close so having another guy around in this situation is comforting for him.

Jerry stretches and yawns before saying, "I've been waiting to call home but her mother will ask me a thousand questions and I have no answers. I guess I have to deal with that now."

"Let's go on that walk first. Maybe you will get your thoughts together," says Aza.

Jerry stands up and follows Aza outside. Maybe he wants to stretch his legs or delay making the dreaded phone call, but maybe he just wants to get his mind off the situation for a while, so he doesn't hesitate following Aza out the hospital to an outside sitting area.

"Jerry, you know how what's going on with Karlisa is strange and bizarre?"

"Tell me about it."

"What if the explanation and cure is as equally strange and inexplicable? Would you be willing to listen to it?"

"I'd be willing to go to Hell and back, Aza."

"Be careful of what you say," Aza warns. "You are right Jerry, that day you found me I was bound and tied and had been left there for a very long time. A time much longer than you can imagine. It started a very long time ago..."

Aza spent a good part of an hour telling a very tired and sleepy-eyed Jerry the history of Paradise, the Fallen angels, and the creation of mankind. Jerry looks over at Aza not sure how all this is fitting into the situation but he doesn't mind as it manages to get his mind off of the medical emergency. Jerry is amused by the way Aza tells the story as if he was there himself. Jerry thinks the events Aza describes are ridiculous, but entertaining as the story manages to calm him and lighten his mood. Then Aza begins to talk about meeting him in the desert. Still a little drowsy, Jerry begins to connect the dots and listen as if he believes the story. Jerry doesn't know why, but for some reason all the oddities in the story begin to add up to possibilities. The peculiar string of events tells a better story than what could be rational as nothing in the sensible world can explain it better. Jerry recalls the quote, "Once you have eliminated the impossible, whatever remains, however improbable, must be the truth."

"So what are you saying? You are some kind of angel?"

"In the beginning, we all started off as a spirit. Spirits are conscious forms of light. We all are made from the same stuff basically, pure energy," Aza explains. "Omnus himself is a spawn of a great energy source. Omnus spawned off yet more energy sources and molded those spirits into companions, angels." Aza looks to see if he is holding Jerry's attention before continuing. "Omnus shared his power with his divine creations. Then like

140

most omnipotent beings do, they became bored and created other sorts of creatures such as fairies, dinosaurs, dragons, what a mess that turned out to be. Eventually, Omnus created the human man. We all loved man, but he had his flaws."

"I'm sure," Jerry responds, trying to keep some humor in the story.

"Omnus created so many humans until supervising you little mortals was getting out of hand. Your curiosity and constant questioning brought up all kinds of trouble. The balance of nature was becoming disturbed. You didn't get along well with the dinosaurs because you ate and devoured every beast you saw. Your diets and gluttony brought disharmony in the coexistence of man and beast. So that put an end to the creations of dinosaurs, gores, the trolls and finally the dragons." Aza shakes his head in disappointment, "They all weren't so bad you know."

"So, God created dragons?" Jerry asks with a cocked head and a half smile.

"Who? Oh yeah, umm God."

"Why would he create something to hunt us?"

"Well those weren't his dragons, that's another story. Where was I... oh yeah, supervising humans was an honorable task for a select group of angels called the Guardian Angels. The Guardian Angels were given permission to descend and walk the Earth."

"So angels just roam all around us, interacting with us, and traveling back and forth to the Heavens?"

"Not exactly. An angel can always choose to fall upon the Earth, meaning to go without divine permission. Once an angel falls onto the earth it cannot return unless given the power of ascension by the Divine Order or the use of dark magic through the authority of Abaddon, the evil Underlord. As for humans, when they are born they lose awareness of their spiritual wings, this is why humans cannot rise back to the Heavens."

"So how do you fit into this?"

"Underlord Abaddon, who you call Lucifer and Chancellor Sammael, who you call Satan are both powerful angels. They both can rise and fall from the Heavens to the Earth. Abaddon is in Raquia, the Second House of Heaven where he is imprisoned. The Chancellor still walks the Earth. They have plans to bring upon the Apocalypse. I'm one of few angels that know of their plans."

"Ok, so how did you get here?"

"Some angels misused their ability to mingle with humans and became a little too friendly with the women. Omnus forbade this. You see, although we have human qualities our genetic makeup doesn't exactly match and a few overgrown children decided to rule the earth with their freakish height and strength. Omnus destroyed these giants, or Nephilim, and punished all those who took the daughter of man for wives."

"You were one of these angels?"

"Yes, but it wasn't my intent. I sought refuge in a village and naturally I made civil relationships with the villagers. A group of angels called the Watchers discovered how I made a good life for myself here on Earth and the next thing you know the whole dammed choir of angels was falling to the Earth. I warned them to keep it cool, but their damn children kept popping up all over the place. I knew sooner or later Michael, the leader of the Archangels, would catch us."

"So who tied you up in the desert?"

"The favorite four Michael, Gabriel, Raphael, and Uriel."

"So they tied you up in that desert and left you there?"

"Yes."

"Why? Why leave you there."

"Because contrary to popular belief, angels can be quite ruthless. I guess it was to serve as a reminder of how I illegally descended onto the Earth."

"So I came along and freed you?"

"Thank you very much."

"All this time no one else found you?"

"I was covered up until the Chancellor unearthed me."

"Why didn't he free you?"

"Only an Archangel can do that."

"That's not me."

"There's also... the power of love, as corny as that may sound. Only a pure heart can manifest the Power of the Arch."

"Pure heart... Whatever! What does this have to do with me and Karlisa?"

"It's a trade off. You use your dormant power to get me back to Heaven—"

"Wait my power to get you back to Heaven? You were an Angel. so you say... why don't you just go back on your own?"

"The Arch used some kind of magic Angel Dust on me that took away my power to ascend. But you on the other hand, if I get you to realize your true spiritual wings I can ascend with your escort."

"Then what?"

"I entered an Oath of Alliance with my... brethren. It must be fulfilled otherwise they'll avenge me."

"What's the Oath of Alliance?"

"The oath was simple. We all agreed to violate the rules together and to come to the aid of one another if we were caught and imprisoned."

"You expect me to help you release a bunch of God's prisoners?"

"No, I'll do that—"

"Why? Why are you doing this? You are free to just walk away. You don't owe them anything, besides they're imprisoned right?"

"I have to do this to honor the pact, besides the Chancellor will never leave me alone if I don't."

"The Chancellor... Oh come on you are not going to use the devil made me do it excuse are you?"

"That's cute. Who do you think placed a spell on Karlisa?"

"You know this story has been a great distraction," Jerry says while stretching and yawning. "But now my friend I think it's going too far. But thanks for—"

"You don't want to believe, but it's the only thing, no matter how incredible, that makes sense in this implausible situation!" Aza shouts with cold protruding eyes.

"Too far, Aza! Too far!" Jerry shouts back.

"Is it really?" Aza responds. "There something wrong with the world," Aza mimics Jerry's voice. "When I saw you... it looked like you had been there... for a very long time!"

"You bastard! You placed a spell on Karlisa?"

"Not me!"

"The Chancellor?"

"Now you got it!"

Jerry's breathing increases rapidly as he raises his hands over his shoulders to help him inhale air. After gaining control of his breathing he reaches for another pill from his pocket and swallows it dry. "Why help him? Why shouldn't I just walk away and say you, your Chancellor, and all the rest of you and your God forsaken angels can just rot in Hell?"

"That's an option for you if you can live with loosing Karlisa. As for me... I'm the only one who has connections to obtaining the key that opens the prison cells in Raquia so I have to go anyway."

"You're free now. What do you get out of this?"

"Well for one I got out of that hole and I have... I have... This is about your decision. Your chance to save her," Aza points to the hospital. "If you don't want it then—"

"How would my going there help Karlisa? How would I get back?"

"The same Angel Dust that kept me from ascending will help you return back to Earth and release the spell on Karlisa."

"When will I get the... Angel Dust! I can't believe I'm playing this game with you."

"I will show you how to obtain the Angel Dust. There are seven houses in Heaven. Matey, the fifth house, Sandalphon's house is where the Angel Dust is stored."

Holding his hands to his temples Jerry asks, "Who is Sandalphon?"

"He's an extremely powerful Seraph. He's one of the elder class Divinity Angels and a commanding warrior along with his brother Metaphon. He can get you the angelic dust that bends every rule. It can send you back and it can reverse the Chancellor's spell."

"He's just going to hand it over to me?"

"He's a softie. He loves you freaking humans. No offense."

"What if I say no?"

"Then good luck Karlisa. Poor girl."

"Damn you!"

"Damn me? I'm already damned!"

"Is there a gotcha in this somewhere? Now would be the time."

"I'm afraid not." Anticipating his next question Aza pulls a sword out of the air and taps the metal on the ground.

"Whoa!"

"I know... why should you believe me? You want to see something vulgar." Aza spins the sword back out of sight.

"Where... did... that come from?" Jerry asks with a shallow breath.

"The exoverse, a place in between here, the innerverse and out there," Aza points to the stars, "the universe."

"You can do that... but you can't release Karlisa's spell?"

"I didn't cast it."

Jerry thinks for a moment. "There's no way I'm asking a warrior angel who guards the House of God for anything! Especially, after I just helped set his prisoners free."

"You don't even need to talk to him. You just need to get in the house and get a hold of the dust. Bring it to me and I'll show you how to use it."

"Then why don't you go get it?"

"If he catches you he might show mercy. If he catches me... well I'm not supposed to be out of my fucking hole!"

"I can't believe this! How long will all this take?"

"A twinkling of time. Don't worry about it. You'll be back in no time because there isn't really such a thing as time in Paradise."

"OK. I need to go say goodbye to Karlisa then we'll go."

"Not that easy. You must first learn how to fly. Take my vehicle back to the resort. Meet me near the same place you found me in the desert. The pale horse will bring you there. A quick training lesson, then we're off."

On Earth As it is

Jerry stands over Karlisa's bed feeling ashamed for having been away for so long. Jerry is not sure what to believe about himself, Aza, or his story. The one thing he knows for sure is that there's still something not right with the world and maybe he is about to find out what that is and get a cure for Karlisa. He knows there is a risk in making this journey. He thinks he will be taking a chance on not being able to come back, but still it is worth taking the risk if it will save Karlisa.

Karlisa lies in a coma and in a catatonic state. She breathes deeply, rasping for air with each breath. Tubes are providing her oxygen and food supply. Several intravenous medication bags hang from a pole that runs down to her arm. The color in her face has turned pale and her lips are dry with a bluish hue. Karlisa, being a hairstylist and somewhat of a vain person, would have never allowed herself to be seen like this. Jerry tries to brush her hair, but it does little to help and only brings tears to his eyes. "I know we weren't very religious but maybe this can help." He grabs her hand and recites a prayer out loud. "Our Father and angels, which art in the houses of Heaven, hallowed be thy names. Thy Kingdom come, thy will be done, on Gaia as it is in Paradise. Give me this day our daily bread and forgive me for my trespass as I forgive those angels that descended and trespassed against us. And lead me not into temptation, but deliver me from evil. For thine is the kingdom, the power, and the glory, forever and ever. Amen."

He feels cold and helpless, tired and weary, yet hopeful that some miracle will save her and bring her back. Jerry whispers to Karlisa, "If this is the miracle you need, I'll gladly give my life for yours. I'll risk everything with what I must do." Jerry knows he can't tell anyone what it is he feels he must do because there is no one foolish enough to believe it, so he decides to write a letter.

If I'm not here when you wake up it's because I had to do what must be done and what must be done is like our love, inexplicable. Love, Jerry.

It is all he can write without feeling that he'll confuse her and make his absence appear inflammatory and poorly unexcused. He bends over dropping his tears on her face as he kisses her lips for what may be the very last time.

The Rise

Aza, leaving the car with Jerry, travels to his former dwelling place in the desert. He can't help but think of how cool it is to be able to fly again, even if he can't ascend to the Heavens. He spreads his wings and aims high in the sky like a gargoyle trying to not be seen in the light of day. He finally arrives to an isolated and barren place in the desert rocks where he finds a dark figure standing and waiting on his arrival. "If he says one more damn thing about that trial I swear I'll drop him further from the Heavens and the Earth than he knew could be possible, so help me Omnus." Azazel contemplates for a brief moment if he'd rather be back in the hole than to deal with the dark, but that thought lasts only for a brief moment. Azazel treads up behind the dark figure and begins to inform him, "The plan is in place. Through the son of man I should be able to rise to Vilon. We will be departing soon."

"The t-r-i-a-l!" squeals the raging voice as it turns towards Azazel.

"Yeah the trial. As I said, soon!"

Briefly, the figure dims the sky dark as he dissipates into a murky dark haze and fades away. Azazel watches with slight disgust. "Must he be so damned dramatic?" Azazel begins to experience yet another feeling that he is not accustomed to, the feeling of deep animosity towards another Fallen angel. "No one bothered to poof a rock when I was buried for over 5,000 years! I hope someone is considering my trial while I'm digging my hole deeper!"

Jerry makes his way back to the resort's stable where he finds Zelig the stable keeper. Zelig smiles as he leads a white Arabian over to Jerry. "How did he know I was coming for that horse? Another enigma. It's all a part of what's wrong with this world. Now we have Fallen angels and demons amongst us?" Jerry's anxiety and heart rate begins to increase. "How am I ever going to be able to trust anyone again when people are not always what they appear to be?" Without questioning it any further Jerry grabs the reigns from Zelig's hand.

"He's been waiting," Zelig informs.

Silently and without hesitation Jerry mounts the horse and pulls away to the trail. "Ok, I wonder if you know what else to do because I don't." Jerry allows the horse to walk of its own free will for he is too exhausted to care at this point. He has been up for several hours straight and does not know how he can continue on this mission, but time is of the essence. "Alright now horse, move it! Yah! Come on boy!" Jerry startles up the horse in hope that it will run the same way it did the other day and take him to Aza. Eventually, the Arabian runs through the desert as fast as it did that hot sunny day. The horse runs hard against the wind, up an incline into the mountains, and to an off-trail designation where Aza is waiting. The horse, breathing heavily through its wide nostrils, comes to a stop where the sky has already appeared to dusk.

"So are you ready for the training session of your life?" Aza says standing in the twilight.

"No, I just like coming out to the most barren places on Earth to meet up with men who say they work for the devil," Jerry replies as he removes a small pill from his pocket container and swallows it.

"Well you haven't seen anything yet so prepare yourself," Aza warns. "You will see the worst of the worse villains, the baddest of the bad angels, and the wealthiest of the wealthy. We are going to Vilon, the First House of Heaven where all souls must come to enter the Heavens then we are off to Raquia, the second house where they keep the most notorious prisoners. Whatever you do, you stay near me. The Fallen will not be happy to see you, not that they're happy to see anyone for that matter," Aza grimaces before continuing. "Then I'll see you off to Matey, the Fifth House of Heaven where you'll meet Sandalphon who will give you the dust. Then you bring it to me and I'll send you home. That simple."

"Why should I give the dust to you?"

"I need that dust to get free from the binding, to grow my wings again."

"And what about Karlisa?"

"Trust me there's enough to go around."

"And if I run into an Archangel?"

"You do just that! You run! But don't run back to me."

"What am I suppose to do, just run around in the Heavens?"

"You find Sandalphon and kiss the ring of Your Gracefulness. May Omnus have mercy on you, but first things are first. Let's get started, shall we?"

A schoolroom blackboard appears from out of nowhere and Aza changes his appearance. He is now wearing a pin striped gray suit with shiny gray sharkskin loafers, a white shirt, complimenting tie, and accessorized by a gold-chained pocket watch. There are several student desks surrounding Jerry. Aza motions for Jerry to have a seat, "Class is in session! So how does an angel take flight?" Aza lectures while pacing in front of the blackboard.

Aza holds a pointer and points to the word FAITH that mysteriously appears on the blackboard. "Unlike birds and planes, angels use faith to take flight. Believe that you can fly and have faith that you can ascend over any depth. Have faith that you can arise over any occasion. Let faith take flight!"

Jerry sitting at a student desk, "I'm not a man of much faith, Aza."

"Uh... it's Pro-fes-sor Ziel, please."

Jerry smirks. "Please!" Jerry succumbs, "Professor... Ziel you are wasting your faith on me."

"Oh no, my good dear boy. Faith is something you have in abundance. You may not be involved in organized faith, but you have your faith in order. Was it not you who, on a crazy horse, rescued an old man in a desert giving him your last bit of water in hopes that you two lost souls would find your way home?"

"What was I suppose to do?"

"Are you not present in this class today, here in this God forbidden place, on the account of an old man's tale while your comatose wife lies in a hospital bed?"

"Well... that's because—"

"FAITH! Believe in it Jerry and it will believe in you. The next thing you have to have is..." Aza points toward the blackboard again which now mysteriously reads FLIGHT. "Using your faith you take flight. Not any of that air under my wings Wright Brother's bullshit. Your faith will raise you and your wings will guide you," Aza continues as the word WINGS appears on the blackboard.

"So where do I get these wings," Jerry asks as he turns his eyes away from the blackboard, back to Azazel who is now in full angelic form. Azazel stands looking taller and stronger than he ever appeared before. He is like half soldier and have black raven with dark green eyes. The hair on his head even looks more radiant and styled like the head of an eagle. He's a dark Fallen angel with a glowing darkness like the shine on a black corvette under the evening dusk. Jerry is more startled than afraid. Aza escorts Jerry to the edge of a nearby cliff.

"Oh, how long I've been waiting to do this. My true and natural form," Azazel looks around in admiration of himself. His vanity saturates his entire being. "A little darker than I used to be." Adjusting into his old form, Azazel stretches his neck and shakes his shoulders like a wrestler before a fight. "You already have your wings my child. All souls can fly. When Adam and Eve bit into the forbidden fruit and saw their nakedness it was not the knowledge of their nudity that Omnus concealed from them but the knowledge of their spiritual wings. They never completely accepted their ability to know their true selves. They didn't realize what the Chancellor was trying to get them to do, to see that Omnus was not telling them the whole truth."

"What truth?" Jerry asks as he looks down over the edge of a deep cliff.

"Believe, Jerry! For once in your pathetic human life! BELIEVE IN YOURSELF!" Azazel screams in agony. He's tormented by Jerry's human appearance and wants him to believe so deeply in himself that he will activate his dormant powers to transcend into his spiritual form. "Do you believe? You said something was not right with the world

Jerry and here it is before you. All the answers you've been seeking. Now DO YOU BELIEVE?"

"You want me to jump?" Jerry asked with widened eyes and heavy breathing.

"I want you to believe!"

Jerry pauses with eyes closed and takes in a couple deep breaths. He takes a couple twists on his wedding ring while he collects his thoughts. "I believe!" Jerry responds in anguish as his wings begin to bulge out from his shoulder blades.

"Do you believe?"

"I BELIEVE!" screams Jerry, as his wings come out and grow taller.

"Do you have the faith?

"I have the faith!"

Aza pushes Jerry off the cliff and shouts, "Faith Jerry. Faith!"

"Do you have the flight?"

Jerry struggles in the wind of the fall then begins to raise and hover over the ground. "I have the flight! I have it!"

Jerry raises several hundred feet into the air. "That's it," says Azazel. Jerry shows no fear. He is eager to continue on. Azazel flies in full force through the skies. Jerry follows, mimicking Aza's every move. Aza flies up then Jerry flies up. Aza flies down then Jerry flies down. Aza comes to a complete stop in mid air, but Jerry is a little clumsy and out of control and rolls in the sky before stopping. "You've come a long way, baby," Aza laughs before heading into the mountain peaks and caverns. Jerry follows demonstrating his ability to navigate near the tight mountain curves, and the twist and turns. He flies through caverns and holes in rock formations. "Beats mountain climbing any day Jerry," Aza shouts back with Jerry close on his heels.

"If I'd known I could do this why would I have ever wanted to be in the form of a human?"

"It's exactly what Omnus didn't want you to do. He wanted to control you, Jerry," Aza says while coming to a stop on the top of a mountain ledge high in the sky. "You have Faith and flight, now are you ready for the last requirement?"

"Yes. Hell yeah," Jerry says while trying to catch his breath.

"Must be careful in the use of that word, Jerry."

"Yes, of course," Jerry says while calming down and coming back to reality of what his mission is all about. "Don't worry my new friend, my guardian angel. I got you. Now let's go get your wings and save my wife."

"The final requirement is... love!"

"Love? Did you say love?"

"FAITH, FLIGHT, and LOVE, Jerry. Flying won't get you anywhere. To get into the kingdom of Heaven you must have pure love, a quality I once possessed, but have lost in my Fall."

"But I already have love."

"Show me. Tell me what you love."

"I love my wife. I love my children. I love peace, but I also love simple things like... I love my freedom and my country. I love my mother's cooking. I love the puppy that I had in sixth grade, even when he ate my favorite baseball mitt I still loved him. I love the smell of cookies baking in the oven. I love Pepsi. I love the way my son laughs when Jack pops out the box," Jerry smiles and laughs a bit. "I love the Cleveland Indians, I love the Ohio State Buckeyes." Jerry doesn't notice that he has elevated above the clouds and Azazel has caught a hold of his hand as they rise towards Vilon. "I love those starving kids on late night TV. I love the prophets of the world like Gandhi, Martin Luther King, Nelson Mandela, Chelsea Clinton, Mohammed Tantawi, and Liu Xiaobo. Most importantly... I love myself! Is that selfish?" Jerry asks without noticing they have risen to Paradise and are standing on the clouds of Heaven.

"To love your creator, you have to love yourself. You've got to have love, to give love. Love oneself, Jerry. Welcome to Vilon."

ACT II

Angels are bright still, though the brightest fell.

William Shakespeare, Macbeth

CHAPTER XEVEN

Gabriel's Gate

Jerry and Aza arrive on the thoroughfare to Vilon. It's the main path that leads up to the Seven Houses of Heaven. Many souls promenade up the path, instinctually following those in front of them as they walk the incline up into the mountaintops of Heaven where each of the seven houses are located. Each of the houses is engulfed in a cluster of stars, like clouds circling a mountaintop. The Heavens have seven subdivisions with each division rising higher than the one below, like ornaments ascending up on a Christmas tree. The highest peak is the rooftop of the Seventh House of Heaven. From the bottom portal of the path you can only see the rooftops of each heavenly estate. The clusters are strung together by a side-winding path that curls up to the highest house in Araboth. The foremost house is located in Vilon. It is the gatehouse of the Heavens. It's also the home of Archangel Gabriel. This is where souls come if they lose their way along the path.

"No fucking way!" Jerry says as he looks at the vastness of the First House. "We were so... screwed!" Jerry says as he struggles to find the right words to conceptualize the Heaven to Earth comparison.

Jerry is star-struck as he gazes at the sky of all skies. The continuous rainbow-rowed sky of blue, green, yellow, and violet is dashed with a mist of glittering stars that appears as close as a hand's reach. The galactic beauty engulfs him like a blanket of peace. Jerry inhales and exhales deeply trying to fill his lungs with the freshness of Heaven's air, but there is really no air in the atmosphere of immortality.

"Alright snap out of it!" Aza demands. "We have work to do."

Jerry follows Aza into the crowd of other souls traveling up the path to the First House. Along the path there are angel sentries watching over the souls like a flock. These angels serve in the Sentinel, a division of the angelic military under General Seraphiel created for the sole purposes of patrolling the Heavens and preparing for the apocalyptic incursion. They keep the order and watch for damned souls trying to sneak into the atrium, the area outside the Gates of Paradise where all the blessed souls wait for reentry into the post-apocalyptic sanctified Earth.

"Keep your head down, don't look at them, and keep moving," Aza drills. Jerry can't help gazing around at wonder of Vilon. He is not aware that he looks like a tourist at Disney. "Stop smiling!" Aza directs in a low voice as he hangs his head down, avoiding direct eye contact with the sentries. "You are a immigrant in a strange land so try to look lost, but happy. Stumble step a little bit. You're walking to your day of judgment. Look confident with a little bit of uncertainty," Aza instructs Jerry who can't help looking more curious than cautious. "That's it, just look at your feet, keep moving, and follow the crowd." Jerry lowers his head and tries to mimic the souls walking on the path. "When I move, you move. We are going to run off the path to the gate of the First House."

"This is great. The ground feels like that soft recycled material on the exercise trails. I don't think I've ever felt this good. It's like a baby—"

"Will you please pay attention? We don't have any room for error and we just got here."

"I'm sorry. It just... feels... so great!"

"It's the Angel Dust in the atmosphere. It makes you feel energized, replenished, and invigorated. It's made of the same stuff that will save Karlisa."

"Oh God, she's going to feel so great. Just like back in college when—"

"Over there! Run, follow me. Quick!" Aza scurries off the path undetected by the sentries and runs up to Gabriel's gatehouse, Jerry follows. "This is Vilon, the First House of Heaven, and home of Archangel Gabriel."

The gate is tall and made of a strong material that looks like iron rods. The gate is heavy and sturdy. Each rod rises far up into the sky beyond the point of visual acuity. On the sides of the rods are pillars that look like a block of stacked golden bricks molded into one huge and massive amalgamation, towering as high as the rods. On the ground is a well-manicured lawn with grass blades of various colors reminiscent of a garland in a Christmas wonderland. Beyond the gate is a checkered walkway that illuminates in random pastel colors. The tetragons glow is slowly fading from the steps of the last feet to have traveled over the walkway. The curling trail of pastels leads up to an exterior corridor that tunnels down to the main door. Just before you reach the door you have to pass a row of white marble columns that are fixed flush into the face of the gatehouse. Above the columns are several rows of windows topped off way up high with a roof that spikes in several points like a Gothic castle. The gate out in front of the house has a long chain hooked to a large bell.

"Move over behind the pillar and try to stay out of sight," Aza instruct Jerry as he pulls the bell chain to alert the gatekeeper.

"What if Gabriel answers the door?" Jerry asks from around the other side of the pillar.

"Gabe, answering his own door? I think not. At least not in the several 1000s of years I worked in Vilon. I doubt if he's even here. He's probably somewhere moping around, sharpening his sword, and sparing off with Michael. Alright keep quiet, someone's coming," Aza whispers.

Out from the main door a figure appears flickering like a flame. At first the figure flashes at the door, then quickly down the checkered walkway lighting up the pastel tetragons until it reaches the gate. The figure flashes at the gate. "Hello! Blessed one? Are you there? Hello... are you lost? Did you wonder from the path? Hello."

"Hello... Janus!"

Peering through the gate, "Azzzza... What are you doing here?"

"The Trial—"

"What about the trial?"

"You know what I need."

The genie clinches its jaw shut and squeezes its eyes closed with a hard swallow. "Now?" the genie asks through closed lips. "Lord Almighty! Get over here before someone sees you!" Janus scurries to open the gate. Janus flashes outside the gate to look around but does not notice Jerry hiding around the pillar. "I can't believe you even thought to come here at a time like this!"

"Just give me what I need and I'll go."

"Are you kidding me? Do you really think— What is that? There's something... Blessed one... Blessed one, are you lost?" Janus flashes around and locates Jerry on the other side of the pillar. "Oh! You're not... How adorable. It's a... Oh my Omnus... but how?" It has been a very long time since the genie has sensed mortality. Everything Janus remembers about humans is like a fantasy or an exotic creature from another land. Standing back and being careful to not to frighten Jerry, Janus stares and examines him from a distance. Janus detects a sense of fear coming from Jerry. "You... you did this!" Janus says accusing Azazel of mishandling a mortal life form.

"He's alright! You can get closer. He doesn't bite."

"You precious soul. Are you well?" asks Janus while further examining Jerry.

"He can't hear you. Your angelic squeal is much too high for his mortal ears."

"Oh! Yes, excuse me," lowering the pitch, "Are you well blessed one?"

"Yes, I'm fine I guess."

"Yes you are... I'm Janus."

"Oh, brother," sighs Aza.

"I'm Jerry... Jerry Xeven."

"Like five, six, —"

"Yes!"

"We must get him inside right away. His sense of mortality is still strong. I'm not sure how you got him this far without being noticed." Janus escorts Azazel and Jerry up the walkway, down the corridor, and through the large doors into a dark foyer. "Keep your voices down. Look what you've gotten me into!" Janus whispers.

"Just get me the keys and I'm out of here," Azazel whispers.

"There's no keys just one key. The key! The golden key and there's no way I'm letting it get into your hands."

"You took the Oath."

"If I give you that key they'll know where you got it."

"You knew this day was coming. You knew of the alliance."

"That last I heard you were buried in Dudael and Semjaza is in prison, so therefore no alliance."

"Surprise asshole! I've been resurrected!"

Janus

Janus recalls the day of joining the pact and taking the Oath of Alliance. It occurred when Semjaza was just on the verge of his fall. Semjaza was adored in the Houses of Heaven and held with high esteem for he was an elite Guardian Angel swordsman under the tutelage of Abaddon, who at the time was the brightest star in the Order of Guardian Angels. Abaddon and Semjaza were close friends, an accompaniment made in paradise. After Abaddon was imprisoned, Semjaza was assigned under the direction of Michael who was more interested in joining the new warrior class of Archangels than supervising a Guardian Angel apprentice. When Michael resigned himself from the Guardian Angels to lead the Archangels, Semjaza became revered as the next in line to replace him, but his level of talent was threatened. Word came through the Heavens that Semjaza was not the greatest swordsmen ever and that his talent was beneath that of a mortal human sword fighter, therefore he was least preferred to lead the Guardian Angels. Semjaza became furious and visited Sandalphon, the administrator of the Fifth House where all the Choirs of Angels resided. Sandalphon governs over the distribution of divine talents. Sandalphon informed Semjaza that the only way a human could have been granted a gift of talent beyond that of the angels in Paradise it would have to be gifted from the angel who presides over the realm of the craft, but first the prayer request had to be brought before the Prayer Council by one of its messengers. Semjaza knew that Omnus loved the humans so much that such a prayer may be granted. Semjaza had instructed all the messengers to not honor any prayer requesting a talent parallel to his. Semjaza threatened that any angel who would bring such a request before the Prayer Council would be dealt with severe consequences, yet this prayer made its way through.

One evening Janus was working alone in the prayer auditing room where unanswered prayers are stored for conciliation. "A sword of gold," Janus reads from a prayer request. "Who would be so vain as to pray for a sword of –?"

"You! It was you!" shouts Semjaza as he storms through the prayer room doors with his sword drawn. "You delivered that prayer. You have been protecting that boy," he continues backing Janus up against the wall with his arm and sword pressing near Janus' throat.

Janus flickers and flash to another side of the room. "What boy?"

Spinning around with sword drawn, "Don't play games! I've seen you two spending much time together. You are always at his side granting his every request. His next request will be at the mercy of my blade."

"Jazire? You leave him alone!"

"Who granted his prayer? Who allowed a mortal-being to mock me?"

"Only a member of the Prayer Council can approve of a mortal having a gift parallel to those in paradise."

"So who was it?"

Janus hesitates before realizing that flashing and running away will only prolong the chase. "It. It was... Chief Prince Hozi," Janus reports then swallows with a dry mouth full of shame.

"Hozi! He doesn't possess the gift so he can't give it."

"It's not how he fights it's what he fights for that makes his success so attractive. Hozi is the Angel

166

of the Sword who has just invented the astroflare. He needed a noble sword handler to test his new weapon."

"But why? Why a mere mortal?"

"That I don't know! I was wondering the same thing. He was only a boy," Janus explains. "He wasn't even a swordsman. He was a musician by trade."

"A musician!"

Janus was one of few genies that had been assigned to the Watchers, a group of angels that watch over human affairs from afar. Janus was assigned to watch over Jazire's village, a place where the common man was known for his peacefulness and hospitality, in a place where the people lived simple lifestyles and practiced a monotheistic religion. The village was constantly under attack. They looked vulnerable in their worshiping a single god of peace in a land where many villages practiced polytheistic religions. The village was underestimated as their men often returned from battle victorious in defense of their religion and peaceful lifestyle. Jazire's father was an army leader and war hero who wanted a son who could carry the family name in his honor onto the battlefield. Jazire was not talented with the sword and he preferred to play the lute. Wars continued to plague the village turning a once peaceful land into a place known for raising warriors and studying the art of war crafts. The day came when Jazire's father returned from battle critically wounded and was lying on his deathbed. The seed of revenge settled into Jazire's heart, as he knew his father was one of few leaders who only fought in hopes of restoring the people back to a land known for peace. Jazire decided to join the battle to continue his father's mission and to make him proud before his death, but Jazire was an awful fighter. Jazire prayed, requesting a talent with the sword in hopes of returning peace to his village. Jazire was already the most gifted lute player in his village and throughout the lands, but he wished to have the skill of a swordsman, one that would please his father who he felt disapproved of his lute playing. Jazire's father eventually died from his battle wounds, but not before he confided in Jazire that he was in fact proud of him and he believed music brought people and their villages together, increasing the chance for peace. These last words of support swelled pride in Jazire's heart and reinforced his desire to join the army to carry out his father's mission. If only he had the warrior's talent to do so he would. Jazire had never spoken a prayer for himself in all his young 17 years. He had only made prayers for others and those of ritual and routine wellness, but now he prayed for the talent with a different instrument.

Prince Angel Hozi, spawn of Ambassador Jerriel from Persidis was secretly commissioned by Omnus to invent a more powerful weapon that would not only destroy its opponent, but also imprison their soul to be judged before the throne. Once completed one of these swords would be given to each of the twelve house ambassadors. Hozi combined elements from the star clusters with the mystical workings of the divine powers invested in him through Omnus creating the astroflare. The astroflare would remain in the exoverse, a place in between the physical world and the hidden depths of the universe until invoked by its holder into the innerverse. The sword was not completed until after the days of the Great Disturbance. Before introducing the sword to the remaining house ambassadors, Hozi needed a trail run of the sword outside of the bounds of Paradise to keep it a secret. Only the Divinity Angels and Janus were informed of its creation before it was revealed.

In Jazire's village many demons and Fallen angels had participated in brutal outlawed contests where swordsmen fought in a warrior's arena. The winners were rewarded with material wealth and women slaves, two of the most sought after possessions from members of Fallen. These demons, having an immortal advantage, fought mortals under the disguise of human combatants, walking away victorious with their wealth and women. Their brutality and violent behavior became infectious as they were paraded as heroes amongst the humans.

Jazire played the lute for the crowds during the opening ceremonies and at the arena's entrance. He noticed life in the village had changed from the values his father had fought to protect. Jazire began to see that the children in the village were idolizing icons of violence and fighting in place of peace and brotherly love for their neighboring villagers. He felt hopeless in ever changing the village mentality as the peaceful civil and religious structure eroded away.

Janus delivered Jazire's prayer before the Prayer Council where Prince Angel Hozi, Angel of the Sword heard the request. Hozi needed a venue to fight Fallen angels and demons to test his new sword, the astroflare. A fighting arena of Fallen angels and demons presented itself as the perfect venue. Hozi also took an interest in the lad due to

Jazire's act of selflessness. Hozi represented Jazire's request before the prayer council and granted his wish for an enhanced swordsmen talent. This spirit of nobility was pleasing to Hozi and Rachmiel the Angel of Compassion who also supported granting the mortal with the gift. Hozi motioned that the mortal's gift should be sublime. The motion was approved and anointed by the grace of Sandalphon.

One evening after prayers calling for peace, a flicker of light flashed into Jazire's room. "Are you the Angel of Peace?" Jazire asked of the figure shrouded in white smoke.

"I came not to bring peace, but the sword," the figure responded leaving behind an astroflare into the innerverse of Jazire's room.

Soon after, Jazire became legendary on the battlefield and in the arena. He was a masterful swordsman who slew demons and returned the souls of many Fallen impostures back to be judged before the throne. Jazire, who never gave up on his lute playing, became known for playing his injured opponents a final song before providing the mercy of death.

"They all conspired against me," Semjaza accused as he taunted Janus.

"You have become vain like Abaddon."

"I'll show you vain when I get my hands on your Jazire."

"Please don't. I beg you."

"You have become infatuated with the boy. How many wishes had you granted him? More than three I'm sure."

"He's a mortal of peace."

"I will sure bring it to him... unless... you take the Oath of Alliance."

"What oath? Why?"

"Because you have a KEY position. It may be useful to us someday. A few of the Watchers have decided to descend upon the Earth. We may need you."

In the process of investigating Jazire's talents Semjaza found something more appealing to his senses than the boy's music. He found Jazire's ability to attract women astoundingly delightful. While watching over man, Semjaza and the others became attracted to the daughters of man and decided to mate with them and take them for their wives. Semjaza knew this was a violation and needed a plan to avoid capture and prosecution from the Archangels. Semjaza remembered Azazel and his prosecution for the same offense many years ago. He knew that Janus worked in the gatehouse and had access to the golden key that opens the prison cells in Raquia. If he could get Janus to take the Oath of Alliance the genie would be compelled to come rescue him if he was ever captured. In an effort to spare Jazire's life Janus took the oath.

Many questions ran through Janus' mind while pondering giving the key to Azazel. "Why give the key to Azazel? Would the Arch have mercy on me for having taken the Oath? I'll give them the key and I'll alert the guards after giving them just enough time to enter into the prison and attempt to escape," Janus planned. "What will happen to the human? I'm sure he has no part of this. He's just another puppet like me being used to pull off this scheme. I could warn him and direct him to safety," Janus thoughts concluded.

"Fine, wait here and try to stay out of sight." Janus leaves the foyer to obtain the golden key. Janus wanders through the halls taking slow steps with a heavy foot and mind until the genie reaches its destination.

"Do you think he will help you?" Jerry asks Aza.

"He? You mean it? Genies are sexless. They are manipulators of light and can flash and move very quickly. They can project the illusion of any sex. Janus is an illusion of uncertainty."

"Will Janus help?'

"I believe so. Janus has an obligation to my comrade Semjaza who spared a mortal boy's life a long time ago. What Janus doesn't know is Semjaza placed a spell on the boy and marked him so that he was considered an abomination and expelled from his village. The same mark used on Karlisa."

"And this is who you are helping? An evil angel that brings this kind of suffering on innocent human beings."

"It's not your concern. We'll get the Angel Dust, get you home, you'll cure Karlisa, and live happily ever after. None of this is your concern."

"Live happily ever after while I wait for your partners, your alliance, your pact to Fall upon New Gaia and bring on the apocalypse?"

"No need to wait for the apocalypse, they're already there! Now keep your voice down or you will never make it back to New Gaia. Gabriel could come through the front door at any time."

"Maybe he should."

Jerry is starting to feel like he made a mistake. Jerry feels that even though saving Karlisa's life is important she would gladly give it up for the safety of others and would not be in support of assisting anything that promotes the work of evildoers. "What would she have me do?" Jerry asks himself.

Aza feels Jerry's frustration and he starts to have that odd feeling of compassion again, but he knows he must honor the oath otherwise he, Jerry, and Karlisa are damned with the revenge of the Fallen. Aza struggles with the feeling that he does not want to be a part of anything that would bring mayhem and destruction upon the Earth and its mortal beings. He only wanted to enjoy the sensual pleasures from the daughters of man. He never had any animosity towards mortals. He even taught men the power in the use of the sword and shield, which was a forbidden skill to be used amongst the mortals for it promoted war. When the men returned from a battle victoriously they would reward Azazel with concubines and precious medals. Azazel also taught the use of cosmetics to the women. The women who learned the seductive power of cosmetics were also grateful to Azazel who increased their desirability from men returning from war. The humans loved Azazel for his forbidden arts.

Janus enters the foyer carrying two cloaks. "Here put these on. They'll help hide your vile deception," Janus says to Azazel, "and your sweet mortality," now speaking to Jerry. "I'm not sure how you got caught up in this blessed one but when you get a chance I recommend that you run. You run! Run to the grace of Sandalphon in the Fifth house, or to the savior of Sachiel in the Sixth house, or the mercy of Cassiel in the Seventh house."

"Alright already! Where is the key?" asks Azazel.

"Here's the key," Janus says with regret while handing it over to Azazel. "May the Majestic Order of the Arch have mercy on your soul. And mine." Janus hurries toward the front door.

"Mercy? Yeah if it's one thing I haven't been given its mercy."

"You are really going to do this?" asks Jerry.

"We all have our commitments."

"Janus! Whatever happened to that boy? You know the one Semjaza was supposed to spare?" Jerry asks.

"He caught an illness and died a very long time ago," Janus informs with grief.

"Are you sure?"

"Yes I watched over him. How did you know about Jazire?" Janus asks with a blank gaze.

"Never mind a mortal fool. We need to go," replies Azazel.

Aza and Jerry leave the house, run down the walkway, and exit through the gate. Undetected by the sentry angels, they blend back in with the souls on the path. With the golden key in hand the escape plan was about to begin.

Jerry walks up the path alongside Aza who has now become quiet and solemn with heavy thought. "The funny thing is that all those people back on New Gaia, they got it all wrong. They don't believe in any of this," Jerry informs Aza.

"All this is way too vulgar of an attempt to convince anyone of our existence. It's part of why Omnus didn't want us to mingle with men directly, nevertheless have children with his daughters."

"If you understand that then why did you go against it?"

"At the time of my Fall it was only me and me alone. I didn't know everyone was going to get in on it."

"Why did you Fall? Was having a mortal girl that important to you?"

"I didn't fall for love I fell because of it. I wanted a love in Paradise that I was forbidden to have, a powerful immortal being. When our love was discovered I fell onto the Earth. All that I was accused of was due to the Fall, not because of what I did after the Fall."

CHAPTER EIGHT

Sophia

Aza recalls back to the days before the fall when he worked in Araboth at the Seventh House of Heaven. The Seventh House is a house of administration. It is there where the Throne Room, the Prayer Council, and the Supreme Choral Chambers are located. There are several rooms in the Seventh House, but the most mysterious rooms are those that have entry from the Seventh Hall. A Sentinel Guard is assigned to each hall. Azazel was the guard in the Seventh Hall.

In the arts of defense, Azazel was an expert with not the sword but the shield. Azazel being a Cherub angel, a class of angels known for their intellectual qualities, was not usually reassigned to duties that required brute force and physical dominance. He was on his way to great things as he was earmarked for being the next to be appointed to the Order of the Archangels. Azazel was a member of the posse of angels that apprehended Lord Abaddon on the Lakes of Saqun where he and Semjaza held him off in a fight long enough for Michael to come and secure his surrender. Due to his brave and heroic act he was assigned to the prestigious guard duty in the Seventh House.

There are four doors in the Seventh Hall. All the doors in the Seventh Hall glow from frames with golden light. None of the guards assigned to the Seventh Hall are allowed to see what lies on the other sides of either of these doors. The fourth room is the most mysterious of them all, as it comes with a warning that no one is permitted to neither enter, nor look in the face of its occupant. The room is simply called the forbidden room. One evening Azazel observed a nearly scantily dressed spirit with long fire-red hair and sparkling green eyes float out from the forbidden room. The spirit paused and starred at Azazel from down the hall then floated through the door of the Upper Room. The spirit intrigued Azazel who broke the rules by not turning his eyes away and allowing his curiosity to get the better of him. He knew it was forbidden to disturb any of the rooms but he hoped to see the spirit again. The silhouette of the spirits body appeared perfectly normal, feminine, and even attractive. Azazel had become infatuated with its mystique and its beauty. After several days of being miserably occupied with thoughts and visions of the spirits beauty he decided to disregard all the rules and knock on the forbidden door.

He felt ridiculous as he had no excuse to disturb the spirit and it was not in his nature to tell a lie but after he knocked there was no turning back. After a light and hesitant knock the door slightly opened on its own. Azazel knew he was not permitted to enter the room so he turned and walked away.

"Hello... Hello... Azazel? That is your given name?" the spirit calls out from doorway.

Frozen in his steps, Azazel swallows hard with a dry mouth and slowly turns around as his heart begins to beat rapidly. "How did you know my name?" says Azazel without looking up into the spirit's face.

"I know everyone's name," the spirit answers. "Don't be shy now. Please come in."

Azazel looks up and quickly follows the spirit into the room trying to not be seen by any of the other guards who may be passing by. "I was just wondering who was occupying this room so that I could be sure of its safety. I – I've never seen you before until the other day and I wanted to make sure our security had not been breached," Azazel says barely making eye contact with the figure in the doorway.

"That's cute. Who would breach the security in this house?"

Azazel looks around inside the room and notices the room has no walls. From the outside there appears to be within the confines of the house, but on the inside the room looks like it leads into infinite space. "Who are you, if it's ok that I ask?" says Azazel who is now making steady but weak eye contact.

"My name is Sophia and I believe it's the what that you are wanting to know not the who."

"Ok... are you a Divinity Angel like Cassiel?"

"No, but that would be quite interesting."

"Are you an Aeon like Omnus?"

"Not like Omnus... no one is quite like Omnus. Let's just say you are all of me and I am none of you."

Azazel is not sure what to do with that information but he fells certain that on some divine level Sophia belongs in that room. "I have never seen the inside of these rooms. Most of the house traffic is in the other halls near the Supreme Choral Chambers, the Prayer Room, and the Throne Room. As for this hall and these four rooms... I've never heard of any angel having ever entered anyone of them."

Sophia gives a verbal tour of the layout, "The room next door is Cassiel's room, next to that is the Irins' room, and inside the next door is a stairwell that leads up to the Upper Room where you can meet with Omnus when needed."

"Who is Irin?"

"Irins, two of them. They're Seraphim angels that rarely leave Omnus' side."

Azazel finally takes a longer, more direct look at Sophia. He gazes in her green eyes, watches the flow of her radiant red hair, and scans her soft facial features as she speaks. He feels a weakness in his knees as he glances at her translucent cloak exposing her body. "I think I should go now. Sorry for the intrusion." Azazel makes a sharp turn towards the door and marches down the hall.

"Come back soon. It was nice to have company for a change," Sophia shouts after him.

Azazel turns the corner and falls against the wall sliding down, gasping for his breath, and trying to slow his heartbeat. "What have I done?" Aza asks himself as he sits on the floor trying to collect his composure. "She is so beautiful."

Azazel would come back sooner than he thought. In fact he would come back several times. Then finally everyday he guarded the hall he would take time to visit Sophia. It first started out as brief visits then soon became lengthy stays in the forbidden room. Sophia would teach Azazel about the stars and the universe on levels never known to angels before. Eventually more intimate conversations would take place. It started with small compliments for each other's appearance. Compliments would soon resort to suggestions for how each other would like the other to be seen. With the magical powers of Sophia the possibilities of appearances were limitless. She would change her hair her eyes, her skin tone or anything to excite Azazel and attract his attention. Since Azazel couldn't leave the Seventh Hall, Sophia often brought a change of scenery to them. Some nights they would sit on a half crest moon and on other evenings a floating star. Azazel would chase her through the universe without ever having to leave her room. They were like the best of friends, in the best of times, in the best of all places.

"Are you afraid? Are you so afraid of what the Arch will do to you for being with me?" Sophia asks as she gazes her radiant eyes into his like a window to his soul.

"I don't know what to feel. It's easier to not think about it, " Aza replies with wobbly knees and a hollow feeling in his stomach.

In fact, Azazel was feeling something he never felt before – was it passion? Sophia was feeling something she never felt before – was it compassion? Whatever it was that the two were feeling it was forbidden by the Order of the Divinity Angels. Did their rules have jurisdiction over Sophia? Sophia's part in the equation of the universe was an enigma, however Azazel's orders were clear and simple - No one was permitted to go into the forbidden room and no one was allowed to look into the face of its occupant. Very few were granted access to the Seventh Hall in the Seventh House. Azazel was a Cherub Angel. He was working on a privileged assignment normally reserved for Seraphim. The Archangels trusted him and had high expectations for promoting him to the Order of the Arch. He was an angel with firsthand knowledge about the violations of Abaddon and how it was important to maintain a stronghold of the most sacred rules. Azazel was taking a great risk, but Sophia's request for continued contact and visits was powerfully seductive.

"I'm so happy to see you again," Sophia says as she rushes to embrace Aza. "You took a chance with forbidden romance knowing the price is too much to bare."

"Forbidden whispers are worth the dare. I'm so hopelessly drawn to your sunlight eyes and your radiant hair," Aza responds.

Sophia giggles as she finds his words of affection amusing. Having contact with a Cherub was a new experience for her. Azazel's designation to the Order of the Cherubim, angels who monitors the lives of mortals, is thought to be trivial, as she has no interest in the affairs of mortal beings. She does not feel that the rules governing the order of angels apply to her, but she has not considered how her being in his world affects him. She is somewhat narcissistic from her place of balance in the universe.

"I feel things I've never felt before when I'm with you – things I can't understand," Aza informs her.

"Well don't hurt yourself trying to understand it," Sophia requests as she giggles again. "I don't frighten you?"

Azazel looks into her sparkling green eyes and the waves of her fiery red hair that now look warm and inviting. Like a moth to flame he is attracted to her. "Frightened? No. Afraid of losing control of how I feel, yes."

"I have a gift for you," Sophia says as she tugs and pulls on Aza's guard uniform bringing him deeper into her chambers.

"A gift?" Aza feels ashamed, as he has not thought of getting her a gift. Although he didn't know to expect this he feels so close to her he thought he should have been more in tune with her and anticipated this move.

"It's an astroflare," Sophia informs as she opens a jeweled case. Aza's eyes widen. "And a shield of course. I know it's your favorite weapon."

"An astroflare!" Azazel picks up and examines the sword. He swings it to test its weight and equilibrium. As he swings the sword he notices how it flares up from a metal to a flame with the velocity of its movement through the air. "Whoa! I can get into this. Michael is going to be so jealous."

"It belonged to the late great Simkiel of Persidus. Most of the administrators have one that was passed down from the archons of their former kingdoms. I'm sure Michael has an astroflare too. I'm surprised he hasn't shown you."

"When we spar against each other we never use real weapons, but I think I saw something like this when he fought Abaddon."

"Well I thought it's only fair that you have one too. After all, you're the Seventh Hall guard."

"Yeah! I should have this."

"The shield is my special gift. No one has one like it. If you look into its reflection long enough it will show you where to find me. We'll never be lost to each other."

"Oh brother!" Azazel says as he looks over the shield. Azazel lowers the shield, sheaths his new sword, glides over to Sophia and kisses her for the first time. She doesn't kiss him back but she doesn't stop him either.

Escape from Raquia

Aza and Jerry reach the path leading to up to Raquia. The sentry angels along this part of the path are assigned Warden angels that work for the Prison of Souls. The angels guarding over the path stand tall with their wings spread high. These angels have dark wings, heads of sphinx, and red eyes. They hold bows with flaming arrows. Jerry's breathing begins to increase rapidly as he pats his pockets for his medication but he does not find it. The cloaks help mask their identity as the two sneak off the path and head up to the Second House. Unlike the First House there is no gate. Raphael's house is huge and squared off like an institution. The roofs are pointed like in gothic architecture with towers that serve as lookout points for sentry angels. Aza and Jerry dash up the path and through a large garden leading up to the house. The garden looks like a labyrinth with twists and turns that don't appear to have any straight passages. Tall garden sculptures ornament the grounds. Aza and Jerry slowly snake their way through the maze keeping their heads down and hiding in between the sculptures trying to not draw attention from the sentry angels above.

"Are, you sure you want to do this," ask Jerry in hopes of inciting some reconsideration from Aza. Once inside the prison halls and out of sight of the wardens Jerry continues to pressure Aza on his dedication to completing the mission.

"Are you sure about this?" Jerry whispers while grabbing Aza's arm, halting him from going any further into the halls.

"Listen, Jerry! I have no choice! You have no choice! It's a bad deal but maybe somehow you really wanted to be here. You really wanted to know all those concealed factors that were affecting your world. Well here it is! Sometimes the truth is harder than a lie. So get over it and let's do this!" Azazel tiptoes through several tight corridors being careful to not run into any Wardens. Finally Azazel reaches an old armory stockroom used for storage. It is here where the possessions of the Fallen and other prisoners' belongings are kept. Azazel uses the golden key to unlock it. The storage door squeaks and grinds. The hinges respond as if the door hasn't been opened in 1000s of years. The stench of stale dry air greets them at the entrance.

"What are we doing?"

"I'll show you." Azazel searches through the storeroom until he comes upon a shelf with a glowing sword. He grins as he takes the sword from the shelf.

"You can leave me out," says Jerry. "I'm not fighting wardens for doing their jobs."

"This belongs to me. It's my old astroflare. It may not be a bad idea for you to have something as well. It's not the wardens that you should be worried about. We are about to release some of the baddest motherfuckers in existence." Azazel takes a few practice swings with the astroflare then he hands Jerry another sword from off a nearby shelf. Jerry took fencing classes as hobby years ago but it was nothing compared to this. Jerry struggles to swing the sword, as its weight alone is a challenge. Aza shakes his head in disapproval of Jerry's lack of skills. "On second thought you may want to wait here."

"Yeah maybe I'll do that!"

"Fine!"

"Yeah, fine!" Jerry thinks for a moment. "NO! Not fine! This is the first place they'll come to after you release them. Their weapons are here."

"Good point. OH! WATCH OUT!" Aza points behind Jerry.

Jerry turns to look. Aza strikes Jerry from behind knocking him unconscious with the blunt of his sword handle. Aza catches Jerry. "Sorry my friend but I don't need any weight slowing me down in here." Aza lays Jerry on the floor. Aza takes a moment to observe his astroflare like a newly found lost dog. He runs his fingers up the center of the flat side and watches the blade change color along the way. The color of the astroflare is responsive to swing velocity and contact made against its edges. Aza recalls the last day he held the sword in his hands.

The Siege at Zebul's Point

Angels of the Arch Order sit around a round table in Machonon. In attendance are Michael, Gabriel, Raphael, Uriel, Nathaniel, Remiel, and Raquel the only female member. Each angel is dressed in dark gray military regalia with emblems depicting arching swords, indicating that they are members in the Order of the Arch. At the head of the table sits Michael the Ambassador of Machonon who is also the Chief Commanding elder Archangel. They are all waiting on the arrival of the Sentinel Guard, Azazel to consider his appointment to the Order of the Arch. Michael has called the meeting to order and asked that all cast a vote to approve or disapprove Azazel's appointment. When casting a vote each angel may express their position or silently cast a small colored marble into a bowl. A jade marble would indicate being in approval of the candidate and a crimson marble would indicate an objection. The candidate waits outside the voting area until a decision has been reached. Later, the bowl is shown to the candidate without providing any explanation for the results of the vote. To join the Order of the Archangels one must have all jade marbles indicating a unanimous decision. The Arch proceeds without Azazel. Michael who often sets the tone for the vote has taken out his jade marble.

"Azazel is one of our elders from the days of the Abraxis. He was assigned to the Order of the

Cherubim for his astute historical knowledge of the universe. In his leisure time he became an expert sword fighter and brilliant shield defender with rankings competitive to the most elite in the league of Sentinel Guards. In the days of the Great Disturbance he did not hesitate to track Abaddon down in Saqun and attempt to apprehend him even though he knew his skills were outmatched. Through these merits, he was appointed to the high guard at the Seventh House in the Seventh Hall where he has worked admirably." Michael tosses a jade marble into the bowl.

The next vote has gone to Gabriel who also throws in a jade marble for approval. "The choir of angels sings songs that salute his heroics. He has a great many followers in the community. Let's see that leads them closer to Omnus."

Uriel, Raquel, Nathaniel, and Remiel follows suit but do not give an explanation, as none is necessary when one casts a vote in approval.

Raphael stands before the table. "My brothers, it is true that Azazel has acted heroically in his pursuit of Abaddon. It is true that he has completed every task that we have required of him, but..." Raphael looks over at Michael and swallows hard, "I am not so sure that an angel who has spent so much time in the historical archives can make a successful transition into the role of an Archangel." Raphael rolls his eyes up in his head and takes a deep breath before continuing. "Now I'm sure you are aware that he was formerly a Cherub working in the archives department before being trialed as a Guardian Angel but in that alone it says he was not intended to be a warrior! I have nothing against my Cherubim brothers. I'm proud to fight next to them and place my own immortality in their most powerful hands," Raphael says looking around for approval. "I'm not an angel of Abaddon's pride and prejudice, however it is my concern that there are delicate and uncompromising positions that we are often placed in, such as taking the souls of both immortals and mortals, that he may not be able to endure," Raphael says looking around again for approval before continuing his filibuster. "Yes I know he's talented with the sword and has a vast amount of knowledge about the workings of the universe, but it takes more than being star smart and brut to perform the duties of an Archangel. We have to be spiritually rigorous and able to detect the workings of our most clever enemy, the enemy from within. The enemy of self-doubt, pity, and mercifulness cannot interfere with our administration of severe penalties. We need to be firm and unyielding in our disciplinary actions," Raphael says as he looks around for faces of confirmation. To become a Sentinel Guard you have to complete a rigorous internship rotating through various angelic duties. I'm afraid that when Azazel descended on the Earth to intern as a Guardian Angel his submergence into that wayward culture may have weakened him. The Earth is an infectious milieu of mortality that often trials the senses of angels who are frequently exposed to the human condition. For one it makes you lustful and tempted by the flesh. This is how beasts such as dragons and mermaids were created. The angels lost their minds! They wanted pets! Furthermore, Azazel loves to attract the mortals' attention with his use of flair in colors and such. Butterflies! Unicorns! Chameleon dragons! He ripped an arch from the heavenly skies and created a rainbow on Earth. It's all for show! Pure nonsense! I myself find it quite amusing." Raphael takes one last look around, closes his eyes, and inhales deeply. "I will admit that he has one of the finest talents with the use of the sword and shield, but the sword is the least used tool we have in our possession. We must first strengthen our hearts and souls. We must be able to follow the divine rules without hesitation. I don't see this strength in him. It is the very soul of Azazel that has not yet convinced me enough to make this approval therefore I cast a crimson marble."

"So it has been said, so it has been done, so it shall be. The appointment is denied," Michael concludes.

"Commander Michael if I may," requests Raphael. "I am open to revisiting this motion upon review of General Seraphiel's report on his supervision of Azazel's work guarding the Seventh Hall."

"Once again compassion has it. The motion may be recalled upon General Seraphiel's report. Meeting adjourned."

Meanwhile back in Araboth, Azazel has just noticed the time and is rushing off from Sophia's room down the Seventh Hall into the main corridor. He is late and has very little time to spare as the Archangels are in Machonon voting on his appointment and will seek for him to disclose the results. Azazel runs for the doors to exit the Seventh House.

"Halt!" shouts General Seraphiel.

"Oh, brother!" Aza sighs. "Is there something wrong General?"

"Well yes. There is something seriously wrong," Seraphiel says as he approaches Azazel and reaches out to his uniform. "You can't go to that meeting looking like this," Seraphiel straightens Azazel's collar and aligns the medals on his officer's regalia. "You are representing the Seventh House of Cassiel. There are not many more esteemed positions in all of the Heavens than the one you currently hold. So remember that, regardless of what the outcome is," Seraphiel concludes.

"Thank you, sir. I must get going I am running late," Azazel responds but Seraphiel is fixated on his sword.

"Where did you get an astroflare? That's an administrator's weapon."

"It was a gift, sir."

"Omnus gave you a gift of the divine?"

"No sir... it... was a gift... from Sophia."

"Sophia! When did you see Sophia?"

"Sir. I'm running late, sir. I'll be glad to explain it to you later."

"You will tell me now. You should have told me before now. Do you know how many angels in all of the Order of Angels have ever seen Sophia?"

"I understand sir but... she's very powerful. She drew me from the hall into her room—"

"Her room! This is an abomination! You have disgraced me!"

"But sir... listen."

"Surrender your sword immediately!" Seraphiel demands but Azazel hesitates.

"Guards!" Seraphiel arms himself with his sword as other Sentinels enter the room. "I am placing Azazel under arrest! Take him to detention!" Seraphiel instructs the guards who are somewhat confused and hesitant as Azazel is a highly respected Sentinel.

"No, sir!" I may have been appointed to the Arch as we speak. You don't understand. You will have to take this up with Michael later," Azazel pleads.

"You dare to defy me?"

"Sir... You don't understand," Aza says with sunken eyes.

"Seize him now!"

The guards draw their swords on Azazel. The transition to the highly regarded Order of the Archangels was not going well. Azazel knows a Sentinel would not have authority to arrest an Archangel. Azazel draws his astroflare against the guards. "Please! You guys know me well. This is only a misunderstanding." Azazel looks around but the guards are not giving in to his request. "Semjaza," Azazel calls out to one of the Seventh House Sentinels. "Brother! You know me! I ask that you hear my plea."

"I'm only following orders. I suggest you surrender. Your quarrel is a matter for the Throne Room now, Azazel," Semjaza informs.

"You're making a mistake!"

"Orders are orders!" shouts Tubiel a captain in the Sentinel. "Enough of this!" He shouts as he attacks Azazel with his sword, but Azazel makes a defensive move. Click-ety-clack! Click-ety-clack! The swords strike as moves and counter moves are made.

"I urge you to cease this action!" Azazel requests as he defends Tubiel's aggressive pursuit. Click-ety-clack! Click-ety-clack! The two dance in a duelers groove across the main hall while Seraphiel, Semjaza, and some of the other Sentinels follow nearby. Soon Tubiel learns that his sword is no challenge for an astroflare as Azazel swings a destructive blow to Tubiel's sword and snaps it in two pieces. The pointed end half of Tubiel's sword hits the ground, but he does not cease his pursuit and charges towards Azazel with the dagger portion of his broken sword. Azazel swings a fatal blow to Tubiel who falls to his knees severely wounded. "I warned you! It didn't have to be this way!" Azazel screams as he hangs his head and drops his shoulders.

The hall falls silent. The death of a Sentinel is a rare sight to be seen. Death itself is extraordinarily surreal especially in this house, in these halls, and under this circumstance - murder.

"You've done it now!" Seraphiel warns Azazel. "Send for Commander Michael and alert Your Mercifulness Cassiel," he orders the guards standing over the deceased angel's body. "There is nowhere to run now Azazel. You Abaddonite! There's nowhere to hide."

With tears in his eyes, Azazel can barely stand. He drops his astroflare, stumbles, and staggers with a heavy heart as he flees down the Seventh Hall. He finds his way to Sophia's door. Sophia conceals him inside. She is aware and almost omniscient in her response as she comforts him without any exchange of words.

"I knew this day would come. Yet I did nothing to stop it," she confesses as she holds him close in her bosom. The two stand together in silence as Azazel weeps. An angel knocks on the door. It is Cassiel, General Seraphiel, and Prince Angel Metaphon. Sophia looks into Azazel's green eyes, "You know what you must do," she asks but he is not sure what it is she thinks he should do. Sophia points to the Paradise below, Zebul and the mountaintop roof of Sachiel's Tower. "Go to the tower and wait for me on Zebul's point." Azazel holds Sophia close, he looks into her gleaming green eyes, and kisses her long and deep feeling the heat from the fervor of her caress. "I will see you again," she assures as Azazel flies through the barrier of her walls and out into the Heavens. Sophia watches him as he disappears through the distance of the sky. She is hoping to fulfill her promise of seeing him again. She already misses the forbidden romance and the secret whispers that he was so brave to persevere because she was worth the dare.

Sophia stands and watches as Azazel disappears into the expanse of the universe. She is thinking, "You always want something more when you can't have it, then when you have taken it for granted." A pounding on her door interrupts her thoughts. "I'm coming," Sophia says as she heads to open the door. "He's not here," she responds as she opens the door. "How dare you! Never in over the 10,000 of years since I've been here have I been disturbed," She scolds.

Seraphiel lowers his eyes away from the face of Sophia as the Divinity angels Cassiel and Metaphon and address her.

"Pardon me, but we have an epic disturbance of a proportion similar to the siege of Abaddon," informs Cassiel. "I must secure the house and make sure all my guests are safe."

"I know what you came here for and you are too late."

Metaphon is a powerful Seraph angel whose appearance is rare, like that of the Irins. Metaphon is one of the eight elder class Divinity angels, the other seven being his brother Sandalphon, Archangels Michael and Gabriel, administrating angels Cassiel and her brother Sachiel and the twin Irins. His powers are only needed in the most extreme of circumstances, but even still he is not certain of his role in a situation regarding Sophia for she is an enigma in the balance of the universe. He stares into Sophia's uncanny green eyes and she stares back. A showdown has begun. Sophia's hair flares wild and stands in a fiery frizz. A glowing halo appears over Metaphon's head as his skull polarizes into a florescent blue hue. "Zebul's point!" He informs Seraphiel.

"You are an abomination! You are beneath me!" shouts Sophia.

The three angels turn and leave the hall. The fight with Sophia is not the fight for which they came. Azazel awaits Sophia at the revealed location. Sophia flies through the walls of her room to the Heavens outside where she rushes to be at Azazel's side. She fears she is too late as she approaches the tower of Zebul for she does not sense his presence. "I failed to save him again? I can't be inferior to this world." Sophia begins to panic. The sky above becomes volatile as the atmosphere changes to a disturbing darkness never seen since the siege of Abaddon. The roof of Sachiel's tower attracts lightening from the near skies above. It is Zebul's highest point. A mist of star clusters engulfs the tower rooftop providing a cover for Azazel's hiding place. Sophia feels Azazel's presence and drops out of the sky in front of him. Azazel is startled by a presence but is relieved to see its Sophia. "Metaphon and Cassiel came to see me Aza. They know. Somehow they know. They are on their way here."

"You don't happen to have a spare astroflare do you?" Azazel asks with a half smile trying to lean on humor to support his nerves.

"Fighting your way out of this will not work. You'll have to Fall unto the Earth and go into hiding."

"Fall! There is no way! I don't deserve this!"

Michael and the Order of the Archangels riding fiery-eyed horses of gray, black, white, and red are closing in on the Tower. There are too may Sentinels filling the skies to flee from the tower through the air. Sophia recommends that they run on foot. They will need to exit the tower and take the main throughway all the way to Vilon until they get to the path in front of the gatehouse and then Fall onto the Earth.

They proceed down the stairwell trying to avoid the pursuit of Sentinel Guards along the way. Azazel obtains a sword from an angel he has overpowered. Making an attempt to not cause any further deaths he wounds pursuing Sentinels enough to stop them as he and Sophia keep running down the stairwell. Zebul's tower was built 200 floors tall by dragons and masonry angels. The builders swore there would never be another like in the entire universe. On this day the tower is an exhausting 50 feet too tall for Aza. Sophia and Azazel make it down the first 150 floors and almost out to the main path before running into Sammael.

"Going somewhere my brother?" Sammael asks with sword drawn.

"I'm warning you," Azazel answers, "I know you are following orders but this is all a misunderstanding. Please don't make me do this."

"I was never too good at taking orders." Sammael informs Azazel as he lowers his sword and allows them to pass. "Hey, brother! Good luck!"

Azazel tightens the grip on his sword as he and Sophia pass by Sammael on the stairwell. Azazel never takes his eyes off him. "The universe has gone mad and they are chasing the wrong angel," Azazel says to Sophia as they continue down the long spiral of stairs.

"This universe is full of imperfections. It's the nature of its existence. The balance of good and evil in the universe does not exclude these Heavens," Sophia informs as they continue running.

Sophia and Azazel scurry down the tower stairs until they finally reach the exit. Sophia and Azazel look out the exit door and notices the tower is nearly surrounded.

"So this is what it all boils down to? One moment I'm on the verge of being an Archangel, to the next moment being an archenemy. What is it about my love for you that is so forbidden? So forbidden I can't look upon your face. Why?"

"It's not you. It's a lot to explain." Sophia wrings her hands as chest rise and fall rapidly with building anxiety. "The omniscient one will never allow me to speak of it."

"Even now? What do I have to gain or you to lose?"

"We have everything to lose. I should have never let this happen," Sophia says with a flush face and widened nostrils. "Just stick to the plan and Fall to the Earth.

"Without you? They'll find me. I'd rather die here and now with you then not ever see you again."

"Whatever they do, they will not keep me away from you."

"Remember when you asked me if I was afraid?"

"Yes. Don't be afraid. I'll find you. I promise. I'll find you. Now run before they get here. Run and keep running. I'll find you." Sophia urges Azazel. They embrace for a moment forgetting about the urgency of time. "I'll find you."

Azazel flees through the dark stormy heavens. The darkness provides just enough cover for his discrete descent down the throughway and down onto the Earth. Sophia raises her hands and startles the sky. She turns and twirls her body in a frantic spin moving the stars and planets off balance. There has not been a shake up like this since the Paroxysm of Abraxis. Angels run for safety as the grounds shake and the skies whirl above the Heavens. Her anger erupts and explodes into the universe creating several new planets and galaxies. The search for Azazel is successfully stalled as he flees to an unknown location but this guise, no matter how spectacular, may only serve as a temporary deterrent for the Archangels are relentlessly in pursuit. Sophia steps outside into the crowd of patrolling Sentinels while holding her abdomen with one hand and her head with the other. She looks up far and deep into the unstable sky at Earth.

"Am I becoming more like them or am I realizing more that they are a part of me? This war must be stopped."

Sophia leaves the Heavens and enters into the expanse of the unknown universe to find a refuge, a new place to call home.

CHAPTER NINE

Paradise Lost

The Archangels were concerned about Azazel's fugitive status in the universe. Sophia had concealed him in some undisclosed location that mirrored other galaxies and other Earth-like planets, thereby creating a problem with Paradise. Paradise is an extension of Heaven located on Earth through a direct portal in Machonon called the Gates of Paradise. On one side of the gates is Machonon, the Fourth House of Heaven and on the other side Earth. It was planned that blessed souls would wait in Machonon, in the atrium outside the Gates of Paradise and once the Earth was reclaimed in the days after the Apocalypse, blessed souls would reenter into the newly sanctified Earth. Omnus installed a gate around the most lush and fertile area on Earth and called it Paradise Garden. A man could walk directly from the Heavens to the Earth to keep close to Omnus. Now with Sophia's creation of multiple galaxies, the original Earth had been lost along with the location of Paradise Garden.

The Divine Order of Angels convened in the Upper Room to discuss the problem with Paradise and it was suggested that Omnus should choose any of the other Earth-like planets to replace Paradise Garden, but this only angered Omnus. Without knowing the whereabouts of the original Paradise Garden the sanctity of the Heavens was vulnerable for any soul that finds it could breach the Heavens through the portal on Earth and into the Gates of Paradise in Machonon. To prevent this, Omnus placed two of his best guards, Metaphon and Uriel at the gates. Sophia is the only soul that knows where the original Earth is located. She alone knows the location highly sought after by the Order of the Divinity Angels as well as Abaddon and those who have Fallen with a desire to retake the Heavens.

Stump! Stump! Tap!

With Jerry lying unconscious in the storage room, Azazel makes his way to the East cellblock where Semjaza is imprisoned. The cellblock locking mechanism is located in a master control room. The turn of a key will unlock one or more of the warden-selected cellblocks. Raguil, a Warden angel sits in the master control room while others patrols the cellblocks.

Raguil is careless and inattentive as if a long day's work has gotten the better of him. Raguil has found his uneventful job of 500 years boring and calm this evening as he slouches back in his control room chair yawning and sleepy-eyed. Azazel easily enters into the control room and sneaks up on Raquil who quickly refocuses and retaliates with his sword. Click-ety Clack! Clack! Raguil finds that his sword is no match for an astroflare and even without it he is no match against a former Seventh House Sentinel.

"Peace, my brother," Raguil says while kneeling and surrendering his sword to the ground.

"I've been waiting 5000 years for a fight and this is what I get? Peace!" Azazel steps closer to Raguil and an elbow strike him to the head render him unconscious onto the floor.

Azazel sits at the control desk, places the golden key into the locking mechanism, unlocks the cells, and transmits a signal faintly over a loudspeaker using the Chancellor's rhythmic stomp and a tap onto the master control microphone.

Stomp! Stomp! Tap! Stomp! Stomp! Tap!
Stomp! Stomp! Tap! Stomp! Stomp! Tap!

"Do you hear that?" a member of the Fallen asks his cellmate as they both stand still and listen attentively.

Stomp! Stomp! Tap! Stomp! Stomp! Tap! Stomp! Stomp! Tap! Stomp! Stomp! Tap!

Most of the Fallen are now paying attention to the faint rhythm while other imprisoned souls aimlessly continue their routines.

"It's faint, but familiar."

Stomp! Stomp! Tap! Stomp! Stomp! Tap! Stomp! Stomp! Tap! Stomp! Stomp! Tap!

"It's the signal!" shouts Armaros, a Nation class Fallen angel.

"It can't be," says Balberith, leader of the Fallen Cherubim.

"Yes! It is my brethren. Everyone prepare. Tap the signal throughout the prison," commands Armaros.

Stomp! Stomp! Tap! Stomp! Stomp! Tap! Stomp! Stomp! Tap! Stomp! Stomp! Tap!

Armaros in sight of the Northward prisoners does the rhythmic stomp and tap with his foot and fist up against the cell bars. The signal is passed on throughout the prison.

Northward Fallen Guardian Angels.

Stomp! Stomp! Tap! Stomp! Stomp! Tap! Stomp! Stomp! Tap! Stomp! Stomp! Tap!

Westward Fallen Nations.

Stomp! Stomp! Tap! Stomp! Stomp! Tap! Stomp! Stomp! Tap! Stomp! Stomp! Tap!

Eastward Fallen Powers and Dominions.

Stomp! Stomp! Tap! Stomp! Stomp! Tap! Stomp! Stomp! Tap! Stomp! Stomp! Tap!

Southwestward Fallen Thrones and Cherubim.

Stomp! Stomp! Tap! Stomp! Stomp! Tap! Stomp! Stomp! Tap! Stomp! Stomp! Tap!

In the Southeastward Abaddon grins an evil grin as he looks up at the guard. Abaddon joins in on the rhythmic stomp and tap with his foot and his fist up against the side of his cot rail. The wardens find his behavior uncanny and unnerving but that's nothing new.

Stomp! Stomp! Tap! Stomp! Stomp! Tap! Stomp! Stomp! Tap! Stomp! Stomp! Tap!

The Fallen scuttle around the prison making shanks and weaponry from anything they can find.

Many of them begin to roughhouse and prepare each other for battle.

Stomp! Stomp! Tap! Stomp! Stomp! Tap! Stomp! Stomp! Tap! Stomp! Stomp! Tap!

"What do we do now?" asks Rameel, a female Dominion class angel.

"Alert every leader, in every cell block, in every gang whether they be demons, beast, or belong to any angelic order. We must have Abaddon's assistance to distract the guards," commands Armaros.

Stomp! Stomp! Tap! Stomp! Stomp! Tap! Stomp! Stomp! Tap! Stomp! Stomp! Tap!

As reports are whispered down the block they are reported to Armaros. "The demons in the Northward are reporting that they are ready. Belphegor, leader of the Nations in the Westward is reporting that they too are ready. Reports from Gadreel, the leader of the Powers in the Eastward along with Baraqel, the leader of the Dominions say that they are ready. Kokabel, the Throne leader is reporting that they are ready and my Cherubim are standing by as well," reports Balberith.

Stomp! Stomp! Tap! Stomp! Stomp! Tap! Stomp! Stomp! Tap! Stomp! Stomp! Tap!

"What's this stomping and banging?" A warden asks the crowd, "I command that you stop at once!" The rhythm grows stronger and louder. "I said now scoundrels!"

Armaros recites the Oath of Alliance out loud and the Fallen join in slowly until they are all in unity.

Stomp! Stomp! Tap! Stomp! Stomp! Tap! Stomp! Stomp! Tap! Stomp! Stomp! Tap!

"From heavens above us,
To Mountain we fall.

The Fall,
The Call,
This pact shall be the law.

I descend with my brethren,
And rise to his call.

The Fall,
The Call,
The pact of us all.

I bring one to the legion,
The legion brings all.

The Fall,
The Call,
The pact will stand tall.

Through Houses of Heaven,
Every room and every hall.

The Fall,
The Call,
We break every wall."

The cell doors are pushed open and the riot
begins. The wardens slay many of the Fallen, but
others flee out onto the house grounds. Azazel
opens all the armory storage rooms except the one
where Jerry is being kept. Swords are passed
throughout the hands of the Fallen, who then fight
back and slaughter many of the wardens. A full-
scale assault is underway. Azazel searches the
grounds for Semjaza.

"Where is Semjaza?" Azazel asks Armaros.

"He has already been taken to Anahel's house, you know the one out back."

Azazel becomes frustrated as he now has another rescue attempt to execute, but this time under the alert of the Archangels. Fighting his way back he returns to the storage room where Jerry is sitting awake.

"Sorry about that load. That old shelf gave away before I could push out the way. How are you now?" Aza asks.

"A little dizzy, but I'll be ok." Jerry looks around. 'A load of what?"

"Forget it. We must hurry. We have to make another stop to complete the oath and it's not going to be easy."

"Great! Who are we kidding we are never going to make it out of here. I may as well lock myself in a cell."

The Sphere of Death

Janus is restless and worried. It is not only the violation of giving out the golden key that has the genie worried, but also the last words of Jerry inquiring about Jazire that is bringing up old memories. Why did he ask about Jazire? Is there something I should know about Jazire's death? The questions relentlessly weigh on the genie's mind until Janus can no longer stand it. The only way Janus can learn about the details of Jazire's death is to summon Miriam the Genie of Death. Miriam will want something in return for the gift. Janus conjures up the genie with an enchantment.

"Father Barcus hear my call,
Send my summons through the halls.
Let the soul I desire to appear,
I request for Miriam to bring a sphere."

"This is going to cost you!" Miriam says as the genie enters the room in a mist of blue smoke.

"I have information to exchange for the cause of death."

"Information? Do I look like the resource hotline? What kind of information?"

"Information that will make you pleasurable in the eyes of the Arch Order."

"The Arch? Raphael and Michael?"

"Yes! Especially in the eyes of Michael."

"Umm... this better be good."

Janus makes a request to have verification on the cause of Jazire's death. Miriam searches for him in the Sphere of Death, but the vision is cloudy.

"The sphere is not very clear since it was so long ago but... It appears that the boy had a skin condition—"

"Yes leprosy—"

"No... not leprosy," Miriam informs as the sphere begins to clear. "Oh my... he had... yes I see it clearly now. He had the mark."

"The mark?"

"He was cursed with the mark of affliction."

"Are you sure?"

Miriam shows Jazire with the circle-tailed rash. "The sphere don't tell lies, babe."

"Who put it there?"

"That's going to cost you extra."

"Don't screw with me!"

"Alright! Hold your dragon's breath. Give me a minute." Miriam continues navigating through the sphere. "Oh! Ah ha! Should have known."

"What? Who?"

"It was from the poison of Armaros, the root cutter." Miriam spins the sphere around to Janus to show the vision of Semjaza poisoning Jazire with Aramos' special concoction. The hideous rash covers Jazire who becomes a miserable recluse and outcast living inside a cavern. His facial hair is long and he walks with a limp under an old raggedy cloak. He stands on the side of a cliff overlooking the violent waves crashing onto a rocky seaside below. He disappears.

Janus weeps. "He made me leave. He didn't want me to see him that way."

The genies pass a moment of silence.

"I'm sorry to interrupt your mourning, but it's time to pay up!"

Fighting back the tears and trying to speak, Janus gives Miriam the information about the jailbreak. "If you run and tell Raphael now it may not be too late."

"It's been a pleasure!" Miriam flickers and flashes out of sight.

Hell House

Aza and Jerry make their way up the path to the Third House of Heaven in Saqun. It's Anahel's home. There are very few sentry angels on this part of the path as most souls stay away from the Third House unless escorted by Wardens from Raquia. Aza and Jerry enter the main path leading up to the house.

Like Raphael's house there is no gate. Jerry is again amazed at the grand scale of the Houses in Heaven.

"What in the hell is that?" Jerry says after being startled by the blowing vents of Hell's fire randomly shooting up throughout the landscape surrounding Anahel's house. Jerry's breathing begins to increase rapidly as he pats his pockets for his medication, but he does not find it.

Anahel's house is a grand lake house built on the edge of pooling pits of hot steamy hell water that was once Lake Saqun. The water was blue and clear before Abaddon spilled the blood of former angels during the Siege on Lake Saqun. The home has symmetric shapes, soft two-tone pastel colors, and big bay windows. The large pot-gardened grounds are made of smoothen granite. The lively florescent glow of star plants bring in serenity until venting fire shoots up out of small fountain pools surrounding the home. Around the back of the lake house, a long dock leads out to Hell Island where Hell House stands in the middle of the pit. The Hell House is surrounded and engulfed in steam, like a thick fog on a lighthouse bay. On the perimeter of Hell Island there are large bell towers that ring every time a soul's fate is committed to its pit. The Hell House is made out of dark lava stones. The house is circular with hot glowing orange streaks from the burning decay splashing up out of the pits. Inside there are several stalls where chained souls wait to be cast into the pits.

To get up to the house you have to navigate a long narrow stone pier extending from the main house. There is a cryptic raft used to float on top of the pit. Azrael uses the raft for maintaining the layers of buildup molten bone crust.

In the front of the main house, if you can find your way around the vents, you will find a path that leads up to the front door. The home is elevated on a stone foundation that raises the house up off the ground to protect it from the occasional hellfire marsh overflowing from the surrounding pools. Steam rises from the pool vents, but that gives no indicator to which vent will blow the molted lava of decaying bones and hell stones. The reddish-orange muck blows up and quickly dribbles back down into the pools. Occasionally several vents will blow at once creating a hell shower of scorching steam and bits of soft orange magma.

Jerry and Aza need to devise a careful route around the lake house to gain access to the pier leading out back to the Hell House where Semjaza is being imprisoned. The steam hides their presence in the lake house yard from the sentry angels on the rooftop towers. Their angelic cloaks provide protection against the hot steam and liquid fires.

"Why put hellfire vents in the front of a beautiful home?"

"The irony I guess. They do things like that. When I run, you run, but follow my steps exactly around these subterranean vents or you will have your stay cut short... in that case you will end up back here as an invited guest."

"Not funny."

Aza and Jerry wait for enough steam to blow up from a number of vents to hide their dart through the front passageway and around the lake house to the pier outback.

"Give me your wedding ring," Aza asks.

"What?"

"We need to pay a token to the ferry driver?"

"Ferry? What ferry?"

Out from the hot steamy mist a dark cloaked figure pulls closer to the dock on a raft. The ferry driver extends his ash-tarnished hand to receive a token.

"No fucking way am I giving you my wedding ring," Jerry says to Aza with a shaking head.

"You are willing to come this far to save her and you're going to stop now because of a ring?" Aza asks while waiting for Jerry to change his mind. "He's not going to wait for long."

"Fucker!" Jerry says as he takes off his ring and extends it over to the ferry driver but after catching a glimpse of its red eyes he quickly decides to hand it over to Aza.

Aza shakes his head and drops the ring in the palm of the ferry driver who allows them to board the raft.

The ride feels long and hot. Jerry stands on the side of Aza away from the cloaked raft driver and tries to not stand too close to the edge. He watches the waves of molten lava splash across the side of the raft as they draw nearer to the Hell House. The three souls in cloaks stand quiet in the hot mist of Hell until they reach the Hell House docks. Aza and Jerry exit the raft and run quickly into the Hell House.

The house is steaming hot like a sauna. "Be careful to not touch anything including the walls," Aza warns.

Azazel uses the golden key to open the door then the two head to a side stairwell that leads down into a dungeon. Azazel slowly makes his way through the dungeon where he finds several cells of souls waiting to go out to the pits. Azazel begins quietly asking the inhabitants if they have seen Semjaza. Most of the occupants don't even bother to look up. They are quiet and miserable, as they have no hope of ever being spared from their hellish fate. Some of the souls detained there are deranged and look as if they have been waiting there for a very long time. With Jerry close behind, Azazel keeps searching the cells, checking every soul, and looking in all their hell-bound faces.

Jerry pulls Aza's arm, "You know if you would have told me that we would have to take a quick swing over to Hell on the way back I would've called this deal off," Jerry whispers.

"All that matters is that I told you this would save Karlisa."

"Well hurry up! It's hot as hell in here."

"Now who's got the jokes?"

"Make the lie big, make it simple, keep saying it, and eventually they will believe it," says an imprisoned soul in a Nazi uniform standing with his face pressed against the cell bars.

"Is that who I think it is?" Jerry says while shaking his head. "I hope there's a gift shop or no one is ever going to believe I was here."

"If you don't keep your voice down you might get a chance to open that gift shop. Now shut up and follow me so we can get the hell out of here."

Azazel and Jerry run through the Hell House until they come to another large block of holding cells. Azazel searches more faces of damned souls looking for one that is familiar. Finally, Azazel comes across a cell with a soul sitting in the corner. Like the other souls this one sits hopeless, slumped over holding his head into the palms of his hands staring into the ground with vacant eyes. It is Semjaza who now believes the Oath of Alliance was a failed dream of the Chancellor.

"I descend with my brethren and rise to his call!" Azazel whispers.

Semjaza looks up with widened eyes of hope like a child being rescued from a lost and found. "The Fall? The Call? The pact of us all! My brother! My brother Azazel has come for me!" Semjaza expresses a new found joy. He jumps up and runs to the cell door.

"Before I free you I need your word."

"What! What is the meaning of this? Fulfill the oath you fool. Let me out of here!"

"Your word!"

"Yes my word... anything you'll have it."

"After I free you I have fulfilled the oath, right?"

"Of course. You've done it!"

"Do you see this mortal?"

"A mortal? Here?"

"You will have the mark of affliction removed from his wife Karlisa and you and your brethren will not bother Jerry's family ever again. Do I have your word?"

"Jerry? Who is Jerry?"

"Jerry Xeven."

"Like He, Vav, Zayen?"

"Yes!" Both Jerry and Aza respond.

Semjaza takes a closer look at Aza's cloaked partner and senses something he hasn't seen in a very long time. "He's human... how did you get a human?"

"It's a long story. Now promise me he'll come to no harm."

"Yeah. Yeah. No problem with me, but I don't know anything about an affliction. It wasn't me." Semjaza looks at the cell lock and back at Aza. "All I know is you need Angel Dust to remove one of those and I don't have any... but I know a place if you would kindly GET ME OUT OF HERE!"

A Mortal's Soul is at Stake

A flash appears in the Halls of the Raquia outside Raphael's administration room. It is Miriam who stands before the entrance of the door. Standing with clenched hands that repeatedly release and make a fist again, Miriam breathes deeply trying to formulate a speech. Motioning to knock on the door then hesitating once again, Miriam cannot feel ready enough, but the urgency of the situation has come to a point that does not allow any alternative action. Taking in another deep breath and raising a knocking hand to the door, Miriam now feels it is time to do what must be done. Miriam knocks gently then repeats the knock with more vigor and urgency. A voice from the other side invites the genie inside. Miriam only has to turn the handle to begin the pursuit of the Arch upon Aza. Swallowing hard and turning the handle, Miriam opens the door and flashes with the spirit of a critical situation before the presence of Ambassador Archangel Raphael. Above the head of Raphael is a large orb of light that projects a visual on New Gaia of a running herd of animals as a storm forms over the skies. In another visual there are people calmly shopping at a nearby major Asian market place. Raphael laughs as the orb projects a visual of

Rimmon the Angel of Lightning, looking frustrated as he scared the beast but failed to warn mortals of the coming storm.

"I told him twice that if he doesn't make the thunder loud enough he won't warn anything but the beasts in the field. It's a Holiday. The mortals are not going to stop shopping. This is going to be a mess." Raphael continues watching the orb. "So Miriam what did I do to deserve the honor of your presence?"

In an effort to not make Janus appear scandalous in the eyes of Raphael, Miriam begins with the story of the Pact of Alliance and how Semjaza threatened Jazire to get Janus to take the Oath. Although disturbing, this was of no surprise as Raphael suspected that Choir of Angels and the children of Barcus were contaminated with some deceitful souls. By the time Miriam revealed Azazel's being unearthed and his visit to Janus, Raphael had become angered and upset, but not as upset as he was when he was finally informed that Azazel had used a mortal to rise to Vilon in his attempt to rescue Semjaza from prison.

"A mortal's soul is at stake?"

"Yes, Ambassador. That's why I didn't hesitate to tell you."

"Janus allowed this?"

"Only under the threat of Azazel."

"You take this information to Gabriel immediately. He is in Machonon with Michael."

"Yes, Raphael."

"Michael will know what to do. I must go search the cells... Miriam... Good job! Thank you for having the courage to come forward with this information in spite of your loyalty to your sibling."

"It's my duty. I will go to Machonon at once!"

CHAPTER TEN

Hell's Bells

Semjaza now freed and anxious to leave Saqun wastes no time as he makes his way through the steamy hot cells of Hell and down the corridor up to the front entrance of the house. Hell's bells clattering with a metallic clang ring disturbingly down on the ears of those below. Semjaza and Azazel run through the main entrance and back out to the docks. Jerry follows close behind as they struggle to concentrate and keep their balance against the large bell's vibes and clatter that is so loud it's producing a disturbing mental effect on the ears and minds of listeners. If they can maintain any concentration they still have to overcome the challenges of the physical environment. Cinders and splashes of fiery orange hell dust braise their cloaks as they make their way to the docks that lie across the pit, leading away from Hell House.

Semjaza looks around at the terrifying place that was scheduled to be his eternal home. The gratitude for his freedom is given to the Chancellor and his allegiance to the Fallen. Semjaza tugs on Azazel's cloak to get his attention over the loud bells. "Azazel, my brother. We may run into some trouble out here. It may not go well for me if I have no way to protect myself," Semjaza gripes as he stares at Azazel's astroflare.

"There's no way I'm giving you my astroflare," Azazel shouts.

"You'd have me defenseless brother?"

Azazel can barely hear Semjaza's plea for obtaining a weapon over the loudness of the bells. In hope to end the losing conversation he shouts, "I'm not your brother! I'm doing what I must do to fulfill this pact, then I'm out of here!"

Semjaza stops running and slows the caper. The mission to escape Saqun comes to a halt.

"Brother! You would deliver me from just to lead me into danger?" Semjaza shouts trying to be heard over the loud and nauseating hell's bells.

The inability to communicate over the sickening loudness of the irritating bells forces Azazel to give in and he hands Semjaza a small dagger.

The bells, in the midst of their swings, freeze in a time suspended motion. The entire area seems to go lifeless. The hot fog dissipates and reveals a figure standing on the dock in the path of their exit. The figure, tall and dark is no stranger to Semjaza and Azazel who kneel down in servitude. Jerry mimics their position out of concern for his safety and ignorance as to what it is exactly that he's suppose to do. Jerry's breathing begins to increase rapidly as he pats his pockets for his medication but he does not find it.

"The Keyyyy," squeals the figure with a phantom screech that irritates the ears and frightens the soul.

"Oh, brother," Aza sighs.

With no eye contact Azazel raises up the golden key while continuing to kneel. The key disappears from Azazel's hand.

"I have the pass too just as you requested my Lord," says Semjaza pointing over to the human.

"The pass! What pass?" Azazel shouts.

Semjaza smiles. "Did you think we would have you bring him all the way out here to this dreadful place for nothing? Mwahaha." Semjaza laughs.

Azazel stands up from his kneeling position and draws his astroflare, "I've fulfilled my oath and I've had enough of your trickery," Azazel informs the dark figure.

"Bring the pass!" squeals the dark figure as it disappears leaving in its place two cloaked members of his entourage. Semjaza and Azazel try their best to see through the distance of hell's fog. Azazel can barely make out the faces of the two members of the Fallen. A slow cryptic grin comes over Semjaza's face as the fog's intensity lightens up enough for him to recognize Auza the Fallen Angel of Injustice and his twin brother Uzza the Fallen Angel of Immorality.

The Watchers

Azazel recalls his last encounter with Auza and Uzza in the days after the Fall of the 200. Early one morning, Azazel awakened to the sounds of a great many troops tramping across the land near the Dan River. Azazel took to the village to investigate the rumblings and found an army of 200 Fallen angels pilfering and raping a small Akkadian tent community. As a former Guardian Angel, Azazel served and protected humans as a duty, a mere requirement of the assignment, but as a simple dwelling member of the mortal community he began to feel something that morning that he had never felt before, a sense of compassion and responsibility for humankind.

Azazel somehow figured that he had brought the attention of the Fallen on the village. Before the 200 fells upon the Earth some of them served in an angelic bounty unit called the Watchers who were assembled to find and apprehend him. During their duties they were exposed to the human culture while seeking him out. If it weren't for these bounty hunters, the Fallen would have never been made aware of the humans in the village, most importantly the daughters of man. He himself had made several trips into the village to woo women and to mingle amongst the men. He posed as a sojourner, a mere traveler from a far away land. He traded angelic secrets in exchange for their company and female companionship, which was plenty to be had in a village where most of the men were often away at war against neighboring lands. The men were taught angelic battle techniques, which they used to come back victorious. They were grateful to Azazel and rewarded him generously. Azazel was offered a chance to pitch a tent within the village and to further become a consultant in their army, but Azazel refused stating that he was only passing through as he planned to meet up with his family in a faraway land, a place from which he had been gone for far too long. This tale wasn't altogether a lie as he was waiting to be reunited with Sophia in a faraway place, but nothing as farfetched as what the humans could have imagined to be true.

For the most part, with the exception of catering to his growing desire for female companionship, Azazel kept his distance from the village. Azazel felt the less involvement he had the less chance of being discovered by the Watchers, but Azazel had not been careful enough. The Watchers had noticed the evolution of man's use of weaponry, clothing, and makeup that was all too similar to those used in the Heavens. The Arch Order sent Guardian Angels to mingle with the humans and to investigate the evolution of their mortal development. The Archangels also sent the Watchers to look for signs of Azazel's involvement however; this group too had become suspect and weakened by temptation and desire for the daughters of man.

Azazel had notice the influx of travelers coming into the village. He figured that allowing an angel or two to visit every now and then to fulfill their lustful desires would be less harmful then confronting them and alerting the entire Order of Watchers to his presence. Azazel had in fact traveled away from the village and found cultures surviving on every corner of the Earth. He would often take on the role of a sojourner to exchange angelic trade secrets for the company of women and then move along to another village. He repeated this pattern all around the world. He became an avid world traveler. Azazel always came back to the Dan village and Mount Hermon west of the lands considered to be the cradle of humanity.

One day Azazel came across two angels posing as travelers in the Dan village. The men were the twin brothers Auza and Uzza. The two angels did not attempt to arrest Azazel, but instead stated that they had come to inform him about Sammael's plan to Fall onto the Earth. Sammael felt that Azazel's familiarity with the land would help him find a place for safe refuge. Azazel did not like the idea of having company to draw attention to his presence, however he knew that if Sammael had figured out where he was hiding, soon so would the others. Azazel decided that it might not be a bad idea to have an alliance with other angels in the Heavens or those who had Fallen to the Earth, to update him on the status of the Arch Order's plans to capture him. Azazel toured Auza and Uzza around the world showing them many primitive cultures and the beginnings of civilizations who were all vulnerable and naïve. They became a small adventurous group of world travelers. Azazel introduced the twins to the foul in the air, the forest creatures, and the beasts that roamed the land and the sea. The day came for Auza and Uzza to leave the Earth and report to Sammael all that they had seen. Azazel knew that soon he would have more company than he ever wanted. He hoped his time to be reunited with Sophia was drawing near and that he would not have to share the Earth with Sammael and the influx of Fallen angels that would be soon descending down onto the Earth. However on that day it was clear that his time to leave the Earth had not come soon enough, yet he was still convinced that Sophia would soon come to find him there so he stayed.

Several moon rotations later two tall statues were erected up on top of a distant hillside. It was a command post for the Watchers. Azazel knew by their actions that this group was not the Watchers in the employ of the Archangels, but a rogue group who had descended upon the Earth. Azazel was not going to allow a major disturbance in the village so equipped with his astroflare he felt he had all he needed to engage in discussions about his concerns for the Dan village.

Walking through a campsite Azazel spots an old adversary. "Are you looking for someone?" asks Azazel with sword drawn.

"Azazel! My good friend welcome to Cain's Point," responds Semjaza. "Let the past be the past. No need for aggression. We are just having a little randy fun."

"You are raping and plundering through a village of mostly harmless women and children and you are concerned about a show of aggression. I demand that you stop this at once!"

"I'm touched! You actually care for these humans."

"I'm keeping the peace as to not disturb the land and bring attention to my presence here. So again I demand that you stop!"

"Alright, anything for a brother of the alliance."

"What alliance?"

"You didn't forget about the alliance you agreed to with Auza and Uzza did you?"

"With the oath came an understanding that Sammael would seek quiet refuge in areas away from the Dan."

"Well... that's when there was only a few, but now there are over 200 of us and we all have needs. You should be grateful. We have held watch over this Earth for several hundred years and concealed the secret of your presence from the Order of the Arch. It was brilliant to hide in plain sight. I would have thought you would have taken refuge in one of those dark and cold planets with Sophia."

"Enough of your ramblings. Call off your comrades at once!"

Semjaza signals the leaders of the Fallen to cease their activities and to regroup at camp. "Let me introduce you to the other leaders of the Fallen Watchers," Semjaza continues. "I believe you've met Seraphim Auza and his brother Uzza. From the Nation crew we have Armaros. We also have some of Barcus children Araqiel, Gaap, and Penemue. It's always good to have a genie or two around for good measure." Semjaza continues as he escorts Azazel through the campsite. "As to be expected we have never been able to recruit any Virtues." Semjaza points out some more of the Fallen leaders. "Gadreel heads up the Powers and Baraqel the Dominions. From the Thrones we have Kokabel and most importantly for you we have the scripter, Balberith of the Cherubim who can certify that you entered into the Pact of Alliance."

"What pact! All I offered was a safe hiding place for Sammael only. That's it! So nice meeting you all, good luck, and get out!"

You can't have total dominion over the Earth,"
informs Baraqel. "The honeycomb is much too deep
for one Fallen brother."

"You better take this up with the Chancellor,"
says Semjaza.

"Chancellor? What chancellor?"

"Chancellor Sammael."

"Sammael? A Chancellor? Really?"

"Auza! Uzza! Take him to see the Chancellor."

Azazel follows the twin escorts to a dark tent
where Sammael is taking up temporary housing
while he oversees the Fall. The twins motion Azazel
to enter the tent while they remain outside. The
tent's interior appears much larger in size from the
inside than the perception from the outside. Azazel
feels as if he stepped out of Dan and into another
dimension. The inside of the tent is lit with
torchlight. The inner ceiling has a translucent-like
quality that shows the planets and stars
throughout the universe. Azazel hasn't seen
anything like it since he was last in Sophia's room.

Azazel finds a familiar dark figure sitting on a
throne. What is not so familiar is an eerie feeling of
evil and unnerving danger that cringes Azazel's
toes and sour his stomach. Chancellor Sammael sits
on a throne between two wild white sphinxes with
red eyes. In his left hand Sammael holds a two-
plunged lance with two sharp tips of intertwined
serpents at one end and an eyeball handle on the
other. The lance's handle is made from a large
creature's eyeball that rolls as if it's still alive and
seeing. In his right hand he holds a purple chalice
filled with blood wine. His seemingly boneless, long
fingers wrap around the chalice perfectly tight. He
wears a skull ring on his middle finger and his nails

are dark gray contrasting against his pale white hand. He is dressed in a dark pitch-black cloak that conceals his dark blue wings.

"Interesting look, Sammael."

"That's Chancellor Sammael."

"Chancellor? Whatever. Just call your entourage off the village and keep down the ruckus."

"Azazel you are a legend in the Heavens. You were the second to defy the Arch Order and the first to escape, unlike Lord Abaddon who rots in Raquia."

"Lord? If you think Abaddon lies in the prison cell because he can't escape you are not a very good understudy... Chancellor!"

Nodding his head in confirmation of his thoughts, "I knew you were very perceptive beyond the rest of them. You are an insightful warrior. This is why we need you. Why we need your leadership skills. The other are good, but they'll be better under your direction."

"I'll have no part of this. I just want to be left alone."

"No one truly wants to be left alone. How long were you out here waiting for her?"

"I don't know what you think you know about me, but that's far enough. Now call back your entourage. I don't want any harm to come to these people."

"You care for them?"

"Listen! If you want to destroy mankind just do it all at once. Why make them suffer?"

"Suffering is the point! Killing them quickly is much too vulgar and impulsive. I need prayers and pain. I need for them to see their prayers unanswered as they flood the Prayer Room floors. I need them to feel pain for them to come to the realization that Omnus has forsaken them."

"That's not true. You ever heard of sacrifice, endurance, and faith?"

"Faith! That's the lie you tell yourself when you can't stand to hear the truth. The truth hurts more when it comes from a liar than a lie hurts when it is told by someone who tells the truth, because the truth is always a lie."

"Enough of your trickery!"

"You will join us Azazel," says Chancellor Sammael as he raises his lance to transform the sphinxes into upright swordsmen.

Azazel draws his astroflare. The swordsmen advance and attack. Click-ety-clack! Click-ety-clack! They exchange sword hits and blocks as they swing back and forth. Click-ety-clack! "Call off your girlfriends before it's too late for you, Sammael!" Azazel makes a sudden striking leap that kills the first swordsmen. He continues the assault on the last demon. Click-ety-clack!

"How do you think I possess this power? Do you want to know where Sophia is hiding? Do you know why you haven't been reunited with her?"

"No more lying, Sammael!" Click-ety-clack! Fighting with the lone swordsman continues.

"They rapped and bound her before they threw her in the desert."

"Shut up! That's not true!" Click-ety-clack! Azazel twirls and lunges killing the last swordsmen.

The Chancellor throws away his chalice and draws his sword.

"I should have wasted you at Zebul's point!" screams Azazel. Click-ety-clack! Click-ety-clack! The

Chancellor advances toward Azazel but he does not retreat.

"I knew one day you and your precious Sophia would need me." Click-ety-clack!

"Need you? Never!" Click-ety-clack! The dueler's dance continues.

Azazel lands a cut on the Chancellor's arm and advances with several fletch and lunges until the Chancellor begins to retreat. "Killing me will only stop you from knowing the truth. You will wait here for all of eternity, but she will not come because she needs your help." Click-ety-clack!

"Why should I believe you?"

"I have the shield." The Chancellor mimics Sophia's voice, "We will never be lost to each other." He laughs, "Ha! Ha! Ha!" Click-ety-clack!

"You bastard!" Azazel remembers those words from the last time he saw Sophia. "That's my shield!" Click-ety-clack! The duel resumes.

"You want the shield? Join me! Take the Oath of Alliance. The pact needs you! Sophia needs you!" Click-ety-clack!

The duel continues but their swords barely touch. Click! Clack! Click! Azazel feels defeated and overcome with sorrow mulling the possibility that Sammael may be telling the truth. The attacks and parries come to a near end. Click! Clack! Azazel feels that if Sophia is out there in need of his help he must do what has to be done to help her.

He drops his sword and falls to his knees distraught. "I will join you... Chancellor."

"My brother. We will be victorious!" the Chancellor responds as he extends his hand out and exalts Azazel into the dark.

Auza and Uzza enter the tent along with Semjaza and Balberith. Behind them comes the Chancellor's entourage known as the Four Fiends of Fury: Xaphan, the second in command of the Fallen Cherubim Order; Eblis, the angel of despair who along with Sammael refused to worship man before Omnus at the veiling of humanity; Iadalbaoth, the archon of darkness and liaison for Lord Abaddon; and Rehab, the angel of violence. With their fist pumping over their hearts and their feet stomping onto the ground they cite the Oath of Alliance to enter Azazel into the pact.

Stomp! Stomp! Pump! Stomp! Stomp! Pump!
Stomp! Stomp! Pump! Stomp! Stomp! Pump!

"From heavens above us,
To Mountain we fall.

The Fall,
The Call,
This pact shall be the law.

I descend with my brethren,
And rise to his call.

The Fall,
The Call,
The pact of us all.

I bring one to the legion,
The legion brings all.

The Fall,
The Call,
The pact will stand tall.

Through Houses of Heaven,
Every room and every hall.

The Fall,
The Call,
We break every wall."

Azazel looks up to the heavens and whispers,
"Forgive me for I know not what I have done."

Mêlée at Matey

From out of the cover of Hell's fog Auza and
Uzza continue to move toward Semjaza, Azazel,
and Jerry. Their smooth irregular, sidewinder-like
movements make their approach strategic, as they
appear to approach in an unpredictable, yet direct
motion. The twins speak in a tandem, switching
speakers in an unpredictable pattern to distract the
listener's attention. The alternating speakers are
able to hide their approach in the fog from two
different locations.
   "It's time to,"
   "bring."
   "The son of,"
   "Man!"
Although their movements are unpredictable,
Auza and Uzza's approach become sharper and
quicker as they move closer.
   Semjaza and Azazel draw their swords and place
themselves on opposite sides of Jerry.

"Oh brother," Aza sighs. "Don't let them confuse you. Concentrate on Auza and I'll take care of Uzza," Azazel informs Semjaza.

Semjaza breaks from heavy thought, "Sorry, Azazel. I descend with my brother and rise to his call."

"Don't be a fool!"

"Change of plans!" Semjaza grabs Jerry and holds a dagger to his neck. "Never trust a Fallen no matter what you do!" Semjaza taunts Jerry as he uses him for a shield between him and Azazel. Semjaza buries his nose into the back of Jerry's neck and takes a deep sniff of his mortality. "You make me feel closer to God. Mwahahaha."

"What are you doing? Release him!"

"Oh no, I was told to bring his mortal ass. He is my key out of here."

From the mist of the fog two angels appear. It's Sheburiel and Hadrial, Warden angels from Raquia. Auza and Uzza engage in battle with the wardens.

"You know what I didn't like the most about Sammael? He was selfish, Semjaza. He was only interested in his own gains. Did you know he let me go that night in Zebul? He said it wasn't his fight," Azazel informs Semjaza.

The Wardens and the twins fight in the background. Their swords strike and defend against the assault. Click-ety-clack! Click-ety-clack!

"I'll never go back to being Michael's peon. I'll die with dignity under the Chancellor rather than live with humiliation under Michael."

Azazel and Semjaza dance in a circle as Semjaza keeps Jerry closely in between them. Azazel waits for the opportune moment to attack, but Semjaza keeps Jerry close.

"Dignity? Where is he now? He left you here. Why do you think he took that key? He wasn't going to take you with him. He's headed for the Paradise Gate!"

"I have the pass."

"You never were very smart. He wants to use Jerry in exchange for safe passage through the gate. It's the only way Metaphon and Uriel will let him pass through."

"But I have the pass!"

Azazel asks as they continue circling around Jerry, "Don't you know anything? Capturing Sammael isn't the priority anymore. It's the human's safety. Sammael can't take on both of them. One of them is going to run to the rescue of the innocent mortal and guess who will be caught holding him at peril?"

"You think you know everything."

"It's over, Semjaza. Give me the human. One way or the other you are not walking out of here," says Azazel while twirling his astroflare to taunt Semjaza.

"Take another step and he gets it old friend. I don't need to be too fancy at this distance," Semjaza threatens as he holds the blade closer to Jerry's neck.

A sudden flash from out of the fog reveals Janus who stabs Semjaza in the back with a dagger. "Stabbing you in the back is more courageous than what you did when you killed Jazire with your cowardice spell," Janus mocks as Semjaza falls to the ground on his knees and drops his knife.

Jerry quickly pulls away to safety.

"A genie!" Semjaza looks at Janus with squinting eyes and clinched teeth. "You can't kill me you inferior—"

"Don't you know anything about who you are?" asks Janus. "You have Fallen and when you Fall you are no more powerful than a mortal soul, unless you have been anointed by the light or exalted by—"

"The dark!" Interjects Azazel. "Oh don't tell me... Let me guess, Lord Abaddon didn't fully bring you into the dark because—"

"I helped pursue him in Raquia," answers Semjaza.

"He would have killed Jerry so he could impress the Chancellor. He's still trying to buy his way in," informs Janus.

"Oh great!" exclaims Jerry as he pats his pockets for his medication but he does not find it.

Azazel looks over at Sheburiel and Hadrial who have defeated and killed Auza and Uzza.

Jerry stands over Semjaza as he lies on the ground dying. "Shouldn't we offer him last rites or something?"

"He sold his soul a long time ago," Azazel replies.

"I'll see you in... back here some day," Semjaza whispers as he finally slips off to death.

"So what do we do about this situation?" Azazel asks.

"His soul will be captured in the Sphere of Containment," explains Hadrial.

"No, not that situation," informs Azazel.

"Oh!" Hadrial says as he rolls his eyes up into his head and sighs heavily. "This situation... well... our orders are to detain you and bring you in to the Arch—"

"Wait a minute!" Jerry interjects. "I know you have jobs to do and Aza is your fugitive and all but... I still need him to get home and to save my wife!"

"Isn't he adorable?" says Janus.

"He's not just any fugitive," Sheburiel explains.

"So you mean to tell me you would risk putting him into prison with the Chancellor's disciples, knowing the Chancellor is out to kill him? Whose side is he on anyway? In this battle between good and evil where does he fit in that equation?" Jerry asks.

"Are you saying you are not his prisoner?" asks Sheburiel.

"Prisoner? No! He's helping me save my family," Jerry pleads.

"Don't be a fool. It's you who are helping him save his comrades. You only have one savior!" informs Hadriel.

"I've literally been caught between a rock and a hard place for a long time. The cells of Raquia don't look that bad right about now. I fulfilled my oath and I have nothing else to do here," Azazel says before surrendering.

"What about Sophia? What about my wife? And did you forget that the Chancellor has the golden key?"

"The Key!" the two guards shout.

"This day can't be over yet. I'm not done yet! I'm not leaving without that dust!" Jerry informs Azazel.

"Aww... sweet passion. I remember passion," says Janus while looking at Jerry with glossy eyes and one hand over its heart.

Azazel ponders Jerry's comments for a moment. "You're right. I can't allow the Chancellor to get away with that key. I guess there are some loose ends, but we must get you out of here first." Azazel turns toward Sheburiel and Hadrial and pleads, "We are on the same mission like it or not. Above all else Omnus would not want this human to be harmed. I must help him complete his mission and return him to his home. Then I... we must get the key back from the Chancellor. After that you can do with me whatever you feel has to be done."

"These affairs are no longer yours. We will see that the Arch—"

"Wait!" Sheburiel interrupts Hadriel. "Are you willing to give up your life for this human and return your soul to the sphere?"

Azazel pauses and sighs, "Yes, I am. I lost my soul a long time ago."

"Aza! No!" Jerry pleads.

"This day was inevitable," says Sheburiel. "...And it still will be if you had somehow eluded us—"

"Say no more," Janus responds and flashes Jerry and Azazel to the foothills of Matey.

Meanwhile back deep in the galactic forest of Machonon, Michael and Gabriel are sparring and practicing as they often do. Miriam enters Michael's house with wide and glowing eyes. The genie looks to the left and quickly to the right in search of Michael's sparring room. As Miriam approaches the sparring room doors the genie pauses and takes a few quick breaths, inhaling and exhaling through the lips. "I must collect my thoughts," says Miriam's inner voice as various strategies for delivering the message runs through the genie's head. Miriam knows Michael has been waiting for the Apocalypse, the day when he can have his battle with Abaddon, so his escape is of supreme urgency. "Stalling on this information would not look favorable in their eyes but how must this information be delivered without implicating Janus' involvement?" the genie ponders. "Azazel could be freeing Abandon at this very moment," the genie further contemplates. "Father Barcus would not like it if I make a mess of this." Miriam sighs and takes a deep breath. "Azazel, Sammael, Abaddon! Oh... my lord! This is way more important than Janus who should have known better. This is an emergency," says the voice in the genie's head. "I have to disturb them and I have to tell the facts and try my best to not implicate Janus. The details can be sorted out later, just stick to the urgent facts." The genie flashes ferociously into the room between the middle of their sparring.

"Pardon you!" scolds Michael.

Gabriel asks through his teeth, "What! What is this—"

"Sammael and Azazel kidnapped a HUMAN and brought him to RAQUIA! They FREED the prisoners! There is CHAOS everywhere!! They are LOOSE! They are ALL loose!"

"What's this madness!" shouts Gabriel.

"WAIT! ...Something is not right," says Michael feeling the galactic energy in the air.

"Raphael sent me. He said you must come at once!"

"Azazel? Attempting to free Abaddon? He's in Dudael! You can't believe that he's—"

"Azazel or Sammael, I don't care who sets him free! I just hope I get there in time to track him down before the coward runs and falls," Michael exclaims. "Pachdial! Oumriel!" Michael calls out to two Seraphim Sentinels. "Alert the Chalkydri Army and tell Israfel to sound the horn."

Now buying into Miriam's report, Gabriel snaps orders. "Pachdial! You must also tell Seraphiel to send extra guards to the Fifth, Sixth, and, Seventh Houses then inform the other Archangels and meet us on the foothills of Matey."

"Miriam! I need you to go tell Uriel his watch over the garden may be threatened, but he and Metaphon must remain at their post," instructs Michael.

"I'll go now!"

"Miriam!" Gabriel urgently shouts. "You've done well to bring this to us so expeditiously, now continue to be quick. Time is of the essence!"

In a glee of proud smoke Miriam flashes away to the Gates of Paradise. On the foothills of Matey, Azazel, Janus, and Jerry make their way to the Fifth House of Sandalphon. The house sits high up on the peak of a hill. The house is not like any other in all of the heavens. The house is smaller and round with a mist of stars rooftop. The front of the home does not have a door, but only a large multicolored circular window. The pane is not made of glass, but an energy field that radiates various psychedelic colors like a kaleidoscope. The pathway leading up to the home is covered with stepping platforms made of light and galactic dust particles. There are galactic flowers along the side of the path. The galactic flowers glow in many bright colors. The galactic grass is dark green but its tips glow starry bright and fade back slowly as the wind passes over the blades. The galactic grass and flowers move together when drawn to any interactions along the path. They move in a synchronous fashion like a sway in the wind as travelers move up and down the path.

Walking up the path to the Fifth House Azazel turns to Janus. "How did you know?" Azazel asks.

"How did I know what?" responds Janus as they continue to walk.

"About Semjaza's mortality?"

"When you are the gatekeeper between the Earth and the First House of Heaven you need to know everything about those who rise and those who fall."

"So when angels visit the Earth they lose their immortality?" asks Jerry.

"An angel can visit in full angelic strength. The Guardian Angel was created for the purpose of consummating Omnus' grace, power, and protection. A Fallen angel has been stripped of their power and therefore their immortality. The only power it has is through the in depth knowledge of how the universe works, unless it has been given some additional power through the adulation of darkness. But even then it's nothing more than Black magic at its finest, which any human can learn to use."

"Yeah, but teaching it to them isn't exactly supported," Azazel adds.

The three continue up the path towards the front of the house.

"What about flying?" Jerry asks. "Aza could not fly."

Azazel corrects, "I could not ascend! Angel Dust sprinkled during a ritual they like to call the Prayer of Binding strips your ability to use your wings or become aware of your angelic potential. All beings have spiritual wings and the potential to use them if they only believe in the faith of flight. It's how you got here."

"This same Angel Dust will cure Karlisa?"

"It also gives you the power to fight off evil. She will realize her true self. Like your... Holy water," laughs Azazel. "It serves as a motivator to realize your own inner power to overcome evil."

"So I'm to go in and just ask for this precious Angel Dust? Hi I'm Jerry Xeven, the human who helped Azazel break your most infamous criminals out of jail. Will you give me some Angel Dust so I can complete my mission?"

"Remember what I told you about His Gracefulness. He's very forgiving," Janus informs.

"Yeah but he just set free 200 Fallen angels and helped carry out the work of Abaddon's darkest protégé," Azazel adds.

Janus pauses. "On second thought, you might want to try begging and batting those pitiful human eyes at him," Janus advises.

"And if that doesn't work don't come running out here to me!" demands Azazel.

"But I was only an innocent bystander in all this scheming," Jerry pleads as he pats his pockets for his medication but he does not find it.

"That's it! Start building your case. Play the victim," encourages Janus.

The three make it to the front of the house. "Why can't you just flash in and flash out with it?" asks Jerry.

"The Angel Dust can't be taken. It can only be given."

"Great! So I guess I'll just have to go in and ask for it."

Azazel stops the group behind a tall row of galactic bushes. "Ok. This is close enough. Be quick about it! I'm not exactly wanted around here. Not in a good way."

Jerry looks at the circular structure and examines it carefully. "There's no door. How do I get in?"

"Free your mind, think only pure thoughts, then walk through the pane," instructs Janus as they hide behind the row of galactic bushes.

Jerry walks to the house, steps up to the entry pane, pauses, and takes a deep breath. He takes a step into the pane and bumps his head on the force field that denies his entry. Jerry turns around holding his head. "Now what?" Jerry shouts back.

"I said free your mind, not clear it!"

Jerry turns towards the pane, pauses, thinks of his family, takes another deep breath, and steps through the pane's field.

"Oh, brother!" sighs Aza.

Meanwhile above the throughway, a chariot driven by four white horses rides forcefully over the Heavens, like a solar flare escaping from the sun. Aboard the chariot is Archangel Michael with his six wings spread tall and high. Michael pulls and guides the harnesses with a firm grip as he yells and directs the angelic beasts to fly faster, climb higher, and travel further from the forest of Machonon to the lower grounds of Raquia. Michael's eyes are wide and round as he fixes them on his destination. He licks his lips under his arched eyebrows as he zeros in on Raquia. Michael has been waiting for this moment for a very long time. This is a race to settle an old score, to end an old debate, and to finally lay claim as the brightest star in the Choir of Angels. Patience has finally paid off and Michael is ready to be remunerated with the reign of being, the undisputed victor of Seraphim supremacy. No more will Michael have to rule with Abaddon lurking in the background.

Michael despises Abaddon's claim of being a lord to any realm of angels. Abaddon was the first and original leader of the Seraphim Order and the first chief commanding elder in the Order of Divinity Angels. He was the bravest, the brightest, and the most talented in all areas of Omnus' pride and pleasure. Abaddon was admired and looked upon as the big brother, loving protector, and mentor of all angelic orders. Some even began to admire him over Omnus, like a toddler clinging to a preferred sibling. Michael is afraid that some of those followers may still be around in the background, in silent support, and disapproving of Abaddon's replacement. Michael knows as long as Abaddon is around, whether free or imprisoned, control over the Arch Order will be at risk of mutiny and divided loyalty. Although most of the unfaithful and disloyal betrayers have already aligned themselves with Abaddon or Sammael and have fallen from the grace of the Heavens there is always a threat of lingering doubters of the current Arch leadership.

For Michael this is a time to purge the angelic order of pretenders and infiltrators. This is the beginning of Abaddon's final demise. "How wonderful it would be to catch him fleeing like a fugitive," Michael thinks as he drives the chariot harder and faster. Michael has prepared and trained for this day for years as he always knew Abaddon would not go out without a fight and that a battle makes the victor more esteemed than an opponent's surrender. Michel was growing weary and restless waiting for the Apocalypse and now he feels that Janus has done him a favor by assisting Abaddon with his escape plan. "Very clever," Michael thinks as he rolls Miriam's story through his mind. "Taking a human hostage, using him to raise Azazel to Vilon, obtaining the key from Janus, and freeing the Fallen to distract the guards was a devious plan. How else would the Fallen obtain a key but to use the innocence of a naive and free unsuspecting spirit? Who else but Azazel would know Raquia's layout, how to get by the sentry angels along the path, and all the prison schematics? A clever but futile result to the conclusion of his legacy." Michael reflects on the plan with some admiration, but more so with appreciation for this ploy brings forth the finality of iniquity.

Israfel blows the trumpet of the Apocalypse. An army of Seraphs and Chalkydri soldiers fly through the Heavens securing the seven houses and searching for any fugitive angels on the run. The skies are filled with fleeing fugitives and the wardens who are chasing them. Chaos fills the Heavens. Michael's chariot is the fastest of all in the sky. Behind Michael's chariot is Gabriel on a black horse with red eyes of fire. Gabriel tries hard to keep up with Michael and his four-horse chariot but he continues to fall behind. Gabriel's horse, Kafziel is the fastest horse in heaven. Kafziel has the speed of three horses. Gabriel is the best horse trainer in all the Heavens. He rides Kafziel hard and strong yelling, "Mahir! Mahir!"

For Michael and Gabriel their angelic horses just can't seem to move fast enough. Gabriel can't stop thinking of Raphael fighting off a pack of fugitives all by himself with none of the Archangels there to help him. "How many have escaped? How many have Raphael had to fight?" and finally the thought of "Have they overtaken Raphael and hurt or killed him?" a thought that pushes Gabriel to drive the horses even faster, even when he feels they have reached their limit. When Michael and Gabriel finally reach Raquia the celestial grounds are in chaos. As they had expected many of the Fallen were out of the prison and engaging in battle with the Warden angels. The Fallen, armed with swords have outnumbered and slain many of the Warden angels, but the fighting is continuing on as a few of the remaining Wardens bravely hold on to their positions. Some of the Fallen have noticed Michael's chariot arrive on the scene and begin to scatter and runaway. Other members of the Fallen are not so lucky and only notice Michael after he has dismounted the chariot and has begun to engage into full assault against the fugitives. Only the fugitives who were in Michael's path to the prison met the brutal force of his swinging astroflare for Michael is not interested in the field battles, but only in searching the prison itself to verify that Abaddon is in fact on the loose and therefore under warrant for arrest.

Gabriel arrives on the scene, dismounts, and searches for Raphael. The Fallen knows it will not be long before the arrival of the entire Arch Order. The Fallen have begun to Fall onto the Earth. The Chalkydri Army has finally arrived and begin to pursue those Fallen members who have run away. There is isolated fighting and small fires as the Fallen have begun to burn everything in sight to distract the Arch angels away from fleeing fugitives and to mock Omnus' omnificent power by destroying his beautiful things.

After seeing the house grounds secure in the hands of the Wardens Gabriel makes his way inside the prison where he finds Raphael assisting Raquil who informs them of Azazel's involvement and that his intent was to free Semjaza, not Abaddon. Raquil further informs them that Azazel was too late because Semjaza had already been sent to a holding cell at Hell House where he would be sentenced for eternal imprisonment.

"Brother," Raphael says to Gabriel. "It was Janus who gave Azazel the key."

"I know... I'm sick with it," Gabriel replies with a sour mouth and a heavy stomach.

"Let's go prepare a cell for the fool."

"What about the human? Has his soul been tainted or has he been brought here against his will?" asks Gabriel.

"It doesn't matter. The three of them will be punished before the throne," Raphael warns.

"He must be frightened. How could we ever return him to innocence after being exposed to this level of enlightenment?" says a concerned Gabriel. "Where's Michael? How does he suggest we proceed?"

Michael continues thoroughly searching the prison looking in all the empty cells as they begin to fill back up with captured fugitives. Michael proceeds rampantly with his search until he reaches the Southeast point of the prison pentagon where he finds Abaddon still sitting in his cell.

Michael pauses in shock as if all the air had left the room. "WHY?" Michael screams with his hands raised to his temples. "WHY ARE YOU HERE?"

Michael screams again in agony. "The cells were open! Chaos had cleared the way! WHY? Why didn't you RUN?"

Abaddon stares back at him with cold, dark, and tranquil eyes resting over a cryptic grin.

Michael enters the cell "You filthy, rotten, dirty, evil, scoundrel!! You had your chance! You could have escaped!" Michael paces the floor back and forth as he tries to calm himself, catch his breath, and gain control of his anger. "I just don't understand. The cell was open. The path has been cleared," Michael says breathing heavily with a shallow breath as he staggers to a cell bench across from Abaddon. Michael sits on a bench with his head hanging down. Trying to calm himself he begins twirling the tip of his astroflare on the ground and watching it sparkle with tracers of energy streams as it spins and stops. He looks up towards Abaddon in amazement. "You had a plan, the son of man, and the key. What were you waiting for? What am I missing?"

Abaddon replies with a solemn voice as if to console Michael, "Sorry, but this isn't the Apocalypse my young and eager friend."

"I'm no friend of yours!"

"You will join me," Abaddon says with confidence.

"Never!!"

"In time."

"Never! You're up to something!" Michael's anger was beginning to calm, but now it has become perturbed again. He stands up energized with his new wondering. "Where are your comrades?" Michael calls out for the Arch, "Raphael! Gabriel! Come quickly!" Raphael and Gabriel run into the room and they too become shocked at Abaddon's presence. "Find Beliar, Wall, and Mephistopheles. I need to know if they are on the run or have been recaptured. Immediately!"

"Lit-tle Mic-hael." Abaddon shakes his head in discontent. "You're always a step behind and always missing the key—"

"Shut your mouth!" Michael caught himself from allowing Abaddon to get him upset and quickly calms himself back down again. Breathing deeply and trying to control his emotions, he returns to sitting on the bench. "You have no power in here. You are just a sorry soul waiting to be reclaimed." Michael nods his head as he assures himself of that statement. "Yeah... quite pathetic. So pathetic that I'm going to let you in on a little secret, well it's not really a secret but we just don't bother giving out the details. Today is your lucky day."

"Luck!" Abaddon says. "Luck has just run out on you fool! Now kindly do the same!"

"Would you like to know what happens to souls after they are cast into Hell? Of course you do!" Michael answers for Abaddon. "Some say Hell is just a horrid state of being without Omnus' good grace and vulnerable to the evils of your kind. But we know that due to the blood you wasted on Lake of Saqun such a place does actually exist. But did you know that after souls are tormented in your blood-stained lake they are returned to the great cycle of energy and reconstituted into new souls?" Michael informs. "So I guess it's you after all who will be rejoining us."

"Splendid. I think we all should recycle."

"In time," Michael mimics. "I don't know what's most pathetic about you, your sense of ignorant pride or just your ignorance?

"Careful, choir boy!"

"See! There it is... that innate deep down pure but simple jealousy. It's not even complicated. I can understand it. You were the first. How exciting that must have been. Watching all these marvelous creations spur up around you. The creativity, the unlimited possibilities... Oh, how exotic and stimulating that must have been."

"It was quite titillating. Now leave me in peace."

"Hmm... hmm," Michael snickers. "You know what's most interesting about it all? You thought that if he shared his power with you, you could also possess it for yourself. To control it at your own will."

"I controlled more than you ever will, you insubordinate bastard! And I'll control more when I get out of here! You'll always be a peon, but I'll save a place for you in my concubine! You filthy crying infant!"

"I used to admire you big brother! Oh, how I thought you were so fun and exciting. I looked forward to the days we spent creating all sorts of beings, flowers, birds, and trees—"

"Cockroaches, dragons, and cancer were my favorites!"

"We needed you! I needed you! Now you are just insignificant!"

"Just wait till I get out of here."

"You had your chance. Just face the truth. You have nowhere to go and your comrades have abandoned you. Sammael is only interested in his own survival," Michael laughs. "You gave your trust to the second most selfish being in the universe!" Laughter continues as Michael exits the cell and calls for the guard to secure it behind him. Now speaking through the cell bars, "You could have been the brightest light of us all but now you're just dim, dark, and pathetic."

Abaddon rushes over the cell bars as Michael walks away, "Hey Michael! Tell your human we'll never let her go. We'll be seeing you. Both of you real soon." Abaddon laughs and returns to his cot.

Michael shouts back, "We both know you are never getting out of here!"

"I don't have to participate in my victory to enjoy it!" Abaddon continues to laugh.

Michael hurries down the prison corridors to the master control room where he finds Raphael and Gabriel. "He's up to something! Where are the Fiends of Fury? It's bad enough that his Triad of Terror are still on the loose!"

"Yes, especially Xaphan who tried to burn the houses down before, do you think he'll try again?" Asks Raphael.

"The First and Second Houses are secured. We must search the remaining houses and verify that they are being well guarded," Gabriel informs the others. "Let's start in Saqun then work our way up to the Seventh House and circle back."

Michael recalls in his mind the words of Abaddon stating that he was always a step behind and always missing the key. "No! That's exactly what he's expecting us to do. He wants us to spend our time searching the Heavens while they plan their escape." Michael ponders on his thoughts for a moment. "Why would you hang around a place that has imprisoned you?"

"You wouldn't," answers Gabriel.

"No, you wouldn't but you also would not travel down the most obvious path and out the front entrance... so how would you escape?"

"With a hostage! They used the son of man to rise and they'll use him to Fall again," Raphael says with certainty.

"Not necessary," Michael explains. "Once they escape they can fall again without a hostage. We'll just follow their path. It will be easy especially with the scent of a human on the trail."

"They'll have to leave discretely," says Gabriel.

Michael replays his conversation with Abaddon stating that he was always missing the key. "Or... with the Golden Master Key!"

"The garden? They'll never get through the Garden. They'll never get by Uriel and Metaphon!" Raphael informs.

"There are many of the Fallen to assist and eight comrades of inequity. Beliar and Xaphan alone could be enough," Gabriel warns.

"So where's the key," asks Michael.

"Azazel took it to free Semjaza. I sent two of my best swordsmen, Sheburiel and Hadrial to investigate and report back," Raphael informs.

"Let me remind you that Janus assisted Azazel," says Gabriel. "This was partially an inside job. So we don't even know who we can trust anymore."

"It's the Great Disturbance all over again!" Raphael shouts.

"Sheburiel and Hadrial may not be enough. He has a human hostage," Michael informs. "We need Miriam to work with Nathaniel our historian and Judiel the angel of Spheres to find the scrolls of all those who took the Oath of Alliance. Only then will we know exactly who we are looking for and who we can still trust." Michael sends a guard for Nathaniel and conjures up Miriam, "I call upon the progeny of Barcus! Take my call into the winds and bring me forward an angelic friend. On divine spirits this message should fall. Let it be Miriam who hears my call."

Out from a flash of galactic light appears Miriam proud and pleased. "Michael, you called on me? I don't believe you have ever summoned me before," says Miriam bubbling with honor.

"You have been very helpful in assisting the Arch and we seek your aid again," Michael informs.

Looking around and finally resting gleeful eyes on Raphael, the genie says, "Anything you want, you got it. I'm always willing to do anything for the Arch."

"I need you to work with Nathaniel by roll calling the missing Fallen and those who helped them. You will need to check the sphere to witness their presence at Cain's Point and verify their alliance," instructs Michael.

"Can you check now to see if any angel has recently descended upon the Earth?" asks Gabriel.

"There is constant traffic between the First House and the Earth. How will I know who descends there on official angelic business?" Miriam asks.

"Gabriel you will need to stop all passages to and from the gatehouse. We must put a hold on all mortal births, deaths, prayer deliveries, and any worldly business throughout the universe," Michael instructs.

"This is going to cause quite a disturbance and interrupt the nature of mortality. We must act quickly and Janus, the one who can manage this the best, has abandoned post," Gabriel gripes.

"Umm... about Janus..." Miriam says. "I believe Janus was caught under the same influence as the human. Please allow mercy--."

"There will be no mercy for treason!" Michael scalds.

"Janus has a lot of explaining to do and only then will we decide what is to be done," informs Gabriel. "Janus disappointed and embarrassed my authority over the First House."

"I'm just saying I believe evil influences were at play," Miriam pleads.

"Here comes Nathaniel and the others. Now let's stop wasting time. We'll deal with Janus later," orders Michael.

Miriam invokes an energy sphere and begins the task. "Energy sphere, great mighty ball, show me the ones who took oath and joined the Fall." The sphere flashes the faces of all those who took the Oath of Alliance while Nathaniel checks the list for those who have been captured and those who are still on the loose.

"The list is long and I'm afraid that many of them have already Fallen onto the Earth," Nathaniel reports to Michael.

Michael returns to the business at hand. "We must go to Hell, it's there we shall find Azazel."

The Arch stands in a round prepared to cite the Sacred Prayer of the Apocalypse. Swords are pulled in the air.

"Omnipotent, Eon of Abraxis defend us in battle;

Be our protection against the wickedness and snares of those who have fallen from grace.

May your omnificent glory rebuke them, we humbly pray:

And do thou, O Prince of the heavenly host, by the power of Omnus, thrust into hell Abaddon, Sammael, and all the evil spirits who prowl about the world seeking the ruin of souls. So mote it be. So mote it be. So mote it be."

Michael concludes, "Time has come to bondage and shackle the sons of inequity!"

Celestial dust flies and engulfs the trail as six horses led by Kafziel forcefully pull a chariot of Archangels down the path destined for the hell pits of Saqun. Gabriel and Raphael ride with Michael in the chariot as Remiel, Raquel, and Nathaniel follow close behind. The three Archangels stand shoulder to shoulder as if there was a single charioteer driving the horses. Michael yells and pushes the horses harder and harder until the chariot flares like a darting comet.

Michael remembers the days of the Great Disturbance when there was much discord amongst the balance of power in the Heavens. Abaddon had secretly begun to roundup a group of followers who had pledged to back him in the event of a divergence from the angelic order. Many of the angels including Michael, Sammael, and Azazel had held Abaddon with high esteem and adored him as their leader. Abaddon was their leader and the great giver of light for he taught them knowledge of their own existence. Being one of the oldest angels he was closer to Omnus, therefore the other angels clung to his light and like a bug to a flame they were mislead by his growing, secret desire for complete control. Abaddon had mistaken their loyalty to him as a replacement for the love they had for Omnus.

In the days of the Great Disturbance, Abaddon lost to Omnus the control he had assumed he gained over the various angelic orders. Abaddon became spiteful and filled with vengeance. Michael and Azazel were distraught over Abaddon's departure from the grace of Omnus. Michael who had remained loyal to Omnus was risen up into the leadership position while other angels like Beliar, Wall, and Mephistopheles chose to follow Abaddon and Fall onto the Earth.

As the chariot enters the celestial yards of Saqun, Michael notices how quiet the home of Anahel remains in the midst of all the chaos. Most of the fugitives left Raquia and headed directly to Vilon, to the end of the path where they will Fall into the universe and out onto the Earth. Michael deliberates, "Did Azazel run with the others to Vilon or could they have waited for me to leave Machonon to exit through the Gates of Paradise?"

Extra security has been provided around Anahel's house but there does not appear to be a need. The Sentinels and Chalkydri army appear to be bored and restless. Michael feels compelled to search the grounds and the Hell House out back to be assured that Azazel is not there and that Semjaza remains in place, but his chances of finding any of Abaddon's disciples in there is becoming unlikely.

Michael, Gabriel, and Raphael dismount the chariots and run around the Hell vents blowing in the yard of Anahel's house. They keep running even though the vents blow Hell fire near their tracks as they run up the path to the main entrance. Raphael runs ahead of the group and signals them to follow him as he goes around the main house and takes the path out to the docks that lead to Hell House.

"Where's Anahel?" Raphael shouts while scanning through the thick fog.

"He's always out there somewhere rowing the raft and working on the pit. He'll be here soon," Michael informs the group.

Up from behind the three Archangels comes Ambassador Anahel. "If you are looking for Azrael you will have to blow the bugle hanging off the dock post."

"Anahel! My boy! How are you?" asks Gabriel.

Anahel laughs in a boyish giggle as he always does. "Gabe! Michael!"

"Hello, neighbor," says Raphael as he reaches toward Anahel, extending his hand with the grip of the fraternal Arch.

Extending the grip and the subsequent Arch embrace Anahel reports, "I feel violated! Downright violated!" Anahel says while throwing his hands up. "Azazel breached my house and freed my prisoner."

"Semjaza!" The three shout.

"Here comes the raft now," Anahel says as Azrael approaches.

The raft approaches from out of a thick wall of fog. A tall dark cloaked figure rows the raft with a long oar made of molted metal. On the raft next to the tall figure are the two Warden angels Sheburiel and Hadrial. They stand over a pile of slain Fallen angels lying on the floor of the raft. Their solemn expressions indicate bad news. As the raft makes it to the edge of the dock Michael can see the two slain Fallen angels on the top of the pile are Auza and Uzza. This for sure is a contrasting sign that indicates a great victory for the Arch order yet Michael cannot figure out why warrior angels are so gloomy with faces of defeat. Gabriel too is feeling a sense of triumph over the demise of two of the closest comrades in Sammael's entourage.

Raphael can no longer hold his excitement and greets the two with congratulatory welcome. "Job well done! It's about time we had some good news today!"

"Two of Sammael's most prized or is it three?" asks Gabriel.

"Yes, who else is it that you have slain down in battle?" asks Raphael.

Hadrial and Sheburiel toss Auza and Uzza off the raft, and then slowly roll over the third Fallen angel revealing Semjaza. The Archangels jump and cheer in joy, celebrating a victory unforeseen without a great battle. Michael is so happy he embraces the two angels and raises their arms in victory, but their arms fall immediately back to their sides.

"It's not our victory!" shouts Sheburiel breaking the cheers of the festive moment.

"Well explain! Tell me who?" Demands Michael.

Sheburiel continues, "We ran into Azazel and..."

"And who brother?" ask Gabriel.

Sheburiel responds, "Auza, Uzza, and Semjaza were attacking Azazel who was defending the human. We aided and won battles against Auza and Uzza, but Semjaza was slain by Janus."

"Janus?" the trio asks.

"Yes, Janus. Something about revenge for Jazire."

"So let me get this right," says Michael. "Is the human not a prisoner?"

"The human is not a prisoner, but a traveler in search of light. He seeks possession of Matey's Angel Dust. Azazel used the human's need to rise to Vilon for Angel Dust. Azazel's intent was to free the Fallen but... I feel he holds no allegiance to the Fallen," explains Sheburiel.

"It's the same that Miriam reported. Janus felt no obligation to act without being under duress of the oath," Gabriel further reflects on the situation.

"Azazel and Janus should have come to us," says Michael.

"There's one more important issue," says Sheburiel. "Azazel mentioned something about the Chancellor obtaining the key—"

"The KEY," the trio responds.

"He can Fall to any place in the universe if they open the gates with that key. Sammael can find Paradise," informs Raphael.

"Thanks to Sophia, Paradise is lost," responds Gabriel.

"But he could Fall onto the Earth? In the portal there are too many possibilities of where he could go!' Raphael says while taking short pacing steps and breathing rapidly.

"He'll never, I say never, get pass Uriel and Metaphon. He'll run into his own demise," Gabriel asserts.

"We can't put our own affairs over the safety of the humans. We must go to Matey. That's where the dust is and that's where we will find Azazel," Michael instructs. "This is the divergence Abaddon was hoping for to buy the Chancellor time. Sheburiel you come with us. Anahel, have Azrael dispose these shells in the pit. Hadrial have the Chalkydri army meet us in Machonon and hurry, if Sammael and his disciples try to go through the gates Uriel and Metaphon will need their help."

CHAPTER ELEVEN

The House of Sandalphon

Jerry crosses through the energy pane into the House of Sandalphon. He feels a new sensation unlike any he has ever felt before. He feels a whole body transition. A naked sensitivity radiates over his body like a tingly hair-raising energetic vibe that makes his skin feel brand new. He feels odd and unfamiliar with his newness. He opens his new eyes like they have never seen anything before.

The transition into the interior of the home serenely greets his new eyes with pastel colors like a floral gathering of carnations. Jerry continues further on his journey. Walking inside Jerry feels light and weightless as each step sinks into the floor like a soft sponge. His steps grow softer and softer until he feels like he's walking on sunshine.

The softness of each step leads Jerry into a gentle fall. Jerry smoothly falls down onto the floor like sliding into warm water. The spongy floor cradles him like he's sitting on a cloud. The house makes him feel like he is floating and falling all at the same time. Floating and falling down, down, down into the house's tenderness like a dewdrop into the center of a flower.

Jerry is not afraid, as the walls of the house grow narrower and closer until it envelops him into a tube of soft serenity and pure peace. The walls surround him with a loving warm embrace that holds onto him and brings him further into the home. Jerry feels like a baby in a soft and gentle womb. He feels peaceful. He feels at home.

Falling down, down, down, into the tenderness of the soft walls Jerry has no fears and no worries as he release control of himself into the gentleness of the slide, like a cozy drift off to sleep. "I have made it to Heaven," Jerry says as if he has truly arrived for the first time on this trip. Jerry weeps. He weeps without sorrow and without pain. A cry that releases all of his humanly worries and concerns. He cries for his return to innocence. Jerry is at ease. Not a concern in mind. Not a worry in his head. Finally the true feeling of being happy has arrived. "I'm in Heaven... finally."

A new sensation of light enters Jerry's eyes. It's a golden light that shines from an angel's sword. A sword is raised high and then swiftly swings down towards Jerry who has only begun coming out of his haze of happiness.

Abruptly breaking out of his cloud of joy, Jerry is startled with fear and screams, "Ah!"

Jerry moves out of the path of the sword's strike and rolls over onto his knees quick enough to miss a swing towards his head.

"You are in violation of a holy sacrament," says a voice from behind the bright glare of the sword.

Jerry eludes several more swings towards his head. "Oh my, God! Oh my, God!" He shouts. His chest rises and falls rapidly as he tries to catch his breath. The swings stop while he sits on his knees wide-eyed with heavy breathing. Jerry ties to focus beyond the glare of the sword to see the face of his attacker.

Jerry pleads, "I just need... I need... some Angel Dust." Still on his knees, Jerry raises his hands as if he's being arrested. Breathing heavily Jerry tries to explain his presence. "I..." heavy panting, "I didn't mean..." panting continues, "I didn't want to bother... I wasn't going to steal it. Are you Mister? I uh... mean to say... Your Honorable... Your... Your Excellency... Are you Sandalphon?" Jerry asks while kneeling, trying to catch his breath, and squinting to see beyond the sword's shimmer.

"You have violated... ahem... violated—"

A slight giggle interrupts the statement.

"You are in violation..." A child's laughter breaks from behind the shine of the sword. "A human," says the Seraph while giggling. "You are as fragile as Omnus said you'd be. Oh, I'm sorry to have frightened you. Don't be afraid."

"Who are you?" Jerry asks while batting his eyes trying to adjust them from the gleam of the sword that has lowered from over his head to the floor.

"Well... I have many names, but I like to be called... well I'm not sure if there is a name for it in your vernacular." The Seraph pauses for a moment then exclaims, "I know!" While raising his pointing finger in the air he says, "You can call me Victoriconvivacilousgracalotory! Yes I like that! You got it? Repeat! Repeat!" demands the Seraph. Jerry swallows hard and remains silent. Still trying to take in all the sweeping changes he finds it too hard to concentrate at all. "Are you still scared?" the Seraph asks. "I wasn't going to slay you. I thought you wanted to play. Don't worry. You are safe here. This is our house. We all live here."

As the psychedelic colors of the tubular walls fade and draw away, a home of sorts is revealed. Visual acuity and mental clarity slowly returns, but Jerry now becomes more mystified by the Seraph's youthful appearance. As he tries to refocus his eyes the Seraph comes into view in the form of a young child, not a powerful warrior angel that Jerry was expecting.

Victoriconvivacilousgracalotory toddles about the house with his powerful astroflare hanging from his holster. The astroflare is almost as long as he is. The astroflare hangs with its tip dragging on the ground, like a child that has found a toy too big for him to play. The Seraph attempts to ease Jerry's fear by offering to show him around the Fifth House.

"Come now, come. Let's go!" the Seraph demands. "I must show you everything. There's so much to see."

Jerry rises to his feet and follows the young Seraph as he is escorted through the house. The Fifth House of Matey is the main angelic residence in Heaven. It's where all the angels not residing in the other Houses of Heaven call home. The residents in the other Houses of Heaven each serve a particular duty, such as Wardens and Sentinels. Most of the angels here in the Fifth house have no other heavenly duties, or interest in the Earth or other parts the galaxy. This is Heaven, so there is no other place they'd rather be and no other pure form of concentrated bliss, peace, and loving energy. All things adored and valued on Earth are present in abundance in this House of Heaven. A great quantity of jewels, gold, silver, sardius, topaz, diamonds, beryl, onyx, jasper, sapphire, emeralds, carbuncles, and other unknown materials ornament this celestial home. The home glitters with a dusty sparkle that shines throughout every hall, on every wall, and every marble embellished floor. The shiny residue reminds Jerry of his mission.

"It's Angel Dust! That's the shimmer and glistening that I see. It's everywhere. It's naturally abundant here," Jerry thinks to himself. "Um... excuse me... Victor," Jerry says trying to be polite about not remembering the young Seraph's long and elaborate name.

"Who!" The Seraph responds.

"Ahh... Vic...tor—"

"Victori-con-vivacilous-gracal-otory! You must get it! You must get it right!"

Jerry continues following the young Seraph. "Is there a... is your father around?"

"He's always around silly."

"It's important that I speak with your—"

Jerry's thoughts are interrupted as spheres of light zips through the room and travels further into the house. Some spheres come closely up to their heads then quickly zoom away. Each sphere is bright and glows with an electric hue of various bright colors before fading to a white light as they disappear off in the distance leaving a trail of Angel Dust.

"Don't mind them. They get into everything. It's just a game. It's just a game!" says the small Seraph, as he waves off two more spheres zooming nearby. "So what's so important? What do you need to speak with father about?"

"I need some... I need Angel Dust to save my wife. Something placed a spell on her. She is very ill," Jerry explains.

The Seraph stops walking as they arrive inside a room filled with vases and several chests. "Well why don't you just take it? Look around there's plenty," says the Seraph while stretching out his arms pointing out the abundance of Angel Dust all around them.

"I was told it can't be taken, it can only be given."

"You're scared!" the Seraph taunts while pointing at Jerry. "I knew it!" shouts the Seraph.

"No it's not a matter of being scared," Jerry quickly explains. "I just want to follow the rules."

The Seraph projects a high-pitched squeal toward passing spheres, "Eeekkkkk!" He darts his eyes at the spheres as they zoom further into the house then turns his attention back towards Jerry. "Do you know what that means?"

Quickly shaking his head then responding, "No... no I don't."

"Victoriconvivacilousgracalotory!" screams the Seraph holding his hands to the temples of his head. His body illuminates with a fast pulsing glow of light that slowly fades away. "So you're a rule follower? Well follow this..." the Seraph pulls an astroflare out of his holster, waives it in the air towards Jerry, and commands, "Gather up this Angel Dust in one of the golden vases from this room and go save your wife." The Seraph looks around at all the various jewel filled vases in the room then further instructs, "Don't empty the vase just take the jewels too. That's my rule now follow it!"

"Will... will that be alright with your father?"

"Just like a human... you follow the rules when you fear the consequences. No matter how difficult or misunderstood the rule is, if you fear the consequence for noncompliance the rule is followed and gladly accepted! No matter how ridiculous!"

"No, that's not always the case."

"Oh...?"

"Sometimes we refuse to follow the rules if they are not fair and justified," Jerry answers.

The Seraph's body swells with pulsating light. "Did you not feel the rules were fair and justified when you illegally entered the kingdom of Heaven!" screams the Seraph.

"I didn't know it was... illegal. I didn't even believe it was possible." Jerry continues to explain, "Once we arrived all I could think of is the reason for why I came here. I had my moments of reconsideration but I was already here. The Angel Dust was all that I could really think about—"

"Well take it!" Sandalphon quickly demands of Jerry. "You could have chose to stay behind and refused to enter the Kingdom of Heaven, but you didn't! You didn't because all you can think of is your own needs! Right?"

Jerry pauses and tries to gather his thoughts. He relies on his trial training from law school. "There are a lot of different theologies and opinions about our creator. There has not been any single accepted decree governing how to understand or even believe in the existence of such things. There is not a precedence set on how one is to enter the kingdom of Heaven. There certainly haven't been any--"

"Here it comes," the Seraph interjects.

Jerry continues, "Any evidence to guide us on this issue. All we have is our faith."

"Faith can be a powerful thing for the plight of the mortal soul!" the Seraph replies.

"It didn't serve us well back before the days of the New Gaia, a time when wars--"

"Your wars!" the Seraph firmly substantiates.

"Faith-based wars!" Jerry quickly challenges before changing his tone. "Pardon me. Um... religious wars Victori... grace... they were global conflicts of utopian ideology. We finally got it right!" Jerry proudly expresses then continues in a modest tone, "The only threat we have now is your war." Jerry looks away trying to not look accusatory.

"Our wars?" the Seraph asks while his wings glow brighter with vigor.

"This battle of good versus evil. It's not our fight!" Jerry explains. "This battle between Michael and Abaddon, Sammael and Gabriel, and Good versus Evil. We didn't ask to be a part of this!"

The Seraph pauses to think for a moment then responds, "You're right." The Seraph takes another moment for deep thought then he continues, "Father was going to scrap the whole project, but... he was asked to forgive you." Recalling a quote from the past, "For you know not what you have done. Because of your ignorance is what was given as an reason to save you." The Seraph's wings begin pulsating slower while he reminisces. "Father seemed to have lost interest in mortals. He left us in charge." Pausing with heavy thought before continuing, "The project was to... die by attrition, just go away on its own."

"Project!" Jerry says while leaning back with a wrinkled nose. "Good to know we're just some damn pastime! Ah... I'm sorry—"

"You are loved!" The Seraph responds. The young Seraph continues touring Jerry through the house. "Very, very much so, but you were suffering in willful transgressions and ignorance. Your souls come from the same source as mine. It's cherished and a very important part of the universal light."

"Then why are we still suffering?"

"You have the right to live out your destiny. In the end those with faith will rejoin and those who have lost their faith will perish in the light," the Seraph explains trying not to scare Jerry. "Don't worry it will be peaceful. We are not the barbarians some of you make us out to be."

"So now that Samuel and his followers have Fallen onto the Earth we'll have to fend for ourselves?"

"I... think it may... push up the clock a bit," the Seraph responds while still trying to approach the discussion with caution.

"What! Victo..." The Seraph stares at Jerry with eagerness and hope.

"Victori...con..vivacilous...gracalotory?" Jerry says with some confidence.

The Seraph glows bright with joy spreading his wings high and proud. "Yes! Yes! I knew you could do it! You mortals always come through in a pinch!"

"Victor... let's cut to the chase, Sandalphon," Jerry says trying to sound firm but subordinate.

"You're smart too. It takes a while, but nevertheless impressive," Sandalphon responds.

"You mean to tell me because your battle has once again spilled over onto the Earth we have to suffer the Apocalypse? It's our demise?"

"You knew this day would come," Sandalphon warns. "It's in your literature. In some form or another all humans fear a day of destruction by way of natural, supernatural, or man-made events."

"It doesn't have to be like that! We just need protection from unforeseen events. We need some understanding and awareness of outside threats. Some damn DIVINE intervention would be nice!" Jerry catches his tone again. "Excuse my manners... Victor, Sandalphon, Your Gracefulness. What I'm saying is, we need some reason to have faith again."

Sandalphon stops the tour inside a room with a large sphere that depicts several images of scenes on Earth. Sandalphon pages through the scenes showing various images of past notable mortals as they deliver speeches and address the human culture in various times out the existence of humanity. "We have given you many protectors, saviors, pundits, priests, clerics, preachers, ministers, pastors, saints, monks, prophets, and clairvoyant people. We even sent angels and various other creations that were rejected and ousted by mankind."

"Not lately," Jerry corrects. "You are talking about ancient times."

"Not in New Gaia times?" Questions Sandalphon. "In a time where everything is explained by science? Our methods would have to be much too vulgar to not be scientifically annulled and dismissed!" Sandalphon's wings begin to swell with pulsing light again. "Besides it's not about forcing compliance. It's about faith and endurance. It's easier to believe without having your faith tested. If we go showing such vulgar displays of omnipotence we'll get a lot of followers who take sides out of fear. A soldier of fear will lose the fight against evil a lot quicker than a faith-tested warrior."

"Maybe some you can recruit and others you can't, but again we didn't ask to be a part of this war."

"That's why the project is to be discontinued."

"Please stop talking about us like we're a bunch of misfit toys."

"Trust me you are not that fun to play with anymore. In fact, most of us never even mettle in the affairs of the mortals."

"Sorry to have disappointed you all."

Sandalphon stares at Jerry who apologetically drops his head in embarrassment. "It's our failure not yours," Sandalphon mercifully replies.

"I can't believe that you created all this and you're not willing to keep fighting for it. Why did you create us? Do our souls exist only to populate your army like some kind of proving ground?"

"Something like that, but it was wholly intended to be a place where there would be no good versus evil. No wars, no battles, no sides to take, a complete paradise but Abaddon spoiled that for us."

"Now you are just going to allow him to win and throw it all away?"

"We've waited centuries upon centuries before resorting to that, but now with Sammael on the loose the stakes have been raised again." Sandalphon paces the floor. "I know about what you and Azazel did in Raquia. Now the Fallen has increased upon the Earth. There will be chaos like you have never seen before."

"Maybe it will bring us closer together."

"Many of you will succumb to Abaddon's mercy."

"Not if I can help it!" Jerry shakes his head and wrings his fist. "If I only had half the strength I've seen in these angels."

"Ha! Ha! Ha! Ha! You! You would fight Sammael?" Sandalphon walks while shaking his head then he spins around. "You only came here to save your own family not humanity!"

"I didn't know what was at stake! What good is saving her to only see the world around her in chaos?"

"Sammael's disciples will TEAR YOU APART! They'll destroy your body and your mind then they'll go after your soul. New Gaia, Ha! You'd be all alone! A crusade of one! No one would believe you! If they detect your divine mission... they'd reject you. A mortal with angelic powers... your own people will call you an abomination, a freak, and they will destroy you before Sammael could ever get a chance," Sandalphon warns.

"Isn't the rule to be discrete and to act without vulgarity?" Jerry asks before continuing, "I would detect them, lure them out somewhere, and handle the situation somehow out of view of the people," Jerry explains.

"Sammael's disciples are former angels of the warrior class. They won't be easily detected. They'll be so neatly hidden amongst your New Gaia men you couldn't find them let alone fight them."

"Not without some help."

"Even if I gave you the strength of a warrior and an astroflare it takes more than a show of strength. When they can't beat your body they'll test your soul and you are not strong enough."

Jerry and Sandalphon pause in the silence of heavy thought.

Breaking the silence, "I knew... I knew there was something wrong with the world. I knew and that makes me strong enough," Jerry explains.

"Are you sure?"

"Yes."

Sandalphon walks over to a display of several swords. He selects one, brings it over and hands it to Jerry. Jerry holds the sword up trying to look brave but the sheer weight of it reminds him that he has no training. He tries to rely on his old fencing experience to guide him but her realizes this is not a sport. Feeling the weight of the sword and the world on his shoulders Jerry continues to hold onto to his position as the New Gaia protector.

Sandalphon draws his sword and strikes it up against Jerry's blade. "Sammael's demons will tempt you to misuse your power. They will attack your soul. Asmodeus will attack your purity. He'll give you many mortal desires for luxurious possessions and temptation of the flesh. Are you strong with chastity?"

"Yes, without lust," Jerry says as he holds his sword with a defensive stance.

Sandalphon swings another blow towards Jerry's sword "Mammon will attack your self-control and have you indulge in your own gifts. Are you strong with temperance?"

"Yes, without gluttony."

Sandalphon swings harder strikes against Jerry's sword. "Beelzebub will attack your sense of generosity. Can you do it with charity?"

"Yes, without greed."

Sandalphon swings two more quick blows to Jerry's sword testing his ability to keep his grip. "Belphegor will try to make you lazy, weary, and wear down your persistence. Can you do it with diligence?"

"Yes, without sloth," Jerry responds as he moves his feet into a duelers stance supporting his weight on his back leg and holding firmly onto his sword.

"Leviathan will try to make you resentful of those you serve and protect without a return of gratitude. Your reward comes from the Heavens. Can you be patient?"

"Yes and without wrath."

Sandalphon swings his sword harder with several blows closer to Jerry's head giving him enough time to make some defensive moves. "Sammael will test your loyalty. He'll show you those who reap your rewards while your efforts go by defamed and unappreciated. Can you do it with endurance?"

"Yes, without envy," Jerry says as he moves quickly to block the strikes from Sandalphon's sword. Click! Clack! Jerry's breathing increases as he looks over at his opponent who doesn't seem so young anymore.

"Abaddon will attack your modesty and dedication. Are you strong with humility?"

"Yes, without pride."

"If you can fight these seven vices, I'm sure we can work out a plan for your people's salvation." Sandalphon lowers his sword.

Jerry lowers his sword and tries to slow his breathing while noticing how challenged he felt by an angel who wasn't even trying to hurt him. "Even if I could detect their presence I can't fight Sammael and Abaddon."

"I know you can't! They're way out of your league, mortal. Abaddon will be here under guard but still his influence goes way beyond our gates. That's a battle for Michael. I'm sure if you could manage to take the others into custody Michael and Gabriel would be glad to handle the Terrible Two." Sandalphon paces for a while then continues, "It's all very entertaining but it's just that, entertaining."

"Well wait a minute... my world isn't for your entertainment. What if I could actually capture them? How many are we talking about?"

"Oh, yes!" Sandalphon laughs quietly as he takes Jerry's sword. "You'll have to go through Sammael's closest entourage, the Four Fiends of Fury. They'll do anything to protect the Captains of Chaos. Let's see... in the Fury there is the fire starter; Xaphan, the second in command; Eblis, the father of devils; Ialdalbaoth who's quite the charm, and then there is the very volatile and violent Rahab. If somehow you managed to get to them, that's only half the battle. We haven't even begun to discuss Abaddon and the Triad of Terror." Sandalphon looks over at Jerry to see if he has wavered in his bravery. "The Triad is Beliar, the supreme adversary of all angles and quite a nasty handful to capture. She's a Seraphim class angel.

270

Then there is Wall, the Grand Duke of Hell. Last, but certainly not least, is Mephistopheles the destroyer. Before you get to any of them you will have to take out the two kings Araqiel and Penemue who are hidden in plain sight amongst the mortals. They'll be close to the politicians and rulers. By the way, we should not forget Semjaza, Auza, and his brother Uzza they know of you already," Sandalphon warns.

"Well you can check them off," Jerry reports with some relief. "Azazel took care of Semjaza and two of your Wardens took out the twins."

"Poor Semjaza, so many souls, so many losses." Sandalphon pauses silent in heavy thought. "Azazel used to be one of the best. How far he has Fallen... but he showed some merit I guess."

"Does that mean you forgive him?"

"Forgive? Oh no! That's Cassie's game over in the Seventh House. Treason doesn't fly well over here!"

"This is all hypothetical right? You don't really expect me to fight this war do you?"

"Didn't you just volunteer? Didn't you say—"

"Yeah, but I was... it was an analogy of what I would... if I could..."

"Oh, I could train you, equip you, and teach you all you need to know. I can even give you some assistants to take with you. What I can't do is give you the courage and the will, or deliver you from evil when you go into this fight. There will be no mercy. No one will step in to fight for you. But like I said, you are not strong enough."

"Wouldn't it be easier for your TRAINED army to handle such affairs?"

"Like I said... we've lost interest. It has been discontinued."

"We've been discontinued!"

"You can take the Angel Dust and go. Remember it's not your war."

"If the alternative is apocalyptic then give me the power to defend myself."

"Adorable... but first we need to discuss a matter of your own salvation!"

"My salvation?" Jerry says with widened eyes and a gasped mouth. Wondering where this conversation is going Jerry stares deeply into the warm incandescent eyes of Sandalphon trying to look strong and dubiously accused.

Sandalphon relaxes his wings and brings the pulsating glow down to a warm florescent radiance. "Why did you want to end it all? What was so bad about your life that you wanted to throw your gift away?"

"Suicide? I never wanted... I was just--" Sandalphon gazes deeply into Jerry's eyes with his bright pupils mystifyingly piercing, yet subtle, and therapeutically engaging.

Jerry knows he can't tap dance around the truth or tell a lie. "Maybe he only knows my actions but not my motives," Jerry thinks while trying to cleverly find away to avoid the conversation. "Maybe he can read my mind." He further thinks as thoughts began to race through his head. "Suicide? You are referring to the doctor appointments? You must have it all wrong, I mean seeing it from a distant perspective. It wasn't suicidal thoughts really it was... depression," Jerry says trying to be clever. "You know these mortal bodies are prone to all kinds of chemical imbalances," Jerry further states, hoping that he reflected the conversation away from his most private thoughts.

"So it's Father's fault, a flaw in your vessel?"

"No, no!" Jerry quickly corrects as to not sound accusatory. "It may be nutritional and environmental," he replies hoping that he sounded convincing. "The air down there isn't what it used to be with all the industrialization and pollution," Jerry says with a nervous chuckle, attempting to change the topic.

"Oh!" Sandalphon replies while slightly raisings his wings again. "It has nothing to do with your feelings of not fitting in and your anger at not being able to answer the enigmatic predicament?"

"What enigmatic predicament?"

In Jerry's voice Sandalphon mimics, "Something is just not right with the world."

"There's no way around it. This is why he says I'm weak," Jerry thinks to himself. "Look I am much stronger now that I know what I know. Obviously I was right. There was and still is something wrong with the world." Jerry answers as he continues to surf his thoughts for less suspect excuses. "We live in a time where if the answer is not scientifically and empirically supported it's not permitted to be discussed in public forums. There is a very fine line drawn between church and state. Even private religious establishments are frowned down upon. The New Gaia Movement controls political offices worldwide like a global government. It's not that religion is not discussed at all but it's only included in significant historical events and not elaborated on any further than what has been academically supported through the New Gaia World Institutional Review Board. Any further discussion is a violation of the International Guiding Heretic Rule. All these rules make it hard to publicly ask deeper questions about the meaning of life without the risk of being ridiculed or at times, prosecuted. But I knew something wasn't right. I know many people who feel the same way but no one's willing to talk about it except in the shadows of speak-easy academic circles and underground chat rooms. There's freedom of speech, but if you are citing violence and violating the New Gaia Peace you can be imprisoned, or they will say you are crazy and need therapy. Clerics have to be licensed by the New Gaia Discourse and Philosophical Exchange Department and their sermons are monitored," Jerry rambles. "I have said it out loud a thousand times that something is just not right with the world, so it's best to be in therapy in the event I need to say, 'Don't mind me I'm just a crazy man talking!' It's a strategic move not a real need."

"Interesting defense, but I know that Azazel intrigued you about coming to the Heavens because—"

"I was going back. I had to help Karlisa... my family," Jerry quickly replies.

"Jerry! Don't do that." Sandalphon scorns. "It's futile and unnecessary. I know you were hoping that Azazel would go back for you. You trusted him to deliver the Angel Dust while you escaped the wrongness of your world. You had been thinking about it for a very long time now and here is your chance to run away to paradise."

"Get out of my head. You don't know me," Jerry says while holding his hands to his head and clawing his fingers through his hair.

"Who would have thought there'd be a problem with paradise? It's just another war-ridden world with villains and deceptive practices. There's no relaxing on cloud nine and sun bathing in the garden of paradise. So you figured, I may as well go back."

"No! I... was always going back!" Jerry's eyelids become heavy while his mouth dries leaving a lump in his throat. 'I considered it. I was intrigued by this place that held all the answers, but I found my answer and I was going back."

"It is not the answer to what is wrong with the world that you seek. It is the answer to what is wrong with you that you are questioning, is it not?"

Jerry's breathing becomes shallow as the blood vessels in his head pumps faster, beating in his ears like a drum. He swallows with a dry mouth as he stands on frozen knees. Feeling exposed with nowhere to run he stands naked and alone.

"What is wrong with you, Jerry?"

"I don't know," Jerry mutters in a low deadpan voice. Jerry realizes that he's at the end of his diversionary tactics. He must now surrender the truth. Feeling weak and weary while dropping to his knees he gives in to the question, "I... don't know," Jerry repeats.

"You do know and you will tell me!" scorns Sandalphon.

Jerry looks up and cries, "I don't know!"

"Yes, you do!" Sandalphon scalds.

"You don't... love me!" Jerry weeps.

"No! No!" Sandalphon says while shaking his head. "Is it I or is it that you don't love yourself?" asks Sandalphon. "And why," Sandalphon kneels down near Jerry. "Why don't you love yourself, Jerry?'

"I... don't know!" Jerry answers while shaking his head with closed eyes and a quivering mouth.

Sandalphon reaches out to Jerry's chin. "You don't know?" he asks while holding up Jerry's face and looking into his eyes.

Jerry repeats, "I don't know," while staring back and trembling into the piercing luminescent eyes of Sandalphon.

Sandalphon rests his hands on Jerry's shoulders and stares compassionately into his eyes. "Abaddon makes you see only the iniquities of your existence in an effort to make you feel worthless and unloved by your Father, your Lord which art in Heaven." Jerry is speechless as he stares with rapidly blinking eyes. "Love who you are, not who Abaddon tells you to be." Sandalphon continues, "Jerry don't think you need the answers to your world or ours. In the end we will all be brought into the light."

Jerry inhales deeply and blows the air out through his lips to relieve the tightness in his chest. He asks, "Until then... how do I remove these negative thoughts from my mind?"

"Your mind will never allow you to achieve your greatest self-image. It's a trick of pride, Abaddon's favorite sin."

Jerry closes his eyes tightly as a tear escapes the corner of his eye.

"Oh my Lord was so right. You are a delicate little lamb." Sandalphon stands up and continues, "Love yourself son of Omnus for our father has and will always love you." Sandalphon reaches out to help Jerry up to his feet. "I am granting you a pardon for

your violation because I love you. We all love you,"
Sandalphon informs Jerry.

Jerry's body stops trembling as he calms down.
He begins to breath normally again.

"Allow me to show you those who love you."
Sandalphon motions a call and several spheres
zoom into the room. The spheres hover around
them, but now Jerry can see them more defined.
The spheres are embodied faces and wings of
angels. Some of the spheres morph into more
childlike mortal figures like Sandalphon. They gather
around Jerry touching him and grabbing his hand.

"Come all and meet the son of Adam!"

Jerry follows Sandalphon back through the
circular pane from where he made his entrance into
the Fifth House. Sandalphon takes Jerry out into
the celestial yard where Seraphim, Cherubim,
Thrones, Dominions, Powers, Virtues, Nations, and
Guardian Angels greet him. All of the angels are
eager to meet the son of Adam as they step
forward and take a bow. The Archangels gallop
onto the scene and dismount their horses. Each of
the Archangels comes forward to greet Jerry.
Michael and Gabriel step up first and bow to Jerry.
All the other angels bow and kneel down to the
human, son of Adam, and Omnus' most cherished
creation. Some of them had never seen a mortal
before in the physical form. It is an exciting time in
the Heavens,

Jerry tries to humble himself as he becomes
amazed by all of the angels treating him as if he is
royalty. He feels elated and honored to be in their
presence. He gazes around in sheer excitement and
joy for a time has come where he no longer feels
like an intruder, but a guest. Angels crowd in from

every direction as they come to greet Jerry. It's an angelic extravaganza like no other ever seen in the Heavens before. Today Jerry is a big star.

Jerry stands and gazes through the crowds of angels seeing all the various forms from spheres of light to humanlike Guardian Angels. Orbs of light descend down onto Matey and transform into walking angels. The huge crowd lined up to meet him overwhelms Jerry.

"Hello I'm Nephon of Persidis. Welcome."

"Hello I'm Jeuli, a child of Barcus. It's a pleasure to meet you says a genie before flashing away.

Jerry's ecstatic moment is interrupted once he spots Azazel and Janus being held under the arrest of the Arch. "Oh my God, am I one of them now? Is it us versus them? They were my friends." Jerry thinks to himself as he slowly loses his euphoric feelings. "I must do something, but what?" Jerry keeps smiling and trying to listen to the angels as they introduce themselves. "Aza should have known better! Why should I jeopardize myself for him? I can get my Angel Dust and leave. I don't need him anymore." Jerry thinks to himself.

Several angels begin to crowd and make a circular ring of flying angels above Jerry's head. The angels sing a song with some of lyrics in their own language which is beautiful yet indistinguishable.

"Victori-con-vivacilous-gracalo-tory!
Wel-come to kingdom land,
The home of Omnus glory."

As angels sing in the skies above, other angels gather on the grounds below. Several angels are clamoring and making sounds of joy as they talk and chatter about the human.

"A mortal here in Heaven?" an angel says in disbelief.

"First the trail and now the Apocalypse, it's all coming together," another angel declares.

Two large Spheres enter the sky and rest over the head of Sandalphon. The angels circling above stop singing. A blanket of quietness pulls over the crowd of angels. Sandalphon's wings spread higher, wider, and taller. His body glows brighter. An energy field dresses him in military regalia. The pulsating light of his body flashes faster and faster as his entire form transitions into a galactic orb of divine light. He is now Chief Administrator elder angel Sandalphon in his purest form. Sandalphon rises into the sky joining the other to spheres.

"Don't worry my friend," says Gabriel as he strides over to Jerry. "It's the Holiness of Sachiel and Cassiel the Merciful. They are the Chief Administrators and Commanding Elders of the Sixth and Seventh Houses."

"Thanks um…"

"Gabriel. Archangel Gabriel."

Jerry remembers the gatehouse in Vilon and Janus. "Um… I'm sorry about that gatehouse situation. I knew not what I was doing. I was following Azazel but—"

"Say no more. We'll deal with him once and for all and as for Janus, what a disappointment. We'll make an example out of them for all to follow."

"Oh, God," Jerry thinks to himself. "Not to make any excuses, but Janus was under a lot of pressure too."

"Janus could have come to me. Don't worry. It's not your concern," Gabriel instructs.

Turning his attention back to the three great spheres Jerry asks, "What do you suppose they are discussing?"

"I hope it's the start of the Apocalypse. It's time to get this situation under control," says Michael as he walks up into the conversation.

"Michael let me introduce you to Jerry," Gabriel turns to Jerry. "Jerry this is Michael administrator of the Fourth house and Chief Commander of the Archangels."

Michael bows again. "Don't worry. Azazel will pay for what he has done to you. Tricking you to get him here. It's a travesty and an abomination."

"Well he was under the influence of Sammael."

"He took the Oath of Alliance. There is no excuse," explains Michael.

While looking away trying to not sound defensive, Jerry replies, "Except... maybe because... he was bound and left helpless in the desert."

"Where he should have remained!" says Gabriel.

"You sound merciful. That's a good virtuous behavior. It's ok. You don't have the whole story," Michael says trying to be empathetic to Jerry's limited perspective.

"Bring Janus to me," commands Gabriel to the Warden angels. "It's time for you to face your offenders and identify those who have robbed you of your innocence."

Escorted by wardens Janus comes forward shackled in chains of light.

"Bring forth Azazel," Gabriel commands.

The Archangels bring Azazel over to Gabriel. The wardens stand Janus and Azazel side by side. "Are these the two souls that tricked you and brought you into the sanctity of the Heavens against your will?" Gabriel asks.

Jerry swallows hard and answers through his teeth in a low tone, "Well... it wasn't exactly—"

"Wait!" Azazel interrupts. "Do with me what you will, I have surrendered to you, but please I beg of you for a moment to have words with Jerry."

"Silence! You foul beast!" shouts Raphael.

"Give him his tongue for he shall be put into permanent silence soon," says Michael.

"Thank you," Azazel continues, "I know I have done many things against the divine order of the Arch and broken the sacred rules governing the relations with mortals. I have fallen to temptation, indulged my deepest desires, and fornicated relentlessly with no temperance. I did what I've done because I thought it was what I had to do to survive in a foreign land. I was never a victim of Abaddon's pride. Chancellor Sammael never tricked me with envy for neither he nor the son of man had anything I wanted," Azazel inhales deeply and continues. "My failure was falling into Leviathan's wrath and anger for being restricted from a forbidden love. I was full of Belphegor's laziness for I did not fight to stay strong and I took the easy way out by fleeing from my home. I was making it the best way I knew how in a strange land, chased away from the one place I wanted to be. I didn't know it then, but I had a lot of time in Dudael to think about it. My greatest atrocity was being weak to Asmodeus' desire, a desire for a forbidden love. The love of Sophia," Azazel concludes.

"The very thought of it makes me SICK!" screams Raphael.

"Well isn't it a simple... crime of passion?" Jerry defends.

"There's nothing simple about treason," says Gabriel.

The conversation is interrupted as Sandalphon returns to the crowd and walks over to Michael and the rest of the Arch Order. Sandalphon informs, "It has been reported that many of the Fallen were captured, but several of the most notorious fugitives have escaped and have Fallen onto the Earth. According to our Archangel Nathaniel, Eblis, Iadalbaoth, and Rehab have escaped and joined Xaphan completing the Four Fiends of Fury once again. Beelzebub, Leviathan, and Mammon have all escaped completing the Seven Vices. The Triad of Terror has never been captured. The allusive creature Behemoth is still on the loose. Penemue, the infamous child of Barcus has escaped and all seven of the Rulers of Wrath are rampaging on the Earth as we speak. The quantity of intruders that have Fallen upon the Earth is more than any mortal culture can handle. In consideration of this information the elders have reached a decision," reports Sandalphon. "Even with Abaddon safely in the prison of Raquia, the scales of justice have tilted. The Apocalypse shall wait no more!"

There is a rumble and a great commotion amongst the crowd. General Seraphiel and Commander Michael quickly call together the guards and the Archangels. Several spheres zip through the skies while other important angelic figures scurry off to unknown locations. The majority of angels in the crowd remain in a dazed silence while a few others whisper back and forth. Fervent, yet frightened, the crowd awaits further instructions while those in strategic positions run off to their post or other assigned duties. Each of the Archangels mount their horses with Michael in the lead, followed by Gabriel, Raphael, Uriel, Nathaniel, Raquel, and Remiel who has taken out his bugle preparing to signal the march into the apocalypse. In a battalion behind the Archangels, General Seraphiel is comparing a scroll with Jeremiel, the Overseer of Mercy who is accounting for all the souls to be resurrected and judged. Two scrolls are prepared, a black scroll of names for the damned and a silver scroll for the souls to be shown mercy. In the second battalion Azrael from the Hell House in Saqun is riding Hayyoth a fiery horse. Azrael has come to collect the black scroll.

The angels above, still in a circle and hovering over Jerry, are now motionless with faces frozen in solemn expressions. Jerry continues standing next to the Warden angels who have Janus and Azazel in their custody. "I can't believe this is happening," Jerry thinks to himself. "I win a trip to an exotic resort with a return flight on the Apocalypse? This can't be happening. There has got to be a reason for why I am here. Why me? I have to do something."

Now back in his youthful childlike like appearance still equipped with an astroflare dragging from his hip holster Sandalphon tatters up to Jerry. They watch several battalions of angels gearing up like the start of a parade. The energy of prewar tension is in the air. Many of the angels are relieved as they feel this war has been prolonged for way too long. This is the beginning of the end of the war of good versus evil. The praise angels circling above are somber for they are benevolent for the souls of mortals caught up in the coming chaos.

"Are you still willing to take the oath?" asks Sandalphon.

"Are you kidding," Jerry replies, as he looks around at all the battalions of angels. "Look at all these warriors. If it takes all this, what was I going to do alone?"

"A preemptive and quiet strike may be the best strategy. This way is violent and vulgar. There will be mortal casualties, chaos, and disorder, but it will be quick and thorough."

"It can't be done more discretely and without bringing an end to humanity?"

"We tried that before. Now with the New Gaia man there's not much interest in sparring them. Most of this is necessary for gathering up souls and bringing those who need to be judged before the Throne. Maybe a little bit overdone, but they've been waiting a long time for this."

"It's all too much for me. All I wanted was to help Karlisa and now..."

"You did what you had to do because it was what you felt had to be done. Regardless, Abaddon and Sammael knew this day was near. You were only a last minute divergence. These warriors would still be here preparing for this event if you had not come. The question is, what are you willing to do about it now that it's you who has been lead to this moment?"

"That's right put it all on me? I thought the elders have ruled already. I don't see them calling this off and placing such an important mission in the hands of a mere mortal!"

"Mere mortal? Did Azazel not tell you that you couldn't go back as a mortal?"

"What! No!" Jerry responds. "What does that mean?"

"An angel travels back and forth from the Earth because they are immortal. Azazel was bounded to the Earth and yet he was able to rise to Raquia through you. He used you to rise because both of you are immortal."

"I don't understand," Jerry gazes inwardly. "I'm just a human?"

"You have a human form because you ascended to the Heavens in the embodiment of your mortal form," Sandalphon explains. "Your body and soul was never put to rest."

"Well that's because I'm not dead."

"Mortal's have two deaths, a physical death and a spiritual death. If you die without releasing your physical death your body remains with your soul."

"So what you are saying is... at some point I... No! No can't be I would have... No!" Jerry runs over to Azazel. "Aza! You are every bit of the dirty scoundrel that they say you are!"

The Wardens break out into laughter.

"You didn't tell me about my immortality!"

"Oh, brother!" Aza groans.

"You naive humans," a Warden says while chuckling with his peers.

"Did I die back there?" asks Jerry. Aza remains silent. Jerry grabs the already shackled and bounded Aza by his collar. "WHEN? WHERE? Did I get sick like Karlisa? How did I lose my mortality? Speak to me!" You dirty..." Jerry catches himself as he becomes mindful of his surroundings.

"Would it have made a difference? Would you have not given up your life for hers?" says Aza.

"I... I had a right to know."

"I knew the answer. I knew how much you loved her. All that I have done was done because I'm your friend. I adore you Jerry. You are my savior. You set me free from that damn hell in Dudael."

"I should have let you rot there!"

"Jerry I don't know what they've been telling you but they are all wrong! Wrong!"

"Oh..." responds Sandalphon.

"Elder Sandalphon. Your Gracefulness, I have been around for a long time too. I am a Cherub by lineage. I worked in the historical archives. I know there is a way—"

"Don't even speak of it!" warns Sandalphon.

"Jerry! I've been nothing but truthful to you and I'm being truthful now. The Divine Order of the Upper Room. The all powerful! OMNIFICENT!! They give it, they take it away, and they give it back if they want to."

"What is he talking about?" Jerry asks Sandalphon.

"What he's implying has never been done!" Sandalphon informs.

"Never?" Aza questions Sandalphon. "Jerry you are still human because you ascended that way. A mortal can't walk the Earth with extensive knowledge of the Heavens. It has always been forbidden! But an immortal like a Guardian Angel can freely descend. Jerry you don't need mortality to keep your humanity. You only need to take the Guardian Oath of Concealment, a promise to safeguard the secrets that you have been exposed to here in the Heavens. You can be anointed by the light and walk the Earth again."

"A human cannot take the oath!" Sandalphon responds.

Azazel looks at Sandalphon making deep eye contact. "No, not a human..."

"Don't even think of it!" Sandalphon says shaking his head in refusal.

Jerry looks over at Sandalphon then over at Aza. "Think of what! Will somebody let me in on my own fate?"

Azazel nods and announces, "Behold... the Earth Angel."

"What is an Earth Angel?"

"It doesn't exist!" Sandalphon answers.

Azazel explains. "An Earth Angel is scaled down from a two-winged Guardian Angel. It has the likeness of a human. A wingless angel, an immortal human."

"It won't be permitted!" shouts Sandalphon.

Jerry pauses in thought before breaking the silence. "Wait! You knew that I couldn't go back as a human but you were entertaining the thought of me returning. How would I have done that?"

"He... entertained?" asks Azazel. "He knew! Your Gracefulness! You knew!"

"I've always known and little known is that it has been done before. You will never be a step ahead of me, Azazel! Never! The problem is Jerry has not accepted a divine mission."

"If it saves my wife and gives me back my life with her, I'll do it. If it will save humanity from this war, I'll do it!"

"You'll need training and some trustworthy assistance."

"I'll take Azazel."

"I said trustworthy!"

"He has never lied to me."

"Give him time."

"He's a master swordsman and very talented with the astroflare, the only weapon that can slay a Fallen angel and bind it to the Sphere of Concealment." Sandalphon looks up at Jerry with his eyes widened, "That's right I've been paying attention."

"I would have to release his binding, give him back his wings, recommit the oath," Sandalphon rolls his eyes back in his head. "I'll have to forgive him. The elders would have to forgive him!"

"You mean you will have to call upon the... MERCIFULNESS of Cassiel?" Azazel says with a cocked head.

"Shut up! I can't believe this!" Sandalphon paces the ground. "What am I doing?" Sandalphon's wings glows vividly. "Azazel can train you and fight with you but you still need someone I-I-I-I can trust. Someone who can balance out your ignorance and Azazel's weakness so he doesn't go astray."

"Will you take any volunteers?" interrupts Janus.

"You are not a warrior. Your own siblings are amongst the fugitives."

"They... were adopted," Janus says with rolling eyes. "I need a chance to redeem myself. I can ascend and descend the fastest. I can move around the Earth the quickest. Through the use of the sphere I can locate the Chancellor and all those other fugitives. I can –"

"That's enough! I will take this request to the Upper Room. Summon Michael, Gabriel, and General

288

Seraphiel," Sandalphon orders one of the Wardens. "Are you sure you want to do this?"

The three look around at each other for confirmation. Janus looks at Jerry with widened eyes and a nodding head. Azazel stares back at Jerry with his shoulders broadened and his chest sticking out. He stands shackled but straightened and tall. In a moment of silence the two stare at each other with piercing eyes.

Breaking the silence, "I'll stand with my brother. I'll fight with you," Azazel says confirming his allegiance to Jerry.

"We will do it," Jerry answers.

"Do what?" Michael asks after rushing up to them with Gabriel and Raphael at his side.

"Come with me," Sandalphon replies. "We have a great many things to talk about."

CHAPTER TWELVE

The Upper Room

Sandalphon, Michael, Gabriel, and Raphael trek down the seventh hall in the Seventh House of Cassiel. The seventh hall guard escorts them along the way. Sandalphon explains to Michael their purpose for being there and the request that is to be made. Michael listens to his elder Sandalphon, but he is not showing that he is in agreement with the mission. Raphael and the guard trail behind as the three pass the door where Sophia once resided and find it sealed with a radiant energy band. They continue past Cassiel and the Irins' rooms. Finally the group reaches the door of the Upper Room. Raphael immediately takes a door guard position next to the Seventh Hall guard, as he knows he is not permitted to enter. Sandalphon steps through the energy pane of the Upper Room entrance. Michael and Gabriel stall for a moment, take a deep breath, and then step in the doorway and through the energy pane into the Upper Room. They find themselves at the bottom of a stairway and notice that Sandalphon has gone up ahead of them. They continue up the stairway and each step glows a radiant red light when they step on each stair. Finally the two enter the top of the stairs where they find yet another door. They cannot enter through this next energy pane they must be drawn inside by the Irins. Two sets of hands extend from behind the colorful field. Both Michael and Gabriel firmly grasp onto the palms of the extended hands and are gently pulled through the pane into the Upper Room.

Michael and Gabriel gaze from left to right in search for the others, but all they can see is a long stretch of barren rock. The Upper Room appears to be on a mountaintop. The wind is blowing lightly as cosmic clouds of various florescent colors move briskly through the dark night sky. Occasionally, lightning strikes through the sky, but there is no thunder and no rain. Michael turns towards the Irins and asks where the meeting is taking place. One of the Irins stretches out his arm and points his long fingers from underneath his cloak towards a table resting in the middle of the mountaintop plane. Although the sky above is dark a single star brightly lights the meeting area. Michael and Gabriel walk over to the table where they find the other attendees already in place. The table is long, oval shaped, and suspends in the air without the use of legs. The escorting Irin takes a seat next to his twin brother on the thrones located at the center edge of the table. At the east end of the table two six-winged elder angels, Cassiel and her brother Sachiel sits next to each other. At the other end of the table sits Sandalphon, but the throne next to him is empty. Michael and Gabriel take seats in the thrones at center of the table across from the Irins. On the center of the table rests the Right Eye of Abraxis, an optical sphere used to monitor various events throughout the universe. Next to the sphere is a casting bowl used for collecting jade and crimson voting marbles. Each of those seated at the table have one of each colored marble. There is a track circulating the table's perimeter for casting marbles as they roll down into the collection bowl. Voting at this table is democratic and does not require a unanimous ballot.

Sitting at the end of the table with all her six wings spread high and tall in the throne behind her, Cassiel opens the meeting by striking a gavel on the table. Sitting to the right with his hands folded under his chin and elbows resting on the table, Sachiel has his eyes wandering about, not focusing on the meeting attendants but chasing some playful thoughts in his head. With Cassiel's third strike of the gavel he rolls his eyes over at her, sighs, and blows through his lips. Cassiel and Sachiel's wings are very much like elder Sandalphon's glowing bright, light, and lucent yet dense with the radiance of divine energy. Sachiel and Cassiel are dressed in formal regalia indicating a high-ranking position in the Divine Order. Cassiel wears an emblem on her left chest with the picture of a sheathed sword indicating the sign of mercy. Her brother Sachiel wears an emblem that depicts exploding rays of light for the sign of holiness.

Down the table the Irins wear the same regalia but both of their emblems picture swords drawn and pointed up, it is the sign of the Divine Guard. Michael and Gabriel wear emblems with arching swords. At the other end of the table Sandalphon wears an emblem picturing a hand with rays of light being released from the center of the palm, it is the sign of grace. The throne next to him remains vacant.

Cassiel begins the meeting, "This is what we call a clarifying committee. We will enlighten you on the events that occurred as a matter of cause and effect and those events that occurred because they were effected by a cause."

Sachiel looks up at the sky and whispers, "Lord, help us." Cassiel waves her hand in the air and lightning strikes in the distance. "That better had not hit my last Gliese Peg-nosed Mountain Dog!" Sachiel warns.

Cassiel continues, "Because we knew that Sammael was going to attempt to free Azazel we caused the event that made it so by sending Zuriel, disguised as a stable manager with Michael's horse Kafziel, to a resort on Mount Hermon. It was from this location that Kafziel rode into Dudael with the mortal called Jerry." Cassiel looks around to see that all in attendance are paying attention, especially her brother Sachiel who she stares down momentarily.

"Please continue," Sachiel requests.

"By assisting Sammael's ill-fated plans we hoped to foil his ultimate goal and capture him. It is unfortunate that our cause was affected by demons that cast spells on the mortal's wife Karlisa. That event influenced the mortal to seek a cure in the Heavens. It was also highly unanticipated that our very own Janus would later give over the Golden Master key as a condition of having taken the disgraceful Oath of Alliance."

"A crime for which Janus is currently being confined by our Wardens," Gabriel interjects with a nod and smile.

"Was this mortal predestined to take this journey?" asks Michael.

"I selected him myself," answers Sachiel. "He seemed like a good fit with his inquisitive and intuitive nature about the world. He couldn't afford the trip so I let his wife win this contest I set up on the radio. I was so smooth the way I rigged it. It was such a fraud, but quite simple." Sachiel continues, "You see humans love radio and TV shows."

"Are you finished?" Cassiel asks with a gasp mouth and crossed eyes.

"Oh... go ahead... you may continue," Sachiel waves her on.

"Azazel was able to rise to Vilon with the help of this mortal. We allowed it to be so."

Michael looks at Gabriel dumbfounded and shocked. "Why? Why was I not notified of these proceedings? Am I not an elder? Am I not a member of this Divine Order?" asks Michael.

"Your eagerness to fight with Sammael, and most definitely Abaddon, would have caused a ripple in the divine energy. Abaddon would have sensed your anticipation of these events and ceased the plan altogether," Sandalphon answers. "By the way, has anyone seen Metaphon?"

Everyone looks around at each other but no one answers.

"In fact we believe it's why Abaddon chose to remain in Raquia when his path was seemingly clear for a getaway," adds Sachiel.

"Even as our plans became effected by Sammael's maneuverings we felt that it did not matter if Azazel was successful in freeing the prisoners as long as the gateway in Vilon was heavily guarded. The Irins oversaw this duty themselves," continued Cassiel.

The Irins nod in agreement.

"Many of the escaped fugitives were slain or recaptured. None made it through the gateway. What we did not anticipate is Sammael obtaining the Golden Key in Saqun and using the key to get through the Gates of Paradise and out into the universe," concludes Cassiel.

"Impossible, that portal is protected by Uriel and Metaphon, so there's no way they escaped through there!" Sandalphon exclaims.

"The last report from Uriel reads as follows: There was a great many fugitives slain as a decoy while others escaped through the portal. Metaphon was last seen chasing Sammael through the portal but it is not certain where in the universe they have gone."

"I must go assist my brother at once!"

"Slow your chariots! Thanks to Sophia's multiplication of the universe there are numerous places they could have gone. Many of which are still not known to us."

"We sent out several search parties. As soon as we are notified of his location we will send a ready-team of Sentinels and the Archangels," Cassiel informs. "In the meantime I believe you had a request of this council?"

A feeling of tightness in the chest takes the words away from Sandalphon as his nostrils flare with heavy deep breathing. He can barely think of anything else other than running to the rescue of his brother. All else is unimportant at the moment. To think of Metaphon going up against Sammael alone in a place where he could be outnumbered and vulnerable to Sammael's trickery is too much to fathom. Sandalphon feels that he is ultimately responsible for what happens to his brother and that he has failed him.

"All things aside, I would feel angry and bewildered too if it had happened to my dear brother Sachiel, not that it matters as Metaphon is my brother too," Cassiel says trying to extend her mercy to his sorrow.

"This is why we must end this now!" demands Gabriel. "What are we waiting for?'

Collecting his composure, Sandalphon answers, "I have another plan. There have been too many failures in execution, way too many souls gone astray, and much too many casualties of this war. We need to be smarter, less vulgar, and more preemptive. I suggest a radical approach," Sandalphon requests. "Azazel has expressed his will to recommit to the order in an effort to assist with an alternative approach to handling this matter, but it would call for his salvation and reestablishment into an angelic order."

"Never!" says Gabriel,

"It's a trick," adds Michael.

"If it sounds tricky to us, imagine what it does to Sammael. I feel strongly enough to bring it before this council, but yes it is a gamble."

"That's not even the half of it," warns Sachiel.

"No it's not. The human Jerry, he too has pledged an allegiance to this plan, but he will need training that he can receive from Azazel. To further complicate things, as you know he cannot walk the Earth in his human form after having been made familiar with the intricacies of the Heavens."

"So what are you suggesting? An omnificent?" asks Michael.

"Yes, a wingless but immortal, Earth Angel."

Laughter breaks out amongst the order. It is a rare occasion to see an emotion expressed from the Irins, but they too join into the laughter that makes the motion even more humorous.

"What will this Earth Angel do for us? Apprehend a Fallen Seraphim?" Gabriel chuckles. "Xaphan alone will take this Earth Angel out!"

The group comes out of order as they discuss and laugh in disregard of formalities.

Trying to talk over their ramblings Sandalphon shouts, "An Earth Angel trained by one of our most talented swordsmen. They'll never see it coming!"

Sachiel still in the midst of laugher shakes his head and informs, "You've been using too much of your own Angel Dust—"

Laughter erupts again.

Shouting, "Our Divine Directive of Protection is to carry out all that is possible before declaring the Apocalypse! I believe that this is possible and I call upon a vote," demands Sandalphon.

Fiercely striking the gavel, "Order! Order!" shouts Cassiel. "A vote is before us. A vote has been requested and these are the facts: Azazel is to be unbounded and reestablished so that he could descend back to the Earth as an assistant to the mortal we now know as Jerry. Once the mortal

Jerry reenters the realm of the Earth he is to not meet his death, but instead he will become a creation of a new omnificent Earth Angel, physically a wingless class angel, but yet an immortal. Electing these options will delay the 10,000 years trial and brings upon a divergence to the Apocalypse. It requires an anonymous vote of the majority. Casting a jade marble will be a ballot of approval and casting a crimson marble will signify a ballot being disapproved. In the event of a ballot that cannot be balanced one way or the other by Metaphon, Omnus will have to supremely settle any unresolved issue from the Upper Room. Angels cast your vote."

Michael sits quietly in his throne with a marble in his hand. He ponders his vote over and over but can't make up his mind. Michael has been waiting for the Apocalypse for a very long time, but with Abaddon still being held in a Raquia prison cell the thought of the Apocalypse isn't as enticing as he imagined it would be. There would not be the epic battle against his number one adversary. Rounding up the rest of the infamous leaders would be victorious, but not quite the challenge he had in mind. Shameful thoughts of his own pride and vanity begin to eat away at his conscience, but he still waits to think it over a little while longer.

The Irins have no trouble making a decision and simultaneously cast marbles into the tunneled tracks. Gabriel looks over at the Irins and wonders why they were so quick and decisive. He takes both marbles in his hand and rolls them back and forth in his palm. Gabriel reviews all the divine rules of judgment in his head and focuses on Sandalphon's statement about the Divine Directive. His thoughts are interrupted by the sound of Sandalphon placing a marble into the tracking tunnel. He takes a deep breath and releases one of his marbles into the device.

Cassiel looks around the room and monitors the casting of marbles counting those yet to be cast. She looks over at her brother Sachiel who is playing with both the marbles on the table, rolling and bouncing them into each other. She frowns and begins to breathe heavily. Sachiel looks over at her, shrugs his shoulders, casts a marble then rolls his eyes as he notices that she too has not yet cast a marble. Cassiel rolls her eyes back at him and extends her arm as another marble is cast from Michael, then she follows by dropping her marble into the tracking tunnel. All the marbles roll down track into the collection bowl like children on water park slides, falling into the pool one by one.

Cassiel nods signifying the start of a ritual. The Irins stand and proceed over to the collection bowl. One of the Irins lifts the bowl and brings it over to Sachiel for inspection.

"Have all the marbles been collected," asks Cassiel.

"Yes," responds Sachiel.

"There is a member of this order who is not present. Will the casting of that marble be required to balance the vote?

"No," Sachiel responds. "The vote is not unanimous but an additional vote one way or another will not change the results."

"Irins do you agree with Sachiel's report?"

The Irins nod their heads in confirmation.

"What is the leading vote?"

Each of the members' eagerly awaits the results, but no one wants to look overly excited or supportive of any result. The Order of Divine Angels has always been one of harmony and accord with every decision as it is accepted as a divine judgment and not one of a personal agenda. Sandalphon sponsored the vote so there is little question about how he cast his marble, although it is kept a secret assumptions have no place in the workings of the Divine Order. Sachiel takes his time with the announcement and Cassiel can't help but wonder if he is trying to build anticipation, or is purposely making an attempt to annoy her. She sighs, rolls her eyes again, and then raises her hand in a similar fashion as before as if to threaten Sachiel's Mountain Dogs. Sachiel's eyes widen then he quickly focuses on the marble count.

"The motion has been supported by a majority vote," Sachiel quickly answers as he looks for Cassiel to drop her hand.

"With the power invested in this Divine Angelic Order we will initiate the omnificent ritual of producing... ah what did you call it?" Cassiel asks Sandalphon.

"An Earth Angel."

Light snickering is heard from the council members.

"An Earth Angel," Cassiel continues. "Let's site the prayer to lift the bounding of Azazel and to restore him to his original state of a Cherub."

Gabriel's face becomes hardened, but he remains quiet. Sandalphon reaches over and places his hand on Gabriel's hand. "You will not be disappointed in the end my brother," Sandalphon comforts.

"No brother, it's ok. I need to be merciful and forgiving, but most of all I need to put my complete trust in you, especially in a time like this," Gabriel responds looking over at Metaphon's empty throne. "I'm here for you my brother."

Cassiel continues, "Unbound the chains that cling to Dudael! Free the damned soul Azazel! Release the binds that kept him there and allow his wings to soar free and clear!"

The skies darken outside the House of Sandalphon. The angels hovering above Jerry and Azazel stand shoulder to shoulder holding hands while spinning in a circle like horses on a slowly moving carousel. The chains on Azazel's arms and the shackles on his feet fall off on their own. The Wardens sense something extraordinary in the divine energy. They stand back, observe, and wait for orders from General Seraphiel who keeps them at ease and refrained from making a move.

Cassiel continues, "Restore the energy from the Cherubim class. Give four wings to this angelic mass!"

Azazel slumps to the ground into a deep sleep.

"Bring the light of Abraxis the maker of beings! Make a mortal immortal let him realize his spiritual wings, but when in the physical form the wings shall not be seen."

Jerry falls to the ground next to Azazel and both are in a deep sleep.

General Seraphiel and the others back away until Azazel and Jerry are left alone under the circle of hovering angels. A great energy sphere enters the center of the circling angels. The sphere slowly darts rays of light that float through the air and down into the bodies of Azazel and Jerry. Each arrow of light is emitted in tiny streams that float in single file lines until they reach their bodies and penetrates through their mass. Their bodies radiate with a blue hue of light as each ray breaches through the outer shells. Azazel and Jerry's bodies pulsate and glow like flashing beacons.

General Seraphiel steps up into the front of the crowd that has formed a circular perimeter around the two bodies. "A miracle is upon us. Come witness the Omnipotence work with thine own eyes. Let us be thankful and glad to have been here to see such a miracle carried out before us."

The carousel of angels hovering above is circling as they begin to sing.

The angels sing, "O-ri-or."

General Seraphiel complements, "Bring us into your glory."

"O-ri-or."

"Bring us into your presence."

"O-ri-or."

"Bring us into your power Lord."

"O-ri-or."

"Provide us with your majestic protection."

"O-ri-or."

"Bless us with your grace upon this most holy place."

"O-ri-or."

"Have mercy on us Lord."

"O-ri-or."

"You are the holiness of our existence."

"O-ri-or."

"Bless these sprits with your omnipotence Lord."

"O-ri-or."

"Bless them with your omnificence."

"O-ri-or."

"Bring them into your omnifarious angelic order."

"O-ri-or!" The angels above continue singing as they circle faster and faster.

"Let them rise up!"

"O-ri-or!"

"Orior!"

While still in a deep sleep, Azazel and Jerry's bodies rise off the ground.

"O-ri-or!"

"Rise!" Seraphiel shouts.

Their bodies rise higher and higher.

"O-RI-OR!"

"RISE!" he screams.

"O-RI-OR!"

"RISE!" he wails.

There is silence.

Silence continues.

The great energy sphere zooms out of the sky and disappears into the distance. Azazel's body animates as four wings sprout from his shoulder blades. The crowd bursts with excitement and chatter. Azazel flies out over the crowd in fully restored angelic form. General Seraphiel tosses up Azazel's astroflare. Azazel catches the astroflare and swings it with a pose of grandeur and grandstanding splendor like a parading champion.

The body of Jerry Xeven remains suspended high in the sky and continues to rise up through the center circle of the hovering angels. Finally he stops rising and seven of the angels reach out into the center and touch Jerry's body with the tips of their fingers. Jerry's body glows brighter and brighter with each touch of an angel's hand. Soon after the seventh touch Jerry's unconscious body springs into motion, flying higher and higher over the angels and far into the sky.

Jerry opens his eyes when he notices the warm galactic atmosphere breezing over his face. He is awake and aware that he has changed. He looks at his arms and legs as if he is seeing them for the first time. He waves his hand in front of his face and watches the hazy glare of his angelic ambiance flutter in front of his eyes. He notices that he is floating far in the air, but he is not afraid. Jerry soars through the sky. Jerry rolls and twists his body through the galactic energy force in the sky as he flies proudly above the House of Sandalphon. His new angelic body streams Angel Dust created from his very own life-source as he flies in the sky. "My own Angel Dust and plenty of it," Jerry says smiling as he recalls his reason for being there. "Hold on Karlisa. I'm coming."

Jerry joins Azazel and the two fly down next to General Seraphiel who stares at Azazel with a wrinkled brow and a tight jaw. There is silence as the General recalls Azazel's wrongdoing in the Seventh Hall of Araboth and the years of pursing him after his Fall onto the Earth. Seraphiel swallows hard and takes a deep breath before allowing himself to declare, "It's all forgiven. Welcome back, brother!"

The two shake hands and embrace. The crowd applauds and cheers, "Grace! Grace! Grace! Grace!"

Seraphiel turns to Jerry, grabs his hand, and holds up his arm while announcing to the crowd, "Behold an Earth Angel!"

"It is done," reports Cassiel to the others in the Upper Room.

The meeting is adjourned and all rise from the table to prepare for exiting the Upper Room, but Sandalphon is still in his throne with his head hanging down and his body slightly slumped over onto one side. Michael looks over with the intent to congratulate him on a referendum sanctified by the order, but Sandalphon does not appear to be well.

"Sandy," Gabriel shouts, but gets no response except from Sachiel who lets out a small snicker.

"VICTORI... GRACALOTORY!" shouts Sachiel while giggling lightly to himself. Still there is no response.

"Can't you see the poor boy is sick with grief and worry?" says Cassiel. "Irins, please see him back to Matey."

"It's all my fault," Sandalphon mutters. "I should have gone," he says with an inwardly gaze.

"We will accompany you back to Matey," informs Michael as he and Gabriel follow the Irins who have Sandalphon slumped in between the two of them as they leave the room.

Looking around and seeing that they are alone Sachiel says to Cassiel, "You should have told him. Metaphon's dead and you know it!"

"We do not know! I sent a search and rescue team."

"He should have known better. He ran through the portal into an unidentified universe in pursuit of Sammael. Sounds like a death trap to me."

"A trap we didn't have to set."

CHAPTER THIRTEEN

Dissentions and Dimensions

Michael and Gabriel return to the grounds outside of the House of Sandalphon while Raphael and the Irins see the Gracefulness to his home. The angels are all gathered together to receive instructions on how to proceed with the Apocalypse. Battalions of soldiers all dressed and equipped with their gear are becoming restless and disgruntled. The excitement of the omnificent act only created a temporary diversion to the assembly of the guards who are now becoming impatient and agitated. Michael and Gabriel are in a private conference with General Seraphiel. The General's face slowly changes from one of a commander ready and eager to serve, to one that appears deflated of emotion.

"And you want me to go out there and tell them this?" asks General Seraphiel.

"You are the commander aren't you General?" replies Gabriel.

"In the past 10,000 years that has not been very evident," says the general as he inhales deeply and turns to go prepare for addressing the troops.

The rumble grows louder from the restless crowd of warriors as they wait on instructions for deployment. General Seraphiel plods his way to the center of the battalion staging grounds just under the hovering circle of singing angels. Azazel and Jerry join him and wait for his instructions.

Seraphiel steps forward while raising his right hand in commanding everyone's attention. In the palm of his right hand he holds a hot chunk of crust-covered, dark brimstone with orangish-red streaks of lava glowing from its crevices. "As I look out over these corps I cannot help but to be arrogant enough to proclaim that WE CANNOT be defeated!"

The crowd cheers.

"We are eighty divisions strong. We have all the houses represented here. All the orders of angels are present, standing tall and ready, willing and able, united and FORTIFIED!"

The crowd applauds and yelps sounds of military jargons.

"In one field group we have 100,000 warriors from the Chalkydri Army. We have 100,000 Guardians, 100,000 Nations, 100,000 Virtues, 100,000 Powers, 100,000 Thrones, 100,000 Cherubim, and 100,000 Seraphim. In all we are 800,000 angels congregated here on this place that from this day on shall be called Gracalot."

There are whispers within the crowd as the angels try to confirm the name with each other.

"Angels! Angels!" Seraphiel shouts trying to regain their attention. "In my hand I hold a piece of the molted crust from the pits of Saqun. The red lava you see oozing from the pores of this rock is from the blood stained grounds where many of our brethren fell slain by the sword of Abaddon. The very sword I have sheathed and hanging from my left hip."

The angels gaze at the sword in solemn silence.

"It's not the sword that I am concerned about, but this rock. This piece of Hell! It is this molted hell fire that concerns me." Seraphiel looks around holding the rock high so that everyone sees it. "The problem is..." Seraphiel crushes the rock in his hand and the molted lava leaks out and runs through the fingers of his crushing grip. "HELL is just not hot enough!"

Seraphiel looks around through the crowd as he rubs and shakes the pieces of rock and molted lava off his hand. "If Hell is not hot enough we are not ready for this battle."

The crowd erupts with gasps of shock and waves of disagreement rolls through the corps of battalions. The discontent grows louder and louder with unsettling anger.

"I beg to differ, sir! We are ready!" shouts an angel in the crowd.

"YOU ARE NOT! You stand down!" orders Seraphiel.

"ATTENTION! ATTENTION!" Seraphiel commands over the loud angry crowd. The crowd slightly quiets down.

"Twenty-four fugitives are on the loose throughout this universe because you have failed! Many of them have fallen onto the Earth. That is no surprise yet they still ran to where we knew they would go. Why? Why would they go there?" Seraphiel looks around for an answer from the quiet crowd. "Because they knew you would follow. They knew you would chase them right up to the front Gates of Gabriel while their Chancellor Sammael escaped out through the Gates of Paradise," Seraphiel reports. "It was a failure of imagination. We never thought they would challenge the guarded gate. Our brother Metaphon is missing. Uriel was seriously wounded. Sammael now has possession of the Golden Master Key. With that key he escaped through Gates of Paradise, a portal to various unknown places in the universe. The others ran right through you and fell onto the Earth. So now you want to go to war! Now you want revenge!"

The scorned angels stare down away from the eyes of General Seraphiel. Feeling deflated they remain silent and less enthused. Wings that were once spread high and wide are now hanging low and tucked in close to their bodies.

"Don't worry my brothers. The day you are waiting for is inevitable for it has already been foretold in the prophecies. As for now there is a new plan in place," Seraphiel informs as some of the angels begin to look back up at the General.

"You have seen an omnificent miracle to honor a vow of protection sanctioned by Your Gracefulness Commander Sandalphon. The Divine Directive of Protection over mortals has provided, when possible, an alternative, safer, and less vulgar way to capture our enemies. We MUST stand down in honor of this directive. If I may quote the writings of the great late Prince Hozi who said, 'Wars are not won by the swing of the astroflare but by the swing of the changing heart and the flare of the enlightened soul.' If you didn't know you should realize by now that a containment sphere will only capture the soul, not the spirit. A resilient prisoner plants the seed of patience and harvests the flowers of revenge. This war will never end if it's not fought from all sides. We must attack from the Heavens and from the heart. We must meet them where they are and avenge from within. Jerry, the Earth Angel is that attack from within. Along with Azazel who was amongst them, but is now one of us again, we will be stronger and wiser."

The angels stand in attention as their wings relax and spread out and up high. Several battalions whisper amongst themselves as the entire corps chatters with light discussion. A battalion pushes a single angel up front.

"Sir. General. I was there at the lake in Saqun that day our brethren were slain. I've seen the Fiends of Fury in action. I've fought with some of the Triads of Terror. No offense to Azazel and this Earth Angel, but alone they are no match for these fugitives."

The General nods in confirmation of the soldiers concerns. "We will be assigning a special unit, a team of Watchers will be on the scene at first notice that any of the Fiends or Triads is spotted. At that time Azazel and Jerry will step aside and allow the Watchers to intervene. Janus will accompany these two and serve as a scout to

310

locate the fugitives and as a messenger to bring status reports to the Heavens."

Janus, still shackled and cuffed, looks up wide-eyed and mouth opened. "Take these chains off! You heard him. I'm a messenger of Heaven. We are on the same team!"

Descent Through the Garden

An outlying planet in the universe is strategically hidden away leaving the budding of a psychedelic tropical forest unnoticed. Green shrubbery and pink trees complement an indigo blue sky in a way that is peaceful and placid, until commotion from below distracts its tranquility and replaces it with elements of disarray and lifelessness. The usual serenity of this obscure territory has become agitated by a foreign intrusion. The once lively, blowing, and refreshing air of this warm breezy tropical wonderland has now gone stale and dry. Branches and leaves are disturbed and shaken as a force rampages through the thick foliage, blazing a manic trail of erratic twists and turns. Turned up dirt, broken twigs, and crushed flower petals are suspended into to air before landing in a scattered freefall of muddled dust and grime. A trailblazer leaves behind a continuous path of ruined plant life and extends destruction across acres of thick bushes into a low-lying grassy plain. The hustle and scurry continues relentlessly for miles and miles with no predictable pattern. The scythe of a swinging astroflare destroys all that's in the way of penetrating deeper into the psychedelic coppice of harlequin greens and magenta bushes. Finally the trail stops.

In the midst of the bushes a floating astroflare is seen suspended in the air, hovering and bobbing on its own. A radiant golden halo appears, followed by a set of piercing silver eyes. Subsequently a silvery translucent outline of a six-winged angel comes into view holding the astroflare. As the body becomes more densely and fully defined the florescent blue skull of Metaphon appears. His nostrils flare open and close in rapid repetitions.

"Air? This is impossible!"

Metaphon has run himself into an unfamiliar environment that is detrimental to his immortality. The unfortunate need to breathe air is overwhelming and new. Metaphon pauses to catch his breath before continuing on with his search. He fiercely swings his astroflare with determination that something is to be found in the shrubs, but his dwindling immortality impedes his physical strength.

"I know you are around here somewhere."

Metaphon keeps searching and swinging the astroflare, clearing a path through the high greenery and pink thistle shrubbery. Soon he makes his way back out onto a grassy plain and starts running across the field. Metaphon runs up to a large rocky incline protruding from the ground. He climbs to the top to get an overview of the lands lying out ahead of him. He stands at the top and slowly scans the landscape. He sees fields of tall green grass, thin pink trees, and small blue birds flying away in the distant skies, but nothing else of interest. A thought comes to mind and he observes the scene once again.

"Life?" Staring into the distance. "In this uncharted territory?"

Metaphon looks around at the desolate and lifeless area immediately surrounding him. He closes his eyes, pauses in deep meditation connecting into the divine energy force. He is silent and still. He waits. He grips tightly onto his astroflare then swings around in a defensive move startling his lurking attacker, Chancellor Sammael.

Sammael with his six dark blue wings extending high up from his back is crouching in a warrior's stance ready to attack. A cloak covers Sammael's head but his identity is no mystery to Metaphon, his long time adversary. The time has finally come to make a stand for the moment of divine vengeance is near at hand. The skies above this arena, already still and stolid have now become bleak and dim. The Chancellor spear-holds a serpent-laced electrified lance cocked back over his right shoulder. Metaphon assesses his opponent and inspects his weapon, speculating on how Sammael may use it. He knows that even without a direct hit from the lance's dual serpent-tail tips he cannot endure many blows from the lance's electroshock.

Metaphon takes a step to the right maneuvering off the rocky surface to step back onto the ground but for every step he takes the cloaked figure takes a strategically opposing step. Metaphon knows it's not only a matter of who strikes first, but who has the leverage of higher ground and a supportive surface. Sammael has the advantage of standing closer to the firm support of the grassy ground but Metaphon has the higher ground advantage if the rocky surface is stable enough as to not cause him to slip on loose gravel. Both opponents are very aware of all the calculated points that advance or weaken their chance for a successful fight. Metaphon takes another step to towards the low grounds preferring to fight on a leveled battlefield. The cloaked figure takes a step back allowing him to lose the higher ground advantage. Metaphon continues to step towards the ground and his opponent makes the subsequent tactical moves. Metaphon finally steps off the rock onto the grassy land. A warrior's dance has begun as more frequent sidestepping and posturing transpire in the course of their positioning themselves for the initial strike.

Metaphon swings his astroflare around and tosses the handle from his left hand to the right hand while all along keeping his eyes fixated on his opponent. The dark figure holds his lance up in front of his torso, releases it with his left hand, twirls it around in a propeller-like cycle, and grabs it again. The center of the lance blazes with an electrifying red core covered by the twined body of two snakes. The two snakeheads on the staff are now animated and hissing while the tips of the snake tails remain sharp and pointed at the end of the lance. A large creature's eyeball, fixed as a handle on the lance, is in sync with its master, Sammael. The creature eyeball spins adjusting itself as the lance moves so that it never allows its master's opponent out of its sight.

"So, Sammael… I see you've been keeping your eye on me."

The dark figure removes his shroud with one hand while keeping a firm grip on the staff with the other. "It's you that needs to see the face that defeats you," scowls Sammael in his raspy voice.

Sammael lifts his lance up and out to the right thrusting a hit towards Metaphon's chest but stopping in mid strike to force a blow with the other end. Metaphon is quick and counter defends both strikes with his astroflare.

"I've waited all this time for that?" Metaphon taunts before plunging a series of blows towards Sammael's head and torso.

Sammael successfully blocks all of Metaphon's strikes. The two continue to dance the dueler's duel of bobbing, ducking, and swinging strikes only to be shielded from making bodily contact by the opponent's weapon.

"Come on, Sammael. You've waited all this time to prove your incompetence? I already knew the stench of it."

"The only stench you will know is the reek of your own rotten soul in this universe and it's Chancellor Sammael for when you start begging for mercy."

"You brought me here to this filthy, repugnant place to drain my immortality? You thought you could bring me down to your level and still you are beneath me!"

The two warriors dance and exchange more blows, at no avail.

"I brought you here to show you how foolish you are," Sammael responds in his usual grimacing squeal as he takes his lance and plunges the serpent tail end into the ground. The lance stands up straight with the creature eyeball handle still fixated on Metaphon, watching his every move. Sammael removes an astroflare from underneath the back of his cloak. "Maybe an old warrior needs to die the old fashioned way."

"So you think you can slaughter me with an astroflare? You want to return my soul so we can fight again?"

"You still haven't figured out where you are fool!"

Metaphon advances several more strikes towards Sammael's head and torso, but still he is not able to land a single deathblow onto his body. He heavily forces his way onto Sammael trying to overpower him and distract his ability to think of subsequent strategic defensive moves. He swings one strike after another over and over again backing Sammael up, causing him to stumble backwards, and lose his footing. As Metaphon's skull glows brighter it blinds Sammael and causes him to become disoriented. After being overpowered by rapid subsequent blows Sammael falls on his back giving Metaphon the advantage he's been waiting for to make a final strike.

Metaphon raises his astroflare high and angles it for the fatal thrust but he pauses momentarily as he is distracted by a third presence. The eyes of another entity have entered the arena. The distraction pauses Metaphon just long enough for Sammael's lance to quickly uproot and plant its serpent tail spikes deep into Metaphon's back. The sudden shock of pain sends a piercing jolt down Metaphon's spine. While contorted with pain he is perturbed by the mysterious eyes he has seen in the near distance. Sammael takes an advantage of Metaphon's weakened state by quickly scuttling to his feet. The snake tails of Sammael's lance releases continual electroshocks into Metaphon's back until he is feeble and worn. Metaphon, on his knees whaling in agony, drops his astroflare, reaches behind his wings and with painful apprehension pulls and rips the lance from his back.

Staring into the distance Metaphon can see flaming waves of red hair over a set of green eyes and a silhouette of a body hiding behind the rocks. Metaphon feels his immortality slipping away and his spiritual vitality fading. He holds his head back, panting for air to fill his near mortal body while he pats the ground around him in search of his astroflare but his recovery is too slow.

"It's a little to the left. Go ahead and grab it. The least I can do is allow an old ally to die like a warrior," Sammael offers as he prepares his astroflare for the victory swing.

Metaphon's fingers find his astroflare and grasp it firmly into his hand. "Omnipresence will shadow you," Metaphon warns.

"Whatever!" Sammael swings his astroflare and severs the head and soul of Metaphon. A piercing scream is heard in the distance.

Sammael raises his hand initiating the lance to automatically float through the air and land securely in his hand. "Good look out," he praises the lance.

"I know you are out there!" Sammael shouts while preparing for his departure. "It's quite a fantastic place you've created here. It sucks out one's immortality so no fool would dare come looking for you here. Brilliant! You figured them out too well. They adore the humans, yet they don't want to be them because like any other creation they too love eternal life." Sammael continues shouting into the distance. "To show you my appreciation for this horrid creation I'll let you in on a secret. If you are still looking for your boyfriend you may want to rise to Vilon."

The dark figure disappears into the universe.

Sophia's radiant eyes and fiery hair moves from behind the rocks, over to the beheaded body of Metaphon. She picks up his soul-vacated skull. "Sorry my old friend. Now the divinity wars will begin."

A brave man is a man who dares to look the Devil in the face and tell him he is a Devil.

President James A. Garfield

ACT III

CHAPTER FOURTEEN

Road to Damascus

General Seraphiel prepares the three souls to descend onto the Earth. Jerry, Aza, and Janus stand in The Circle of Divine Descent with their arms arched across onto their neighbor's shoulder. Gabriel leads the angels of Gracalot in The Prayer of Divine Descendent giving the trio divine permission to walk the Earth. They will not Fall, they will descend upon the Earth.

The prayer is cited:
"Take on this journey the blessing of Omnus, and may your travels be filled with providence. Take on this journey the message of Omnus, And may your words be spoken with eloquence. Take into your hearts a love that never parts, Then spread it throughout human condition.

Descend on a mission with a clandestine intention,

Then rise again with Omnus' permission."

The troika of retribution slowly descends onto the Earth like a space capsule floating back in from outer space. Gracalot and the images of Matey fade away in a vortex. Passing scenes of Machonon, Saqun, Raquia, and follows until they finally reach the exit through Vilon. Janus watches the gates of Vilon close behind them and disappear in the void like a child looking out the back seat window, watching a loving home gradually vanish into the far distance. Jerry is eagerly looking ahead for his return to Damascus and furthermore home to Cleveland.

Descending on the Earth was very much like entering the House of Sandalphon floating and falling down, down, down onto the Earth. A kaleidoscope of psychedelic color schemes pass by, engulfing the three descendants in a dwindling funnel. On this trip Jerry is as amazed and overwhelmed with ecstasy. He is happy to be going home. He closes his eyes and takes deep, long breathes with a smile. Jerry can't wait to tell Karlisa how insightful he was about feeling something not being right with the world, but most of all he just can't wait to see her. From this day on all in the past is forgiven, nothing in the past matters anymore.

Aza is not eager to leave the Heaven, the place he once again can call home. Aza knows that visiting the New Gaia will be nothing like it was thousands of years ago when life was simple with farmers, trade markets, and tent dwellers. In the hours after being rescued by Jerry, Aza took refuge in his room at the Tower of the Sun Resort taking in large amounts of data on life in modern times from the Gaia Net. The information he obtained supported the position that most angels have about mortal life on Earth, boring and overly complex. Again he visits the Earth alone without Sophia. Being estranged from his only true love, Jerry has become his only companion.

"How can I help," Aza asks. "What's your plan?"

"I was hoping you could tell me."

Aza is silent before finally suggesting, "Well we go get the girl... I mean... Mrs. Xeven. We get the heck out of... what are they calling it now... the Confederate of Arab States?"

"You know a lot for someone who was deserted for the last 7,000 years."

"Well I was a little bit of an icon and a pioneer for the Fallen. Demons loved to visit me to keep me updated on their evildoings and the current state of affairs," Azazel reports.

"None of your groupies attempted to rescue you?"

"I did say they were demons?" Aza responds with raised eyebrows. "They didn't know exactly where I was located. They knew the grounds were evil and spoiled out there due its desolation. The locals called the place... The contaminated garden."

"Oh, trust me I know. I never felt such thick bleakness until that damned horse ran off and lost us out there."

"Horse...?" Azazel says quietly, "Kafziel."

"Who?"

Aza stares at Jerry then replies, "Never mind," as he shakes his head. "The grounds were kind of a sabbat for demons and witches. They would talk to the ground never knowing exactly where I was buried, but I heard them."

"And now you're free to save the world."

"Now YOU are going to save the world. I am just here to assist you in any way I can."

"What do you get out of all this?" Jerry asks with a stern stare into Aza's eyes.

"You don't think my freedom after 7,000 years isn't enough?"

"Aza... It's going to serve our mission best for you to know... I may be human, but I'm not stupid."

"Good... Good," Aza repeats while nodding his head and rolling his eyes up into his head as if in deep thought. "There's a great many things we will need to discuss, but first let's get Karlisa back to Cleveland."

Jerry mimics Aza's nodding head. "OK... OK. So what do you suppose we tell Karlisa and the kids about you and Janus?"

"There's a great many things the children of New Gaia will need to be told and the truth will not set anyone free," Aza warns.

"You have children?" Janus asks with a big grinning smile.

The tunnel of psychedelic descent continues as they approach New Gaia into the Confederate of Arab States. The tunnel of descent beams into the Earth's atmosphere like a falling star.

"Um... well we are business partners. I just invested a huge amount of gold, uh... credits into your business and I'm overseeing my interests," Aza elaborates further on the plan.

"Oh, yes 100,000 credits. Where exactly did you get those credits?" Jerry inquires.

"The Chancellor. Apparently, evil has a platinum card," Aza informs with a tongue-in-cheek smirk. "The credits, coins, and the bank accounts. It's ridiculous how you humans have created so many ways to barter wealth."

"What do you suppose we say about Janus?"

The two look a Janus in silence.

"Mrs. Ziel?" Jerry suggests.

"I think not!" replies a slightly disgusted Janus.

"Gay hairdresser?" Aza inquires.

"I'm not gay. I don't have a sex," Janus informs.

"But you did have an attraction to Jazire?" Jerry asks.

"So! Anyone would," Janus replies with a snap and slight twist in the hips.

"Well for now you are a hairstylist. You do know how to do human hair?" Aza asks.

"I'm highly skilled in all the human arts... well not in anything violent or gross."

"And you're here to save the world?" Jerry sighs.

"I'm not saving anything. I am the messenger," Janus corrects.

The tunnel of descent rockets into the Damascus skies onto a hilltop overlooking the city. To anyone who may be watching the pierced sky, the descent is so subtle and quick it barely draws anyone's attention long enough to cause a stir. The descent barely registers as a weather anomaly, but somewhere some radar technician monitoring the skies with his advanced New Gaia technology notices the blip on his screen then turns away when there is no signs of repeat irregularities.

"We have descended," informs Aza.

The psychedelic funnel slowly fades away revealing a new scene from a hilltop in Damascus.

Janus, with eyes clinched tightly closed before looking out onto the foreign environment, slowly peers out onto Damascus. Soon after seeing the New Gaia for the first time in over 5,000 years Janus breathes in a sequence of taking long inhales, pausing, and blowing air out through the lips repeatedly. The breathing sequence repeats faster with each breath and each inhale becomes deeper, followed by faster exhales. Aza clinches his fists in preparation of conjuring up his astroflare as he looks out over the hilltop.

Jerry has his eyes closed too as the funnel dissipates and reveals his home planet. He has that feeling you get when a commercial airline hits the tarmac of your final destination. Jerry sighs with relief, although he has not yet reached his home in Cleveland. Jerry opens his eyes and now he is frozen with a dropped jaw, shallow breaths, and widened eyes.

The three stand together on a hilltop overlooking the city. Their bodies are silhouetted in the dimming darkness by an emerging moon. They have arrived shortly after nightfall. The mirror in Jerry's astonished eyes reflects no place like his known home. The three stand frozen by moonlight. Small drones zip through the sky only a few feet above their heads. The drones are so small and thin they cannot be manually driven from the inside. Electronic beeps from the drones with their flashing blinking lights whiz by every few minutes. Maybe it's the same drone. It's too hard to be sure in the twilight sky. The beep, beep, beep, beep sounds cold and unwelcoming, but not as uninviting as the scene in the distance. Across from the hilltop helicopters and military hovercrafts surround two large humanlike figures standing over 700 feet tall. Beams from large searchlights projected up from the ground cross-stream with spotlights shining down from the helicopters onto the protruding anthropoid structures.

"Oh, brother!" Aza sighs as he flexes his grip in a continual preparation for calling up his astroflare.

The mirror of Jerry's eyes becomes softer with the saturation of lightly budding tears that deflate the fervent mission to proceed onto a happy reunion with Karlisa. His heart begins to race with anxiety and fear. Janus and Jerry make subtle attempts at controlling their breathing with long inhales, a pause, and finally blowing the air out through their lips. They are challenged by the human condition.

"Everyone just relax," Aza says as he tries to unglue his eyes from the large humanoid structures.

Aza roamed this area for thousands of years before being apprehended by the Archangels and he has never seen these structures before now. Aza cannot determine if the structures are manmade, or how long they have been there, but he oddly finds them familiar. He wants to get a closer look at them but he knows there is a more important mission that they must begin.

"Ok... OK guys focus! Let's get Karlisa back to Cleveland," Aza reminds the team of the plan.

"There's something wrong here," Jerry says finally snapping back into action.

"I know!" Aza replies trying not to allow the feeling to stall their mission. "We need to find out what year it is—"

"Year!" replies Jerry. "It's Sunday! I came to the resort last week. I rescued you on a Monday and we had diner on Thursday. Karlisa became ill Thursday night and we drove to the medical clinic here in Damascus on Friday morning. Saturday morning she fell in a coma and we left that evening to Vilon. I can't account for the time we spent in Heaven but it can't be any more than Sunday evening or maybe Monday!"

"It's not the same," Janus informs. "A rotation in Heaven can be several days in Earth time. That's why your prayers come across as so impatient."

"What! AZA! You didn't tell me that! You said I'll be back in 'a twinkling of time' and 'don't worry about it'," Jerry says trying to mimic Aza's voice.

"It's been over 5,000 years since I've been there!" Aza explodes. "I forgot some of the details."

"Some details—"

"Let's just calm down and find out what date it is and where to find Karlisa!" Aza directs Jerry while trying to keep his cool in embarrassment of his oversight. "At worst her mother came and took her back to Cleveland."

"Is that the extent of your imagination in the face of 700-foot frozen giants and hovering surveillance drones? I mean what the fuck! Last week there was not 700-foot giants ripped up out the earth!"

"Maybe it's an art exhibit," says Janus.

"Shut up!" Aza and Jerry snap.

"Ok… Janus, clothes, cash, and car can you get that?"

"Your wish is my—"

"No... please no. Just get the stuff, don't add to the madness," Jerry requests of Janus.

With both hands raised in the air Janus takes a moment of silence before conjuring up a spell of human wealth.

"Agla Agla Agla O'God Almighty Omnus,
who art the life of the Universe, and who
ruleth over the seven houses of its vast form
by the strength and virtue of the divine angels
in thine Upper Room. Bring forth your mighty wings,
In your name we beg for these most fortunate things,
Garments of grandeur, Treasures of Parasiel,
Our mission has been sanctioned,
By the mercy of Cassiel."

A wardrobe change is granted in an instance.

"And they said I was vain," responds Aza as he looks down at his new garments.

"We look like pimps," Jerry critiques as he rubs his hands over his blue silk blazer. He checks the pockets of the complementing blue silk pants where he finds his old wallet, a roll of cash, and a set of keys.

"I work at the gate of the FIRST House where it's always expected to give new arrivals the very best first impression," defends Janus dressed in an all white silk blazer, shirt, pants, and shoes outfit.

"And that car?" asks Jerry pointing over to a very luxurious red hovercraft sedan.

"I don't drive! I don't know what to do with such things. It was all in the spell."

"Well fortunately I do," Aza informs. "It's one of the many things I learned all on my own in my brief time before the rise."

Jerry reaches across and places his hand on Aza shoulder, "I got this. I'm the only one with a license."

Jerry stares at Aza's maroon and black silk combination suit. He recalls how nicely Aza was dressed in the days before the rise. Oddly, the flamboyant attire wears well on him, but who wouldn't look nice in high-end fashion?

Jerry and Aza sit in the front seat while Janus takes the back. Each of them looks around at the luxurious accommodations and their nicely dressed attire. "Maybe we are over doing it a bit," Aza says as memories flash in his mind of how he paraded his riches to attract women back in his days when he lived in the Dan village.

"Janus can you look into that sphere of yours to see where she is so I don't have to drive this bourgeois vehicle all over town?" Jerry requests.

"Good idea," replies Janus as the genie conjure up an energy sphere. "Father Barcus here my call and bring into my sphere a mortal soul. Where art thou Karlisa? Show me your dwelling as I bring peace amongst the living. Janus waits but there is no vision to be seen. There is only a mass of gray clouds in the sphere. Janus repeats the spell then waits a while before screaming, "Father!"

"Is there a problem?" Jerry asks.

"This is not good... there is... nothing there. It's like she's not—"

"There is another explanation," interjects Aza. "She could be blocked. It could be a part of the curse. They're trying to conceal her soul."

"Well... I guess, but Father would never allow—"

"Barcus is a mere... no offense, genie. He is not exempt from the Chancellor's evil hex. Let's just go

330

to where we last saw her and start from there." Aza looks around to collect their nonverbal agreements. "We should really ditch this vehicle. It draws too much attention. It's way overdone."

"If you think we've overdone it then you haven't seen anything yet," says Janus while pulling a briefcase off the back seat and showing it to be full of jewels, credit accounts, and other sources of currency. The very fashionable alligator skin case has a golden letter "A" attached to the interior floor.

"That's my old briefcase," informs Aza. "From whom exactly did you conjure up that spell? That was a gift from the Chancellor."

"All my spells are sent to Father Barcus, approved by the Almighty Agla, granted through the divinity in the most Upper Room!" Janus says with a tight jaw and flared nostrils.

"Throw it in the street," Aza instructs.

"No! Best to have it and not need it, than to need it and not have it," Jerry instructs the team.

Greed

In a dim torch-lit private room at the top of Zebul's point, five masked and red-cloaked Seraphs sit around a table. In the center of the table rests a device called the Left Eye of Abraxis. Near the Eye of Abraxis stand seven rugged and cooled brimstones each shaped in the image of a man. A black masked Seraph extends a hand and knocks one of the figurines down.

"When you give to those who have so little, they always tend to take too much. Greed my brothers' greed is a sure bet every time," a black masked Seraph says before returning its attention back to the Eye of Abraxis depicting a red sedan pulling into the parking area of a Damascus hospital.

2171

Jerry exits the red sedan followed by Aza and Janus as he strides towards the hospital entrance. He looks up at the bright blue emergency entrance lights illuminating the name Damascus Medical and Wellness Professional Arts Center. The heavy traffic of people going in and out of the hospital entrance indicates a buildup of precarious activity in the local area. Several sets of families and friends drag out of the hospital entrance, consoling each other. It appears as if no one who enters leaves with any good news. Jerry's pace slows and his breathing begins to increase rapidly as he pats his pockets for his medication but does not find it.

He continues through the entrance and steps up to the reception desk. The receptionist and the nursing staff behind the desk are busy running about in several directions. The receptionist is on a holographic communication device. The receptionist takes one quick glance over at Jerry before holding a single finger up, requesting him to wait a minute. The receptionist continues her conversation with a caller, redirecting the call to another department. Jerry examines the scene in the lobby where he finds many patients speaking with triage nurses complaining of symptoms that don't appear to be emergency-worthy complaints. He does not see a single injury, wound, or symptom of an obvious illness. Aza and Janus enter the lobby and stand off to the side watching the distressed patients and families. Jerry notices how out of place and silly they look in their nice modern suits amongst all the traditional thobes and shalwars but as he laughs internally he remembers his own similar attire. He also notices a few patients making attempts to start conversations with Aza and it reminds him of how attractive he found Aza's pleasant nature when he first met him. The nurse gains Jerry's attention by addressing him in Mandarin. He pauses and stares at her trying to formulate his awkward question before she repeats the greeting again in English.

"MAY... I... H-E-L-P YOU?" the nurse says again.

"Sorry I'm visiting from out of the country—"

"Obviously," the nurse interrupts while rolling her eyes down at his clothes.

Jerry continues, "My wife was being treated in this hospital. I had to leave for a while and now that I'm back I would like to know in which room she is staying."

"What's her name?"

"Karlisa Xeven."

"Like five, six—"

"No. Its x-e-v-e-n."

"Spell the first name, sir," the nurse requests as she rapidly types in various commands on her digital input device.

"K-a-r-l-i-s-a."

"We don't have a Karlisa five, six, or Xeven." The nurse smirks.

"What about Sevien? S-e-v-i-e-n."

"No! I did think of that too. What is her date of admission?"

Jerry pauses and inhales deeply. "Um... well... I can't remember. A week ago maybe."

"Here she is... no, no that was nearly 10 months ago. Sorry no Karlisa."

"Wait!" Jerry requests. "There was a Karlisa Xeven here 10 months ago?"

"Well yeah but that was last summer! Maybe you were on vacation back then?"

"Can you tell me to whom she was discharged?"

"Excuse me!" the nurse replies darting her eyes and snapping her neck.

Jerry eyeballs the nurse's nametag, Jezzie Bell. "Please... Jezzie there probably isn't a coincidence here so maybe it's a mistake. Can you tell me when and to whom she was discharged?"

"She's your wife?"

"Yes!"

"I'm not telling you anything before I see some ID."

Jerry presses his thumb on an ID scan box. The nurse reads the Gaia ID display as he stares at her with a titled head while biting his inner lip. The nurse examines the ID with an eye roll and pinched lips.

"She probably doesn't want to be found," Jezzie concludes by saying, "sambool," under her breath. "But it says here she was discharged on August 11, 2170 to a Mr. Samuels."

"Who? Samuels? Is there a discharge address?"

The nurse types a little then makes a cryptic smile. "The Tower of the Sun Resort," she replies before saying softly, "You go, girl!"

"Is there anything else you can tell me?" Jerry asks as he pats his pocket for his pill container.

"Nope! That's all there is."

"Was she well?"

"She probably is now," replies the nurse without checking the display. "You will have to check with Patient Records tomorrow!"

"Thanks, you've been very—"

"Next!"

Jerry starts out slowly but picks up his pace as he hastens toward Aza and Janus. He looks to his left and then to his right until he sees a sign pointing towards the restrooms. He signals the two to follow him by using a head bobbing motion to the side. He continues at a swift pace until he reaches the restroom doors. He takes a quick peek inside and finds it empty. Jerry stretches his arm across to open the door for the other two but Janus stops at the door and points to the gender sign.

"Um... I'm not quite sure—"

Jerry reaches over to Janus' arm and pulls the genie into the restroom.

"Not now!" Jerry says stopping any complaints from Janus. "Keep anyone from entering," he demands.

"Oh! A gate spell! I can do that!"

"No! Just don't let anyone in gatekeeper!"

"Ok, but boring."

"You know I could wait in the car if you need to do something in here," Aza informs Jerry.

"Yeah I need to do something!" Jerry swings and punches Aza in the face.

"Whence hell you come!" Aza responds.

"It's twenty-one seventy-one!" Jerry screams. "We've been gone for..."

"Forty weeks to be exact! I know! I saw the date on the news."

"Forty WEEKS!"

"I told you before that I didn't know. I meant no harm."

"Harm? This is not harm! You took me from my wife and my kids for a year! We're way past harm. You've ruined my life!"

"Me! No! Them! I was under a rock!"

"Oh, there you go again with that the devil made me do it!"

"The... Sammael? Oh... you got a lot to learn my friend. Do you think Sammael set this up all on his own? Ha! Ha! Oh, brother!"

Janus standing by quietly with an increasing heartbeat and shallow breath interjects, "You're not suggesting that—"

"Don't even try it Janus. You know how the Upper Room operates. Nothing gets by them and I do mean nothing!" Aza responds.

"This is blasphemous!" Janus sulks.

"If you bury your enemy for 5,000 years, you're not going to allow one chance of mortal bravery to undo all that effort?" says Aza.

"As I said before... I may be human, but I'm not stupid," Jerry reminds.

Still perturbed, Janus replies, "I can't believe any of this."

"Can't or won't?" asks Aza.

"Whichever! Can we go?" asks Janus.

Shaking his head and marching towards the door Jerry informs, "I can do this on my own. We can't work together if we can't trust each other."

"Trust, Jerry?" Aza asks. "Not only do I trust you but I've been protecting you! I trust that you will be a fool! I trusted that you would be lead by the lies and the deception!" Aza paces the small confinement of the two stalls bathroom. "OK! I honestly didn't count for the time lapse but they knew, Sandalphon knew, Cassiel knew, Sachiel knew, they all knew about it!" Aza paces over the tiles some more then stops behind Jerry who is turned towards a mirror, resting his hands on the sink countertop. Jerry looks up through the mirror at Aza who stares back at him with eyes swollen with moisture. "It's been 40 weeks, but she can still be out there. I've been separated from my girl for 7,000 years. I could leave now but I don't where to look, where to go, or if she still loves me," Aza impresses upon Jerry's sympathy.

"Eww... this humanity is starting to become infectious... Oh my Gracefulness! I need some space. Lots and lots of space!" the genie informs the crew while fanning itself with flapping hands near its neck and face.

Jerry turns towards Aza. "A Mr. Samuels checked her out 40 weeks ago. She was discharged back to the resort," Jerry reports.

"We'll go to the resort then we'll, if we have to, we'll make contact with her mother," Aza plans.

A red sedan glides down a road less traveled at night. The rudders squeal through twists and turns constantly warning the driver to slow down in this unfamiliar territory. The road is dark but the lands off to the sides are darker. The sedan cuts through the thick coppice of untamed woodlands that are barely contained from overtaking the unpaved road. In these modern times of highway travel and hovercraft technology these forest roads have been relentless to change as the local legend has held steadfast against demands for civil advancement, surveying, and mapping by either land or skies above. An anxious foot presses down harder on the pedals switching frequently from the break to the gas as Jerry accelerates through the darkness, through the wilderness, through the unfamiliar. No one in the vehicle is as concerned about Jerry's driving as they are about what lurks on the sides of the road, in the dark.

Aza flexes to draw out his astroflare but then decides that it may be too paranoid of a move. Aza finds a small degree of insecurity in this precarious journey through the darkness. He looks around at the faces of his traveling companions hoping to mirror their strength but he only finds tension that brings him back to the edginess of dread. He thinks to lower his window a bit to give the travelers some fresh air but the thought quickly fades as his finger meets the button. How dare he let in the contents of the dark? There are no comforts in the dark. There are only the remains of a nefarious and legendary cryptic past that conditions the outside air of the dark.

Finally, a green neon sign on the side of the road that reads, "The Tower of the Sun Resort ahead on the right," pierces the dark expedition. The rhythmic exhales in the sedan signify the relief of its passengers as the resort's lights illuminates the journey's end. Jerry drives into the lot up to the guest services building. The grounds around the stone cavern building are poorly lit except in the areas where the resort's neon sign wards off the dark. The three divine missionaries run from the sedan into the resort's lobby only to find more darkness as the resort is shut down at this time of night where they rarely, if ever, get visitors coming in from out of the dark. The lobby is elegantly decorated in rich emeralds and dark blood-orange textures that are dimly lit this time of night with green shaded torch lamps. Inside the entrance of the door a long 75-foot wool runner stretches to the end of the check-in counters to greet its guest. The runner that covers the shinny jade marble floor is designed with repetitive interlaced orange circles, four-sided emerald polygons, ubiquitous bluish-green star patterns, and multisided amber polygons. The two-toned mint cream walls fade into the shroud of darkness beyond the torch lighting and the dimmed, dangling crystal chandelier.

The lobby is empty as it usually is this time of night. At the service desk sits a figure that is familiar to Jerry. It is the old man who is one of few staff members who stay on site overnight with the resort's overseer. The old service attendant sits behind the counter on a stool hunched over as if he's nearly about to lose his balance and fall over asleep. His head hangs low, pushing his long goatee into his green blazer uniform covered chest. Jerry, Aza, and Janus step up unnoticed to the front of the counter opposite the old man who is still snoozing. Jerry clears his throat to gently awaken the old man but his efforts are delivered with no avail. Aza reaches over and slaps the service bell.

"An angel just got his wings," Janus gushes as Jerry and Aza snap their necks to look at the genie with their late night travel worn expressionless faces then return their attention back to the attendant.

The equally expressionless and drab face of the old bearded attendant slowly comes to life as his eyes widen and focus in on the late night guests.

"What the HELL are you doing here this late!" the old man asks as he animates into action.

"What a way to greet your guests," replies Jerry.

"Don't no God-fearing guests come a calling this time of night! How in the hell did you crawl out of that darkness?"

"Aww... poor child. Did he say God FEAR-ing?" Janus asks but no one is listening to the genie.

"I need some information!" Jerry demands of the attendant.

"I don't have any information for you! I told that damned Araqiel to stop sending his demons here. Now you two take that damn spirit out of here!" the old man gripes as he stares at Janus.

Aza is confused and disturbed by this mortal's exclamations. He rapidly turns his head towards Jerry and Janus and then to the old man. "What demons are you speaking about?" Aza asks. "Who is this Araqiel?"

"Araqiel!" Janus shouts. "Child of Barcus?"

"What!" Jerry shouts.

"What is it you know about Araqiel?" Aza asks again.

"Mmm... mwahahaha!" the old man laughs. "He said you'd come for her. Wahahaha!"

"WHO?" Jerry shouts. "Where is my wife?" The old attendant doesn't respond. "Listen, old man, I was in this resort several months ago. Jerry and Karlisa—"

"Sevien! Mwahahaha!" the old man laughs again.

Jerry reaches over the counter and grabs the old man by his jacket, pulling him off his feet and up onto the counter. "Where is she old man?"

"The spirit, like that one there," the old attendant says pointing at Janus. "They came here, three of them in all. They took the girl. I was never told the other spirit's name. He was quite a fancy fella and the quiet type—"

"Penemue! My siblings were here!" Janus informs.

"The other one was a Mr. Chance Samuels."

"Chancellor Sammuel," Aza interjects.

"They were here, but now they are gone with the girl."

"Was she ok? Did she leave a message?" Jerry asks.

"Mwahahaha. No, there was no message. There was only... the stench of death. Mwahahaha!"

"Did she leave anything behind n the room," Jerry asked the old man while pulling his jacket harder.

"We've had to seal the room off," the old man continues. "Like many things around here it's been marked with the curse. Mwahahaha!" the old man continues to laugh hysterically as Jerry holds his body down onto the counter.

"This fool makes no sense," Jerry says to his crew. "Aza please make him talk!"

Aza hesitates to move as he stirs in place, anxiously wanting to assist. "You have to put your work in on this one Jerry."

"What?" Jerry asks.

"Just do it," Aza demands.

"Listen, old man! You think you know something? Look at this spirit!" Jerry says pointing his eyes to Aza. "Do you know who he is?"

"Oh... He knows the towers. I assume we have... children to see in the garden? Mwahahaha!"

"Oh, brother!" Aza says.

"What's this nonsense?" Jerry asks.

"Oh, no! The old man is insane," Janus reports.

"Listen, old man. My wife's life may depend on what you tell me," Jerry informs. "You will give me that room key and tell me what I need to know or... I'll... I'll... I'll kill you!" Jerry threatens.

"That's it!" Aza approves.

"Oh, my Mercifulness!" Janus responds.

"I'll... never! Never tell!" The old attendant says. "Things were promised! Many... wonderful things. Many... horribly wonderful things. I'll NEVER TELL!" shouts the old man.

"Oh... oh, my Gracefulness!" responds Janus.

"Do it, Aza! Do it!" Jerry pleads as holds the man over towards Aza.

Aza stares at Jerry with his fist clinched. "What is it you expect me to do?"

"Do what you're good for!" Jerry shouts.

"I've... I've been absolved by the grace of Sandalphon, besides I've never... I've never taken a mortal life before. That wasn't my crime."

Jerry stares back at Aza batting his eyes with disbelief. "If you can't take a human life how are you going to—"

"Jerry!" Janus interrupts. "The astroflare captures souls into a containment sphere where they are held, judged, punished or exonerated and therefore restored to their former lives. It's not the same as killing. Killing separates the body and the soul permanently."

"This man is keeping secrets to the whereabouts of our adversaries," Jerry argues as he stares at Aza.

"I never said I wouldn't do it, I just need to know that when we are surrounded by the Chancellors men you will have no trouble doing what must be done. The Chancellors entourage comes in many forms from pretty women to elderly men like this one. If you can't put your own work in, how can I trust that you will fight by my side when I need you?" Aza asks.

"Mwahahaha you can't do it. Rooh entak!"

Jerry places his hands around them man's neck and squeezes firmly causing the old man to turn red, but Jerry hesitates to apply any further pressure. Janus turns to look away while Aza grimaces with a slight grin and darting eyes onto Jerry hands squeezing the man's neck. Jerry looks into the old man's eyes trying to convey a clear and present warning into what will follow next if he doesn't comply, but even under the agony of Jerry's tight grip the old man mocks Jerry's threat with a smile and eyes that invite a chance for death.

"This is your last chance, old man. I only want to find my wife. Please don't make me do this."

"Go ahead! You'll only bring us closer together," the old man pleads.

"You and the Chancellor?"

"You and us! Mwahahaha!"

Jerry grabs the old man's neck and strangles him harder and watches his face turn from red to purple as the old man kicks his legs and squirms frantically. Jerry envisions Karlisa being held captive, being assaulted, and calling out his name. He feels that she believes he has abandoned her. The thoughts make him squeeze the old man's neck tighter and tighter. Aza grins and deeply inhales the sweet smell of death quickly filling the air like an aroma of fresh baked bread. Aza wants to give Jerry the astroflare to finish him off quicker, but he feels that there is no better warrior's lesson than to feel the soul leave your opponent's body by the force of your own hands. Aza closes his eyes, leans back, and nods with a high chin.

"STOP!" Janus shouts. Janus has conjured up an energy cube scrolled out like an old newspaper. "Which room were you in?"

"Room 212," Jerry answers as he slightly loosens his grip.

"The key is behind the counter taped under the floor of that center drawer. It's marked with a red X," Janus reports before heading behind the counter.

"Your timing is impeccable," Aza taunts.

"Every spell I cast comes at a great cost from father Barcus!" Janus snaps. Janus looks under several center drawer floors before finally finding a key. Janus examines the key and reads a red X and the number 212 then slaps the key on the counter. "You may not find anything that will help you in there so I will be waiting in the transport in case you decide to kill him after all." Janus flashes across the marble floor and back out into the darkness.

"Let's go!" Aza instructs the old man while pulling him across the counter onto his feet. "Dead man walking!" Aza shouts as he shoves the old man.

Jerry and Aza push through the resort to the sealed room escorted by the service attendant. As the three souls hurry through the plush carpeted and wall ornamented halls it's hard to imagine that anything less than complete tranquility and calmness could ever be contained in the rooms of this luxurious resort. The resort has two center elevator shafts one for each building erected on the opposite ends of the lobby. The elevators are completely interior and open-air so that the riders inside can be seen from the lobby. Those who do not take the elevator can use one of two ornamented and wood carved staircases on each side of the elevators. The attendant, being an older man, chose to use the elevator. At the top of each set of elegant stairways in front of the elevator doors there is a large 15x10 foot self portrait of General Almrei or his great-grandson Amir Almrei. Jerry's elevator opens up at the end with the portrait of Amir.

Jerry looks up at the large antique framed portrait of the grand opening owner, the late Amir Almrei. "You'd think he'd spend his money on a better location than this God forsaken place," Jerry says breaking the silence of the stroll to the sealed room.

"It's just the opposite. This is the one place that has not been forsaken. Mmm... mwahahaha," the old man laughs.

They continue their short passage down the lavishly decorated hall until they come to a room that does not appear to be out of the ordinary. The esthetic value of the hall has not been diminished by this room's exterior doorway. There are very few signs that the room has been sealed off except a glimpse of a light that catches Aza's attention. A small glimmer of a golden light surrounds the edges of the door reminding Aza of the doorways he once saw in the Seventh Halls of Araboth. Jerry takes out the passkey and tries to open the door but it does not unlock. The door is equipped with an electronic lock that is opened by a key code and shaped like a real house key for that "at home" feel. Jerry turns the knob repeatedly and tries applying pressure to the door, but the door does not budge.

"I don't believe the key is going to work on a sealed door," Aza reports.

"Is this key still coded for this room?" Jerry asks.

"The door is sealed by the Chancellor of the underworld. Mmm... mwahahaha."

"I've had enough of you and this Chancellor shit! By the power of Gracalot! Open!" Jerry shouts as he kicks the door.

To Aza and Jerry's own surprise the force of the kick swiftly and ferociously swings the door open and nearly off its hinges. Aza with his jaw dropped, rolls his eyes from the door, over to Jerry, and back to the busted door.

"By the power of what?" Aza asks.

Slightly energy depleted, Jerry stops and stares over at Aza nodding his head and calming his breathing. "Gracalot! Yeah that's right," Jerry confirms.

Aza slowly beams his eyes and shakes his head, "Who do you think you are?"

"Jerry Xeven... Earth Angel," Jerry swaggers.

"Uh, yeah! Sure! Let's go in," Aza says as he motions the way with his hand.

Jerry grabs the old man by his jacket and shoves him through the door first.

Aza stands back momentarily and watches Jerry enter the room. "Earth Angel," he mutters.

Jerry finds the room very different from how he last left it and very different from all the other guest rooms. This room that was once lavishly colored with amethyst silk linens, Byzantine carpeting, and lavender curtains all accented with gold trimmings and two-toned purple cream walls is now barren without any carpeting or furnishing with the exception of a bare mattress on the floor. The wall paint is faded and peeling. The wood floor is dry and cracked. The room's stale hot air is barely breathable and unconditioned by the sealed air vents. Jerry attempts to switch on the room lights but they are not working. The windows are boarded up with dried and uneven wood slats so inelegantly done it appear that sloppy work was accepted to get the job finished fast.

"Why were all the amenities stripped from this room?" Jerry asks the old man.

"No one comes in this room anymore. The room and all its properties were defiled. Everything was taken away and burned. No one would touch the mattress. It was considered desecrated and—"

"That light in the closet! What is that light?" interrupts Aza.

Jerry shakes his head and shrugs his shoulders recalling that the lights were not working. Aza tilts his head to the side, requesting that the two step aside while he investigates. Aza places his body behind the door with his hip angled to apply force to close it quickly if needed. He slowly pulls the closet door open while peaking around to see the inside. Aza moves from behind the door and stands directly in front of its opening.

"Did they plan on coming back?" Aza asks the old man.

"They'd never tell me. They just show up unannounced, but they promised to take me to the underworld so that I may join them."

"Shut up, old man!" Jerry orders. "That's enough of your madness."

"When was the last time they were here?" Aza asks.

"What is it Aza? What do you see?" Jerry asks.

"Something that hasn't been seen for a very long time." Aza reaches into the closet and pulls out a shining golden astroflare.

"An astroflare left out in the innerverse?" Jerry responds. "I thought only angels carried astroflares."

Aza holds the astroflare looking at it up and down with admiration. "This is not just any astroflare. It's one of the lost Swords of Destruction," Aza reads an inscription on the handle. "It's the sword of Zimkiel, a former Divinity angel and Ambassador of Vilon."

"So you are thinking whoever left it here is coming back to get it?"

"I'm not sure, but this not a weapon one would leave behind. I have one of the three lost swords of Persidis and this is one of the other two, but how did it get here?" Aza still admiring the sword swings it around to test it out. "Take it. Feel its power," Aza tells Jerry while handing him the sword.

Jerry swings the astroflare around several times. "Yeah! It's like it knows what you want to do and swings on its own." Jerry switches the sword in and out from the exoverse. "I feel the power! I really feel the power."

"Ok, old soul. This is where you tell us exactly who was in this room?"

"Like I said, the two spirits, Mr. Samuels, and the girl."

"Was the girl ok? Was it my wife?"

"Mmm... mwahahaha! She was everybody's wife! Ha! Ha! Ha! Ha!"

"WHAT!"

"We all had our pleasures with her! HA! HA! HA! HA!"

Jerry takes the astroflare and swings it at the old man's neck, severing his head from his body. "Wow you are right! This is a great sword," Jerry informs Aza.

Aza stands frozen and speechless as he rolls his eyes down to the floor where he sees the headless old man lying slain and then he rolls his eyes off into the distance gazing away and disconnecting from the event.

Jerry continues swinging and admiring the sword then he stops, looks down at the slain old man, then up at Aza. "He had it coming. Talking about my Karly like that!"

Aza snaps out of his distant place, "Ok, let's go Earth Angel."

Wrath

A Seraph wearing a gold mask and a blood red, dark oval ring extends over towards a statuette and knocks it down. The angel wearing the ring boasts, "Now that's what I call the human condition. Place a human in the right circumstance and it will respond accordingly in spite of its previously stated code of ethics," the red-cloaked and gold masked Seraph concludes.

A second cloaked and white masked seraph adds, "It was ultimately inevitable as it has always been one of the first vices to afflict humans."

"Don't try to degrade the potency of my wisdom. None of you knew that wrath would come so quickly."

A third cloaked red-masked Seraph interjects, "It's all situational. All the vices will fall in line, as the seed is planted the flower will surely grow and blossom."

CHAPTER FIFTEEN

Smell the 22nd Century

A radio tuner moves rapidly from station to station, stopping briefly before moving on to another channel. "This is The Mix where you can always find the hottest, greatest, latest—"

The tuner abruptly moves again then tuning in on a broadcast to hear a song singing, "Ohhh myyy... I got a funny feeling when she walked into the—"

The tuner moves again to another song singing, "Anything you want, you got it! Anything you need, you got it! Anything at all—"

The tuner moves yet again to a broadcaster shouting, "My God... Are you serious? I mean really? No matter what you call us Gaian Humanist, Gaian Free Thought, Gaian Agnostic! WHATEVER! Citizens! What's the point? Are we really going to have this conversation again and revisit outdated thinking, irreverent views, and digress BACK into the whole way of DIVISIVE and PREPOSTEROUS behavior that TORE us apart just because some protruding geological anomalies HAPPEN to look like human features?" a raspy voice concludes.

Another voice interjects, "You know this reminds me of those scenarios that you may have heard of wayyy back in the early twentieth century when a stain on the wall looks like Mother... Terry—"

"No, Mother Teresa or wait no... Sister Mary you know that virgin woman—"

"Yes! That's her. So the stain has this shape, always of her for some reason, and the imbeciles from back then in a time when they were still using tissue to wipe their ass—"

"Oh gross!"

"They would pray to the stain on the damn wall! Kid you NOT! People! Are we back there because of some damned archeological protrusions?"

"You know you have to admit, geological anomalies or not, human features or not, the fact that these 700-foot protrusions can just rip up out of the ground overnight without any earthquake or signs of plate shifting is just eerie and fantastic," the second speaker concludes.

"Fantastic, yes! But not an act of GOD! For all we know the government or some rogue art group planted those things there. I heard that the carbon dating is older than the surrounding crust. You would have to go deep down to the lithosphere to find something that old. In the end, science will reveal the FACTS! People, science will tell us this has nothing to do with any god. You know WHY?...

People! Gaians! Wake up and SMELL the Twenty! Fifth! Century! THERE IS NO GOD!"

The radio is turned off and Janus is sitting alone in a dark car breathing heavily. "Oh, my! It's worse than I thought." The genie sits with its hands held to the temples of its head. "If they've been listening and I know they have... they're coming. They were always coming."

Click! Click! Thud! Sounds erupt from the back of the sedan. Janus quickly shrinks down into the middle of the back seat. Clunk! Clunk! Swoosh! The sounds continue as the car shakes while something is stirring in the dark outside. Janus reaches over to check the locks that the genie has repetitively checked every few minutes since first entering the vehicle. Janus can see the lock button in a downward position and a red LED indicating locked, but in this place, in this dark one cannot be too sure.

"I knew I shouldn't have come out here alone. Why didn't I just wait in the lobby?" the genie thinks to itself as it swallows hard and extends its shaking hand to check the lock. Sloshed down almost onto the floor Janus reaches for the lock button and with closed eyes pushes the button, but it is already locked. The lock pops into the unlocked position and the green LED glares a sign of fear. Janus mouths the words, "Oh, mighty Abraxis!"

The front doors swings open and Jerry and Aza enter the front seats of the car. Both Jerry and Aza look over their shoulders and check to see that Janus is in the back. "Why are you sitting in the dark?" Jerry asks as he reaches in the back and flips on a holoscreen behind the headrest. "There you are the comforts of mortal technology. You can see anybody anywhere, no spells required."

"You can't see... anybody," Janus responds with a slightly defensive tone and roll of the eyes.

"Right you are!" Jerry says with a finger pointed up while looking at Janus through the rear view projector screen. "You know I was thinking. If this Omnus—"

"Watch it!" both Aza and Janus respond.

Frozen in his thoughts, he thinks to himself before continuing out loud, "Oh yeah... these guys aren't my mortal friends. I must be more careful." Jerry softens his tone. "If Omnus can turn me into an immortal, trap you under a rock quandary for five THOUSAND years, and Janus you can conjure up this vehicle that I could never afford, a trunk load of cash, and anything else we can think of, but you can't find Karly in your damn crystal ball—"

"Only mortals use crystal—"

"Whatever! Why is the great honorable Omnus making this so hard for us? Why can't he just snap?" Jerry snaps his fingers. "There's your Karly."

"Please allow me," Azazel says holding up a yielding hand at Janus. "As an elder angel who worked in the prayer room and the historical archive, let me explain something to you." Jerry turns his attention towards Aza. "In the beginning there was the great Aeon Abraxis who created Omnus and other Eons, Gods, or Lords whatever you mortals may call them. There was an incident, an explosion of some type that... destroyed the other Eons and disintegrated Abraxis leaving Omnus, the only survivor," Aza looks Jerry in the eye to confirm his understanding before continuing. "Since the reign of Omnus the creation of immortals was ceased giving way to the creation of mortal men—"

"The new objective is about the self-sustaining and purification of the Heavens since the fall of the Twelve Houses of Heaven," Janus interjects.

"Twelve? I thought you said there were seven?"

Aza continues, "There once was twelve before the very souls that captured Karlisa burned five of them down. Destroyed by factions that were lead into the dark by Abaddon. Since then, Omnus has not granted any individual prayers. He only honors those for the greater good of souls. So a vulgar display of snapping Karlisa here for your benefit is not an option."

"Speaking of leading into the dark, can you lead us out of here?" Janus requests.

"So are we alone on this mission?"

"The elders assigned Watchers over us to be used in battle. Our prayers and requests will be generously supported, but there are rules against vainglory and vulgar displays of power," Aza explains.

"But what about this car and the cash."

"Jerry, be careful of what you ask for and know that all of what you receive is not a gift."

Jerry mulls over to himself, "That sounds cryptic."

"I was thinking..." Janus says then returns to a downcast stare. "I can't find Karlisa without removing the block but... if I cast a counter spell it will open up my ability to at least see her."

Jerry turns around to face Janus. "You can cast a counter spell! You never said you could counter a spell!" Jerry shouts while breathing heavily, then conceding to a smile.

"What I said was that all my spells are granted through the Divine Upper Room and every spell I cast comes at a great cost!" Janus snaps back.

"What cost?? We're on a divine mission to capture Heavens most wanted!" Jerry huffs as he pats his pockets for his pill container. "Where are my damned pills?" Jerry stares at his shaking hands. "I get immortality but I can't get rid of my anxiety."

"You're afflicted, Earth Angel," Aza respond as he glances at Jerry through the corner of his eye and back to Janus while shaking his head in frustration. "All you get is immortality so you can live long enough to fail and you're going to lose that if we don't get out of this forsaken place! Do you want me to drive?"

"What! Why would I fail?"

"It hasn't clicked for you yet, Earth Angel? All they want is their damn war! You're the last hurdle they need to jump to please Omnus. Every time someone like you, Jesus, Gandhi, King, or Xiaobo comes along they have to..." Mimicking an elder's voice, "'Give them a chance. Let the mortals work it out,' But some of them are tired of giving you a chance! They were hoping you would run home like a little bitch so they can get on with the Apocalypse!"

"That's a lie!" Jerry says squaring his chest at Aza. "Sandalphon loves us. Just like the Chancellor, you resent that! You have been despising me this whole time. You only want to get out of here and go find your Sophia. You don't want me to succeed. You don't think I have what it takes to be a warrior of the light."

"Warrior! Right... you killed your first mortal and now you're a warrior?"

"YOU... Ki...killed him?" The wide-eyed Janus stutters.

"Just so that you know, Sandalphon is not the only divine angel in the Upper Room and not every angel in the Upper Room is all that divine," Aza reports.

Jerry closes his eyes and shakes his head while he thinks to himself, "I'm not going to be tempted by lies of a former Fallen. I've given him way too much trust already." Jerry starts the car then turns to Janus. "I did what I did because it was what I felt had to be done. If you have nothing to contribute but criticism for what I've done then we've failed, you can go back to Gracalot, you two can go back to jail, they can have their war, and we can all go to hell." Jerry's eyes fill with moisture. "But I'm going to Cleveland to see my kids." Tears roll profusely out of Jerry's eyes as he fights a losing battle to keep them away. "I-I... I promised myself I would not leave here without her."

Jerry continues wiping as they all sit in a somber silence. Aza glances at Jerry, shakes his head, and then turns away to look out the window into the darkness.

They sit in the pretty cash filled sedan, engulfed by the darkness.

Janus speaks slowly and softly, breaking the silence, "What... I... was going to say is..." Jerry and Aza turn to give attention to the low speaking voice from the back seat. "If I counter a blocking spell it will open a direct line into her mind. The problem is... it will be open for me and for the

Chancellor. Once you counter a blocking spell it can't be removed. It's sealed to the initial spell."

Aza adds, "So we would have to defeat the Chancellor after we rescue Karlisa or she will always have... the devil dancing in her head."

"Great!" Jerry grimaces. "I can't defeat the Chancellor. You're right." Speaking to Aza without facing him, "I was trying to get you to do my dirty work in there because I was too afraid." Jerry looks out into the darkness beyond the beams of the sedan headlights. "Earth Angel... I'm not made for this shit."

"Well... not yet!" Aza replies as he turns to Jerry. "The way I see it... we are damned either way and I'm not one to give up without trying! Right?" Aza asks Jerry for his confirmation.

"Yeah. I guess you're right."

Aza turns back to Janus. "What do you need to counter that spell?"

Janus rolls its eyes around and then up at Aza. "I-I can't do it here. The grounds are tainted. I don't imagine anyone can get a prayer out of this forsaken place."

"OK, so what do you need?"

"To counter the Chancellor's spell it's not going to be easy." Janus sits up straight and leans in closer to Aza and Jerry. "I will need a sanctuary of some sort."

"A mosque or a church," Aza clarifies.

"In twenty-one seventy-one? Are you kidding me?" Jerry answers. "You have more sanctity in a brothel."

"A brothel?" Aza grins.

"Stay focused!" Janus snaps. "What about a place where religion or spiritual practices are still permitted without restriction?"

Jerry rolls some thoughts around in his head while biting the inside of his mouth. "A cemetery."

"Oh, brother!" Aza says as he rubs his hands through his hair. "We have to trade one dreadful place for another?"

Jerry types in cemetery on the dashboard GPS. The GPS responds, "Current location not found." Jerry types in Damascus and cemetery then the readout gives over twenty locations.

"Any particular kind of cemetery," Jerry asks.

"The bigger the better," Janus responds.

Jerry reads the map and presses a few buttons to turn on the GPS driving assistant. "Take me to the largest cemetery in Damascus," Jerry says out loud.

The device responds, "That would be the Commonwealth Gaia War Memorial and Cemetery. Would you like to go there now?"

"Yes."

"Sorry. Directions are not available from this unknown location. Please drive into the nearest Auto Detect Zone."

Jerry places the car in drive. "Buckle up! Let's get the hell out of this place!" Jerry drives back out of the parking spot, moves forward for a while, and then slows as he looks over to Aza. "Do you need to stop by the garden to say goodbye to your children?"

"Yeah funny... Earth Angel."

Jerry drives past the Welcome to The Tower of the Sun Resort sign along the same path that they arrived. The break of dawn is still a few hours away but in this darkness you'd think you would never see the sun. The wind picks up slightly as Jerry maneuvers the sedan down the winding dark roads. Jerry feels no confidence in having before driven up this path. The sky shimmers with signs of an approaching storm. The wind picks up more as Jerry proceeds down the path. The riders are more relieved to be leaving than they are frightened of the treacherous path through the dark. Janus, with eyes closed, tries to not to listen to what sounds like voices howling across the trees. The breathy voices grow louder and clearer as Janus becomes certain that the voices are saying, "Leeaave..."

As the voices grow louder Janus places both hands over its ears. Aza squirms in his seat frequently feeling a need to readjust his posture as he shakes the voices from his head. Aza bats his eyes and shakes his head over and over again. Jerry looks over as Aza, shrugs his shoulders, and rubs his forehead. Aza eyes widen as he determines that the voices are saying, "Daddyyy don't leave."

Jerry, trying not to take his eyes off the windblown road, asks, "Did you hear something saying 'Jerryyy help me?'"

"Don't listen to it," Aza warns. "It says whatever scares you. It's an auditory hallucination."

"A wind demon," Janus informs.

"Yeah, great! Wind demon!" Jerry says before mimicking something Karlisa must have said prior to the trip, "The history, the mystery, it'll be so romantic."

Jerry continues down the twists and turns of the resort's path through the wind and darkness. Condensation builds on the windshield triggering the automatic bladeless air wipers. An automatic alert in the sedan turns on, "This is the Auto Safety Advisor. The current weather condition requires that you proceed five miles under the speed limit for safe travel. Would you like to hear the local weather report?"

"Jerry and Aza turn and look at each other. Aza arches his eyebrows and shrugs his shoulders. "Yes," Jerry responds.

"Sorry, a weather advisory is not available for this area. Please proceed to the nearest Auto Detect Zone."

"Next time I'll just ask the wind demon," Jerry says while looking over at Aza who manages to crack the first smile Jerry has seen since their return from the Heavens.

Jerry continues driving down the path at the speed limit as a light rain begins to cover the sedan with an increasing build up. "Slow down. Slow down," the Auto Safety Advisor alerts.

"I'm not slowing down until I get us out of here," Jerry thinks to himself as he continues to fight the sharp turns on the dark road.

The rudders keep squealing, sudden turns keep appearing, and the rain keeps pouring. Lightning strikes the road near the sedan. The lightning strikes from the ground up opposed to striking from the sky down. Jerry maneuvers the road conditions and keeps going, not allowing the lightning to distract him. "Good job," Aza compliments.

Jerry remains silently focused, grinding his teeth, and griping the steering wheel tightly with both hands. The rain, mist, and lightning strikes blur the already darkened road but Jerry is determined to get out of Golan and into Damascus. Finally, a sign signifying entering into The Syrian Arab Confederated States and exiting the Unincorporated Territories of The Arab Confederated States is seen from the roadside. An alert is triggered on the sedan's Auto Detect Zone. "Bing! Would you like to proceed to the Commonwealth Gaia War Memorial and Cemetery? Bing! Your weather advisory report is ready."

Jerry inhales and exhales deeply producing a sound that is echoed from the other two riders. Condensation rolls of the window as the automatic bladeless wipers turn off. The road is still dark, but not pitch black. There is an airy breeze rolling through the rural grounds along the highway. Streetlights illuminate the roadside and small drones beep through the Syrian skies. In the distance the peaks of the archeological anomalies can be seen. "Well... I would like to say things are back to normal but that wouldn't be exactly... accurate," Jerry says as he loosens his grip on the steering wheel and allows the tension in his shoulders to drop. "Actually, I have to rethink what normal really means now."

"Well that certainly doesn't appear to be normal," Janus says pointing out a winged figure in the distance waving and standing near the middle of the road.

Jerry tightens back up on the steering wheel and slightly slows the vehicle before looking over at Aza with widened eyes and a dry, gasping mouth.

"I think it's ok, let's see how this plays out," Aza says while conjuring up his astroflare on the side of the seat.

Jerry powers down to a stop and lowers the driver's side window. A tall ruffled winged figure wearing a traditional Arab keffiyeh runs up to the vehicle after disengaging his wings from the innerverse. "The Call! The Fall! The pact of us all! Whoa! Whoo!" leaning in through the window close up to Jerry and shouting over at Aza, "I knew it was you! Who in the hell else would be coming down that God forsaken road this time of night except a forsaken! Ha Ha Ha Ha! Whew! Hew! It's an honor to meet you! A God damned legend!"

With eyes darting and forehead wrinkled up Jerry looks over at Aza who shrugs his shoulders and frowns his face up in question. "Who in the hell are you?" Jerry asks.

"Who in the hell are you?" the figure replies. "You smell pretty boy," the figure says while inhaling deeply. "Oh, yeah! I SMELL... mortality! Ha! Ha! Ha! Swwweeet mortality! BUT I can see your light! Ha! Ha! Ha! Ha! Oh, yeah! I can see your light from up the road, son!"

Jerry shakes his head and locks his jaw while pushing the button to raise the window. "I've had enough of this!"

"Wait! Wait!" the figure pleads. "I'm Zophiel! Zophiel of the great late kingdom of Persidis!"

"Zop?" Aza exclaims. "Well damn soul! I haven't seen your arse in over five thousand years!" Aza shouts as he propels his astroflare back into the exoverse and opens the door to hustle around with his greeting. Aza and Zophiel embrace. "Whence, comest thou?"

"Thy be hindered by thine divine me fere!" Zophiel reports. "So what rock did you crawl out from under? Ha! Ha! Ha! Whew! Wee! What kind of shit is that? Place a damned soul under the damned

Earth just because you Fall upon it?" Zophiel speaks loudly in Aza's face.

Aza squints his eyes, wrinkles his nose and backs up. "Been drinking from the elixir of souls much my brother?"

Zophiel tilts his head and cracks a half smile with his eyes pointing over to a smoking vehicle smashed into a light pole. "It said the Emergency Auto Driver would navigate the vehicle all by itself. Well... it did! Ha! Ha! Hell! I had nothing to do with it!"

Aza quickly conjures his astroflare and wings from the exoverse and maneuvers himself behind Zophiel with the flare to his neck. "And I suppose that you just happen to be on this very road on this very night is all a coincidence?"

"Oh, my Mercifulness!" Janus screams.

Jerry jumps out the car and conjures up the sword of Zimkiel. He stands on the other side of Zophiel breathing heavily and turning his head to the left and to the right looking around as if he's expecting some other angels to come out of the dark.

"Yeah! Sort of... I-I I've been looking for you ever since Penemue told me you were out and exalted by the light again," Zophiel answers while swallowing hard and looking at the night sky with his hands up in a surrendering motion.

"Penemue!" Janus shouts before flashing out in front of Zophiel. "Where did you see Penemue?"

"The genie runs through this forsaken place every now and then," Zophiel reports. "I saw both your siblings down at the speak easy. They said I may be able to find you up here, but as you see the vehicle went in the wrong direction."

Jerry inhales deeply and shouts on a single breath, "He's a pact member! He... He's one of them? We should expend him into the sphere!"

"No! No! No!" Zophiel pleads. "I answered my call a long time ago!" he responds. "I've actually been adjudicate and released!"

"No one is released after judgment!" Aza disputes as he holds the flare closer to his neck. "One either goes to prison or to Hell!"

"Not if you have a divine appointed representative!" Zophiel responds.

"A what?" Trio responds.

"Daniel! Daniel, the Angel of Judgment Laws. He's a Fallen," Zophiel explains. "He was captured and ordered to provide representation to all the Fallen and other souls waiting to be judged."

"Hell has an attorney?" Jerry shouts with his eyebrows arched and raising his palm to the sky.

"And a damned good one!" Zophiel responds. "I took the oath and I answered the call, but those bastards never knew I was working for Cassiel."

"What's this nonsense?" Aza asks. "Janus! You ever heard of such Dragon shit?"

Janus takes a long inhale. "I'm afraid he may be right. Michael is always coming up with some clever trick to balance the scales of justice."

Aza rolls his eyes and releases Zophiel then pulls his wings and astroflare back out of the innerverse. "So are you working for the Archangels now?"

Zophiel collects himself and bends over with his hands on his knees trying to gain control of his breathing. "Me, working... for whom?" Zophiel straightens his stance. "I'm... uh... in between lords at this time I'm afraid," Zophiel smiles as he returns to his former jovial self. "Damn soul! You are a legend! I was just hoping to see you free with thine own eyes once more."

"This Penemue. I hear that he and his brother may be kings or rulers of some sort. Where can we find them?" Jerry asks.

Zophiel cocks his neck back and responds, "Kings? Kings of what?" Zophiel pauses with an inward gaze as he rolls the thought around in his mind. "Ha! Ha! Ha! The only thing those guys are ruling is a franchise of the finest gentlemen clubs in the world. But... here in this place! They have old ways so it's a speak easy near the other edge of town."

"Did he have a girl with him?" Jerry asks.

"Girl? They have plenty of girls."

"No! My wife! Karlisa! She is about—"

"Look soul! Who are you?" Zophiel asks.

"Jerry Xeven. Earth Angel."

"Like one, two... um... four?" Zophiel says while rubbing his head in thought.

"Yeah! Yeah! The girl have you seen her?"

"Maybe... a mortal girl?" Zophiel squints his eyes and shakes his head. "They don't have any mortal girls," Zophiel elaborates. "They use all she-demons and Fallen whores. All the best desires of lust a soul can afford. You, you're not going to find any decent daughter of man in that place."

"Well we'll just have to go and ask them ourselves," Jerry asserts.

"Oh, you are not getting in there... Well you are dressed for it! Ha! Ha! Ha!" Zophiel notices he is the only one laughing. "These brothers are serious," he thinks to himself before surrendering an explanation. "You are not getting in there without a secret password, handshake, or some shit!"

"Well, we'll see about that!" Aza threatens.

"You can take me! Your brothers always let me in for free," Zophiel says with a wide grin looking over at Janus. "Besides... I need a ride. Can you help a brother out with a magic carpet or something, damn? Ha Ha! Ha!"

"He may actually be useful, but first we have a stop to make," Aza says while nodding as he looks over at Janus and then over to Jerry.

The four passengers load into the vehicle. Sitting in the back Zophiel looks around at the vehicles amenities and electronic gadgets. "Man these brothers are on a mission," he says to himself as he looks around in awe of the luxury and comfort. "Yes I believe I will be... useful." Zophiel taps Jerry on his shoulder and asks, "Earth what?"

CHAPTER SIXTEEN

Memorial Gardens

The glare from the LED headlights cut through the cemetery's early morning gloom with the precision of a surgical laser. Jerry parks the sedan off the side of a long entrance road beyond the gates leading up to the cemetery plots. The moon is set low, dimly illuminating the flat headstone lined grounds that appear to stretch far up to where the edge of the earth meets the horizon of the moon. The white moonlight and the gray sky silhouette the grave markers protruding up from the ghastly grounds. Cast iron black gates extend up for miles around the cemetery perimeter. The gates built so tall and so strong that it wouldn't be too much of an assumption to think that they were installed there to keep something inside the memorial park.

An arched sign above the narrow entrance off the main street reads, "In memory of souls lost but not forgotten." Immediately inside the entrance there is a memorial wall and fountain listing the names of those souls lost in the 40 Years New Gaia War of 2105 - 45. The foregrounds of the cemetery are nicely maintained with clean short cut lawns, precision sharp bush trimmings, and immaculate horticulture. A red ribbon, possibly leftover from a recent ceremony, slowly floats in the settling morning mist across the grass.

"Is this sanctified enough," Jerry asks as the four scrolls down the walking path.

Janus swallows with a dry mouth and heavy eyes as the genie evaluates the sanctity of the grounds. "There is a lot of grief here and the souls are resting peacefully but many of the graves are memorial markers. There are no souls in them."

"That's what happens when mortals die in an atomic blasts. There are few relics to bury outside of small body remains, jewelry, and memorial items," Jerry explains.

Turning and holding a hand out to stop the group from proceeding down the path, "So are you saying this deadly place isn't deadly enough?" Aza asks.

"Well I was hoping for more restless souls," Janus answers. "Those that have a stronger connection between the living and the dead."

"Ha! Restless? You haven't seen anything yet!" Zophiel responds. "This is the memorial park. The old burial grounds are back there," Zophiel says while pointing to another opening in the cast iron gate. "Those souls died a lonnnggg time ago! Well... mortally speaking."

The fearless four hustle to the back of the memorial park. Along the seamless continuation in the cast iron gate, a rusty-hinged door is bolted lock with a chain. The graves are marked with old broken headstones and overgrown weeds that can be seen through the gate poles. Some graves are unmarked while others have headstones that are broken and illegible. Aza conjures up his astroflare and swings at the chain, splitting the links apart. Sparks fly as the chain falls to the ground. Janus pulls the gate and a loud screech of rusty deteriorating hinges grind away as it opens. No one has visited these souls for a long time. The group enters the backyard burial grounds.

Janus looks left and then right with a solemn frown. "We need to find the most restless and sinister soul to open a channel to the Chancellor's spell."

"There are a lot of sinister souls in this place," Zophiel replies as he rubs the bottom of his goatee.

"I suggest we spread out," Aza directs.

While placing a hand up against his stomach and breathing in short breaths Jerry grimaces over the sight of the graves. "What are we looking for exactly?"

"You'll know when you feel it," Janus answers.

"Souls, son. Souls," Zophiel responds.

"I thought when mortals died their souls ascend the path up to the gate house?" Jerry questions.

"Many will come, few will be chosen—"

"The others don't even bother making the trip! Ha! Hek! Hek!" Zophiel interjects.

"Cut it out and get to work," Aza orders.

The posse of four spreads out as they each takes a row of headstones and plod in between them slowly while reading the names and inscriptions. No one was sure what it is exactly they were looking for but they tapped into their best intuition for guidance. Trying not to feel trite as a holovision psychic, Jerry senses the area deeply while taking in its ambiance with every step. Feeling a sudden bout of deep depression, Aza comes across a grave that has potential. When he reads the inscription on the tombstone he discovers the grave of a small child so he continues on down the row. In the next row over, Zophiel walks slower and slower before coming to a complete stop. He takes is hand to his head and then to his chest while breathing heavy. In observance of his actions, the others stop and wait for confirmation that he has found something, but he snaps back shaking his head explaining that he's had way too much to drink.

"We need to hurry!" Janus informs. "The best mystical energy occurs right before dawn. Don't be overly discriminatory we don't... Oh! Oh my Holiness!" Janus stops and trembles at the knees. An old cracked tombstone next to Janus is marked with writing that is indiscernible. "You! You murdered them!"

"Sounds like a winner. Can we go now?" Zophiel asks.

"Janus!" Aza shouts, but from out of the frozen terror there is no response. "Janus!" Aza tries again. Janus' teeth chatter as words are fighting to break out. "Child of Barcus!" Aza shouts.

"This, this is it!" Janus replies. Janus immediately begins the counter spell to remove the block on Karlisa. "Lord Abraxis, almighty spirit of the universe. I do exorcise and command thee, by the divine Upper Room before the throne, having eyes before and behind." The night clouds above move in a fast circular motion. "By the holy angels of Omnus I do potently exorcise thee that thou appearest here to fulfill my will in all things which seem good unto me." Thunder rumbles in the sky above. "Wherefore, come thou, visibly, peaceably, and affably, now, without delay, to manifest that which I desire, speaking with a clear and perfect voice, intelligibly, and to mine understanding." Lightning strikes and the clouds grow larger and change to purple with a pulsating dark orange shimmer. "Give me the power to open this channel into the mind and body of Karlisa Xeven and keep at bay those whom are forbidden the grace of the throne."

Lightning strikes from the grave up into the sky as a dark cloaked figure appears in the distance. The figure raises a rod up to the sky. An eyeball on the handle of the rod projects an energy beam into the sky that opens a sphere. Strong winds blow in from every direction. Aza conjures his astroflare and wings from the exoverse. Jerry follows Aza's lead and conjures the sword of Zimkiel from the exoverse. Zophiel hides behind a tall tombstone. The sphere flashes a scene of Karlisa being tied and gagged. She is being pushed and shoved down a hall by Penemue and Araqiel. Karlisa is thrown on the floor in a room and then a door slams shut, trapping her inside.

"You bastard!" Jerry screams through the thundering storm. "Where is she? Where is she you God damned bastard?"

The dark figure tries to close the sphere with the energy beam from its rod but Janus fights with a counter spell to keep it open. Janus throws up two hands and shouts, "The power of Barcus!"

The sphere blurs but remains open showing Karlisa crying and looking through the sphere as if she can see Jerry. She whimpers and tries to speak through the gag but her voice is muffled. Her eyes are wide and red while her face is stained with running mascara and tears. The sphere begins to fade again.

"I'm coming! Karlisa, I'm coming!" Jerry shouts before turning to the figure. "Damn you!"

Janus tries to keep the sphere open. With two enchanted hands raised to the sphere in the sky Janus shouts, "The Grace of Sandalphon!"

Jerry runs toward the dark figure with his astroflare raised.

"No! No! Jerry you are not ready!" Aza shouts.

"It's just an aberration!" Janus shouts through the wind. "It's not the Chancellor! It's an illusion Jerry!"

Jerry swings the astroflare at the dark figure's body but it disappears along with the sphere. With no target to strike, the force of Jerry's swing lunges him onto the ground. He looks up and watches the sphere zip out of the sky. Dawn breaks as streaks of the morning sun pierce through the darkness. The wind and storm clouds fade away as quickly as they had arrived. Jerry looks up at the sunlight rays shining into his eyes while birds chirp in the distance. The others stand in the light of dawn with the fading mist of the passing storm quickly dissipating around them.

"Well that was fun! Hell! I need to hang out with you boys more often. Ha! Hek! Hek!" Zophiel laughs away the last remnants of the event.

Janus flashes over to Jerry as he crawls up off his knees. "Sorry I couldn't keep the sphere open," Janus apologizes. "The sun broke the channel. The spell only works at night when channeling evil entities."

"If we find your siblings, we find Karlisa?" Jerry asks feeling self-assured.

"Well that's the easy part," Zophiel informs. "They have a not so gentlemen's club not too far from here. They call it the Thirteenth House of Heaven."

"Can we find them there during the day?" Jerry asks.

"Oh... the Thirteenth House never closes. The Thirteenth House is off the grid. It's need-to-know only, VIP admittance, and password required entry," Zophiel explains with a smile.

"Sounds like we are taking you home," says Aza as he motions the others to follow him to the exit. "Let's get out of this dreadful place. It even stinks in the sunlight."

13th Heaven

Jerry parks the sedan on a side street near a row of old mom and pop retail establishments. The street is located in a historic district that was an old venders market where the trading and selling of old world goods once took place. Most of the storefronts now look worn as business transactions in these shops use outdated methods from the past. Many of the vendors still barter and use a form currency in exchange for goods and services. In most modern 2171 markets all merchandise is mail ordered after shopping through display only models. The transactions are digital and the credits are not tangible but scanned from a bar scan mark embedded in the hand. The customers in this district are mostly undocumented citizens who have not embedded finance and ID chips in their hands so they can stay off the New Gaia grid. They prefer to exchange goods and services at the point of transaction using some bartering power.

"Ok, all I see is a tobacco shop, a spice and oil shop, a textile shop, an un psychic shop; that I thought were outlawed, and a fine spirits and liquor shop," Jerry reports.

"Do you see any gentlemen clubs?" Zophiel asks.

"Ah... no!" Jerry responds.

"Then you are in the right spot. Ha! Hek! Hek!" Zophiel laughs. "Let's go get some spices."

The four immortals enter into the small spice market and discretely shop the shelves while Zophiel speaks with the head merchant. The shop has many old oak shelves with glass jars and other dark vessels made of clay. Under each container is an inscription of the jars contents. Janus reads the shelf labels and begins to chuckle. Janus quickly moves through the aisles with excitement looking at the labels indicating various types of Love Potions, Anti-aging Lotions, Enemy Repellants, Career Tonics, etc., Each label causes the genie to cover its mouth to avoid laughing out loud but Janus can barely control it and lets a few giggles out for all to hear. A store clerk comes over to Janus and asks if she can be of any assistance, but Janus politely turns down the offer and keeps shopping. Zophiel speaks with the head merchant but does not make any headway into gaining entry beyond the secret door to the underground gentlemen's club. Aza pretends to shop through the spices but keeps a watchful eye on Zophiel who doesn't appear to be making much progress. Jerry browses through the bubbling mist potions where the jars are all over flowing with vapors, offering mystical cures for illnesses and other physical disorders. Janus picks up an oil vessel that reads, "Libido Power." A sudden burst of laughter is heard throughout the store.

The store clerk, a short woman barely tall enough to reach canisters on the shelf, comes across the room to Janus. "May I help you," the store clerk asks with a stern and unwelcoming tone as she stands with a hand on her smock-covered hip looking up through her eyeglasses at Janus.

"I'm sorry. No... I'm fine really," Janus replies.

Looking at the jar Janus is holding, the storekeeper asks, "Are you looking for something to increase your sex drive?"

"Well I was thinking of maybe making some kale and carrot soup," Janus chuckles. "It says olive oil," Janus laughs hysterically. "You can't increase ones libido with olive oil. Huh ha!"

"If I had a credit for every novice who thought they knew everything from reading the Gaia Net I would be a rich person," the store clerk responds. "Olive oil increases the blood flow to the sexual organs and it is very potent when mixed with the secret quantities of the other ingredients."

Trying to sound less critical while fighting to straighten its smile, Janus replies, "Yes... olive oil with the right amount of dead sea salt will make a... delicious Huh! Ha! Libido! Ka Hee! Ka Hee! Hee!"

Cocking her neck back and sticking her nose up with her head slightly turned to the side the store clerk asks, "Maybe if you purchased a bottle you could come back and tell me what ingredient you believe to be missing."

"I'm not purchasing this salad dressing, but I'll tell you that none of these potions are going to work without a root stem from Yellow Rock Weed and no love or libido potion is going to work without a binding agent from Bee Vomit and Balsam Orchid Pedals."

With her mouth frozen open the store clerk removes her glasses and demands a response. "Who are you? From which convent are you from?"

"Convent?" Janus grabs its chest as laughter and breathing becomes difficult. "Ka! Hee! Hee! A witch? Do I really—"

"Janus!" Aza calls.

"Umm... thanks for the laugh. It's been great!" Janus says to the store clerk before heading over to Aza. Still chuckling from the question Janus glides over to Aza who has also been joined by Jerry. "What's the hold up?" Janus asks.

"The holdup is everybody is having such a great time doing everything but penetrating this place," Aza says with his teeth clinched speaking under his breath while looking around trying to be discrete.

Jerry shouts over at Zophiel, "Hey! What's up?"

Speaking to the head merchant, "As you see my friends are anxious to spend their credits," Zophiel informs the merchant. "Why don't you just ask the twins to let me in? I'm on the list."

The old merchant wearing his smock over a gray vest and white shirt points to two levers protruding up from the floor behind the counter. The clerk's hand with black painted fingernails is wrapped firmly around the right lever. "Citing the correct password allows one pull on the lever to the right. One pull releases the locking mechanism that unlocks that door." The merchant points to a door with a glowing light around its perimeter. "One pull, one entry. If you have the correct password you will get one entry not four!" The merchant shouts at Zophiel, as he has now grown weary of the conversation. "The lever to the left... well you don't want me to pull that lever." The clerk stares at Zophiel as he switches his hand to the left lever. "You need to give me a password, make a purchase, or leave now."

"The old lever trick," Janus discretely informs Aza. "The secret is he can pull anyone of those levers, it has nothing to do with opening that door. The door has been spell sealed."

"It's useless brothers," Zophiel reports. "I've tried."

"Maybe you don't mind if I try," Aza says as he turns to Janus. "Gate keeper, will you please attend to the front door?"

Janus throws a locking spell at the door that seals the entry. Aza conjures his astroflare from out of the exoverse then turns to the merchant. "Look you can pull any fucking lever you please but you will let me speak with the club owners so either you get them out here, or you let me in there. You tell them an old friend, Azazel, is here to see them!" Aza demands with the astroflare pointed at the merchant's neck.

The merchant's eyes grow larger as his chest swells with a deep breath. "Sire! You are... Azazel?"

The merchant asks as the inner light in his eyes sparkle brighter.

"What is it you know about me?"

"My lord, you are a legend!" the merchant responds as he fights to keep his chin up off the blazing astroflare.

"And this one is some kind of demon!" the storekeeper shouts across the room pointing at Janus who immediately fights the urge to release a giggle. "You will lower your weapon now or face my hexing!" the storekeeper shouts as she transforms into an pale green hag with black nails and long old fingers that she claws towards Aza.

"It's Xirce, The Dan River Witch, Aza!" Zophiel warns.

"You're not my first witch!" Aza informs. "Who do you think taught you all these black magic spells?"

"Xirce, he is a leader of the Fallen," The merchant informs. "The door was sealed by the Chancellor. Only Xirce has the spell to release the seal." The merchant turns to the witch. "He's a leader of the Fallen so maybe we should just let him in?"

"He may be a leader, but I've been trained through the lineage of Master Semjaza, the greatest of all the Fallen!" the witch informs.

"HA! Hek! Hum! Hmmm," Janus laughs out loud. "I'm sorry! I'm sorry I just can't take it anymore."

"Yes, he has fallen to this genie's sword and you are about to do the same!" Aza warns.

The merchant raises his arms and cast an energy sphere at Aza but Janus quickly counters and casts an energy sphere that consumes it with an explosion that blows the merchant back into the wall, shattering all the glass jars and containers in the room leaving a mist of dust and glass shards. Aza, Jerry, and Zophiel duck for cover as Janus turns and prepares to throw another sphere at the witch who attempts to hex Janus, but nothing comes out from Xirce's casting fingers. Xirce repetitively makes gyrating hand motions throwing her hands, but nothing has an effect against Janus.

"Mortals!" Janus shouts at the witch. "What's wrong, witch? Your old black magic won't work against the true power of the divine?" Janus taunts. "Now get your ugly ass over there and open that damn door!"

The witch looks at her hands in defeat with sunken eyes and a shallow beating heart. "I'll never open that door. I'll die first, you filthy creature of the light."

Janus flashes across the room and stands over Xirce as the witch looks up in fear. "The BITCH of Dan River!" Janus mocks. "Look at your snake oil shop now. You will need to rebuild. Hopefully there's a deli nearby that will sell you some olive oil and sea salts."

The witch looks around at the remnants of her destroyed shop. "With the right libido spell I can rebuild much quicker," The witch says staring at Janus. "If you give me the right ingredients I will open that door."

"I don't teach sorcery to mortals. It's forbidden!"

"Are you kidding me!" shouts Jerry. "I just killed a man, fought with the devil in a midnight cemetery, and now I'm covered with glass," Jerry pleads as he brushes dust from his clothes. "That's the easiest thing we've been asked to do all night."

"Give her the spell! She's just letting people get it on! Doctors sell that shit all day! It's not like

she's asking for the secret of eternal youth,"
Zophiel adds.

The witch's eyes widen, "Actually… that doesn't
sound—"

"Shut up! Now write this down," Janus instructs
the witch who searches for a pen and paper in her
smock. Janus turns towards Jerry "This is not right.
This is highly vulgar and forbidden!"

"I think you killed the warlock over here and blew
up a spice shop. You're way pass vulgar! Forbidden
depends on how you interpret the law," Jerry
responds.

"I'm ready," says the witch.

"You will need: one cup of virgin shark oil, three
pinches ground Nile River Snake spit, two pods of
cardamom, the egg of a desert tarantula, one pinch
of dill weed, and two pedals from a purple dragon
tulip. Stirred it with four dime sized jasper stones
from the red sea caves. The libido elixir should be
drunk at the point of arousal. The lust for ones
partner will last for four days so it should only be
shared with a lover."

"Where in the hell am I going to get purple
dragon tulips?" the witch asks.

"In Hell indeed! You're a witch. Go get it!" Janus
follows Jerry and the others through the secret
door that has now been opened but not before
shouting back, "Without the tulip the rest of the
potion is merely a marinating sauce at best."

Jerry steps through the club entrance with his
newly found posse. The first passageway is a softly
lit foyer where guest are greeted by modestly
dressed women in elegant attire and a master host
who looks more appropriately suited for a five star
steakhouse. The foyer is decorated with chic

golden paisley embroidery on pink silk fabric padded walls. The carpet is a plush metallic gold Saxony with nylon hand sewn patterns and silky threading that feels better on bare feet. Your steps sink in the comfort like walking on clouds in Heaven. Jerry notices the feeling and reminisces about his first steps into the house of Sandalphon, but the comparison is a far second.

Jerry looks up and notices a large dangling chandelier that reminds him of a story he once read about the restoration of furnishings excavated from out of a nightclub in the memorialized war-torn buildings in New York. The hostesses offer to take the gentlemen's jackets but they refuse. Then the ladies escort Jerry and his party up to the master host, Mister Triel. The music coming from beyond the doors separating the foyer from the club is loud and booming. The sound nearly drowns out Mr. Triel's voice when he tries to introduce himself and offer special accommodations to Zophiel, a VIP guest.

"Mr. Zophiel!" Mr. Triel shouts. "It's nice to see you again." Mr. Triel extends his neatly manicured black nail painted hand to greet Zophiel.

"It's always good to come back Mr. Triel," Zophiel shakes his hand while gesturing toward his companions. "This is the one and only, Azazel."

"AZAZEL! No way in Hell! HA! HA! ALRIGHT!" Mr. Triel extends a hand to Aza. "What an honor, what an honor! Girls! Girls!" He calls to the hostesses. "The finest table we have available please. We have a lord in the house."

Aza stares at Mr. Triel with a blank face devoid of emotion. As they loosely shake hands, Aza inhales and quickly exhales while bringing his shoulders down low with his deflated chest. Mr. Triel scuttles off to instruct the girls on the preparations.

"Are you ok?" Jerry asks discretely, up close to Aza.

"I don't need to be in places like this," Aza answers. "Spells, cosmetics, and the art of seduction... I taught them these things. This is my fault."

"Ah... you didn't Fall alone."

"I was the first! It was me and me alone!"

"But you've been redeemed!"

Aza nods his head and remains silent.

Jerry moves closer and places a hand on Aza's shoulder. "I know what it really is," Jerry says softly just under the blaring music that has been covering their conversation. Aza stares straight ahead at the still joyous Mr. Triel and the ladies who are preparing for their VIP entry. "These women remind you of how much you miss her." Aza's eyes widen as he fixate on Jerry's every word. "I feel the same. We are this close to getting some real answers. She may even be in this damn place somewhere." Jerry squeezes Aza's shoulder with a firmer grip. "All that stuff I said in the car... that's just me being scared and without my meds, but I'm learning and I still need you. I knew when Sandalphon offered me this opportunity that it wouldn't be easy but I'm in it for the long haul. After I see that Karly is at home and safe... we'll go find your girl." Aza swallows the buildup of moisture in his mouth as his eyes sink in over his clinched jaw. "But for right now I need you to be THE AZAZEL! That's whom these demons and warlocks want to see. Go give'em a show!" Jerry pleads. "We need to get these guys to come to us! Get up into their backroom or get them alone in the

VIP area. Then you'll see what a little warrior I've come to be! I'm not leaving here without her or one of them!" Aza shakes his head in confirmation of the plan. "Now let's go kick some demon ass!"

"Jerry!" Aza shouts before he walks away. "You're immortal now! You don't need any meds. What you are experiencing is a part of the human condition. You're ok. Angels can get anxious too." Aza smiles at Jerry who breathes in deeply and nods in acceptance of the information. "Now one thing you need to know about Azazel is that he was quite the ladies man. Maybe you will learn something," Aza concludes as he straightens his blazer.

The master host brings a fashionable courtesy jacket to Zophiel. "You know the required dress you Fallen mess. Here, this will suit you just fine," he says as he helps Zophiel into the house jacket. "I see your friends are dressed for the occasion."

"Thank you, Mr. Triel—"

"Stop it! Kay! It's Kay Triel, but all my VIPs call me Kay," the master host corrects. "Now ladies," Kay claps softly, "Take our guests to the Thirteenth Heaven."

"Gladly," the ladies sparkle as they escort the four gentle souls beyond the foyer doors.

The main concourse of the Thirteenth Heaven is a heavenly dreamscape decorated lounge and staging area. The ceiling has an appearance of an open night sky amphitheatre with statues of fallen angels, gargoyles, and demons surrounding the high perimeter. The club is dark with the exception of general torch lighting, table candles, and stage lights. A stage lighting, environmental effects, and sound room is located up high across from the center stage. Over the center stage a digital sign flashes: Vilon. There are twelve other stages. The entire place was intended to ridicule the Heavens. Stages ten through twelve named: Persidis, Dynacia, and Lucimus are elevated higher than the other nine stages. Stages eight and nine are kept dark and it's where nude demons shadow dance in mock of the destroyed houses of Heaven. The exotic dancers come in every race, gender, and sexual orientation but there is only one nationality the club promotes, Hell it's where the dancers will tell you they're from if you ask.

The loud music fades as the master of ceremonies MC Mikael, a childlike figure in oversized clothing, comes out to introduce the center stage performer.

"Witches and Warlocks please welcome to the gateway of Hell the DELICIOUS demon of the DARK, Dilek!" the MC announces as Jerry and he crew is escorted to a private VIP table.

Seductive music played on hand drums and harps play rhythmically as purple lighting accentuates the center stage. A live crooner sings off stage as Dilek slowly seduces her audience with a slow belly dance.

A harp plays and a hand drum thumps:
Bomp!
Bomp! Bomp!
Bomp!
Bomp! Bomp!
A crooner sings:
"Love," Bomp ... Bomp! Bomp! "Don't live here."
Bomp... Bomp! Bomp!
"I'm the lust you want but always feared."
Bomp... Bomp! Bomp!

"Lust," Bomp... Bomp! Bomp! "Knows my name," Bomp... Bomp! Bomp!

"You can't deny the lust to escape the shame," Bomp... Bomp! Bomp!

Dilek continues her dance as the crooner keeps singing. Her eyes fixate on no one in particular until she spots Aza. Bomp... Bomp! Bomp! The rhythmic drum continues. A direct line of seduction becomes obvious as her eyes return to him after every twirl and turn. Her body moves and her head spins but her eyes never leave Aza. Members of the audience soon catch on to the lust connection and turn to look at the lucky client who has caught the dancer's attention.

"Do you know her, Aza?" Jerry asks as he catches on to her attraction.

"Yes. To no one is to know all, for they are a legion," Aza answers as he keeps his eyes glued to the hips of the delicious Dilek. "To know one is to know all."

"May I get you warlocks a brew of one of our finest potions?" a voice asks, interrupting the mesmerized guests.

Jerry responds, "No thank you," without turning away from Dilek's show.

Aza, stuck in Dilek's entrapment, does not respond. Zophiel answers, "Get me my usual poison please Ishtar," as he grins wide at the thrill of his companions. "Get them a goblet of the same goop."

Turning away from the stage show towards Ishtar, Janus eyes widen and the genie flickers while placing a hand over its chest. "I... I-I," Janus swallows, "I'll have a chalice of wine please."

Dilek's show ends and as usual there is silence as it is against the house rules to applaud or to show gratification. This crowd takes pride in not having any good manners.

"Did you see her?" Janus asks as he stares off in the distance at Ishtar. "She's the reason why so many fell. She is why so many were tempted to fall."

"So I take it that you liked the show. Huh ha! Ha!" Zophiel laughs.

"No... not the dancer, the waitress, Ishtar," Janus explains.

"Waitress?" Zophiel ask looking across to Ishtar. "Auh Ooo... you mean waiter. Look a little closer next time. Huh! Ha! Gets'em every time! Ha! Hek! Hek!"

"Waiter or waitress I don't care what kind of demon it is," Jerry snaps getting back on track with the mission. "Get us in the company of the owners!"

"Don't worry... I-I think I got this," Janus replies as the genie straightens its attire. "This place is infectious. The longer we stay here the more we are vulnerable to seduction."

"The soul is right!" Zophiel confirms. "They change the seduction scheme every twelve minutes until you pay a toll, sell your soul, or sign up on their you-owe-me scroll, no body leaves clear and free," Zophiel smiles.

"If I find out you helped lure us here to pay your tab... your bill is going to be long overdue," Aza warns.

"Oh you don't have to worry about that. Whatever it is they think is still of worth from me they withdrew it a long time ago," Zophiel says with his eyes hanging low.

"Your refreshments are here warlocks!" Ishtar announces as she serves a round of drinks.

"Excuse me temptress," Janus calls to Ishtar. "If my friend here wanted a more private arrangement with... ah let's say... Dilek, how is that arranged?"

"That depends on how many will be attending this... private arrangement. You will have to discuss the details with Dilek. Shall I send her over?"

"Yes, please. Umm... Ishtar! If the arrangement was with you how would you accommodate me?"

Ishtar moves in closer and swings her way onto Janus' lap. "Well if it's for you exclusively, I can accommodate you here or in one of our more private booths."

"And if I want to bring a friend?"

"Eww you are a little demon," Ishtar says with her finger rubbing down Janus chest. "I would suggest a private booth."

"Ishtar. Let me be more direct," warns Janus. "What I want is sodomy and terror! But most of all... I want to indulge in group sadistic MURDER!" Janus requests with one eye cocked and widened as the genie leans in closer to Ishtar's face.

With eyebrows arched and eyes blinking under his wrinkled forehead Jerry turns to Aza and mouths the words, "WHAT THE FUCK!"

Aza grins, but not as wide as Zophiel's smile that is leaning in closer to hear the answer to Janus' request.

Ishtar backs away from Janus face, swallows hard, and removes her hand from Janus' chest. "Well... we, we can accommodate most anything but who is it you want to murder?"

Janus leans in closer again, "A young mortal woman. One who is unsuspecting and spellbound to not resist anything I may request."

"Ok... but what does this have to do with me?"

"Everything!" Janus answers. "What good is sadism without an audience?" Janus asks with a smile. "There's nothing like having a beauty such as yourself arouse me then set my desire for the flesh loose. You will join us of course."

Ishtar stares at Janus with questioning eyes, "Are you kidding me?"

Janus pushes Ishtar off its lap hard onto the floor. "I knew this place was a faux!" Janus says standing up as if preparing to leave.

"Oh, you think you are the first to make that request?" Ishtar shouts from the floor. "It's going to cost you!" she says as she stands up, brushes herself off, and straightens her dress. "I'll have to go get it approved in the Lower Room first!"

"The Lower Room?" Janus asks.

"Downstairs with the owners," Ishtar explains.

Aza looks over at Jerry. Jerry stands up and approaches Ishtar. "Excuse my comrade's behavior. Are you ok?"

"I'm fine! I've been treated worse!" Ishtar smiles.

"Listen, Ishtar. This venture is very important to us. It would mean a great deal to us if we could make our request ourselves to make sure the details are clear."

"No one meets the owners without prior approval," Ishtar informs.

"Look, do you see this damned soul here?" pointing at Aza. "This is one of the oldest lords of the underworld. I'm surprised your owners haven't come up to pay their respect. I find that quite offensive!"

"Please accept my apology. I'm aware of his legend but I was hoping to give you a variety of demons to choose from before sending you off to the dark dungeon," Ishtar explains.

"Ishtar. I'll give you 5,000 credits if you allow the legendary Azazel to make his own introduction," Jerry says holding out his palm for a credit scan.

"Five? Are you kidding me? 12,000 credits! I'm breaking the rules."

"I'll give you 8,000 now and you keep it regardless of the results, but if they permit our request I'll give you the additional 4,000 for your participation," Jerry barters.

Zophiel leans over to Aza. "Where did you find these souls?" Aza smiles and shakes his head.

Ishtar pulls a device from her dress strap. "Swipe!" she requests of Jerry.

Jerry swipes his palm then presses his thumb over the password identification scanner. Uncertain that the credit or his personal scan would work, Jerry holds his breath as he waits for the results. Aza looks over at Janus who is conjuring up a silent spell. The device lights up one of three green lights, then two as Ishtar waits for the final transaction approval. Jerry turns and looks at Aza who stares back with a puzzled look as he too waits for the approval. Janus notices that Aza has prepared his hand for conjuring his astroflare out of the exoverse. Zophiel backs away from the table and they all wait tentatively for the final green light.

The led flashes green. "Ok, let's go!" Ishtar instructs.

Aza looks at Jerry and Jerry shrugs his shoulders. The group follows Ishtar to the Lower Room. The group descends down the stairs into the lower level where they come to a hall with various rooms along the side. Each room has a door with a small window.

"This used to be a very prestigious lunatic asylum," Ishtar informs as she tours her guests through the building. "The upstairs area was the auditorium and the store fronts were administrative offices."

Jerry takes a quick look through every window on the right while Aza glances through each window on the left. On the right, Jerry finds what appears to be dressing rooms for the stage shows upstairs and on the left, Aza discovers cells where men sit in the dark muttering and frantically pacing the rooms.

A captive stands in a cell talking to himself, "... when he went in unto his brother's wife, he spilled it on the ground! He-he-he should have given seed to his brother," the captive says as he paces the room, "Mwahahaha! The thing, which he done so displeased the Lord wherefore I slew him!" The captive runs up to the glass window and shouts at Aza, "I slew ALL OF THEM!"

Dilek pops out from around a corner standing in front of the group with her hands on her hips and her head cocked back preventing the group from proceeding down the hall. "We had a DEAL!" she shouts at Ishtar.

"Things have changed. We have a situation." Ishtar says calmly as she monitors her breathing and speaks through her teeth.

"Two of them are coming with me or we are going to have a problem!" Dilek says as she flings a small radiant light scepter from out of the exoverse.

"Bring it BITCH!" Ishtar says as she transforms into an old cracked and pale-faced demon with dark blood red colored eyes.

"Wait!" Jerry shouts. "Maybe Zop and I should go with the lovely Dilek," Jerry offers as he stares at Aza and nods slowly with connected eyes. "You and Janus go and make the arrangements and we'll accompany Dilek in one of the nearby rooms here in this hall," Jerry confirms with Dilek.

"Sounds like a plan to me," Dilek agrees.

"Yeah I kind of like it myself," Zophiel agrees.

Ishtar transforms back into a woman. "Save some credits for the main event warlocks," Ishtar says as she proceeds past Dilek to the Lower Room.

Dilek escorts Jerry and Zophiel to a nearby empty cell as Ishtar takes Aza and Janus to the owners. Ishtar arrives at a door marked: MISMANAGEMENT. She opens the door and escorts in her guests as the two owners quickly stand up from behind their desks.

Ishtar introduces, "Penemue and Araqiel this is—"

"JANUS!" the two genies shout.

"Look it is Azazel!" Penemue shouts to Araqiel.

"The Call! The Fall! The Pact of us All!" the two owners shout in unison before hurrying over with quick bows and handshakes. All five souls take seats in a sitting area away from the desk. They are full of smiles with their reunion.

"So... what rock did you climb out from under?" Araqiel laughs as the genie looks around for an audience but only finds straight faces. "I'm sorry," the genie snickers. "I had to, I just couldn't resist," Araqiel says with a shaking head curbing off the laughter. "I mean... under a rock! Really! What kind of cruel shit is that to be placing an immortal soul under a quandary of rocks in an earthly desert?"

"Since he fell upon it, it was meant to ridicule his liking of it over the Heavens," Janus explains before looking towards Aza and then quickly away with jolting eyes. "I-I meant it's what they told us."

"Janus! How are you?" Penemue asks looking over at its sibling with large and moist eyes.

"I'm fine. How come you didn't come up to greet me?" Janus snaps.

"They told us two Fallen VIPs were in the house... this place has been a magnet lately for Fallen V-I-Ps. Pleeeaaase spare me from all the Prima Donna self-absorbed demons!" Penemue answers. "They should have said a child of Barcus!"

"Or... THE One! And only! Second after Lord Abaddon to Fall... AZA... ZEL!" Araqiel announces with a master of ceremonies shout.

Janus looks at the genies and notices how nicely they are dressed. The finest silk suits and leather shoes that a mortal can buy cover these two from head to toe. They are similarly dressed in stylish suits, similar to Janus and Aza, but their colors are brighter and their silks are shinier. Penemue is a very metropolitan high fashion genie and former assistant ambassador of the now destroyed Tenth House. Penemue is wearing a two-toned burgundy-stripped wool and viscose suit with a slim fit jacket and notched lapel collar. There are two darker flap hand pockets and one lighter colored besom pocket at the chest with a silk pink handkerchief. If he catches someone admiring his suit he is usually quick to inform how it was hand sewn. Araqiel was the former assistant ambassador of the now destroyed Eleventh House. Araqiel wears a greenish-yellow, single breasted, two button light wool and silk micro designed suit with green led pin stripping. The jacket has a highlighted blinking notch lapel, digitized front flap welt pockets, and blinking button cuffs. The pants have a tab waist, a lighted zip closure, digital belt loops, and led lined pockets in the front and the back.

"So... how did you escape, what happened, I-I was told you were captured in the last revolt then I was told you were out in the dark expanse," Penemue asks.

Aza explains, "Well once I got out from under that rock pit—"

"Which I visited the grounds to inform you of all the latest developments," Araqiel interrupts. "I didn't know exactly where you were but I knew you'd hear me." Araqiel smiles. "I just thought it was important to say at this time."

Penemue does some discrete eye rolling.

"As many others did, but thank you! Thank you very much." Aza continues, "I traveled to Heaven, freed Semjaza—"

"How did you get to Heaven once your body and soul had been bounded by light?" Araqiel interrupts again.

"I was unbounded by a pure hearted mortal and through that mortals belief in the faith of flight he..." Aza pauses and looks over at Janus before continuing. "He came to realize his spiritual wings—"

"The jump trick! You made him jump? Ha! Ha! Haaah! Whew!" Araqiel laughs.

"He killed himself and you rode his soul to Heaven! I love it!" Penemue shouts.

"YOU killed him!" Janus scorns. "That's why I didn't sense damnation. He didn't know!"

"I simply did what had to be done," Azazel explains. "What was I to say. 'Hi I'm a Fallen angel and if you jump off this cliff I'll take you to save your wife?" Aza pleads to Janus. "If I didn't get him to do it the Chancellor would have killed him and his wife anyway."

"Still it's the oldest trick in the book with these damned mortals," Penemue says as it adjusts itself in his seat. "They believe they can fly."

"Ha! Ha Ha," Araqiel and Penemue laughs.

"Well as it happens to be," Azazel continues, "I freed Semjaza and the others, I believe one of you were able to get out during that revolt."

"Yes, I did! Thank you," Penemue says. "Our sibling Gaap was not so lucky."

"Thank the Chancellor that one of you escaped. The USA has been without a leader for so long," says Araqiel.

"What do you mean?" asks Penemue. "This New Gaia godless man movement has been crazy cool!"

"So you guys are not kings anymore?" Janus asks.

"Kings? I was hoping to be a Queen sweetheart," Penemue responds.

"Kings. Ha! Those days are over. Mortals don't elect men anymore, they elect money," Araqiel answers. "We finance campaigns in over fifty developed nations around the world."

"So Janus you blew your assistant ambassador job to answer the call?" Penemue asks and answers with a nodding head in confirmation. "Now that's what I call a loyal member of the Pact!"

"I guess we have to do... what must be done," Janus responds looking over at Azazel then lowering its head.

"Hey where is Semjaza?" Araqiel asks. "He should have been here by now. The Apocalypse is coming soon so this is our time to terrorize! Our time to rule before the big battle!"

"Lord Abaddon didn't get out so there is no Apocalypse yet," Azazel informs.

"He was not supposed to leave. It's part of the bigger plan," Araqiel informs. "Didn't the Chancellor update you?"

"Once we get the Second and the Third House we'll control the prison in Raquia and the Hell House of Saqun. The twins assured us they'd get a house for their brother in exchange for freeing Abaddon during the Apocalypse," Penemue collaborates.

"Which twins!" Janus asks as the genie comes unglued from its passive role-playing.

Araqiel wrinkles its forehead up before answering. "Hey why don't you guys know the plan and why didn't you bring Semjaza?"

"I'm sick of this shit!" Janus informs Aza. "Because I killed him that's why!"

"No Janus!" Aza pleads but it comes too late as Janus springs into a rant.

"He killed Jazire and I killed him!" Janus shouts after jumping up from the chair.

"What!" Araqiel and Penemue shout.

"He was a captain! You can't kill a captain!" Penemue shouts.

"He was not exalted by the dark. He pursued Abaddon at Lake Saqun," Penemue informs with a forward cocked and swaying head. "He was vulnerable and trying to win his way into the dark."

"So you killed a Pact member?" Araqiel disdains.

Aza prepares for drawing his astroflare from the exoverse. "Let's just cool it now!" He warns the genies.

"If you wanted a Jazire you could have had 50 of them!" Araqiel informs. "There's a whole heirloom full on stage four!"

"Where's the girl?" Janus asks.

"What girl?" Araqiel responds.

"The mortal! The bait you used to draw out Jerry."

"Oh! That bitch!" Penemue answers.

"We gave her to the Chancellor. What concern is she to you?" Araqiel further says as it throws up its hands and prepares to cast a spell. "I think its time that you go!"

"Oh, please lower your hands!" Janus informs. "I was elected to the FIRST house of Vilon because of my skills."

"You might be skillful, but you're not too bright," Ishtar says as she sneaks up behind Janus with a dagger.

Aza conjures his astroflare and wings as Araqiel and Penemue conjure up scepters. Ishtar holds the blade tighter to Janus' throat. Aza feels confident with taking on two genies and a demon, but it would come at the cost of Janus' immortal soul.

"Drop it Azazel or my dear sibling gets it!" Araqiel informs.

Aza ponders it over for the moment but he knows one way or the other there would be no getting out without a fight.

"Ishtar, listen to me," Janus requests. "Who will be the new owner if these two leave?"

"Maybe... Kay Triel," she answers.

"Not if you and only you possess the spell for attraction and desire. Think about the power that would bring you over repeat customers," Janus offers.

"You'd teach me?"

"That's forbidden!" Araqiel reminds Janus.

"You bitch!" Penemue calls out.

"Oh! Really?" Ishtar responds while darting her eyes at Penemue. "Kill'em!" she demands as she lowers her blade.

Aza jumps and swings his astroflare into the torso of Araqiel instantly killing his body and sending him into a cloud of smoke. Janus throws an energy sphere at Penemue disabling the genie's ability to vanish from the room. Penemue flickers and flashes across the room to the door and attempts to run out but finds itself in the path of Jerry's astroflare pointed at the genie's chest.

"No Jerry!" Janus shouts. "This one is mine." Janus takes the astroflare from Aza and drifts over to Penemue. "You disappointed Father. Now redeem yourself and tell me where the girl is and I'll let you go!"

Jerry holds his astroflare closer to the genie's chest in a stabbing angle as his face frowns up and his breathing rapidly increases.

"Cool it, Jerry," Janus pleads.

"An Earth Angel?" Penemue says with widened eyes and a gasped mouth. "What kind of shit—"

"Tell me now!" Janus shouts.

"Honestly, I don't know," Penemue answers before seeing Jerry's eyes squint with a death-striking stare. "Wait!" the genie quickly stalls. "It's a monastery somewhere in town."

"Tell me where."

"I don't know! Find it yourself!"

"Wrong answer," Jerry informs.

"Fuck you Earth Angel!"

Janus plunges the astroflare into Penemue's back and the genie's soul swarms away in a cloud of smoke.

"You promised to spare me," Penemue yells as it falls to the floor and slowly dies.

"And you said honestly!" Janus answers back. "You never had an honest day in your life."

"I know the monastery," Ishtar informs. "But it's going to cost you!"

Janus raises the astroflare to Ishtar's chest.

"You guys sure know how to barter!" Ishtar says with a smile. "It's the abandoned old world monastery in Saidnaya. It's the only one standing since the war. It has angel statues lined up in the front entrance. Be careful. It's dilapidated and the grounds are cursed," Ishtar informs.

"Oh, brother!" Aza replies.

"The spell you promised me..." Ishtar reminds Janus.

"I'll say this once!" Janus says in hesitation of breaking a sacred rule.

"Drink the elixir of an aphrodisiac potion then bring your lover to a prepared room. In a dark room set four lava rocks from a red sea volcano in each corner of the room. Make sure the room is no more than 10 feet across. Burn an orange frankincense candle inside the room surrounded by five 12 pounds amethyst stones in the form of a

Pentagram. Light the candles and recite while your lover is in the room:

"I call upon Abraxis in this magic hour on prepared grounds within my bower.

Give my companion the will and desire and let it ignite like a raging fire.

Allow no escape no chance to resist, bring vision during the day of our late night kiss.

Trapped inside this ordained spell lovers will return to where I dwell.

Forever trapped in lust and desire, their fantasies shall run rampant, yearning for my hire."

Janus finishes the spell. Using supplies from the office desk Ishtar writes enthusiastically, fixed on every word. "The spell will only work on a client who asks to be your lover. So you must seduce them into a commitment for it to work," Janus concludes.

As Jerry, Aza, and Janus pace their way through the dark halls headed back upstairs they pass several cells along the way. "Zop is ahh... using this cell here," Jerry informs as he stops outside a cell door with sounds of heavy panting coming from inside. "While the demon was occupied I slipped out to search those other rooms. When I came to realize that she is not here I found myself outside the office door... just in time."

"Ewww! Yes!" a voice screams from inside the room.

"Maybe we should just leave him here," Janus says.

"Never leave a brother behind," Aza contests as he opens the cell door and sticks in his head. "Abraxis ye soul! Be careful of what thy place in thou mouth!" Aza exclaims as Jerry and Janus look on from the hall at Aza. "We are departing! Coming art thou?"

"Ohh... ha ha ha yesss! I've been coming huh! huh! Whoo!" Zophiel answers.

"My credits have stopped!" Jerry shouts from the hall.

"WHAT! Out Zophiel! Good bye!" Dilek is heard shouting from the room.

Zophiel exits the room and is soon followed by Dilek. Zophiel waives goodbye and says, "Next time you are going to owe me. Ha! Hek! Hek!"

"Um... Yeah! Sure!" Dilek responds as she wiggles three fingers goodbye.

The four immortals hasten down the hall past cells where they find imprisoned men muttering and talking to themselves. The same captive they passed on the way in continues to pace the floor, grumbling, and talking to himself while rubbing his hands together frantically as he stares at the floor. "When the sons of God came in unto the daughters of man they gave birth to children who became—" the old man abruptly stops, runs up to the cell door window, and points at Aza. "Your children rise again! Father! FATHER!"

Lust

Five red-cloaked and masked Seraphs stand around a table in a dim torch-lit room watching the events at the Thirteenth Heaven unfold before their eyes on the Eye of Abraxis. One of the Seraphs wearing a red mask stands and begins pacing and circling around the table.

The pacing Seraph breaks a long-standing silence, "I knew it!" the Seraph says while coming to stop back at the original point in which it broke the group. "They just couldn't keep their mouths shut!" it says while slamming a fist down on the table.

"Why worry about it?" a red-cloaked, black masked Seraph says. "Do you know how many twins there are amongst us?"

"The legend has it that even Abraxis has a twin out there in the expanse," a gold masked Seraph adds.

"Legend?" the initial pacing Seraph asks. "Who cares about legends? This thing is about to come undone every minute that it takes for any of them to figure it out!"

"I'm afraid by then it'll be too late!" says a red-cloaked and white masked Seraph as it extends a hand over to knock down a mortal figurine. "While wrath is certainly continuing to go strong, lust was aroused!"

"Don't worry," the silver masked Seraph comforts to the one who was pacing. "When you see what I have planned... you'll know... it won't be long now. The Houses shall be ours."

CHAPTER XEVENTEEN

The Valentinian Order

A red sedan travels down an early morning highway. The sunlight dawns through the sky and wraps itself around the tall buildings in the distant cityscape. The red sedan leaves behind the dark road and drives into the sun conquered, divided highway. Small surveillance drones fly through the sky in groups before splitting up into separate patrolling zones. Highway traffic steadily increases by the minute as small low flying hovercraft passenger transports enter the inside express lane and larger hauling, massive transit, and utility vehicles enter onto the outside lane headed to the city's underground tunnels. Jerry uses the two center lanes for standard drive transport vehicles. Aza rides in the front passenger seat while Janus and Zophiel sits in the back seat. Jerry uses the rear view projection screen to see that his back seat passengers have loosened up, relaxed, and is nearly off to sleep.

"Wow!" Jerry says softly to Aza. "I didn't know immortals could become so exhausted."

Aza turns and glances at the back seat passengers. "You ever heard of the phrase 'sleeping like an angel?' Well there you go," Aza enlightens. "This mortal environment is infectious to immortals. The longer we are here the more we become vulnerable to the human physical condition, like the need to sleep and the feeling of hunger. You'll find that a visit to Heaven and a little angel dusting can be extremely rejuvenating."

Jerry moves he eyes as he minds the traffic and watches for road signs to Saidnaya. "Why aren't you tired?"

"After 5,000 years of lying around I'm well rested." Aza glances down at the GPS holomap. "You know this monastery is going to be well guarded. Even if we find her there, we still may not get out alive."

"I was thinking that," Jerry replies as he continues minding the traffic. "Sandalphon said if we come up against the Triads of Terror or the Four Fiends of Fury we should call upon the Order of the Arch, but we don't yet know who's going to be in there. Jerry shakes his head and exhales heavily. "We could really use some help now."

Breaking the sleepy silence from the back is broken as Zophiel utters, "Triads and Fiends! You guys are way too exciting for me, but... I can get some help." Zophiel twists the face of his wristwatch, holds his hand up to his ear, and speaks into the inner side of his wrist. "I need level two support. Possible Triads and Fiends. Lock in on this beacon. Yeah... correct... If that's all you got ok. It's a monastery in Saidnaya. Listen to this, Azazel and you know Janus the gatekeeper from Vilon... umm yeah that's right. Oh yes, and an Earth Angel. Yes Earth. You heard right. Oh I've had plenty of strange tonight. See you there."

Jerry looks back at Zophiel and asks, "What the—"

"A few of us who received pardons in the Throne Room dispersed throughout the universe," Zophiel explains. "A faction of us, The Valentinian Order chose to no longer fight for the light or the dark, but against the conflict itself. Our numbers have grown with those whom have become opposed to the idea of an Apocalypse. They look to me but it's more than what I ever expected. We are in need of new leadership." Zophiel leans in toward the front and looks at Aza. "That's why I was looking for you brother. Like us, we figured you've been played by the inequities on both sides."

Aza rolls a thought around in his head and sighs, "I'm not the leadership type."

"How many are coming?" Jerry asks.

"It was too short notice and too far of a destination. Only a few of my closest companions will make it." Zophiel checks his communicator device. "Yeah they are using the hovercraft express lane. Hey Azazel you remember Raziel of Dynacia?"

Aza thinks for a moment then shakes his head. "Ah, no!"

"What about Caliel?"

"Mmm No."

"Astarphon, I'm sure you remember her!" Zophiel says with a nodding head and widened eyes.

"Astar... from Lucimus?"

"Yeah!"

"I think she works back there at the Thirteenth Heaven!" Aza reports as his eyes widen with assurance.

"No, Your Honor! She cleaned it up! She's a fierce warrior of the truth!"

"What truth?" Janus asks as the genie wakes up. "Everything I thought was the truth has been turned upside down."

"Now you are awake. Hum hmm hmm," Zophiel chortles with his lips pressed together.

Jerry signals to change over to the exit lane after seeing a sign for Saidnaya. "I need to get word to Sandalphon. I have a bad feeling about this."

"Me too!" Janus agrees. "I'm calling on Miriam."

"I wish you could call on some nourishment? I'm feeling a little less immortal," Jerry asks.

"Oh, sure! Hmm the human condition," Janus teases as the genie materializes bottled water, pomegranates, and pita chips into the vehicle.

"Whoa!" Jerry exclaims. "What happened to forbidden vulgar expressions of power?"

"You walked the Heavens and tried to fight the Chancellor... you still think this is vulgar?" Janus asks.

"Your right," Jerry ponders over the thought. "Do you think I can get a slice of pepperoni pizza?"

Janus materializes a slice into his hand.

"And a cold one!" Zophiel smiles.

"One what?"

"A brew mate!"

406

Janus materializes a beer into the grasp of Zophiel's hand.

"Well damn! You all right!" he shouts with a wide grin.

Janus sings, "Anything you want, you got it! Anything you need, you got it! Anything at all."

Jerry waits for Janus to finish, then helps by concluding, "You got it?"

Janus shrugs, "I don't know... I never heard the rest of the song."

"Do yourself a favor and don't listen to songs on the radio archives. They'll just confuse you."

The red sedan pulls off the highway and heads into an area where several signs are posted warning vehicles to proceed with caution. The area is moderately populated with floating digital translucent signs that vehicles bump or pass-through as they bob along the road. The signs move along slow and aimlessly like goldfish floating in a pond. The fluorescent digital blinking signs read: HAZARD ZONE. The area is a historic war-zone area where the buildings were intentionally left dilapidated as a reminder. The memorial zone is also a drive through museum area financed by the Our Gaia Now International Humanist Society, a secular group that has rigorously opposed religion-based wars worldwide.

A drifting sign bumps up against the sedan windshield. CAUTION it blinks once then flashes HAZARD ZONE before transcending over the sedan roof. Jerry continues through the memorial zone until he reaches an old road that has not been restored for travel. A rudimentary painted sign on the side of the road reads: Vagrant Domiciles. Large tents and flimsy cardboard housing structures stretch out for miles into the distance. There are no other vehicles on the road except sporadic sightings of small social service hovercrafts. Lines of destitute people wander up and down the street seemingly with no particular destination. The further Jerry drives down the road the more the area becomes less populated with vehicle traffic and pedestrians. On this part of the road the path and the decrepit war-torn structures are covered with a fine dust from dirt and powdered cement. Large boulders from the crumbling buildings lay in the footprints of what used to be a busy metropolis. The sky has a gray haze left over from the periodic falling of decaying walls and cement that send a blast of pulverized sheet rock and grime into the air. This was one of the areas hit the hardest by the war. Jerry proceeds slower with more caution while driving over the bumpy, pothole ridden path. A surveillance drone zips into the middle of the road and stops 20 feet ahead of the sedan. The drone's sleek silver body flashes with blue and red LED lights. "Warning, Warning," the electronic voice alerts as it hovers in the road waiting for the sedan to stop. "You are entering a vehicle free zone. Please proceed back to an authorized travel route for your safety."

Jerry returns to the authorized area and pulls over to the side of the road. "It's right down there, damn it!" he says while gripping the steering wheel of the parked sedan. The group sits in silence. You can hear Jerry's anxious breathing forcefully exhaling every few seconds. Jerry loses the grip of his right hand from off the steering wheel and rubs his chin and facial hair. He twists his finger where his wedding ring used to be as he contemplates his next move.

"Well... I guess we're walking. Ha! Hek! Hek!" Zophiel informs as he reaches for the door handle but he is distracted by a presence.

"Uhh! You came here to save this?" Miriam snaps into the sedan.

Both Jerry and Aza jerk and turn their heads towards the back seat to see that Miriam has made an unexpected entry.

"Thanks for taking your time," Janus responds.

"I came as quickly as I could. That place is a madhouse. Very few of the ambassadors can be found. It's a total lack of leadership." Miriam complains. "The good news is... Father Barcus has been overjoyed and every since Penemue and Araqiel showed up in the Containment Sphere the houses have gone berserk!" Miriam looks around then whispers, "Do you know they are actually taking wagers on how many fugitives you can capture? I lost already."

"Enough!" Janus replies. "We need your assistance."

"Anything you want!"

"We are about a mile away from a monastery where there is a chance that either the Triads or the Fiends may be located. Even worse, the Chancellor may be in there."

Jerry turns himself around in his chair to fully join the conversation. "Will you give Sandalphon an immediate update? We might need some assistance."

"I can try, but Sandalphon has been bed-ridden with grief over the disappearance of Metaphon," Miriam reports. "He has been hiding in seclusion being very antisocial. He's terribly distraught, the poor thing."

"Well he must be monitoring our requests," Jerry asserts. "We've had our prayers... our... um conjuring... The car, the clothes, the cash all of our requests have been granted."

"Your requests have been directly routed past the Prayer Tower to the Upper Room as ordered by Sandalphon but he has not been involved in any of your requests," Miriam informs.

"Interesting!" Aza interjects now turning around to face Miriam. "Sandalphon has not been involved? No one has been watching our mission?"

"Ahh... that's not what I said," Miriam responds.

"We don't have any assigned Watchers?" Janus says with vacated eyes and a gas mouth.

"Yet you were still able to capture Penemue and Araqiel," Miriam reminds Janus.

Aza replies, "Penemue told us that the twins were attempting to secure a house for their brother."

"Which twins?" Miriam snaps with widened eyes.

"Twins who could free Abaddon in exchange for an ambassadorship. Who, they never did say," Aza answers.

"Well which one of the twins has a sibling who is not an ambassador?" Janus asks.

"There are no such twins," Miriam responds. "Don't believe anything Penemue says. They are both liars."

"Wait!" Aza asserts. "The twins are all elders who were born in the time prior to the Paroxysm of Abraxis. During that time great galactic collisions created spawns. Sometimes spawns clung within one star kingdom." Aza looks at each of the passengers confirming their attention. "The spawns were not able to leave their star kingdoms until after Omnus gave their souls life forms. It was not until after that when souls were able to traverse throughout each other's kingdoms and allow spawns to meet their other creators," Aza concludes.

"Ok..." Miriam says.

"What if a spawn never left its kingdom," Aza says. "When I lived in the Kingdom of Omnus I never knew of Sachiel of Cassiel from Dynacia or Sammael from Lucimus."

"How do you know all this?" Miriam asks.

"I've been around for a long time. I worked in the historical archives before there was an Order of the Cherubim," Aza reports. "These Seraphim, Throne, and Cherubim Orders were only given to us to mask the fact that we originated from different kingdoms. This was done to unify the Houses and to make one Paradise."

"What a wonderful rendition of the Paradise story, but what does that have to do with this?" Zophiel responds. "We know all the divinity twins."

"The question is... do we know all the spawns?" Aza asks.

"What if some never joined Paradise?" Janus asks while looking around for understanding. "How would we know if one of the twins has another sibling?"

"And deceive Omnus?" Zophiel asks while shaking his head in disbelief. "No way—"

"Omnus did it!" Aza informs. "The Irins rarely leave his side and although we knew of Sandalphon we didn't know there was a Metaphon until after he was given the Ninth House."

"So how can we find the existence of an unknown elder?" Janus asks.

"We were told that the mighty Aeon, Omnus is the father of all the elder Divinity angels. What we don't know is who are the other Eons," Zophiel asks.

"Brothers... What I'm about to tell you must remain with us and only us!" Aza informs as he looks into each of their eyes for sincerity.

The others look around at each other to get a feel for unity.

"So mote it be?" Aza asks.

"So mote it be!" each one of them reply except Zophiel.

"Zop! What's up?" Aza asks.

"Soul... I just got out of a pact!" Zophiel says shaking his head and batting his eyes. He takes his hand to his head. "Augh! So mote it be. Man! Keeping secrets! Keeping damn secrets!"

Aza turns to Jerry. "You're in this too now."

"Yeah man! Whatever!" Jerry responds. "Somo—"

"So mote!" Aza corrects.

"So... mote... it be!" Jerry replies.

Aza looks around at each of them while rubbing his hands. In a lower voice he begins, "Souls... Sophia is an Eon."

"Yeah right!" Miriam responds.

"She's an Eon and... the matriarch of many of the Divinity angels."

While the others are starry-eyed, Zophiel smiles and replies, "There's something else to this. It's not fair, not to share—"

"Listen!" Aza demands. "Why do you think they kept her locked up in Araboth? They said it was forbidden to even look upon her face!"

412

"This is blasphemy!" Janus asserts.

"Really!" Aza asks. "Do you think they hated me so much for Falling onto the Earth, loving mortal women, and trying my best to make it here!" Aza darts his eyes around at the group breathing heavily with a rapidly beating heart. "They isolated me on the Earth and not in their prison so I couldn't tell their dirty secrets!"

"This is so wrong," Janus responds shaking its head in doubt. "No offense, but Sophia is an abomination!"

"Says who!" Aza responds. "You were never allowed to lay eyes on her, let alone get to know her!"

"The matriarch to which angels?" Zophiel asks.

"I don't know… because she didn't know except to say they were spawned into the Kingdom of Omnus."

"Ok! OK!" Miriam begs. "I'll look through the historical archive of zodiacs, locate where all the Divinity angels come from and both of their lineages from where they were spawned."

"And then what?" Janus asks. "What does all this blasphemous talk mean?"

"I don't know…" Aza says as his heart rate and breathing slows down. "I don't know what any of this means but that someone has some explaining to do."

"OK, well—"

"Wait Miriam!" Aza requests. "That information isn't sitting around in the zodiac. You need to search higher. You said Barcus may be in a generous mood so maybe he'll let you in the Imperial Archives without question?"

"You need approval from the Divine Order for that but... there's an elder genie that maintains the Imperial Archives," Janus reports. "Maybe Barcus can tell Miriam how to find the old soul."

"OK. Good luck with the monastery!" Miriam wishes as the genie zips away.

The four crusaders exit the car and troop down the road on foot. The Syrian sun is high and hot as it shines down on the dirt road through the gray sky. As the crew trots through the ruins of the old war torn territory the gray cement dust lifts from their shoes and blows in the wind. The misty gray camouflages and covers everything in sight. Shells of destroyed civilian vehicles and military all-terrain vehicles lay on the side of the road as untouched war relics. The grayness of the dust floating in the hazy sunlight provides a smokescreen for three figures in the near distance. Aza stops and stares as he tries to focus his eyes through the haze. Jerry and the others stop when they notice Aza's hundred-yard stare. They too take notice of the figures in the distance.

"Behind me," Aza shouts. "A two-by-two cover formation! Now!"

"Are they mortal or immortal?" Janus asks as the genie moves into the back of the formation.

Jerry and the crew fall in behind Aza who takes point. Aza stares more tentatively as he inhales deeply. He senses something about the figures that doesn't feel human in their walk or their stance. "No! Not mortal I don't think," he reports as he draws his astroflare from the exoverse.

Jerry follows suit and conjures up his astroflare too as Janus invokes an energy sphere.

"All right! Let's get it on!" Zophiel says as he pulls an energy scepter from under his clothes.

"Shut your mouth Zop!" Aza says quietly. "You are going to alert the whole damn compound."

Masked in the gray road dust, the three figures move faster up the road towards Aza. One of the figures runs ahead of its group straight up the road with a sword drawn but angled towards the sky. "OK! This is it!" Aza warns his crew as the figures move in closer.

"Zophiel! Zop! Is that you?" one of the figures calls out from the dust filled air with labored breathing.

"Astar?" Zophiel calls out as he squints through the haziness of the sunlight and dust.

"Yes sire," the panting Astar answers as she waives in the rest of her comrades. "Is that him? Is that one of the Fallen captains?" Astar asks with a smile as she moves in closer and stares over at Aza.

"The one and only. Aza, meet Astar," Zophiel introduces. "And this here is Caliel and Raziel," he continues as they approach.

Without maintaining steady eye contact Astar looks up at Aza then quickly down and away again. "It's an honor to meet you, Your Excellency," Astar greets as the other two bow and kneel on one knee.

Aza withdraws his astroflare. "Um... it's Aza and there's no kneeling and bowing necessary." Aza looks over at Zophiel. "They're merely kids."

"Yep! Less than 10,000 years old. The last of the immortal spawns," Zophiel reports. "But they kick ass like they're over fifty."

"Well this is Janus of Vilon." Janus steps forward and nods. "And this is Jerry an Earth Angel," Aza introduces.

"Crap! No wings?" Raziel comments.

"Great! An old legionnaire, a house genie, and a wingless angel," Caliel whispers to Astar. "These guys are one pilot short of a cancelled sitcom."

"Shhh!" Astar responds in an attempt to stop Caliel from being heard. "Just wait and you'll see," she whispers back.

"Well I hope you guys are ready," Aza asks.

Caliel sighs, "Huh! Are YOU guys ready," while starring down their attire.

"Someone was thinking of vanity and not utility when it conjured our clothes," Aza responds while rolling eyes over at Janus.

"As if you are not vain," Janus smirks. "I served a House in Heaven I didn't fight for it."

"So... anyway you look prepared," Aza comments on Caliel's attire.

"Yes, and I already scoped out the exterior layout," Caliel reports. "For a compound this place was quite spacious and luxurious back in its day. The only remaining part of the monastery is the chapel. The outside of the chapel is safe. There are two patrol guards from inside that take turns walking the perimeter every twenty minutes. There's a large garden and pool in the backyard. It's an indoor and outdoor pool that extends into the interior of the building from underwater. The back is fenced in but the fence is old and has a couple of openings where it has caved in overtime. In the front there is a path leading up to the front door. The path is lined with statues of... some angels. I've never seen them before so I guess they're just old mortal artwork. The monastery has three levels, one up and one subterranean cellar. The cellar can only be assessed from the back of the pulpit or from a door in between the front interior stairways. I know that from old pictures I saw on the Gaia Net," Caliel concludes.

"I scanned the layout into my communicator." Raziel displays a rotating holographic image projection from his wrist device.

"Great! Now all we need is for Karlisa to walk out into the front yard," Janus responds.

"Or..." Aza adds. You can flash through there and scope out the interior. Find out where she is exactly and who is guarding the place."

"I know you can elude mortal technology, but can you get around immortals without being detected?" Raziel asks.

"It depends on how fast I move, but the faster I move the less I see."

"Cool!" Raziel replies.

"So you are willing to go?" Zophiel asks.

"I am a part of the team... so ok."

"I'm giving you twenty minutes then we are coming for you," Aza informs.

"Ok..." Janus takes a deep breath. "Here I go." Janus zips out of sight.

Jerry sits on the curb and looks up at all the team members. He counts a combined joint of seven missionaries, but he is still concerned that some of them may not come back. He notices how confident they are in their skills. He watches Raziel play with his wrist device projector flipping and twirling the holographic image of the monastery as he reviews every strategy for entry into the building. Jerry observes Astar who pulls a sword

from the exoverse and practices fight moves and
sparring with Aza. Jerry also looks over at Caliel
whom is discussing possible attack tactics and
escape plans with Zophiel. Each of them looks
seriously motivated to fight against the Disciples of
Doom to help get Karlisa back. Jerry could not
recall ever having six friends in his former life that
would take up such a risk on his behalf. A lump
swells in Jerry's throat and his eyes become heavy.
He is afraid of becoming too emotional. He wants
to keep frosty so he stands and makes his way
over to Aza and Astar.

"Do you think you can show me some moves?"
Jerry asks.

"You may want to stay close, get the girl, and let
us do the fighting," Astar suggests.

"I'm not ready yet, but I can hold my own," Jerry
defends.

"He's actually quite surprising," Aza informs.

"Oh yeah..." Astar responds as she takes
defensive stance at Jerry with her sword drawn.
"Ok how about we practice some basic maneuvers."

Jerry receives a small training session from Astar
and Aza, just the basic stuff like holding a sword,
proper stance and defensive moves. Aza keeps
reminding him that all he needs to know for now is
how to survive. Once they rescue Karlisa and get
back to Cleveland the real training will begin.

After a few minutes, Jerry becomes a little
fatigued. He sits out for a moment while Astar and
Aza continue to spar.

Astar hands Jerry a scarf. "Try to cover your
nose. You shouldn't breathe in too much of this
dust, Earth Angel," Astar warns as she
demonstrates with her veil. "You may be an Earth

Angel, but your body is still vulnerable to the human condition."

"Hey, why are you guys helping us?" Jerry asks. "There could be Triads or Fiends in there. We may not make it out alive."

"Well we have a lot to discuss later," Astar informs as she continues sparring with Aza. "Let's just look at this as an act of kindness inconsideration of a future proposal. Besides, it wouldn't be my first time going up against a Fiend or a Triad. I pursued them during the Siege at Lake Saqun," Astar informs as she breathes heavily from exertion.

"Let's take a break," Aza requests.

"With such a show of generosity why did you Fall from the Heavens?" Jerry asks as he looks down at the ground, not feeling sure if the question is appropriate.

"Hey, Earth Angel, don't raise me on a pedestal just yet. Fighting isn't the only thing I like to do with bad souls. Right Aza?"

"Well—"

"You'll have plenty of bad souls to fight with in there," reports Janus while flashing out into the encampment.

The crew eagerly fires questions: "Did you see her? How many were there? Are there any Triads?"

"Whoa! Easy! Let the genie speak!" Zophiel directs.

"Good news: the girl is there. Bad news: the place is cursed and thoroughly guarded. The inside of the place is laid out in a pentagram design," Janus reports. "I don't know if the old congregation knew that because the points of the star are on different levels. The two sets of stairs in the front are the

Southwest and Southeast points otherwise known as Earth and Fire. In each of these stairways there is a gang member from the Seven Rulers of Wrath. To traverse these stairways you must carry the corresponding element in a calf skull otherwise... something horrible I'm sure."

"Where do we get a calf skull?" Caliel asks.

Janus continues, "The skulls are either at the top or at the bottom of the stairway where the last Wrath member left it, so you would have to get the creep to come back down the stairs to obtain possession of the skull. Once you make it to the top you are in the sanctuary where a... Triad is standing guard in the pulpit."

"Just one Triad?" Astar asks.

"Yes, but this Triad member is Mephiz. He is one of the rookie Triads and possibly assigned the crap job of supervising this place, but nevertheless he is a powerful Seraphim class angel. His favorite weapon is a flail. He usually carries one in both hands. Taking him out will not be easy."

"So two Wraths and one Triad. Where is the girl?" asks Zophiel.

"Between the two front stairways is a door that leads down to the cellar. Another way to get down there is by using the two narrow stairways extending from the North point of the pentagram that is in the pulpit behind the Triad. If you use the north end stairs you are surely to be seen from the top by the Triad or from the bottom where two more Wrath gang members are standing guard."

"What's down there? Is there any way of sneaking around these two soon-to-be hell bound bitches?" Raziel asks.

"That's the interesting part... there's nothing down there. Once you get down to the floor there is a three-foot ledge then a pit of murky dark sludge.

"Oh, brother!" Aza says with his eyes rolled back as he places his hand to his head. "The Behemoth! The hole for a deep-sea demon, that was thought to be extinct," Aza reports.

"Great!" Jerry responds. "So where is Karlisa?"

"Once you get onto the three-foot ledge of the pit's perimeter and pass the Wrath on each side, she is on the other end in the center cell under the stairwell," Janus concludes.

"OK! I got it all programmed into the projection... by the way where are the West and East star points?" Raziel asks as he punches programming codes into his hologram keyboard projected from his wrist device.

"Oh, yeah! Air and Water are the elements you need to enter into those points. They are elevated on each side of the pulpit. I think the mortals used them for choir chambers."

"Ok, I say we wait for one of the sentries to come out and rob him of his immortality then we sneak into the cellar, take out the two Wraths of Weakness, grab the girl and run back out the front," Zophiel plans.

"Sure, Zop! We go in there and get eaten by the Behemoth sea creature or get cornered off when they realize their sentry hasn't come back!" Raziel smiles at his superior.

"Let's face it!" Aza commands. "They got it set up so that if you come through you have to go through them any way you plan it!"

"Not necessarily," Raziel objects. "How about we make them come to us?" Raziel looks around at the crew for their attention. "Check it out! Like Zop said, we take out a sentry, and then we send Jerry with a small search and rescue crew into the cellar. Janus if you can attract that creature into the backyard exterior pool the crew can take out the two Wraths in the cellar and run out with the girl. Wait!" Raziel urges before anyone can criticize. "After twenty minutes we call them out. We'll have to battle, but they'll be outnumbered as they have lost one sentry and two cellar guards. While we take them on, the search and rescue crew can run out and away with the girl." Raziel makes a wide, boasting smile.

"What makes you think they'll come outside outnumbered?" Janus asks with a bobbing head and a foot tap.

"Triads are arrogant. Their vices are their own weaknesses. They'll never walk away from a fight on their own turf. Their too proud for that!"

"Younglings!" Zophiel replies.

"I hope you are as brilliant of a fighter as you are a planner," says Aza before giving further instructions. "Alright! Zop, Raz, and Jerry you're going in. Cal you are on that sentry, do it quietly and don't screw up! Astar you are with me."

"I don't do pets!" Janus asserts.

"You better stir that pool with your foot if you have to—"

"I think not!"

"You get that beast out into the exterior pool. Conjure up something!" Aza directs.

"Almighty Abraxis!" Janus mopes. "Fine!"

The wind picks up and blows the gray debris in the air leaving new layers on top of the old dusty crust that covers everything in sight. Everyone from the encampment wears a fine layer of crud on their clothes, their skin, and hair. Astar wipes a film of the gray powder from her face but it is useless, her hands are covered too.

Janus flashes around to the back garden and pool area where the air is stale and dry. There hasn't been any growth of any kind here in a long time. The flowerbeds are filled with rocks and gray dust. An old angel statue, tarnished and worn, stands from inside one of the garden plots. The angel's wings have broken off and lay in crumbles at the foot of the plot. Janus looks to the left, to the right, and off in the distance and cannot find any signs of life, in fact there's no sign that there was ever any life after the war. There is not a bird in the sky or a bug on the ground, just windblown gray dust in the hazy sunlight. Janus feels alone.

Caliel takes cover out of sight on the corner of the chapel near the path of the sentry's route. Caliel stands behind a large dedication boulder with an inscription that reads, "We stand strong in the test of our resolve in the name of our lord and savior. The year of our saint, May 9, 2145."

Jerry, Raziel, and Zophiel hide behind a shell of an old destroyed and demolished military jeep. The dust in the wind nearly conceals the presence of Aza and Astar who have taken cover behind the ruins of a military transport truck. Aza raises a hand signal to Zophiel who turns to see that a Wrath gang member has left the chapel and begun to patrol around the perimeter.

"I hope Cali is ready!" Raz whispers. "Damn we should all have communicators on this mission."

"Shut up!" Zophiel whispers as he watches the Wrath take a turn towards the side of the chapel.

"How will we know?" Jerry asks.

"We won't!" answers Zop. "We just have to pray that everyone does their job."

Zophiel pulls out an energy scepter and sprouts his four wings. Raziel follows suit by invoking a sabre and his two wings from the exoverse. Jerry conjures his astroflare.

"Wow!" Raz whispers. "Where did you get that?"

"Save it!" Zophiel directs. "Let's move!"

The search and rescue team runs toward the front door and gently opens it up. Aza watches them disappear inside. "Ok... twenty minutes then we're on!" Aza informs Astar.

The sentry Wrath member dressed in a hooded cloak treks the dusty trail dropping each foot in a pattern, tracing over the existing footprints. As the Wrath passes the large dedication boulder it stops and looks around. The fallen angel rolls up its eyes and raises a wrinkled nose into the air. Then the Wrath turns around and heads back but soon it stops again, turns and continues the patrol. A few steps later the Wrath stops again and attempts to turn around but an arm is wrapped around its mouth and head.

"Keep your mouth shut and this will be painless," Caliel warns the Wrath as he conjures his claymore sword from the exoverse. "On your knees," he directs.

Caliel pulls down the Wrath's hood and steps around to the front where he finds a crying female angel. Sniff! Sniff! "They made me do it," she cries as tears roll down her soft skin from her glowing angel-blue eyes.

"Who's inside?" Cali asks while holding the claymore against the angel's neck.

"Just me," sniff sniff she cries as the tears roll profusely, "and a friend. Everyone else is out. My name is Amy and I'm not with those assholes," the angel reports looking at Caliel with her moist wide eyes and long thick eyelashes. "I don't want any trouble. All I want is to be left in peace."

With an inward glaze Caliel thinks for a moment then responds, "If peace is what you want then peace is what I want to give you," Cali informs the Wrath before swinging the claymore into her neck, instantly killing her. "Since when does a Ruler of Wrath want peace?" he whispers to himself.

Caliel softly jogs to an opening in the old rusty, black cast-iron gate that opens into the backyard where he spots Janus throwing pebbles into the dark murky pool. Janus, sitting alone, catches a glimpse of a figure out the corner of its eye and jerks with a deep inhale but soon after recognizes Caliel signaling with a frantic waive of the hand. Janus knows that this means the sentry has been removed and the plan is in motion. The genie blows air across its lips and continues to toss stones into the black murky pool. There is no sign of the Behemoth. Casting stones is not drawing its attention. The murky substance swallows up the stones without so much as a ripple left behind in its path. Janus throws a large heavier stone into the pool but it sinks quickly as the dark goop incases it and sucks it down.

Caliel staggers up with a Wrath slung over his shoulder. "Let's try this."

"Ahh! You killed her!" Janus scolds as it looks at the Wrath's face. "She was beautiful and you killed her."

"Don't let her beauty fool you. She's reeking of wrath." Caliel lowers the Wrath member into the pool. She slowly sinks. "Her name was Amy, or so she said. May her soul rest in peace."

The murky thick liquid begins to ripple and wave from the other end. Bubbles rise and pop out of the murky depths.

"Ok! Stand back!" Caliel directs. "This has got to be it."

In the front of the chapel Jerry, Zophiel, and Raziel stand in the foyer before the stairway. On a shelf is a calf skull filled with oil that has been set on fire. They sneak pass the stairway to the cellar door and quietly open it up enough to peek inside. Zophiel, in the lead position, can see a Wrath member standing against the wall near the north end. He looks over to the south end and sees another Wrath standing and sharpening his sword. The pool looks calm, but he cannot tell if Janus was able to get the creature to leave the interior pool. Zophiel looks back at the other two with a confirming nod. Jerry's eyes are fixated on the north end, center cellar door. Zophiel moves in and to the left, treading softly over the three-foot ledge across to the opposite side where Belzar, a Wrath member has detected his presence and picks up his weapon. Raziel immediately goes into full assault with Bal, the other Wrath to the right. The ledges are so narrow Jerry cannot get to the other side on either ledge while Raziel and Zophiel are on it engaged in battle. Stretching high across the pool is a beam and a chain that looks like it is used to lower large objects into the pool. Jerry looks into the pool but he cannot detect any signs of the creature within its deep, dark murkiness. He decides to take a chance and shimmy slide across the beam.

Zophiel slowly approaches his opponent trying to buy time to anticipate his next move. "I know what you are thinking," Zophiel taunts as he looks at the north end stairway behind his opponent. "You can run up those back stairs like a coward and go get some help or you can be a proud warrior and Ruler of Wrath by defeating me." Belzar angles himself to make either decision. The Wrath knows that a Triad is right up the north end stairway. "Let me help you make a decision," Zophiel offers. "If you defeat me I will renounce the heavens and declare my soul to your Lord Abaddon. That's if a coward like you can defeat me."

Belzar holds a voulge pole weapon he pulled from the wall. "I don't need your soul," the Wrath says as he swallows hard and grips his weapon tightly to control his shaking hands. "Your soul is not required to join us, only your death!"

Raziel and his opponent becomes actively engaged in battle. Raziel's rival, Bal is more skillful than Raz expected. They continue to swing equally matched strike and defensive blocks at each other. The metallic clicks and clacks become increasingly more frequent as the match progresses towards a victor. Raziel breathes heavily conflicted with the human condition of exhaustion. He thinks while continuing to fight, "I should have brought my holographic duplication cloaking device."

Jerry continues to make his way over the pit using the beam above. He climbs the support column and pulls his body over onto the beam. Hand over hand he slowly maneuvers his way across the beam until he hangs above the middle of the pit. The pit begins to bubble and ripple below. Jerry takes a deep breath, picks up his pace, and moans, "What's the purpose of being an angel if you can't fly?"

Outside, behind the transport truck, Aza and Astar watch the twenty-minute clock count down. Aza gives instruction on their plan of attack. Astar recalls a history scroll she read called, "The Legions of the Fall," that reported how Azazel was nearly promoted to the Order of the Arch before Falling onto the Earth. He fell for loving the wrong one and she for loving too many. Like her, he was from the kingdom of Omnus and was assigned to the Order of the Cherubim. Astar looks over at Aza and tries to refocus on the conversation, but her attention faded away while stuck savoring their moment alone.

"So do you think that'll work?" Aza asks.

"Ah... I um... Whatever you think would work is alright with me," Astar rolls her eyes up and clinches her teeth hoping that her response doesn't reveal that she wasn't listening.

"Ok then we'll stick to the plan and insult him until he comes out, but I'm only giving it two minutes then I'll have to go get Jerry out of there."

"OK," Astar responds not knowing the other option.

"OK, it's time. Let's do it!"

Aza and Astar proceeds down the path in between the row of demolished relics of angel statues lining the path to the front door. Aza stops halfway down the path, looks around, and then nods at Astar. "OK... this is close enough," informs Aza as he inspects the area. "Remember to keep out of sight and don't get involved unless I tell you differently."

"What! When did you—"

"HEY! All dark dwelling Wraths of weakness come on outside! Don't be afraid!" Aza yells at the top of his breath. "I'll make it quick and painless for all cowards who come out now and if you bring a friend you'll get an ass whooping discount, but only of you come now!"

Aza doesn't have to wait long before the doors burst open and Mephiz, the Triad comes out. He is taller and looks stronger than Aza expected. He's breathing and snorting like he's already been warming up for a fight. His nostrils flare so wide you can almost see the air exhaling from his nose. The veins in his neck are like thick, bulging hoses pumping hot liquid out of his muscular and stout torso. His powerful arms and strong clamping hands don't look like they need a weapon to be any more intimidating yet he swings two poles with chain-linked balls of fire on each end. The flaring and swooshing sound cuts the air with every circulating spin of the flaming orbs.

Astar watches with a gasped mouth and a mesmerized gaze. "There is no way I'm letting him do this alone! No way!" she tells herself.

Inside the chapel's cellar both Raziel and Zophiel are fully engaged in conflict as Jerry continues to shimmy his way across the beam over the bubbling pit. The bubbles blow bigger and the fizzle grows more active by the second. Jerry moves hand over hand as quick as he can but the activity below is bound to surface before he completes his course.

Jerry knows he's within short yards of being reunited with Karlisa and getting on a plane back to Cleveland, but he's afraid it may all end in the mouth of this pit's creature.

"All this for what?" Jerry moans as he tries to hurry across but the pit has become more volatile. "It can't end like this!" Jerry is thinking of swinging and heaving his body the rest of the distance. "By the power of GRACALOT!" Jerry swings but does not let go. "Who am I kidding?"

He closes his eyes to accept the inevitable emergence of the pit's creature.

A large deformed worm-like creature with wings and large clamping fangs jumps out of the pit bringing up a shower of black steamy goop dropping from its massive body as it attempts to devour Jerry's hanging body. Janus flashes into the cellar and throws a blazing energy sphere at the creature shocking and freezing it while suspended in the air merely inches from Jerry's curled up legs. Jerry opens his eyes after he hears the deafening wail of the injured Behemoth creature falling back down into the murky pit. Janus throws its hands generating a continuous stream of energy into the pit electrifying the pool.

"Hurry, Jerry!" Janus shouts. "I-I can't... keep it under... much longer!" Janus strains.

Zophiel and Belzar enter into a bout of attacks and parry moves. Belzar is quick and deadly with the pole weapon. Zophiel evades it from the left and from the right as the pole zzzoops past his head from the left and from the right. Zoop! Duck! Zoop! Dodge! This is how the game is played before Zophiel even swings his first counter attack.

Click-ety-Clack! Click-ety-Clack! Swoosh! Clack! Shoop! Clack! The swords sound from Raz and Bal as they swing and collide relentlessly against each other's strike and parry. The match has become evenly matched. Now the goal is not one of skill but one of endurance, however another presence has entered the match to tilt the balance.

"It's over my lad," the Wrath warns. "You should have brought your skill to the Chancellor but you chose the slavery of submission to Omnus," Bal taunts.

The second patrol Wrath, Pursiphon from the sanctuary stands behind Raziel with a sword drawn prepared for a fatal plunge. "Scream goodbye my young friend," Bal sneers as he gives a go-ahead nod to his accessory, Pursiphon. Raziel turns around quickly with a duck and kneel maneuver but Pursiphon does not move. He does not deliver the fatal blow. Pursiphon stands frozen, staring straight ahead into the pasture of peace and mortality. He sees a young Seraph run through the halls of Matey laughing and running until he is picked up into the arms of a golden light. Pursiphon drops his sword, falls to his knees, and tumbles face down onto the floor with a thrown claymore wedged into his back. A few yards behind him is Caliel.

"No!" Bal screams as he grips his sword tighter and prepares to avenge Pursiphon's death.

Raziel, still kneeling on the ground in front of Bal, angles his sword up and into Bal's torso then pushes it through to the other side. "Fucking... subservient... bastard!" says Bal as he drops to the floor and closes the light out of his eyes for the final time.

Outside Aza gazes at the stout body of his opponent. Mephiz is one of the Chancellor's top three collaborators of calamity. Mephiz's twirling orbs of fire circle fiercely, increasing faster and faster with every pump of his massive biceps. The chains twirl effortlessly rotating the orbs at his will. He swings an orb from the left and quickly from the right as Aza swiftly calculates the timing of his maneuvers just fast enough to adjust for a second near hit. A dance of ducking and dodging, moving and jumping, flinching and running continues relentlessly without a cease in Mephiz's attacks. Aza attempts to block the orbs with his astroflare but the collision only makes a spattering mess of hot flames and sparks that rain down and add on to Aza's hazards. Astar, watching from the side, grips her sword tightly while grinding her teeth and dancing her feet impatiently for Aza's signal to allow her to join the fight.

In the cellar Jerry jumps off the beam safely onto the other side of the pit just as Janus' strength gives in from trying to keep the Behemoth under the murky pool. "Hurry, Jerry!" Janus pants with a rapidly falling and rising chest. "This is the best I can do for now but it won't last for long."

The Behemoth floats to the bottom of the pit injured but rehabilitating with every passing moment. Jerry runs over to the center cell, looks in and sees the body of a curled up and frightened woman he believes to be Karlisa. He pulls the cell door but it's locked.

"Damn it! Damn it!" Jerry groans as he gives up on pulling the cell door. Jerry invokes his astroflare and sticks it in the locking mechanism melting the steel. He continues pushes the blazing flare through the molten metal.

The lock breaks and the cell door opens. Jerry quickly pulls the astroflare out of the innerverse. He pulls open the cell and runs inside. Jerry knows now. He knows with all his heart, without question, without proof, and without reservation. This is his Gracalot moment of blind faith. This is Karlisa.

Jerry gently rolls her over onto his arms and there the journey has been fulfilled. Live or die they are together now. Jerry brushes the hair back from her face and finds her terribly distorted. A cryptic voice squeals, "You left her to DIE!" The demonic voice continues, "You never loved her!"

Jerry is left frozen as the air leaves the room. His heart falls heavily in his chest while the swallow of his dry mouth can barely keep his stomach down. He brushes his hand across her hair trying to remember her as she once was before all this madness began. A shine of hope catches his eyes. It's her wedding ring. "Oh! Oh, yeah!" Jerry exclaims. The shine, the sparkle, and the reason why he left in the first place, he now has the Angel Dust. Jerry waives his hands over her face while wiggling his fingers but nothing happens.

"Clear your mind Jerry," the soft voice of Janus instructs from behind.

Jerry concentrates and recalls the house of Sandalphon. He thinks about the feeling of falling and floating. He remembers the feeling of being free and happy. He waives his hands and the angel dust pours profusely, sparkling, falling, and snowing all over Karlisa transforming her back into a physical being free of demonic possession. Her skin is returning to its original soft complexion. Her hair is frizzled, but not lifeless and fried. Her eyes are tired, but not darkened and dead. She is barely conscious as she blinks her eyes trying to awake. Her head falls heavily on her shoulders. Her body is limp and unresponsive.

"We need to get her out of here right away," Jerry demands of Janus with his eyes fixed on Karlisa.

Zophiel's forehead moistens with a touch of the human condition as he tires from the game with Belzar, a match that he can no longer tolerate. Belzar relentlessly thrusts an onslaught of jabs towards Zophiel who blocks and diverts each strike. Finally, Belzar's electrified pole weapon misses Zophiel and extends far enough across his right to the strategic point for which Zophiel has been waiting. Zophiel tosses his scepter over to his left hand and grabs the handle of the pole weapon with his right, pulling Belzar in closer. Zophiel then stretches out his scepter with his left hand and delivers a fatal stab into Belzar's lower torso. Belzar drops the pole, staggers, and falls against a nearby wall holding his wounded gut.

"I'll tell them you fought gallantly, my friend," Zophiel informs Belzar who slides his back down the wall leaving a smeared trail of blood.

Still holding his wound he blows out with his final breath, "You're... no... friend of mine!"

"I stand corrected!" Zophiel stands victoriously with his blade resting on Belzar's chest preparing for a death strike but he decides it's of no use for his opponent is already dead.

Outside, Astar waits on the sidelines shifting her weight anxiously from the left to the right and mimicking Aza's evasive moods as he eludes swings from Mephiz's orbs of fire. Astar's eyes bounce as they follow the action. "I can't take this shit!" she shouts.

Aza knows he must act quickly to end this battle before Astar's eagerness gets the best of her. Aza thinks back to his training in the angelic guard where he was taught that the Chancellor's favorite weapon is the use of his opponent's contribution to his strengths. In pressured thinking, coupled with defensive strategizing, Aza contemplates, "What am I contributing to the fight?" He continues to struggle in a cycle of defensive moves. "Fear, fear of being struck by an orb," Aza presumes. "Well maybe it's time I shared my fear."

Aza ducks and moves out of the way from a set of fiery orb attacks then takes a couple strikes, not at his opponent, but at the chains that connect the orbs to the flail handles. The friction on the chains sends the balls of fire off course sputtering and spraying molted metal and sparks of fire back on Mephiz's arms and head. Before Mephiz can get his composure and momentum back into the twirl of his flail weapon, Aza takes advantage of the moment when there is no attack to defend. There's just Aza and his astroflare, free and clear to advance on the opponent.

"Yeah! That's it!" Astar cheers from the sidelines.

Aza swing an unyielding onslaught of strikes and hits against Mephiz's ironworks armor until it cracks and shatters, exposing his body leaving him vulnerable to even his own fire orbs that he can't pull back into the throw of action. Mephiz backs up but his large burly body is not made for the agility of moving backwards so he stammers in the blitz of Aza's astroflare swings.

"Finish him youngling," Aza directs his wide-eyed apprentice.

Astar runs, jumps, and plunges her sword into Mephiz's massive chest riding him down like a cowgirl in a rodeo, clinging to her wedged sword while her legs are strapped around his large torso. "When you get to Hell, tell them Astar sent you. They know me well," she taunts as she pushes her sword deeper through his body.

Astar rides the fall of his body down to the ground where his lifeless eyes roll back into the head of his mortal corpse. Astar dismounts Mephiz's remains and steps over to Aza with gleaming eyes, yearning for recognition of her bravery. Aza smirks and rolls his eyes. "Tell them Astar sent you?" Aza shakes his head as he looks over to see the rest of the crew exit the chapel with Karlisa being carried in Jerry's arms.

"We're getting the car," Zophiel announces as he takes off trying to keep up with Janus who flickers down the road.

Aza trots over to Jerry who has Karlisa cradled in his arms barely conscious. "How is she Jerry?" he asks.

"Not good... but I believe she's going to be alright. I have the faith to believe it to be true," Jerry answers.

"Angels and brothers please gather around," Aza calls out. "This is who we've been fighting for," Aza says with eyes resting on Karlisa. Aza continues as he looks in the eyes of Jerry and each of the young angels, "Our fight is for our right to love whomever, whatever, however we want." Aza pauses. "You've been told that love can be forbidden. But we know that love is not about having control. It is unconditional and at times it comes from an unexpected heart." Aza looks at Jerry. "And it often comes from some unfamiliar, untraditional, and sometimes unbelievable sources. When that love comes you must have faith in your fight to keep it." Aza looks around for understanding as the angels look up at Aza nodding with steady eye contact. "Now since we are messengers let us pray in silence and send that message to whoever shall receive it."

Jerry and the angels all bow their heads in silence as they deliver their own personal messages to Paradise. The silence is broken to the sound of the sedan speeding down the road leaving a trial of smoke from the debris and dirt filled road.

"Hurry before those damn patrol drones come back!" Zophiel orders.

Jerry takes a place in the back seat with Janus leaving the driving to Aza and Zophiel, but Zophiel does not enter.

"This is the end of the road for me. Thanks for the ride," Zophiel departs.

Raziel runs up to the sedan driver's side door next to Aza, "When you get home, press this button and we'll locate you when you are ready to begin our training," Raziel instructs handing the wrist communicator over to Aza who hands it back to Jerry.

"Best let you kids handle that," Aza responds. "Ahh... you know we'll be in Cleveland?"

"That rocks!" Astar says.

"Ah, yeah we'll see," says Aza as he pulls off in the sedan.

"Let's get out of here!" Caliel requests as the crew runs down the other end of the street to their vehicles.

Aza drives the sedan off the dirt road back onto the authorized travel route. Janus looks out of the back window at the monastery in the background. "This place is clean," the genie declares.

In the distance the curse is released from the chapel and it crumbles adding a cloud of smoke into the already gray, dust filled air.

The sedan rides through the vagrant domicile area where the faces of homeless people with inward gazes wander aimlessly on the roadside. Some of the people are pushing carts, walking in crowds conversing with friends while others are shouting and protesting their political views. Janus remembers the lost souls walking up the path outside the First House of Heaven. Janus' heart is so full and heavy the genie can no longer look out the window. Aza drives slowly through the crowd as meal lines are forming and drawing many people into the streets. Janus sits up straight and leans up towards Aza. "Stop!" Janus shouts. "I have an idea."

Aza stops the car. Janus continues, "The briefcase. Let's give them the cash!" Janus says with big eyes and a smile. "Let's just give them all the money! We no longer need it!"

Jerry looks and shouts up to Aza, "Keep going. We are not home yet!"

Aza continues down the road. Janus with a gasped mouth looks at Jerry. "For all we did for you and you can't do for others?"

Jerry responds, "Until I get Karly the medical attention she needs and back home to our children this mission is not over! After she's home you can send it back, donate it, drop it out a plane cargo care package if you want, but until this mission is over I'm keeping all my available resources!"

"Fine!"

Lazy and Selfish

"A daily double!" a red-cloaked silver masked Seraph shouts. "Laziness and Selfishness!" the Seraph announces with two bent-arm fisted air pumps.

"You can't set them up for failure. It must be of their free will and circumstance. The plan is corrupted!" the white masked Seraph says as it shakes its head in contempt.

"The game has begun and the game must be done!" a black masked Seraph responds.

Heavy breathing being forced up against the inside of the white mask is heard by those around table. The white masked Seraph shouts, "I will not stand in the way of your game but you will have to play without me!"

"You must reveal yourself!" demands the black masked Seraph. "You cannot be in the Houses!"

"I will be as I have been!"

"You will not be a part of this war!" a gold masked Seraph adds.

"Oh, yes. I will have MY war and all of you are better off not being on the other side of it," the white masked Seraph warns. "I beg you to stop this madness. This is an unorthodox procedure for justifying any war. This game should end!"

"The game that you have been playing?" the black masked Seraph responds. "Is that the game you are referring to? You knew the rules! You knew what was at stake and no one twisted your wings to come here!"

"We are here to balance the scales of justice not to tip it!" the white masked Seraph informs. "I played this game because I believed it was what must be done!" the white masked Seraph shouts from the other end of the table. "All this hiding behind the truth is where we all lie."

A red masked Seraph stands up at the table, "We were careful to allow them autonomy over their own decisions. As always, we only set the scene, we don't make the decision for them."

A silver masked Seraph interjects, "That's where the problem lies. We didn't offer an incentive to make another choice therefore we eliminated free will."

"Incentive!" the gold masked Seraph responds. "Since when do we offer incentives? The air under their wings and the light in their eyes is incentive enough! They are not mortals! They are enlightened! They were on a mission ordained by the Victor... grace... Sandalphon!"

"Only Abaddon or the Chancellor sets one up for failure," the silver masked Seraph responds. "Are you the Chancellor?" the silver masked Seraph asks while extending its head and widening its masked eyes.

"I don't know who any of you are but I will contest and withdraw any involvement with this clandestine cooperative if it is discovered that the Chancellor was present or participating in this enterprise," the gold masked Seraph responds.

"May we all endorse? So mote it be?" the Seraph asks as it unsheathes and raises a sword to the sky.

"Most definitely, so mote it be!" confirms the silver masked Seraph with a sword in the air.

"Inarguably, so mote it be!" agrees the white masked Seraph with a sword in the air.

"So mote it be, for sure!" supports the black masked Seraph with a sword in the air.

"SO MOTE IT BE!" boasts the red masked Seraph with a sword in the air.

The black masked Seraph looks around and confirms, "We are one!"

"Not quite!" the white masked Seraph replies. "It's happy to know that this proceeding has not been tainted by the Chancellor, but... I cannot commit to it any longer."

"But we already have five of seven vices," the gold masked Seraph informs. "It will not be long before we get the other two! We'll present these acts of transgression without you!"

"And maybe I won't be in the Throne Room," the white masked Seraph responds as it hastens away. "Maybe I'm just a just prayer tower guard," the Seraph shouts from a distance.

The remaining four Seraphs are left standing clinch-mouthed and stiffened as the white masked Seraph exits the room. The room is shrouded in silence.

Struggling to break the silence the silver masked Seraph blurts out, "I-I I... to hell with it! I'm out too!" Avoiding further discussion, the Seraph quickly strides across the room with its red-cloak sweeping the floor as it heads for the exit.

"This is absurd!" scorns the black masked Seraph.

"Yet it's of no consequence!" shouts the red masked Seraph. "We will soon have enough evidence to discretely submit to the Throne Room."

"This location is no longer secure," informs the gold masked Seraph. "We should reconvene here." The Seraph points at a location on the Eye of Abraxis. "When the moon is in the Sixth House."

"And we will need a password for entry," the black masked Seraph asserts while holding its head down and crossing its hands behind its back. "Persevero! That's it! For we will continue without falter." The Seraph looks around for signs of mutual agreement. "So mote it be?"

"So mote it be!" the other two respond. The Seraphs rapidly vacate the room.

CHAPTER EIGHTEEN

Dead Star

Three Archangels step through the Gates of Paradise into a portal en route to check out suspicious activity in a distant galaxy. Archangels Raquel, Remiel, and Nathaniel are dressed in full battle regalia and equipped with shields and swords. Remiel with his battalion bugle strapped on and hanging to the side, stands in the portal looking at his unsheathed sword that he is holding up close to his eyes as he closely examines the blade. Raquel observes Remiel's actions then looks down at her own sword. Nathaniel watches both of his partners and shakes his head in disdain of their preparation ritual. The portal continues its descent of falling and floating, down, down, down onto an unfamiliar destination. Prior to their journey, Zacharael, who is also a leader in the Dominion class of angels who oversee galactic activity, noticed a small star cluster disappear from the map of the universe. An event like this does not happen unless a star is lost into the darkness of the universe's expanse. Zacharael called upon the Archangels to investigate and report back on the findings. The portal continue its descent through a kaleidoscope of psychedelic color schemes, a normal process that engulfs the descendants in a dwindling funnel through the portal's entry and exit points.

Shaking his head and inhaling deeply, "We should have astroflares for missions like this," Remiel says as he inspects his sword.

"You don't need an astroflare," Nathaniel remarks with a slight degree of contempt as he shakes his head, inhales, and exhales slowly. "Just stay close. If we run into any trouble you'll use your lurid bugle to gather up the troops."

"Most likely this is just another desolate star cluster that lost its energy and died in the cold," Raquel adds.

"I know, but still... you never know what might be lurking in these dark places," Remiel responds. "With Sophia being on the loose... and Sammuel! You never know... you just never—"

"Relax!" Nathaniel demands. "You are making me nervous and I don't get nervous."

"You know I was thinking," Raquel reports. "There are only 12 astroflares, three in each of the four Kingdoms. How come the seven of us, well... three of us, don't have one?"

"Raphael doesn't have one either," adds Remiel.

"The astroflare was intended to be an administrative weapon to send those who strayed from the light into the containment sphere where their souls would be judged in the Throne Room," Nathaniel explains. "As you both know, initially only the kingdom of Omnus had these weapons, then each of the other three kingdoms was given three swords after the Great Disturbance. During the purge and purification of the remaining Seven Houses the three astroflares of Persidis were lost and Sammael stole another three before his Fall," Nathaniel concludes.

"It doesn't make sense!" Raquel snaps. "Sachiel, Raphael, and Anahel are all administrators, but they don't have an astroflare but Uriel and Azrael who are only assistants—"

"And old former administrators..." Nathaniel quickly adds.

"OK... but when you give up the administrator job, so should you the astroflare."

"He works the pits of Hell... he can have it!" Remiel interjects.

"Absolutely," Nathaniel agrees.

"Uriel uses one at the Gates of Paradise," Remiel adds.

"Maybe, word is he gave it to Metaphon when he pursued Sammael through the portal," Nathaniel informs.

Raquel exhales sharply and shakes her head and comments, "As far as we know Sammael could have all six. There are just too many missing astroflares out there."

Remiel shakes his head in dismay. "That's my concern! We don't know who we are going up against on these dead star missions."

"Feel free to bring this concern up in the Throne Room," Raquel says as she removes her bow hanging from her back and prepares to depart the portal.

"If we run into trouble you can blow your little bugle to send out a cosmic alert or you can run away like a little fairy and let me and Raquel do all the fighting," Nathaniel says as he adjusts his rip on his trident. "Ok stop your whining. We're here." The portal fades away around them. "Let's go baby angels."

The three Archangels slowly step out into the dark star in a strategic search and surveillance formation. Nathaniel leads the way while Raquel follows closely behind. Remiel keeps a lookout from the rear. Nathaniel observes the atmosphere and notices that it has been heavily concentrated with nitrogen, oxygen, argon, and carbon dioxide, but no water vapors. The atmosphere is capable of sustaining some mortal life forms, but there is something else in the mixture that is rather peculiar which Nathaniel could not quite figure out.

The three slowly advance ahead through the dimly star lit surroundings until Nathaniel points out a higher ground, a rock formation peaking over the tall bushy flatlands in the distance. The rock formation may elevate their view over the landscape. The three pick up the pace until Nathaniel abruptly gives the fisted hand signal to come to a complete halt. The thick bush area has a newly blazed trail of serrated trimmings that look precisely cut, Nathaniel makes an inspection and determines that the trimmings were cut by a blade that left a hydrogen chloride residue. The burnt edges were from the light harlequin green and magenta bushes. Nathaniel shows a serrated branch to the others who quickly understand what was most feared to happen has most likely occurred. There was the use of an astroflare here.

Remiel looks down while shaking his head, unsheathing his sword, and silently mouthing the words, "I knew it."

Remiel inhales deeply, looks up at Nathaniel, and nods his head in confirmation that he remains committed to supporting the continuation of the mission. Raquel pulls an arrow from her energized projectile satchel and loads it in her bow. Seeing that the team is ready Nathaniel grips his trident and continues through the previously blazed trail. The team proceeds cautiously through the thick bush that extends up taller than the tips of their wings. The team continues through the trail for miles until Nathaniel again abruptly stops the procession with a fisted hand signal. He turns to the others with arched eyebrows and an inwardly gaze before inhaling intensely and mouthing the words, "Ni-trous ox-ide."

Raquel ponders on it for a moment then replies, "I don't understand... who cares," she whispers as she shrugs her shoulders and darts her eyes at Nathaniel.

"I'm breathing it!" Nathaniel whispers a little louder.

"Oh... Abraxis!" Raquel whispers.

With strong and swift hand motion pointing up, Remiel responds in a louder undertone, "This place is humanizing! We need to get out of here now!"

"I just want to get a better view from on top of that rock formation," Nathaniel points out a short distance away. "Then we can go. I promise."

"If we can go!" Remiel responds before giving his approving nod.

The team proceeds again through the path until they come to a clearing. They scope out the area before continuing then run over to the rock, drop to their bellies with their wings lowered and crawl up to the top of the rock platform to see over to the other side.

"Ok... just more darkness," Nathaniel reports as he scopes out the area.

Lying at his side Raquel confirms, "Yeah let's go there's nothing else here. Whatever happened we missed it. We'll come back with a full team."

"No way! Michael will just let this star die out. Let's go!" Nathaniel informs.

"Wait!" Remiel requests. Peering deeper through the darkness and squinting his eyes Remiel asks while pointing, "What is that?"

Both Nathaniel and Raquel take a deeper glance across the clearing through the dark. Raquel has a sudden change from squinting, to wide opened eyes as she inhales sharply and covers her mouth. Nathaniel, swallowing with a dry mouth, looks intensely over at a stick in the ground holding up a skull wearing a red cloak.

With trembling lips and moisture building in the warrior's eyes, Raquel asks, "Is that... it can't be—"

Snapping quickly into action Nathaniel orders, "Cover me and get ready to ascend quickly!"

The two warrior Archangels get into defensive positions with their wings raised in full battle-ready stances. They follow Nathaniel to the skull poled on a stick. Nathaniel takes the red cloak and wraps up the skull. The team circles in closer together. After confirmation glances from Raquel and Remiel, Nathaniel shouts, "Rise to Vilon!"

The Paradise Portal engulfs the team and sends them back through the Gates of Paradise.

The Secret of Persidis

In the back of an old star mansion on the plains of Araboth, Father Barcus works busily in a galactic garden. Bands of light are twisted and shaped into new flowers and fading atoms are pulled and discarded. Father Barcus smiles and hums while he works. For Barcus this is a moment of rest and relaxation, a time out to reflect on the past, zone out future worries, and meditate on the power of the present moment. Barcus is unwinding from the various events celebrating the capture of Araqiel and Penemue, the infamous genies that tarnished the loyal servitude reputation of the Jinn kingdom. Four of the current assistant ambassadors are genies and they are relieved from the paranoid suspicion that comes when one of your siblings are involved in a revolt. After Janus was arrested for treason many angels had begun to become skeptical about the motives of the Jinn Kingdom. A culture of paranoia had set into the community forcing many genies into seclusion. But today is a new day, a day of relaxation and redemption as Janus has helped to capture the two long time fugitives and restored the genus' reputation in the Houses of Heaven.

A flash and flicker crosses through the garden. "Who can it be now?" Barcus asks as he has already had a visit from Shakinah, the genie who is now the new Assistant Ambassador of Vilon.

"Father!" Miriam greets popping into the garden.

"Miriam?" Father Barcus answers exhaling long and deeply. "What is it now? I wasn't expecting you back so soon." Father Barcus puts away his tools and brushes the stardust off his hands. "Well there goes my meditation," Barcus internalizes. "So how's Janus? How is the mission going? Is it near completion? When will the child be coming home?" Barcus fires on a series of paternal concerns.

"Oh, Father... you know there are many more fugitives to be captured," The genie rolls its eyes and sighs, "But Janus... Janus will be fine."

Barcus smiles with a closed eyes and a confirming nod of the head. "Yes... Yes I know." Barcus turns to look at Miriam. "So why are you here... again?"

"Oh, I just thought I'd visit because... well you're my father and we rarely spend any time alone anymore."

The old genie rolls thoughts of his much clingy and affectionate child Janus through its mind. "Janus is wearing off on you," Barcus smiles. "Ok. Let's go for a walk."

Barcus places his arms around Miriam, "I wasn't born 5,000 years ago. You want to tell me what's really getting at you?"

Miriam places its arm around Barcus' hip and settles its head on his shoulder as they stroll through the garden. "Father, can you tell me about the times right before the creation of the Heavens?"

"That old story? You know it well."

"I want to hear it again from you," Miriam demands as they continue their stroll.

Barcus pauses and takes a deep breath before he begins. "In the time right after the Paroxysm of Abraxis, Omnus came to offer a deal to our small kingdom that was weakened, energy depleted, and unable to spawn. We had lost most of the Jinn kingdom in the storm so Omnus offered to enclose our souls inside these new oxygen and carbon-based humanoid life forms so we could reproduce, but we refused."

Already knowing the answer Miriam asks, "Why?"

"The gender of these new bodies were predetermined and fixed, that's in opposition to our nature that has always been asexual, reproducing only after the age of maturation. Since we refused these new vessels and remained in our natural light-based life forms we lost the ability to spawn. None of the remaining genies had enough of the light energy that was needed to reach the age of maturation. Our lights were fading from the universe. We are 10,000 genies strong but still declining in our numbers as time goes along. Penemue and Araqiel were opposed the elders' decision to not reconstitute into the flesh. They accused us of genocide and... maybe they were right."

"Father!" Miriam shouts. "You know now they desired carbon-based life forms because they were tempted by the desires of the flesh."

"Within every soul there is a light of truth and nobility."

"Father, that's the story about us, but what about the rest of the angels? How were they able to spawn and who are their elders?"

Father Barcus takes a moment in silence. "Is there something wrong? Is there something you are not telling me?"

"Please Father, don't ask."

"We were told to never speak of it," Barcus reports as he looks around for eavesdroppers. "You are older now so maybe... well maybe it's time that you know."

"Father, what I'm asking is for Janus' sake, but that's all I can tell you."

"Then if it helps Janus, it helps us all," Barcus stops and conjures them out of Araboth, through the exoverse and into a secret portal that lands them into the remnants of an old Jinn kingdom.

"Father, what is this place?"

"It's a small part of what's left of the old Jinn kingdom. This is where the Imperial Archives are kept."

"Why haven't I been told about this place before?"

"These archives are the most sacred and they must be protected. An elder much older than me maintains them. Its name is simply Geniel. It will have the answers you seek, but they come at a cost. That's all I can tell you. We will speak of these answers you seek no more." Barcus zips out of the exoverse.

"But Father how do I... where do I find... Father!" Miriam looks around in the exoverse for signs of life but all the genie can see is illuminated darkness. A shimmer of purple lighting circles the genie but outside of the circle there is nothing but darkness.

A light snaps on brightening the space around the genie. "There, that should do it!" says a young soul dressed in colorful silk pantaloons with a matching top. "Travel into the realm of the exoverse much?"

"No. I can't say that I do travel within the... exoverse. How is that even possible?"

"Well someone has to maintain this place," the young girl says. "Do you know how much junk gets left behind in here?"

"Ah, no um... are you Geniel?"

"I'm Charmiel and if you are talking about Jinn, the old genie has gone to align the Gemini. They tend to come apart this time in the rotation," Charmiel says as she wipes her fiery red hair from her face.

"I'm Miriam. How long will it be until Geniel returns?"

"Do you mean in time?" the young one says with widened green eyes. "We don't have time? Not in here."

"Well surely you have some way to measure when—"

"When my mother left me here she said she'd be back in a twinkling," Charmiel snaps. "Now is a twinkling within 1,000 rotations or 10,000 rotations? Because it's been 7,000 rotations and she still has not returned. Jinn says I'm impatient and I'm not allowed to watch the zodiac anymore so it leaves me here like I don't know how long it takes for zodiacs to need adjustments during each rotation. It's all a matter of observational mathematics."

"Well..."

"Well it doesn't matter because you can't leave anyway. No one can until it releases you."

"Great!"

"Anyway, what's so important that you need to see the old Jinn?" Charmiel asks as she flips her shoulder length hair rotating the colors. "No one but Barcus ever visits."

"I need access to the Imperial Archive."

"Those old boring scrolls?" Charmiel stops flipping her now blue hair. "What do you need to know? I can tell you all about it, really ask me anything," Charmiel says with a big eager smile.

Miriam looks around and finds no other soul in sight. Even with the illumination of the immediate surroundings there is still a vast depth of darkness surrounding them. "I would love to say I don't have time for this but seeing how I'm trapped here... ok," Miriam gives in. "Before the days of the Paroxysm of Abraxis how many Eons were there?" Miriam asks trying to sound like it was a game question and not an inquisition.

"That's it?" Charmiel snaps. "Four! As there always were! Come on! Ask me something good!" Charmiel requests now sitting on the ground directly in front of Miriam with big green eyes looking up for a challenge.

"OK... What... were... their names?" Miriam asks hoping to continue the game and not interrogating the child.

Charmiel rolls her eyes signifying that this question too does not challenge her. She inhales and answers, "Well there is mom, auntie Lil, and uncle Aba who really needs to take it down a notch. Um... oh I see. You tried to trick me with the before and after so the last one is Omnus of course." Charmiel shakes her head in confidence, "You know I can imitate that hovering sound he makes. Ommm Mahh ni—"

"Wait! Aba who?"

"Abaddon!" the child scalds. "I'm right! I'm always right!"

"Have you met these Eons?"

"I've only met auntie Lil, but Jinn talks about the others all the time."

"And your mother... where is she and what is her name?"

"Sophia, silly! She..." Moisture fills Charmiel's green eyes. "She hasn't come back," Charmiel dry sobs with a repetitive hiccup sound as she tries to control her breathing. "She said she'd be back in a twinkling. Hiccup! She... said it wasn't safe yet and that I'd be safer here until after the war."

Miriam walks over to hold Charmiel. "Is Jinn your father Charmiel?" asks the genie as it wraps its arms around the young girl trying to soothe her.

"No. I don't know who my father is. The old Jinn won't tell me," Charmiel explains. "But I know—"

"That's enough!" a voice shouts coming from out of the darkness across the room. "Who are you and how did you? The old genie squints. "Wait! I know you!" The old Jinn flickers and blinks as its instable light source fades. "You know this place is forbidden! Why are you here?"

"Great honorable, Geniel. Please excuse my presence but Father Barcus brought me here and left while you were away," Miriam explains.

"Go child! Leave us now!" Geniel directs Charmiel.

"But... maybe Miriam can take me—"

"We will discuss this later! You must leave us NOW! Do not defy me child!"

"I HATE you!" Charmiel screams as she runs off into the distance.

The old Jinn peer over at Miriam with scolding eyes and a raised finger in the air to keep Miriam from interrupting. "She should have not let you into the light space. She should have kept you in the dark of the exoverse, but as all children do they

tend to become defiant when they are bored."
Geniel invokes a table and chairs. "Please," it says
offering a seat as it sits at the table and pours a
warm liquid into a set of cups. "Jinn juice," it offers
as it pushes the other cup closer to Miriam. "She
says... it's my favorite. Hum! Hum!" Geniel laughs
as it sips from its cup. Miriam remains quiet, sits
down, and politely takes a sip of the warm juice.
Genial continues, "This place is sacred not only to
the genus but to the entire universe. It's so sacred
its existence is kept a secret. Only Omnus and
those whom he trusted the most were made aware
of its location. Omnus, Sophia, Barcus, and I are the
only ones that know how to get here. This is where
all the secrets to the universe are kept. These
secrets can turn the balance of power and disturb
the peace if used by the wrong malevolent
individual."

Miriam looks into the eyes of Geniel trying to
gauge if it is OK to speak. "I don't know how Father
Barcus brought me here. I don't even know where
here is," Miriam says hoping to ease the concern
about the integrity of the security being breached.

"I am sure that Barcus was careful when he
brought you here. He must trust you to bring you
here at all." The old genie takes another sip from
the cup before continuing. "The child has
complicated things somewhat but this day was
inevitable. In fact, I have been feeling disturbances
in the energy fields throughout the entire rotation. I
thought there was a misalignment in the zodiac but
when I found that there was nothing out of place it
hit me that the disturbance was closer to home."

"I came for an answer but now I seek the truth,"
Miriam informs.

"The truth? Hum hum hum hum," Geniel giggles. "What lies between the truth is always another lie."

Miriam bites its inside lip and wrinkles its forehead as it rolls up its eyes in thought. Geniel continues to sip the juice while looking at Miriam. "Don't strain your pretty little head on that one."

"The girl. Is her mother an Eon?" Miriam asks.

"As you know, all the divine elders are spawns of the four great Eons. Eons conjugating with Eons spawn off powerful omnificent immortals," Geniel reports while looking deeply into Miriam's eyes. "In the time of Abraxis these powerful immortals battled over power and control of the four kingdoms," Geniel rolls its eyes up in its head recalling the battles in its mind. "When Omnus came to rule he forbade Eons to spawn with other Eons in an effort to prevent a shift in the balance of power. The angelic community was large and growing larger by the rotation. He feared the kingdoms would grow too rapidly and the draw on the energy force would create another paroxysm like the one that destroyed Abraxis," Geniel sighs as it recalls the day of the great paroxysm storm. "Omnus ruled that no more immortal beings would be created. All life forms would have carbon-based mortal forms and all would have to be approved by a series of tribulations to obtain immortality. These trials were intended to determine the purity of the soul and prove the worthiness of obtaining immortality. Pure souls reduce the risk of another paroxysm. Charmiel was born without of the trials of mortality. She is forbidden in the kingdom of Heaven," Geniel concludes.

"When Janus apprehended Araqiel and Penemue they mentioned something about two Divinity twins having a sibling who would be restored during the next revolt to take over the Houses."

"I take it you don't know which of the twins?"

"No. No I don't."

"You don't know all the Eons and their spawns?"

"But you may?"

"I don't! All I can tell you is after Abraxis the next great Aeon was Omnus. The other Eons are Sophia, Lilith, and Abaddon." Genial looks deeper into Miriam's eyes. "Yes, Lord Abaddon."

"If he's an Eon then how can he be contained in a prison?"

"They locked up the idea that the kingdom can be safe again. It's a façade that buys time."

"Time for what?"

"The coming."

"The coming?" Miriam repeats. "The coming of what?"

"Exterminans Perfectus. The complete destruction of all things."

"What's that," Miriam asks with an elevated heartbeat.

"What or whom? I don't know. This sibling? Maybe. To get the information you need would require a very diligent research of the Imperial Archives and it may have been erased."

"Great! There would be no way to prove to Michael that Abaddon is an Eon. He's been waiting to fight with him and Michael thinks—"

"Michael knows! All the Divinity knows these secrets and they must never know that you know." Geniel looks amused at the opening of young eyes. It smiles at Miriam as if seeing a child at play. "Well if the houses are at risk from the top down... we will need Omnus to come home which means I must seek him out. In the mean time... Charmiel must remain in your care."

"My, what?" Miriam explodes. "Oh I-I can't care for a child."

"Care and protect you must. If these entities have ideas about how the houses should be ruled... a child of an Eon will be a threat to their plans, especially anyone from the Kingdom of Persidis where Charmiel is a direct descendent."

"Why Persidis?"

"Omnus ruled that all souls must have their existence purified through mortal trials on Earth, the late Ambassador Jerriel had a lineage of her souls placed upon the Earth. During the Great Disturbance all the house ambassadors from Persidis were destroyed in search for the Hozi, The Angel of the Sword who possessed all the astroflares." Geniel stands and prepares to leave. "Are you aware that an angel can only defeat and Eon by use of an astroflare? But even then it's still a mere containment to imprison the Eon's soul. Abaddon and his Disciples of Doom cannot take over the houses without having possession of these weapons." Genial finishes off his Jinn juice including Miriam's cup. "Cassiel, Sandalphon, Michael, Gabriel, and former ambassadors Uriel and Azrael hold six of the twelve weapons. Sammael stole three and the three from Persidis are missing. Sophia is the great Eon of Persidis and Charmiel is its heir. That makes her a great bargaining piece in exchange for the three swords of Persidis."

"Maybe that's the time Abaddon is waiting for... the collection of all the astroflares. No one could stop him without it."

"To find the answers you seek question the hands that hold the swords. The balance of power is in the distribution of the swords."

"Sophia would know where the remaining astroflares are hidden. Do you know where to find her?"

"If you have her child, she'll find you."

"Who is the father?

"She wouldn't part with it except to say, 'A soul that's old but feels so new,' then she said she'd be back in a twinkling."

The Fall

The nippy wind off Lake Erie blows the orange and yellow leaves across green lawns of New Richmond Heights, Ohio. The fall has come. This season will bring in the grand opening of The Guiltless Pleasures Beauty Salon under the management of Karlisa's new partner, Mr. Aza Ziel. The Xeven family and their guests have just finished having a grand opening eve dinner in their new home secluded out in the rebuilt, revolutionary war-torn hills of what was once the old Richmond Heights. The modest five bedrooms and two car garage home is close quarters for their new housemates but an upgrade for the Xeven family who was happy to move out of the crowded inner city neighborhood. Jerry looks over the blueprints for a new edition to be added to the back acre plot to house a sparring room and headquarters for his new team.

"Coffee anyone?" Karlisa asks as she walks into the room with a dishtowel, rubbing her hands and looking around for responses.

Jerry looks up at the long streak of gray hair that has grown into Karlisa's dark waves like a skunk's back. He chuckles a bit before answering, "You know it's not that bad." Jerry continues starring as Karlisa runs her fingers through her hair over the streak. "Battle scars," Jerry calls it.

"This family will be in therapy for years to overcome these scars," Karlisa replies as she turns to look at her hair in a mirror reflection from the glass doors of the dining room curio cabinet.

"Remember, no therapy for us. We'll have to rely on inner strength and resiliency otherwise we may end up being locked up," Jerry reminds Karlisa.

"I know, I know. I was only kidding," Karlisa says as she looks over to the group sitting at the dinner table. "A psychoanalyst can't remove the voices from my head. It's best to listen to them and learn how to tune them out," Karlisa replies as she dances her head, reciting something she has been told.

"I'm sorry you have to go through this," Aza attempts to comfort her. "As soon as we capture the—"

"Auh! Um!" Karlisa clears her throat. "The children could be listening," she whispers.

Now whispering Aza continues, "Soon... soon," while shaking his head with a nod of confidence. Aza looks over at Jerry with a confirming eye-to-eye nod. "Now, how about that dessert?"

"White cake with peach or strawberry Sherbet."

"May I have a little bit of both?"

"Funny, that's what Charmiel said," responds Karlisa with a twinkle in her eyes and a smirk in her smile.

Aza looks back with his lips pinched. "We don't know. We simply just don't know, not that it matters anyway," Aza says with an inward stare. "A child of Sophia's is a child of mine. It's just nice to see her face again."

Karlisa looks at Aza and Jerry whose faces both drop with solemn gazes and far away eyes. "Come on guys! These are exciting times," she announces. "I just got my mother off my back for not suing the Confederate of Arab States. She believes a remnant Anti-New Gaia revolutionary group kidnapped us. How she got that idea..."

"Sometimes a lie lays better than the truth," says Jerry.

"I thought the truth sets you free," responds Karlisa.

"I spent 5,000 years under a rock for telling the truth," Aza says with a wrinkled forehead and nod.

"Yeah and I'm still getting calls from the N.G.I.A investigators," adds Jerry. "Sorry I can't remember officer," Jerry shakes his head with closed eyes.

"Well I'm excited to start my apprenticeship at the salon," Janus perks while changing the conversation. "My new life as a human," Janus whispers.

"Now let me get this straight Janus," Aza asks. "Your... daughter, Charmiel will attend school with the Xeven children," Aza looks around for confirmation. "If anyone asks she is your daughter and you are her, what exactly?"

"Father," the group replies.

"She's going to be discrete? A child out in the public with her powers?" Aza shakes his head. "Oh, brother! She's too young to control her impulses."

"She insisted on not be locked up any longer," Janus answers. "Miriam says that Geniel kept her secluded for over 7,000 years."

"Lost years," Aza interjects.

Janus adds, "She's much too wise for human schools. I believe they'll say she's academically gifted, but I agree she's also very impulsive and at times aggressive."

"She'll fit right into our public schools," Karlisa says.

"Not for long hopefully," says Aza. "She can read the archive star maps and locate the Fallen. We locate the Fallen and the missing astroflares, confiscate them, and restore the balance of power."

"Restore the balance of power?" Jerry asks.

"Or rebalance it?" asks Janus.

"Provide another choice in the war of good and evil?" Aza questions.

"Everyone should have the right to opt out?" says Karlisa.

Jerry looks around at the group. "A third option?"

"Whatever ends this madness," Karlisa says while pulling on her streaked hair.

"You may not like the ending," Aza responds raising his cocktail glass then finishing the last sip. "This is one of the best of all the human conditions," he adds with a scowled up face and tightly closed eyes as he swallows the last of his scotch. "I think I'll pass on that dessert."

"Is this the end or the beginning?" Jerry asks.

Aza gazes through blurred eyes trying to introduce an alternative view, "In the divine perspective... there is no end. The Earth, the Heavens, and the dark expanse of the Abraxis are never ending. The story itself is immortal."

HOUSES OF PARADISE

BEFORE THE GREAT DISTURBANCE

House	House Name	Ambassadors and Kingdoms	Assistants
01st	Vilon	Zimkiel of Persidis	Eblis
02nd	Raquia	Seraphiel of Omnus	Raphael
03rd	Saqun	Ariel of Omnus	Anahel
04th	Machonon	Uriel of Dynacia	Zacharael
05th	Matey	Sandalphon of Omnus	Daniel
06th	Zebul	Sammuel of Dynacia	Wall
07th	Araboth	Azrael of Lucimus	Azazel
08th	Xevenus	Jerriel of Persidis	Xaphan
09th	Abraxistan	Metaphon of Omnus	Semjaza
10th	Persidis	Eon Sophia	Penemue
11th	Dynacia	Eon Lilith	Araqiel
12th	Lucimus	Eon Abaddon	Beliar

HOUSES OF PARADISE

AFTER THE GREAT DISTURBANCE

House	House Name	Ambassadors and Kingdoms	Assistants
01st	Vilon	Gabriel of Omnus	Janus
02nd	Raquia	Raphael of Omnus	Zacharael
03rd	Saqun	Anahel of Omnus	Azrael
04th	Machonon	Michael of Omnus	Uriel
05th	Matey	Sandalphon of Omnus	Metaphon
06th	Zebul	Sachiel of Dynacia	Typhon
07th	Araboth	Cassiel of Dynacia	Caymiel
08th	Xevenus	Destroyed	
09th	Abraxistan	Destroyed	
10th	Persidis	Destroyed	
11th	Dynacia	Destroyed	
12th	Lucimus	Destroyed	

THE GOOD, THE EVIL, & THE THIRD OPTION

GOOD?

Archangels	
Michael	Divinity
Gabriel	Divinity
Uriel	Elder
Raphael	Elder
Nathaniel	Born a Mortal
Remiel	Born a Mortal
Raquel	Born a Mortal

EVIL?

THE DISCIPLES of DOOM		
Seven Rulers of Wrath		
Armaros	Wrath	The Root Cutter
Amy	Wrath	The Pretender
Bal	Wrath	The Instigator
Belzar	Wrath	The Oppressor
Pursiphon	Wrath	The Back Stabber
Caim	Wrath	The Hater
Paimon	Wrath	The Deceiver
Seven Vices		
Abaddon	Vice	Pride
Sammael	Vice	Envy
Leviathan	Vice	Anger
Belphegor	Vice	Sloth and Laziness
Beelzebub	Vice	Greed and Avarice
Mammon	Vice	Gluttony and Selfishness
Asmodeus	Vice	Lust and Desire

Chancellor's Entourage the Four Fiends of Fury	
Xaphan	The Arsonist of Paradise
Eblis	The Viceroy Malevolence
Iadalbaoth	The Archon of Darkness
Rahab	The Vex of Violence

Abaddon's Entourage the Triad of Terror	
Beliar	The Supreme Adversary of God
Wall	The Grand Duke of Hell
Mephistopheles	The Destroyer of Peace

Prison Pentagram & Leaders		
Northward	Souls	Leaders
	Mortals:	Hitler
	Beast:	Behemoth
	Demons/Genus:	Gaap
	Guardian Angels	Semjaza
Westward	Nations:	Armaros then Belphegor
Eastward	Virtues:	None
	Powers:	Gadreel
	Dominions:	Baraqel
Southwestward	Thrones:	Kokabel
	Cherubim:	Balberith
Southeastward	Seraphim:	Abaddon

The Optionem Terzo

The Valentinian Order	
Zophiel	Fallen and Exonerated
Raziel	Fallen and Exonerated
Caliel	Fallen and Exonerated
Astarphon	Fallen and Exonerated
Azazel	Fallen and Exonerated
Janus	Exonerated
Jerry	Exonerated

Please visit us at <u>rramarr.com</u> for The Xeven Houses of Deception (House II) preview and other story arcs.
Thank You